ONE LOVE AND THE MANY LIVES OF OSIP B.

C.P. SURENDRAN

olive turtle

NIYOGI BOOKS

Published by
NIYOGI BOOKS
Block D, Building No. 77,
Okhla Industrial Area, Phase-I,
New Delhi-110 020, INDIA
Tel: 91-11-26816301, 26818960
Email: niyogibooks@gmail.com
Website: www.niyogibooksindia.com

Editor: K.E. Priyamvada
Design: Shashi Bhushan Prasad
Cover design: Misha Oberoi

ISBN: 978-93-91125-12-7
Publication: 2021

This is a work of fiction. The names, characters and incidents portrayed in it are the work of the author's imagination. Any resemblance to actual persons, living or dead, events or localities, is entirely coincidental.

Printed at: Niyogi Offset Pvt. Ltd., New Delhi, India

the victims

and their

victims

In essence, my father transferred me to a totally alien century, and distant, although completely unjewish atmosphere.

—Osip Mandelstam

It's not what happened in your life, but how you remember it.

—Gabriel Garcia Marquez

Osip Bala Krishnan, Outlaw

Weeks after she went missing, Elizabeth Hill called and said I had no future with her. I was out among the climbing woods at the back of the school, leaning on a rock and watching a pig-shaped cloud spill its guts.

'No, don't say, that,' I said.

'It's wrong,' Elizabeth said. 'You understand wrong, don't you?' Elizabeth asked, her voice husky, almost conspiratorial.

'No!' I said into the phone.

'Osip, Osip.'

Often one's name is one's fate. One had to respond to the particular challenge that it enjoined upon oneself. I was christened Osip Bala Krishnan after Osip Mandelstam, the Russian poet whom Joseph Stalin arrested and exiled, for the second time, to Siberia in 1938—a year that would prove somewhat consequential to me—where the paranoid poet, mercifully, died of the cold and starvation. Please do not take it amiss when I say that M. was a visitant—no, not a ghost—to my grandfather's house in Thrissur, my hometown. As was the presence of the muse of mass murder, Joseph Stalin; also called Iosif or Osip (!), a Georgian variation of Joseph. The poet and the persecutor, free-speech and force, the timeless two-in-one combination, the forked and yoked teamwork of the mind that informs our moment-to-moment metamorphosis and turns us victim, as well as the victor, in our daily lives. I might mention that Stalin, whom I met once in the backyard of my school in Thrissur, was a bit of a nature poet and church singer in his teens. He was briefly in the neighbourhood of god, then, having studied in a seminary before he realized his true vocation as a well-intentioned executioner and thought he was a victim of continual conspiracies. The easier evil is the one we locate outside ourselves; the great purges of Stalin, my grandfather would say, were acts in self-defence. My grandfather was a great Communist leader in Kerala—a state, as imaginary as it is real, where the Revolution was always about to happen, but did not, at the last minute, so it can happen—again. His wife, Gloria Innaley, thought, perhaps out of a necessity to believe her ever-green resentment of her husband was just, or from an instinct for the wronged woman's vengeance, that she was married not just to a Stalinist ideologue, but also a mass killer in his own right in his younger days, a champion of plots and purges; a proper *Vohzd*, a leader. But Gloria praised her husband in public—she had just written a best-selling hagiography of him—and thought the Revolution was an act of eternally delayed gratification, like the Resurrection, perhaps. Her husband is 96 now. Or maybe older. There are no official records of his date of birth. Gloria said he was pretending to be an Alzheimer's patient. Calling me Osip, Gloria said, not without a tinge of hard, impersonal pity, was a painless act of expiation on his part. I did not believe her, of course. My grandfather and I shared a world where centuries fluctuated and flickered, dull one moment, dazzling the next, but never steady, like the filament in a bulb that would blow out at any moment. The air in his study transmitted the virus of other times. I will come to the details of my shared disorder with my grandfather in a moment.

'Why wrong?' I asked Elizabeth. Is feeding stolen sugar to hungry ants wrong? I have been told so when I was in an orphanage, whose recurring image inexplicably had to do with white baby mice and not, as it happened, ants. Kindness, they said, did not sanction theft. How long ago was that? 15 years? Like my grandfather, I too have no reliable birth records. I must have been three or four, then.

'Oh, never mind,' Elizabeth said.

'I was thinking of you this morning.'

'I knew you would. Don't.'

'It's not easy *not* to think of a thing.'

'I am not a thing.'

There was a pause. It seemed like Elizabeth had more on her mind than just severance of ties. I tried to pre-empt the bad news. It would *be* bad news.

'I could come down and visit you.'

'No,' Elizabeth said.

'It's just a bus ride.' I was aware my offer had begun to sound like a threat.

'It's not a question of ease of transport.'

'I can hear the traffic. Are you in Delhi?'

'Can you tell Delhi's traffic from Bombay's?'

'I have been to Bombay.' I thought of the narrow, packed lanes of the city suddenly opening out into the eternity of the sea. I disliked the city. Indeed, I disliked all cities. From a love of cities, came terror. 'Think of the millions killed in the name of urbanization and development,' my grandfather would say in his odd, penitent moment that gainsaid progress.

'Are they saying anything about me in school?'

'No. No one knows.'

'No one knows what?'

'About you and me.'

'We did a stupid thing. Like everything was allowed.'

Surely, love is the most demanding word in any language? What wouldn't people do for the realization of love? What war will they not wage? What seas will they not cross? I cleared my throat. 'I miss you.' I took a drink from my hip flask, a brown leather-and-steel gift from Arjun.

'You are drinking. You should not be drinking. I should be drinking.'

'I could come down to Delhi and we could stay together.'

Elizabeth laughed.

'For a while, at least?'

'And make headlines? We are potentially the stuff of hashtags,' Elizabeth paused. 'I am not sure why I called you. I shouldn't have.' Elizabeth paused. A horn blared. 'This is not a country, but a dusty, colourful chaos.' Last week, she had met a wandering child of five, on the verge of tears, bought him food and waited with him by the roadside for over two hours, panic rising in her, until his father, a construction worker covered in cement, had put in a guilty appearance, and she had felt like slapping him.

'Didn't we have a good time?'

'You are 18, a student. I am an adult and a teacher. And a foreigner. I must have been out of my senses.'

Students fell in love with their teachers all the time, didn't they? Consider your own life, Dear Reader. Look back: the seventh grade, the biology class. Wasn't what she said about genes a coded invitation to share her bed. No? Perhaps not. I am never quite sure of anything.

'Osip, I am carrying.'

The mountains looking down on me swayed a little, shaking off their mask of freak snow, showing the dark face beneath. I looked up at the sky. It was blue, clear. The pig-shaped cloud had disappeared without a trace. The mind is like the sky, Anand, my room-mate, would say in his more enlightened moments, and the clouds are thoughts, and it would occur to me that every time he said something grand, I had read or heard it all elsewhere. Elizabeth pregnant. I was fleetingly proud. And then felt vacant. Up. Down. Mood swings. One mind, two opposite moods. To sing and to fall silent. To be joyous and to cry. To step out of line. To fall back. I listened to Elizabeth's voice and thought of her golden hair, grey eyes, and the scar on her chin, like an extended comma. And her low hips, a little wide for her slender body. To look at Elizabeth was to fall silent.

'Hello,' I said. But Elizabeth had gone offline. I tried to step back into a patch of clearing that had made our conversation possible. I could not find it. The earth had already travelled past it.

This morning, I had gone for a walk up the narrow road behind the school when Elizabeth's call came. From where I stood, I could see most of St George's. The school, all in red brick and glass, was set in the hills of Kasauli, six hours' ride up north of Delhi. It was a quiet, well-maintained boarding school—on the face of it. But after Elizabeth's call, the school looked different, estranged like a familiar building reflected in the windshield of a car; sharp, clear, and distorted. I looked around with momentarily renewed interest. The trees were pruned, and their Latin names crucified to their hearts. There was a neat lawn in front of the school and, round the year, the grass gleamed like knives. A sign in a corner asked you not to walk on it. Another requested you not to spit on it. A third said walking barefoot on grass was good for your eyes. At the back of the school was a well-tended garden. Beyond it was the hostel, built—again—of red bricks. And, after that, nature took over; the woods, wild and deep, to one side. On the other, the Himalayas rippled endless and foamy, like lather squeezed out of a giant tube. From where I stood, I could see the school flashing a coded message through the pine and alder where the sunlight hit the glass of the windows: I had better go in search of Elizabeth, then. I walked down along the narrow track on the side of the kitchen and mess, toward the hostel, hoping Anand wouldn't be in the room.

***

The Saturday after Elizabeth's call, I picked up my overnight bag, my brittle copy of M.'s poems in Russian, and caught a seismic Uttarakhand State Transport bus to Delhi. I had access to Gloria's rarely used email account—I was the one who got her a gmail id (password: 17glorIous1)—and it came in handy: I could put in a request for an Out-pass as and when required. I would also delete or play around with the adverse mails from the school administration to Gloria. I suppose I made her life a little easier.

Kasauli was a cantonment town up in the Himalayas. But little ran on time here. The bus I got on left the sunken, circular, shop-lined terminus late. No one minded. I watched the langurs play on top of parked vehicles, their human faces framed with mischief and fur. A few weeks ago, a driver had taken an unscheduled break, and he had left the engine running. A determined monkey slipped in behind the steering and eased the gear. The bus rammed into another parked vehicle and came to a stop, while his friends watched the driver with admiration at the explosion of character that turned him a man among monkeys.

The night rattled all the way down. I drank on the bus. Some passengers in the back smoked: beedi, cigarette, hash. The driver stopped the vehicle whenever anyone felt like tea.

The conductor's phone sang continuously, Hindu devotional songs. That would be religion. The window by my seat was jammed, so I could not close it. The cold air kept blasting in. I tightened my cap down over my ears. When we finally reached Delhi, it was not yet light, and I had a head-cold.

I checked into a small seedy hotel, Singh's Palace Empire Dx, near New Delhi Railway Station. If I had to extend my stay, I would shift to my elderly writer-friend Arjun Bedi's house in Whispering Woods, near Khan Market, or so I hoped. Singh's Palace was recommended by Anand: 'Cheap, centrally located, no questions asked.' They gave me a small room on the second floor. Behind the paint-peeling door hung a sign: 'Please Do Not Make Unnecessary Noises.' I looked out of the window. It was too early in the morning for the shops to open. Lit red, orange, and green, signs of other hotels lining the street shone weakly through the brown smog, like vague signals of hope to travelling salesmen. Autorickshaws and an odd, illegal *phut-phut* (an ancient Harley Davidson modified to carry about half a dozen passengers), emerged from the fog into a clearing, then disappeared back into it. A horse carriage slowly clacked its way past the hotel from yet another of Delhi's time zones. I switched on the TV, and listened to the popular Avlok Dutta, of the India Post channel, debating on the Kashmir issue, and addressing a young, bearded participant:

'Faizal Rashid, you are on the payroll of Pakistanis, and you are working to separate Kashmir from India. I have incontrovertible evidence you are working against the interests of the nation, and I am,' Avlok Dutta suddenly thumped his chest, and shouted, 'a nationalist, a proud nationalist! I demand an apology and an explanation from you!'

'I am a patriot,' Faizal Rashid shouted back, 'a patriot! My grandfather died fighting the Chinese in 1962. I don't have to prove anything!'

'Faizal Rashid, you poor worm,' Avlok Dutta laughed, 'we are not talking about your grandfather, we are talking about you. Book him for sedition, right now!' Avlok Dutta shook a finger at Faizal Rashid.

Denunciatory violence emanated in waves from the TV. The air was dark and heavy, harbingering Armageddon, demanding nothing less than immediate apocalyptic resolutions. I switched off the TV and fell to the bed, feverish.

Late in the evening, I stepped out in search of Elizabeth. Before I was swallowed by the fog, I had something to eat in one of those quick, dirty, 'pure vegetarian' places down the road. The sign on the wall said, 'Spitting is strictly prohibited.' Rules everywhere.

F128, South Extension, was not hard to find. It was right opposite the main entrance of the community park in that area. From a white, marble-built gurdwara nearby, strains of *Shabd-kirtan* extolled the eternal. I promised to God never to eye my private parts again if Elizabeth opened her door to me, and took it back the next moment as it was an oath that defeated the entire purpose of my life, which was to marry Elizabeth and raise kids. I sat on a bench in the park and waited for the security guard to take a break.

For a long time, it seemed, he was there, rolling a lathi over his thighs, like a pin flattening the dough. What am I doing here? I looked around. Couples were making out. On a bench opposite, a man's hand was seeking a breast. Someone was laughing softly. From the eateries nearby, the smell of kebabs skewered the night. My head throbbed. My heart raced. The fever poured sweat down my face. My eyes came back to the guard. Ah, he was not there. There was god after all.

Thief, thief. I went up three dim-lit flights of stairs. The overhead bulbs had wire cages around them and threw shadows on the roof. The light looked trapped. I listened to my breathing, the unremarkable exercise out of which triumphs and disasters emerged in their full regalia and marched on the world. I rang the bell. No answer. I knocked on the door softly so that it was heard only by Elizabeth and the baby and no other human ear. 'Hello, father is home'. I rang the bell again. Nothing. I waited. I turned around and went down the steps as carefully as I had come up. I counted the steps. 36. I might have missed a couple. I am never sure of these things. Which is probably why I do the same thing several times. I reached the gate, and there the security man was, flattening the invisible dough.

'Where did you go?'

'Upstairs.'

'Who?'

'Hill teacher.'

'It's late. Are you her student?'

'Yes. Her favourite student.' And lover, I announced to the world in utter silence.

'Madam *gaya yahan se*,' (has gone from here) he said, shifting the wad of tobacco to the other side of his mouth with his tongue, spreading cancer uniformly.

'Where? Where has Madam gone? When?'

'*Pata nahin*.'

He didn't know. For him, not knowing where Elizabeth had gone was the end of the race. Mine began there, where he stopped; he touched me lightly with the lathi, now the baton of our relay race, as if to console me.

'She came in-between once to pack up things. I am just a guard. Madam is English.'

Yes, Elizabeth could do anything. She was Elizabeth. Female. English. And white. Could it get more powerful than this? Besides, when you are in love, you cede so much territory to the other. Hate empowers you. Love emasculates. Thief, thief. I turned away from the guard and slowly walked towards the Metro. It was vast, cavernous, empty. I went up and down the escalators, moving between arrival and departure signs in red, until an elderly police officer stopped me.

'Go home,' he said kindly, 'where do you want to go?' I couldn't first remember; then when I did, I couldn't decide. Was I going back to Singh's Palace, or Arjun's? Somewhere else? I looked at the officer. He had receding, curly hair like my grandfather.

'Go home,' the officer said again.

Home. To my grandfather, Niranjan Menon. Tall, emaciated, the rat of Alzheimer's nibbling away at his memories. Memories like 3271, his old landline from which he shouted his reports on the rotary phone—there on his table still, its dial broken, the cable wrapped around it, a monument to his career in journalism—to the news desk in Calicut, over 400 km from his office in Trivandrum ('Hello, exchange, this is a press call, please extend, hello…can you hear me, Calicut, can you hear me now?'): he still stuttered reports, though the events themselves had long dissolved into unforeseen eventualities at once familiar and new and wholly beyond his control, and the past had somehow become the future and then the present; those old copies of the *Pravda* and *Moscow News*, on which I practised my Russian, stacked under his cot; the yellowing writs to the government on behalf of Treesa and her team of sex workers to legalize their trade; a grainy black and white photograph of the long Troitsky Bridge on the Neva in St. Petersburg, M.'s town, on the back wall. That wormhole of a room, his study, where time stopped, moved back, and pitched forward. Both of us shared—if that was the word—*folie a famille*, a non-genetic delusional family disorder. Folie means psychosis; famille means family; and our doctor never explained why it had a French, rather than a Russian, name. Less than two years later, sitting by my grandfather's bed and watching him die, I would think that the disorder the two of us lived by was not much different from what the digital world sought—validation, as Gloria said, while exiting from Facebook, and throwing away her cell phone, 'its every second message a reminder to the desperate self of its anxious existence.'

'You must decide, kid,' the police officer said. 'You can't keep travelling through the night on escalators.'

'Whispering Woods,' I said to the officer when the name came back to me, 'Is the last train gone?'

'Are you ok? Been drinking? You can't be drinking unless you are 25. I could arrest you, but I won't.'

'Just a little feverish.' I wanted to say more: 'I am always reacting, not acting; tell me I am all right.' But I refrained.

He patted me down, discovered the hip flask, and found it empty. He shook his head in disapproval and returned the flask to me. 'In another two minutes. You need to change to Violet Line at Central Secretariat.'

I went down the escalator. The air rushed up to meet me. I had narrowly escaped arrest. It seemed hard to take a single step without breaking one law or another. I rode down for a long time.

FLUX

After the call, I returned to the hostel, to my long, narrow room with its high ceiling, and one window. I found Anand in his bed, filling up the length of it. He was a big man of a boy, perhaps the oldest in the school. His features were as carved in stone, and from under his slightly flaring nostrils and wide mouth, his jaw jutted out like an outcrop. There was a fierce light in his eyes which, he said, was because he practised yoga.

'You look like you have had a revelation or something.' Anand slowly got out of his bed, and as carefully stood on his large, flat feet. He breathed in and out deeply. 'Time for my *shirshasan*.'

'I was out,' I said.

'Out where?'

'Walking. The woods.'

'There is an English test the day after.' Anand said. 'Please get into shape. I can't copy your wrong answers, can I? "There's only one happy answer," as Tolstoy said.' He grinned. 'Besides, as you know, I live in the dire shadow of Ms Yolanda Andrade. I must perform well. Or else. That means *you* do well in the test.'

'I thought your mother was travelling on business?' Ms Andrade was the school principal.

'Stepmother. I have never met my mother. I have no wish to meet her either. I keep telling you that. Yes, but Ms Andrade has passed a message to me through the warden: If you flunk, you are out.'

'That's probably to scare you. To keep you in check.'

'Maybe. But she has never been exactly a source of confidence for me. You know that.' He unrolled his green yoga mat on the floor between our cots. 'I know you will agree with me when I say that the signs of absence of god multiply by the minute.'

'I bet she doesn't mean it.'

'That's the thing. You can never tell. My time is coming, though.' Anand smiled. 'I am working at something.'

A revenge plan. Yet another.

'Are you all right?' Anand asked.

'No. Yes.'

'What happened?' Anand stood up on his toes, appearing taller than me. 'We are both orphans. So much in common…' He expanded his hands to show the volume and size of the things we had in common. 'We share the same room. The same air. Yet, you are wary of me. Trust!' He shook his head in mock sorrow.

'Nothing, nothing. Really nothing.'

'You said nothing three times. That means something.'

'Nothing.'

'Four times nothing is a lot. You had better tell me because I am the only guy who cares for you.' He rotated his hands at the shoulder. First the right, then the left. Five times each.

I told him.

'Scandal. Shame. Sex! Are you kidding? I knew you two were close. But not this close.' Anand looked cheated.

'I don't think she cares for me anymore. I am close to her though. You know that feeling? That you know another person more than she knows herself?'

'An illusion, of course. How was it, making love to her? Was she a bitch? How many times?'

'Oh, just shut up. I am in pain.'

'She is not making up a story? About carrying?'

'What would be the point?'

'Scare you off her back? People are strange. Look at you.' Anand shook his head in pity and admiration. 'You are not strange, you are weird. The conversations you have with yourself! Yet you scored.'

'Why get in touch at all then?' I sat on my bed. I looked at the dip in the mattress where the weight of my back rested when I slept.

'That's what it is. I keep telling you, stop looking for logic. Evolution is nothing if not a series of accidents. Why do people destroy what they create? There is no explanation for everything.'

'True.' The universe we create in the blink of an eye, and wreck in the next, Elizabeth had said in the course of a Shakespeare lecture.

'Anything I can do, let me know. If you had been frank with me in good time, I could have guided you. I am more skilled than you in many respects. But…'

'…I trust no one?'

'Trust and gratitude. You lack both despite the fact that you have been cohabiting with a saint. A tragedy.'

'I need her address. There must be a forwarding address with the office.'

'I advise you against chasing white people even if they are beautiful. Stick to your own race. There is a reason why you are brown and she is white. We are colour-coded for separation.'

'You know people in the office.'

'If it's there, you will get it.' Anand shook his head again. 'You are a quiet cat.'

'My heart is at my heels.'

'You have had your pleasure. Pain would have followed.' Anand pointed to his forehead, at the small wart where his eyebrows met. 'I'm working on my pineal gland as you know. Once it is awakened, you would have nothing to worry, because I will show you a way forward. I am also developing a theory of wellness. Holistic Metaphysics. Helps you to resonate your frequency with that of the Universe. Till then you must bear your cross.'

I watched Anand carefully balance his head on the floor. His favourite yoga position. Perhaps that was the best way to see the world. When he was all set, I knocked him over, and watched his world slowly collapse.

'Hey,' Anand said, 'hey!'

***

At 101, Whispering Woods, poet and columnist, Arjun Bedi, was out. The key was in its usual place on the window ledge. I let myself in and made my way to the bar. It was only months ago that I had met Arjun, but we had become good friends. One day, having read his acid columns over a period, I had knocked on his door and introduced myself. 'I entertain only good and well-behaved souls,' he said, looking up from his armchair. The large room, painted in green, was crammed with books. Late October sunlight slanted in through the windows like muslin. There were books piled up on chairs too. Where a few were shifted recently, an empty square of dust framed their absence. Arjun rested the short quotation marks of his legs on a footstool. His writing pad had a glass of whiskey stuck in its hollow. He had a paunch, loose and re-arrangeable like a half-filled sack. On the carpet, next to his feet, a blue turban lay expectant of his bald head to roll into it at any moment. He looked up from his writing. He had sharp eyes that trapped the world in their black metal mesh. 'How do I know you are a good soul?'

I brush my teeth every day, and look up to my parents. No, not good enough. 'I read your columns. I wanted to meet you.'

He looked at me for a long moment, then pointed to the bar. 'Not my poems? Anyway. Pass. But that's not what you thought to say. I can read a mind looking the other way. All right, come and help yourself to a drink.' It was 11 in the morning. 'As a young Indian with literary and political aspirations, do you believe in Kashmir's freedom? I just finished a column on Kashmir. I must warn you to be truthful,' Arjun had said after his second drink. That day's newspaper reported that Kashmir was under an internet clampdown to quell protracted public unrest. There had been shooting, deaths, arrests, stone-pelting: 'the rituals by which the conscience of the race is administered,' Arjun would say.

'No,' I said, 'because, a free Kashmir will play into the hands of the fundamentalists.'

'Oh, that's what in effect the British said, reluctant to hand over power, that India can't govern itself.'

'But they can't, don't you see?'

'You prefer the Whites ruling over you, then? Well, I don't think you will ever become a politician after all. Besides, are you a separatist, or not?'

'I don't believe in the idea of India.'

'Let me help you. According to Karl Kautsky, a nation is defined by a common language, territory, economic market. India speaks hundreds of languages. And mountains divide many states. As for market, I don't know. Millions don't have money to buy anyway.'

'I guess I am a bit of an alien.' Mostly I thought I was wearing someone else's shirt and that I may have a shot at the real thing in the next life, if...

'The alien thing has gone out of fashion long ago. You can only be a nationalist or a liberal.' Arjun paused. 'And Otto

Bauer talks about the common character that a nationality implies. And there India may be One. We are mostly clowns.'

'Why clowns?'

'Years ago, I visited a village near Madurai—Anamalai—for a report on elephant trapping. It was like one of those terrifying temple festivals. The elephant had already fallen into the pit early in the morning. Now the villagers, half of them drunk, had turned out in strength to haul it up for taming. It was a lot of work with ropes and involved hundreds of people on either side of the pit with the usual drums and shouts. By evening, of course, they had fallen silent because the poor beast had been strangled to death, and its spine severed from its neck. I remember the expression in the elephant's eyes before it gave up its struggle. And all the while the crowd thought it was doing the animal a favour, because they were going to make the wild thing one of them.'

We thought about the elephant's eyes.

'Never articulate your adolescent theories outside these walls. They will lynch you. The Right will lynch you.' He downed his glass. 'The Left, too. They will find some other reason. You and I are the type who will get lynched by one group or the other. The cow vigilantes as well as the cow eaters. If neither, then the State. You and I must offer to each other the solace of affirmation, so hard to come by in these times of universal fear that each heart harbours for the other.' Arjun wiped the tears that had sprung in his eyes from the nobility of his feelings.

He put his glass down. 'I rather prefer free speech, that's about it.'

Arjun showed me some of his old, bitter but funny pieces. 'I admit I would be in jail if I wrote some of my old stuff now. It is misogynistic, I can see that. But misogyny is a kind of sexual orientation, you understand? It is genetic—like homosexuality. But I can't say that. My voice is being silenced! My voice! Who will talk about my transgressions except me?'

'The individual is more important than groups.' I nodded in agreement. My words slurred. 'I am just sad in my country.'

'You would be sad anywhere. That's who you are. Sad people have no country. Indeed, this might well be that epic time in a nation when people wander in body and spirit. Village to city. City to other countries. From issue to issue. Gender to gender. Earth to Mars. There is no fixity in time and space. Just a great continual flux.' He looked around for his glass, but could not immediately spot it. It was on the second rung of the bookshelf, right next to the Philip Roth. 'They just don't know they are adrift, you see? And such paranoia. No one much cares though because we are all growing insane together.'

We had a few more drinks. Arjun read out from his poems. Then threw his book aside. 'Terrible poems,' he said, it would be just if he was forgotten fast. But in these Google times, one had no choice but to remember everything, everybody; he would write to Wikipedia and ask them to remove his name from the files. It was inconceivable that they were making money from such invasion of privacy; it was his life; and they didn't even ask him if his bio-details could be published to the world. 'Is my life no longer mine?' Arjun said, 'Such a long life, too.' Arjun said he was ancient, 70 something. He hadn't reckoned to live to be older than 65. Now he did not know what to do with the bonus, which was another word for decline, decrepitude, and shame.

Arjun put his book back, next to a collection of Dom Moraes. 'I knew him from Bombay,' Arjun said, tapping the Moraes, trying to remember. 'You know what Dom said of the much-furrowed face of Auden, his mentor? No? "A wedding cake left out in the rain."' Arjun smiled, in appreciation.

'You should not be afraid of your detractors.'

'I am terrified of them. "Destroying reputations is how these little nobodies make their little mark." That is Roth in *Exit Ghost*, not me. Two of them, a couple, Dev and Diya, are spearheading the attack against me. They live on the ground floor. They are a very correct couple, and have begun to look like each other at a very early stage of cohabitation. They are kind. I have seen them feed stray dogs. They can't help their dislike of me. I am not easily liked anyway.' He was lost in thought. 'Against clamorous virtue, what defence? Christ, it's like a pack of angels on the hunt for the lone, wounded devil hiding out. Ah, well, I suppose it's not this or that. It is these and those, as they say.'

'Who? Who says that? Roth?' I was briefly awake.

'Oh, never mind. Did you notice that alcohol is a substitute for everything?'

At the end of that long day, Arjun dropped me at the railway station in his old, black Ambassador. The driver said I was too young to drink so much. Arjun asked him to focus on the road.

'I am just a driver,' the driver nodded.

Arjun turned to me and said, 'Kishan is always trying to reform me indirectly. Sometimes I think he is an agent sent by the super-cultivated to convert me, a kind of secular missionary.' Kishan grinned. I watched out of the window Delhi reveal its past in stone; its silent, deserted forts, and the airy mausoleums, round like giant speech bubbles of the dead. Ruins. And ruins of ruins.

At the station, Arjun said, 'Come again. I may not be always of help. But the bar will be open.' Kishan drummed his disapproval on the steering. Arjun asked me if I had ever fallen in love.

'No,' I said.

'It's a difficult art involving surrender; a kind of faith; only a few have that talent,' Arjun said. After a moment, he added: 'I refuse to play your father's role.'

That conversation was a little over a year ago. The Before-Elizabeth days. BE.

***

I dropped the key in a glass on the bar so nobody would miss it. The shape of each bottle on Arjun's bar might well have been the inspiration behind a modern skyscraper. At first, I found the alcohol not going to my head at all. So I made the drinks stronger. It was like water still. It was not biting me at the back of my throat. I had them neat. Oh yes. Where's the washroom? I wandered around Arjun's house in a warm, expanding haze and stumbled through a long corridor into a large hall, where Mrs Arjun Bedi lay in bed. She had no hair on her head. The room was all white. A nurse with a big nose sat on a chair by her bed, holding Mrs Bedi's shrivelled hand. 'Sorry,' I said, 'I didn't mean to disturb.'

Mrs Bedi opened her eyes. Next to her pillow was an empty carton of Mysore Sandalwood soap. On a small bedside table, there was a black and white photograph of a young Mrs Bedi. She looked beautiful. Perhaps black and white brings out the soul in people.

'Is he cheating on me?' Mrs Bedi said. Her voice was rich with agonies of all kinds.

The nurse stood up and said, 'You are not allowed to disturb her; please go.'

'Oh, I am so sorry. What is the way to the reception?'

'She is not a good nurse. She mixes up my medicines,' Mrs Bedi said, her eyes shut again, her voice hoarse. 'Genius writer, who didn't get his due. That's what he is going to take to his grave.'

'Is she talking about her husband?' I asked the nurse.

'Come here,' Mrs Bedi said.

I went up to the bed.

'Mrs Bedi…' the nurse said.

'You are from the living,' Mrs Bedi paused to gather her breath. 'Death is once, but it is forever. You understand?'

The nurse got up with a sigh. She took me by the elbow and led me back to the bar. 'This is the reception, and please don't try room service.' She tapped her nose in thought, set it in the direction of Mrs Bedi's room, and followed it.

I knew I was drunk now because I couldn't find my glass, which I thought I had placed on the bar. Maybe I didn't have my fifth?

Ah, there, my glass. I had found it. It had rolled under a chair. I stood at the bar and had another drink, as ever irresolute and wavering, and distracted myself from near-irresistible despondency, thinking about Elizabeth. She had a habit of widening her eyes when making a special point. It was a source of merriment for the class as we could bet on the number of times she would do it in the course of a lecture. But no one kept a tab, as her lectures were very good and she was too pretty. The first time she entered the classroom at the beginning of the term, she was dressed in a green cotton sari and matching blouse. 'Hello,' she had said.

'Hello,' we sang like a choir. All the 23 boys in the class had the same carnal thought. Hormones jammed the air.

'I am your new class teacher, Elizabeth.'

Elizabeth took note of me only in the evening when her students had tea in her cottage. We introduced ourselves again as we shook hands with her. She said she was good at forgetting. 'You guys have no idea, I move, return, and begin again all the time.' Her palms were large and unfeeling like a pottery maker's. When Anand extended his hand, I mouthed 'No' to Elizabeth and shook my head, thinking an Indian could never overemphasise his noes enough. Elizabeth was quick to see a tiny pad stuck to Anand's inner palm.

'Are you trying to electrocute me? I don't die easily,' she said, 'or far from England's shore.'

'Just a small shock. So you remember the evening forever,' Anand smiled his crooked smile, and everybody noticed one of his canines was just a bit longer than the rest of his teeth.

'Nothing is forever.'

Elizabeth asked us about the unforgettable incidents in our lives.

'What about you, Osip?'

'Pass,' I said.

'Not fair,' Anand said. 'He has many secrets. Many things have happened to him. He is a deeply disturbed man.'

'Really?' Elizabeth asked.

'There is a dark side to him. He is miserable when alone.'

Later in the evening, Elizabeth came up to me and said, 'Thanks for saving me from sudden and certain death. I owe you.' We shook hands again.

'We are shaking hands, not holding them, you know,' Elizabeth said after a moment, withdrawing the two cold fingers she had offered me.

'Sorry,' I let go of her hand.

'You are welcome,' Elizabeth said.

'I will stay back and help you with the dishes?'

The others seemed to have left in small groups. We washed the dishes together.

Elizabeth said she was a fan of Haruki Murakami. *Kafka on the Shore*, she mentioned; a story about a 15-year-old psychotic hero on the run, and of a man who could communicate with cats.

I told her I was an orphan to the sound of water running from the tap. Elizabeth laughed. It seemed the right thing to join in her merriment. I, too, laughed. 'Funny. You like to be at the edge of life maybe? Very Murakami. There is always theatre at the edge of life. But the fact is you are not very good at washing dishes.' Elizabeth held up a red saucer with a stained golden circle at its center.

'I will do it again.'

'You will make a mess of it.' She widened her eyes. 'You know, when I was a kid, I used to have nightmares in pink. It all took place in a courthouse with giant dolls, which was a patisserie that always got my order wrong.'

***

I put the empty glass back on the bar. Nothing mattered now—fifth drink or sixth. I loved everybody. Everybody loved me. It was the world of the Buddha. I must strive, Anand said, for equanimity. But now was not the time. I was charged. Hey? Who are you, whoever you are? I was equal to anyone, even to the overbearing Ms Yolanda Andrade.

Who could deny me anything? No one except Elizabeth. Love is handing so much power over us to others. Have I said it already? But, really, how easily we entrust our lives to people we never imagined existed until just a while ago. Trust is forged before a word is uttered, and instantaneously.

Whose blue-clad dome blooms at the door?

Arjun? Finally? Come, my friend and mentor, make yourself at home, take off your turban, scratch your head, nourish your thoughts. A drink?

'How many have you had?' Arjun shook his head at me, and did not wait for my reply. 'I have had a most enlightening forty-eight hours. Yesterday in Jaipur. Today in Udaipur. The same fake Delhi crowd everywhere, good at holding on to the mic, and no one listening. There was Mitali Jain, though, thank god! Haven't you met her? Of course, you have. The one who runs Femart? The slim, dark, pretty girl? No? She was a relief. And her father, Alok Jain, the business baron. Owns India Post Media. "I am the IP man," he keeps saying. A most volatile person. How does anyone make a fortune with a temper like that? When did you come?'

When did I come? What time is it? It had become dark. Arjun switched on a floor lamp. 'I am in trouble.'

'What trouble? Can I help?'

'The Right is on my back because I don't buy their nationalist politics. The Left because of my gender biases.' He shook his head. 'They have dug up an old photograph of mine at a party, where I had stripped myself to my underwear and was dancing. Once that came up, there was no stopping them. Dev and Diya, and their friends, you remember Dev and Diya, don't you? They burrowed into my old columns and came up with a list of sexist lines and phrases. Ah, but I love them even in my hatred! A panel of progressive men and women are investigating my writing—The Union of Rights and Fairness (URF). They are more powerful than a special tribunal because of the cell phone. I expect the worst. And the thing is,' he screwed up his eyes to recall a line, "the wolf, the snake, the hog not wanting in me." Whitman, I believe.'

'But there must be good people in Delhi, good people among your friends?"

'Delhi! Father owns daughter's fashion house. The critic is the lover of the danseuse. The minister is the uncle of the MP. Nepotism. Corruption. Brazenness. The discreet charms of the Delhi bourgeoisie.' He placed his turban on his desk. 'They have prepared a file on me. All that I have written, said, bantered, joked, the lingering glances and touches, it's all a dossier now. And no, there are no friends. Only good people as you phrase them.' He looked at me for a moment. 'You had better catch some rest. You look all in.'

'There's someone behind you.' I had glimpsed a form, a shape, flitting behind Arjun.

Arjun looked behind him, and then turned around. 'You are seeing things. How long have you been drinking?'

'I just began.'

'You should not be drinking so much. Not on top of those medicines. I bet you are in no condition to spell the name of even one.'

'R-i-s-p-e-r-i-d-o-n-e.'

'Oh, good.'

'O-l-a-n-z-a-p-i-ne.'

'Then you must drink.'

'I think I will take a gap year, Arjun. That's what I will do.'

'Yes. Retire, actually,' Arjun said. 'You are too old not to. In any case, you know basic English. And you know how to add and subtract. Enough. I don't know what you are doing here.'

But did he mean his house? I went up close to the lamp. My own shadow approached the wall, filled it up. I stopped in my tracks, turned. 'I really need a break.'

'I'm turning in. We will talk tomorrow.'

'Elizabeth is not in Delhi.'

'Ah, yes, your teacher and lover. A great combination. How's that going?'

'I looked her up. She's flown.'

'She has some sense, after all.'

'I talked to her security guard. He said she left.'

"She would be foolish to stay back in this country after seducing a minor.'

'She didn't seduce me. I will find her.'

'Only if you are foolish enough to persist in your pursuit. You know that psychosis is another word to describe a maladjusted personality?'

What if the whole society is maladjusted...? 'I met your wife finally.'

'She doesn't like to meet anyone, but you know that.' There was an edge to his voice.

'It was an accident.'

'Get some rest, OB,' Arjun said, one hand on the door to his room. 'We will talk tomorrow.'

Where was the washroom? I had been to that errant space earlier in the day. But it was now proving to be elusive. I looked out of the window. An old man with a flowing beard was walking around in the dim-lit garden, followed by a German Shepherd. A gentle life, with a dog in the fog. Yes, I would retire. I missed my grandfather. I wished he was not so ill. I missed my father, too, whoever he was, though it was odd how you missed people you never would meet all your life. Like a blind man missing a candle. Later in the night, I brought up all I drank, and spent the rest of the night scrubbing the floor. A little of the ejecta stained the carpet. I hoped Arjun wouldn't notice. He did.

Beneath The Skin

Kabuki is done up in pale blue, and the staff wears matching kimonos. A sign on the wall says: 'No Cash, No Narcotics.' A pale blue tatami covers the wooden floor.

Meditative music plays faintly like a mantra in the background. Elizabeth waits for her turn in an inner room of the clinic, thinking all of Japan is deliberate as a spell. Only then do all those rituals and ceremonies make sense. Maybe she will go to Japan next year. One wall of Kabuki is all blue mirrors so cut and arranged that Elizabeth finds herself reflected everywhere, none of the images whole. When she leans back, the half of her face that stepped out returns, like ghosts coming back to their haunt. Weird. Not very different from her thoughts last night, when Osip tapped out on her door his Morse code of distress. She almost giggles at the memory now, but not out of cruelty, but from relief. It was just so close, like the nape of your neck tickling to someone's breath.

She listens to Osip going down the steps. If she puts out a hand out of the window, it would all be different in a minute. But that minute ticked in altogether another clock, measured another reality. Elizabeth thinks of the joy and hurt she could bring to another. No, we are all one man or woman too many, it is impossible to share her goodness with Osip, with whom she would always be seen as the exploiter. That was the situation. She peers through the window curtain. Just a peep; but how much it reveals. Like watching the sky through a keyhole. She can see Osip talking to the guard, who has stopped rolling the lathi over his thighs. In the light of the streetlamp, she can see his strange Bruce Lee hair. He has nice hair. When the conversation with the guard is over, Osip looks up at the window straight at her. She stands still. Elizabeth can imagine his long eyes searching for her. When Osip walks away around the corner, she turns on the table lamp, and feels her face, framed by her hair, luminous like a painting, with nervous fingers. Her forehead is creased by a worry that her impulsiveness, rendered even more impetuous by her loneliness, may have been misconstrued by Osip for a kind of emotional attachment, which was best interpreted as an act of generosity. Elizabeth is aware of her mild obsession with sensations though, the electric stuff of life. She leans back at the thought. All her split images move back, too. Teaching English and sleeping with students. Student. Will it be less of a crime if the boy is English? Well, don't go and try that now. Literature and licence. The two go hand in hand, maybe? There was a licentiousness about the written word. It sanctioned. But, surely, this kind of thing that she got into happened all the time? No, it didn't. How casual she has been. Let it be. One slipped.

Token 11, the Kabuki electronic indicator says. Her turn. 11 is two upright people. 12 would be one standing and the other about to question. 13 would be one standing and the other in shackles. Before she gets to 14, she is guided into an inner room with two doors facing each other. A middle-aged woman serves her San-cha in a tiny cup, also blue. The tea calms her. When Elizabeth finishes her tea, she is surprised to find at the bottom of the cup a cherry tree in violent blossom like a miniature revolution. She is reassured that the cherry blossom is not blue. But, of course, no other colour would be possible. Yes, she would be born a Japanese in her next birth. The woman smiles. She has even, very white teeth. She introduces herself as Sangita Ering. She says there are many services that Kabuki extends besides foolproof pregnancy tests. Delivery. Painless abortions. Pre-natal training. Early and advanced parenting courses. Astro-Club, too. After a moment, Sangita sits closer to Elizabeth on the sofa, legs together to the far side, like an old friend who has been estranged, but still open to overtures. Another woman enters the room. She whispers into Sangita's ear. Sangita nods. 'I will be back,' Sangita says and takes her leave.

***

Ah, yes, one slipped. Elizabeth ran her hand over her stomach. Heavy? Not heavy? For a while back there, she had panicked. A mother. Mothers were stuck. It was a 25-year contract, if anything. And, in this case, the father was a child himself. Face it, she was a pedophile. 'Nonsense,' Elizabeth thought. Those were the days when they thought Lolita obscene. As soon as Elizabeth called up Osip, she had realized she had compounded her mistake. Yes, impulsive.

***

Through the window, Elizabeth watches Osip walk away, and she feels a surge of pity and power, as if it was another person in her place at the window. His future is in her hand. Her hand. It has done things with him. And now it is closing, tight and hard. Open palm. Closed fist. 'The Ulnar Situation,' Kris said. 'Ever since man found he could close his thumb and little finger, wield a stick or cup, a thing, his complications began,' Kris said, 'because consciousness changed.' Elizabeth is closing her fist for Osip's good, though he will not grasp it. For her good, too. Only the hand that offers can withdraw. She runs her hand over her abdomen again. She has morning sickness. Yes, get it over with. She may drop dead the next moment. She can't make the final exit, frightened and anxious, and with a baby to worry about. Responsibility is also doing away with things. She lets go of the window curtain, the rough texture of the cloth dragging its papery weight over her smooth skin, but only after looking momentarily at its movement, as if an act is coming to an end, thinking how in such small gestures a story turns, an asylum refused, a corner of the heart frozen, and returns to her table, older for the stars that have burned out meanwhile, opens her laptop. Her face lights up in its ghost-blue wash. She googles 'friendly maternity clinics near

South Extension'. 'Go to Kabuki,' Google says. She checks the reviews. 'Expensive and excellent,' the reviews say.

***

And here she is, watching her face split in the mirrors. What she thinks of her face is not what Osip sees in it.

'I suffer from an inability to see things for what they are,' Osip had once said to Elizabeth. He had come over to her quarters. They had ended up in bed, and afterward, lay without touching each other, a little estranged, as if all of it had happened to another couple who lived inside a mirror in the far side of a room.

'I had a partner back in London. Oxford, actually. A kind of father figure.' Elizabeth had reflected on what she said. 'It was a bit like sleeping with Plato. No sex.'

'And, then?'

'He began making claims. That was not the deal, you get it? But I realize such claims are an eventuality. I packed up and left.'

'Why India?'

'Kris was Indian, if that's a reason. I doubt it. But I guess I was just waiting for an excuse.' Elizabeth was lost in thought for a moment. 'He would sit still and surprise me saying inane things. It was not expected of him.'

'What kind of inane things?'

'"When you go out of the room, please close the door after you. I think now I would like to be alone." I was going to close the door anyway. Made me extremely self-conscious.

You would think he was the type of man who kept his gloves on all the time.'

Osip had gazed at her in reverence.

'You believe in telepathy, Elizabeth?'

'Only if it's in English.' Elizabeth was suddenly disappointed in Osip, and self-conscious of her intimacy with him. 'I told you I am not good at explaining things.'

'No, I think I get it. I can read minds.' Osip had said, but it was clear to Elizabeth he hadn't understood the spirit of her speech. Sometimes, the distance between two people was more than what a sea could fill, a vastness that came in like a tide and went, and came in again. They had been quiet for a moment. Then Elizabeth said, 'Kris mistook companionship for something else.' Did she encourage Kris? She was not sure. One sometimes took advantage of one's effect on others.

'If humans, my grandfather would say, kept away from falling in love, the world would be a less warlike place.'

'I don't think we should be talking about things like love.'

'We should practise telepathy,' Osip said.

'Yes, you are too young for anything else,' Elizabeth had said, almost out of despair.

***

'Sorry,' Sangita returns, 'a minor crisis.'

Elizabeth notes that Sangita is attractive in a melancholic way. She has an air about her as if she has decided against wanting to know about too many things at an early point in her life. She is neat, too. Her hair is styled like a Japanese doll's. She is fair, and her eyes are a little slanted. She could pass off for a foreigner if she did not speak Hindi and English with an accent, which Elizabeth can vaguely place only as exotic.

Sangita reads her face, nods. 'There's nothing to vorry.'

Her W is light—like it is V, W with helium balloons attached. She hands over a small blue bottle with a wide mouth to Elizabeth. 'Ve will collect your urine. That door there leads to the vashroom.'

'We?'

'You,' Sangita smiles. 'Just a vay of saying.'

'Ah. yes. Where are you from?'

'Purvanchal Pradesh'

'Does the local spirit smell of ants?' Who said that? Osip? No, his friend, Anand.

'No. Vhy?'

'Just. It's far away, though.'

'Yes. Ve are all refugees here, really. Ve get by because ve look like someone else.' She holds up the bottle. 'Ve know how this works?'

'Sort of.'

'Painless. It's painless, that is the most important thing.'

'Explain to me the test, please?'

'Ve will look for a hormone, chorionic gonadotropin, in our urine. Our body only makes this hormone if ve are pregnant.' Sangita smiles her sad smile. 'But ve don't want the baby.'

'No.'

'Babies are tough.' Sangita smiles. 'There's so much to a baby before and after.' She points to the closed door to the side of the room. 'I sit there. Please let me know if ve vant anything.'

'You have a baby?'

Sangita pauses at the door. She turns around slowly. 'Had. Ve don't know where he is.'

'I am sorry.'

'That was many years ago. Ve experience no pain now. It's like magic.' Sangita smiles, and closes the door after her.

Elizabeth gets up. It is a dream, she tells herself. It is the blue theme. The blue and that music. And the baby she is going to kill. A pedophile and a murderer. She pleads insanity before the Honourable Court. 'You temptress,' the judge says, 'we condemn harlotry, it's our bounden duty to protect the flower of our youth from temptresses such as you, we, therefore, sentence you to…' Elizabeth walks toward the washroom. Her steps are heavy. Once there, Elizabeth finds she has not taken the bottle. She goes back. The bottle is waiting. It has not moved at all. The room and everything in it are concentrated in the empty bottle. Elizabeth picks it up as in a trance and retraces her steps to the washroom. She sits on the toilet seat, thinking. A moment later, she stands up and retches without bringing up anything.

Elikalimata

'What time is it?' I ask myself. It's late. I walk. I drink from the flask. There are few people about. Connaught Circus is nearly deserted. When I reach M block on the outer ring, three battle tanks roll past me in the direction of India Gate. A few months ago, the army chief had marched with a company of soldiers along Shanti Path, an avenue in the main diplomatic enclave, toward the president's palace in an attempted coup. It was later reported as fake news. Fake, real; who knows? Fake is real. Seeing is not believing.

I walk a little more. When I am about to give up hope, a ramshackle three-wheeler, green body, yellow top, turns up. It goes a little ahead and waits for me. I see the Prime Minister, from the back, extending his hands in welcome; 'One India, one mind', says the slogan above his head. I get in and ride toward Elizabeth's place in the company of the Prime Minister forging, behind my back, the nation as his will, inviting a chaotic people into his iron, unifying embrace. I look out at the trees speeding past, the shuttered shops, and the sleeping houses. I could spend years doing just this trip back and forth in an effort to close a circle—and the Prime Minister would still be there; or someone like him; most of us would always be ruled. When I reach Elizabeth's place, I think I can see for a moment a light in her room. I cannot be sure. The guard is in his chair, one leg crossed over the other, gazing at his feet sadly, as if they no longer belonged to him. I ride past her place. I don't have the heart to persist. How easily resolves tire themselves out, only to start all over again, like waves in the sea. The auto-rickshaw drops me at Connaught Place. The driver says he will not go any farther. I step out, stumble. 'You don't look too well,' he says. I pay him. I watch the Prime Minister recede from me. 'In the last count, a leader must elude the grasp of his followers to keep his mystique intact,' Arjun said.

The white colonnade of Connaught Circus is now empty. The fog is thick, but does it justify what seems to be a vast exercise in evacuation as perhaps befitting a war, or a lockdown in the face of a contagion? Right in front of me, across the road, is a high-rise, circular building. The Statesman House, huge, spectral, waning and waxing in the fog. Unreal. I look around. I am back at the corner of M Block. I walk around the Circus. I am exhausted. I want to sit down, surrender to the night. But if I do that, I may not be able to get up. Hours later, so it seems, near Janpath, I see a shop is open. A cubbyhole of an office. A sign says, Kashmiri Travels. Next to it, from a hook, hangs a lantern draped in black crepe. Kashmir in mourning? I hesitate, then step in. A small, dark man sleeps on a longish, glass topped-table, right over the Dal lake. His head rests on a mountain peak. On a chair next to the table sits a jar of water. I would like to have a drink from it. I stare at him. He is snoring. When he snores, his lips flutter. What's his breath like? I will wait for five minutes. If he wakes up, I will ask him for a ticket to Srinagar. I will join the separatist movement. Free Kashmir. Free Osip. This is my moment of truth. Kashmir's too. Shaheed Osip Bala Krishnan. I shall redeem honour by throwing myself in the way of bullets fired by the Indian army. Someone will take a photograph as I leap, firing my last volley, at an army jeep, and win a Pulitzer. Your karma is another's destiny. Elizabeth will eventually read about my epic heroism. Only she will know I travelled to Kashmir, my Spanish Republic, fought another's battle, for another's freedom, because she did not open her heart to me. The consequences of denied love are historic, Ms Hill. I concentrate my energies on the sleeping Kashmiri travel agent. I use my telepathic powers. Everything depends on him. If he wakes up, I am going. Enough of these vacillations, mood swings, and half-life. I stare at the sleeper. 'Wake up, I dare you. Wake up, and I will deliver Kashmir for you. To you.' He turns to one side and slips deeper into his sleep. I extend my deadline by another five minutes. I feel weak. I hang on. But he doesn't open his eyes. I turn my back on my militant future. I step out, look up at the sodium-light drenched night sky and see over the Palika Park, the Prime Minister rise in the air in a massive white balloon. Didn't I just see him drive away in a rickshaw? The Leader is everywhere. There is no other way for a Leader to be. The balloon is flashing-white in colour. The portrait on it is gigantic. I watch the PM rise and rise, an inflated benevolence over the capital, rising. I watch still my neck hurts. Then I walk away, fever bright in my blood.

When I enter my room at Singh's Palace, crossing the grey watery line that marks dawn from the night, I collapse into the bed. I don't want to get up ever. My body is hot to the touch. I am a felled tree. Through my bones spread the branches of ache. The room spins. There is a smell of poultry in the air. Feathers swirl like cotton from a split pillow. Elizabeth and I walk in the dust with the chickens. We look for eggs in the coop and they warm our hands with their life. The cobra hatching them in her folds licks our hands with her blue-forked tongue. 'Never fear, darling,' Elizabeth says. How easily my hands slip into your silken sleeves, Elizabeth? What can be more unreal than life? Than you, Elizabeth. I hold your wrists, look into your great eyes. I will be anything you want me to be. This surrender is so easy. I speak in many languages, I tell her; I love Elizabeth in all of them. Delirium tremendous, Elizabeth smiles. 'Feel my pockets,' I tell Elizabeth. They are heavy with precious coins. A man in a tunic, a *vozhderka*, with his withered left hand shoved into his pocket throws his shadow on the red wall across a street. It feels like the Kremlin, but it is not—almost; it could be the Central Secretariat. He walks fast, all of him together, at once, forward. As I watch, he metamorphoses into my grandfather. No, it's not him. The shadow is two people in one. I sit up in a sweat, my head clear like rinsed glass, certain my grandfather is pretending to be an Alzheimer's patient to cover up for the real thing, though what the real thing is remains vague, like fog.

***

The house in which I lived in Thrissur had a basement and an attic beside the floor in-between. It had a broad veranda running around it, and the high roof was tiled. It had a big backyard with a barren mango tree at the centre, and an old swing that sometimes hid among the branches, and fell to the earth like an invitation from heaven. 'Ascend', it said. The backyard opened out to the paddy fields and, on the far side, to the low hills. From the small horizontal windows in the attic, you could see the tiles over the veranda sloping down and, in the monsoon, the rain ran down in furious little currents and plunged to the earth in a deadfall, shaking the terrified plants. Most of the time, I was at the frontline down in the basement: snow, slush, soldiers, and pogroms.

On the main floor, in a study lined with books, my grandfather lay on his cot straight as an arrow, shot from another millennium. Just one person stood between Mr Menon and me and abject surrender to the visitations: Gloria Innaley. 'It's all an act,' she never tired of saying, 'and he has been at it for decades, ever since his one trip to the Soviet Union in the winter of 1961, when he was in his late 30s, just in time to witness in person the unbelievable sight of Stalin's exhumation from the special mausoleum and reburial under the Kremlin Wall. It must have been a bit like opening the tomb of a Pharaoh centuries later to see if his sway still held the same dread,' she said. Mr Menon had gone for one month on a kind of state visit. And then disappeared for a year. When he returned, he never spoke about the trip. Nor did the local Party. He continued to play an even more active role 'in the murderous politics of his party,' Gloria said, 'but he had changed.' He was meticulous in carrying out his orders as ever. Keener even. But he had turned vague about many things. She had often wondered if he was a killer first and an ideologue later. Of course, every party needed both: without murders, human sacrifice, no party could rule, no State exist. After a while, Gloria stopped asking what was wrong. He was some 20 years older to her. She was married to him when she was 15 or 16. Once or twice, she heard him utter in his sleep a name, Eva, or Iva. Ava Lenk. By the beginning of the 1980s, Mr Menon was becoming a 'the longest willed act in senility,' Gloria said. Then the Berlin Wall crashed, and soon the Gorbachev presidency had more or less dismantled the Soviet Union. It was like a slow lobotomy for Mr Menon, an operation by other means carried over the decades. It was simpler for him that way, Gloria said. She did not care. In any case, their married life was a sham. Gloria tried to do the practical things, little things that the moment demanded, and never gave her game away. Which consisted of running the house within her means and keeping his name up as a great revolutionary leader. She expected the others to be as practical as her. 'If you have nothing to do but mope, please dust the house.' That was her way of staying sane, keeping things going.

'Go, have a shower,' Gloria now issues yet another diktat for being human, from above.

'After some time!' I shout from the basement. Personal hygiene can be easily construed as corporal punishment in many situations.

'Don't shout at me,' Gloria says.

It was 1941 down in the basement. June. Hitler had launched Operation Barbarossa, opening the Eastern Front of the war, and Stalin was going through a nervous breakdown over the Nazis reneging on the peace treaty. The only time he had no idea what to do, my grandfather said.

'Why not now? You haven't had one for days.' Gloria has a shrill, impatient voice, an alarm alerting you to your constant follies.

'I had one yesterday.'

'Are you sitting on a pillow by any chance?'

'No. Why?'

'Because I have seen you doing it. Don't sit on a pillow.'

'I am not sitting on a pillow. By why can't I sit on a pillow?' I was sitting on a pillow.

'Because it brings you bad luck and you will be in debt.'

'How?'

'Never mind. Just go have that shower.'

'I had one yesterday.'

'Conserving water? A soldierly thing to do.'

'You said days. "Days since I had a bath", you said.'

'Balaa!'

I count up to five. So that the response doesn't come across as irrational. 'Yes.'

'Are you deaf?'

'No.'

Years later, as I entered my late-teens, Gloria would be still at it.

'Balaa, come up and have your dinner.'

'Not now.'

'Why not now? You have had nothing the whole day.'

'I had.'

'What? Breakfast?'

'Yes.'

'That was when? In the morning? Do it before the winter begins in the Soviet Union.'

I waited for more. Waited for her to make fun of things she could never get used to, such as other people's lives. I guess we tend to mock what we can't understand. Perhaps that is how we come to possess our allotted share of secrets, by not being understood. I waited for Gloria to go. It was about time for her to call for an auto-rickshaw and go on her rounds. She did it every day. 'I have to air myself,' she would say, 'or I grow musty.'

'You know what the doctor said?'

'No.'

'Of course, you do. Your social skills are poor. Your attention span is fleeting. In school, you have no idea how to compose answers to questions even when you know them. And you are slow.'

She was wrong about the language part of my skills. I took her delusions about me to be a part of my camouflage. It was not as if I did not know that not everything was right with me. I was there with Doctor Ratnamali Nair when he said I was likely to be borderline, psychotic. Years earlier, I had watched him ask test-questions to my grandfather. On that occasion, Mr Menon had got both the day and the year right. I had sighed in relief. Then the doctor asked him my grandmother's name, and my grandfather had looked helplessly at Gloria and me. Gloria took it personally, I think; it was another slight, perhaps. Later in the consultation, I watched my grandfather draw a clock and get the hour hand positions all wrong, after much thought. Because I saw that he did get his two o'clock right, but then he struck it out and brought it forward. I didn't see it symptomatic of his condition. 'Only Salvador Dali would appreciate Mr Menon's clock-work,' Doctor Nair said to my grandmother to make it all appear not so dark and final. When we stepped out of the clinic, my grandfather and I followed Gloria at a respectful distance. Gloria had become the new leader—'thanks to the bloodless coup by General Alzheimer,' as my grandfather whispered. A few steps further, he said: 'I am relinquishing my rank as the supreme commander, but I will continue to be your Russian teacher.'

'And your great escape is the personalities that your grandfather introduces to you in his study,' Gloria continues from above, relentless as an oracle, a disembodied voice that spoke the truth at the cost of broken kings.

She makes it all sound a matter of choice, I would then think, when you were already what you are. But there was a reason why she had been even more persistent with me of late. A few days earlier, for the first time, I had run into Stalin—just as my grandfather promised I would—in a shower of red petals at the deserted Gul Mohar garden, at the far back of the school. Gulab Archipelago, my grandfather rechristened it in my ears, when I narrated the incident. The man in the garden was still as a statue. Then he suddenly moved to fall in step with me, as I walked past him, and he turned stiffly, first the neck, then the head, then the whole body. 'People like him don't die,' my grandfather said. 'They just wait. And when the time comes, there they are, again, history like putty in their hands.'

'Is it true,' I asked the man standing in the garden, 'that from absolute loyalty and faith come absolute punishments?' I was only repeating a question my grandfather murmured to himself. He turned his face in my direction, but said nothing. A group of kids came around, stood in a circle, clapped hands, and sang, '*Shiroka strana moya rodnaya*.' Thank you, comrade Stalin for a happy childhood. 'Ask him about his Siberian exilic experience in Tukhharansk,' the children said. 'Oh, I fished alone in the frozen Yenisei River, read alone, and wrote alone. I rang the bell of my own door. I have been more alone than any poet you care to name. Go on, children,' he said in a low, dull voice, cold and inexorable as steel, 'go to your classes.'

He watched them go with his empty eyes. 'Every one of them is a dictator, let me tell you, every one of them, clinging on to their little power. чистка. *Chistika*. Purge. I did it for a reason. There is no beauty without blood and sacrifice, comrade'

When my teachers got to know of my conversation with the new (deaf and mute, as it turned out) guard in the garden, they didn't let me attend the class. Two of them accompanied me home. My grandfather assumed an authority I had not seen for a long while and talked in my defence. But the school insisted I needed a break.

That night in the basement, I read out M.'s 1933 epigram on Stalin (Мыживем, подсобоюнечуястраны,/Наширечиз адесятьшаговнеслышны,/А гдехватитнаполразговорца,/ Тамприпомняткремлёвскогогорца./ (We live, not feeling the earth beneath us/At ten paces our words evaporate./But when there's the will to crack open our mouths/our words orbit the Kremlin mountain man./Murderer, peasant killer). I was thinking, was this a poem to die for really, when Gloria came down, took a cold clinical look at me, and said I was having an episode. She came back down and with the help of her maid and secretary, Makkam (of yellow eyes and long, matching, teeth), tied my hands behind me, and placed a block of ice wrapped in a towel on my head. I apologized. When the ice had melted, they brought another and kept it long enough on my head, and I apologized again. Outside, it had begun to rain, and I apologized for that. Then there was a peel of thunder and, I said, it sounded like God's house collapsing. I apologized for that, too. And Gloria said, 'we are all left-overs from one man's breakdown.'

Dr Ratnamali Nair came the next day. He forced some medicines on me. When I woke up hours later, Gloria was sitting next to me, reassuring me it was nothing, just an incident. 'But listen, *folie a famille* requires a physical separation between the patients. You and your grandfather are doing no good to each other. I am looking for a boarding school. Far from here. I think I know who to talk to. You can pay us an annual visit. If you stay here, you won't able to break out of his world.'

The effects of poetry are incalculable, Dear Reader.

'It's for your good,' Gloria said.

I nodded, my face to the wall, raised two fingers: victory. I was under medical observation for weeks. Meanwhile, Gloria spoke to the Party Secretary, who knew someone close to Ms Andrade. They put me on a flight to Delhi. A Party contact collected me at the airport and escorted me to St George's, waved, disappeared. He seemed relieved that the mission he was entrusted with had got over without incident.

***

I am down with chickenpox at Singh's Palace for seven days. Arjun knows where I am, but he doesn't come calling. He must be upset about the carpet. I don't blame him. That's fine, really, I don't want to meet anyone. Not even Elizabeth. She can keep her great secrets to herself, the deep mysteries of her womanhood. Am I emotionally blackmailing her, instead of appreciating her generosity of body and spirit? 'Hey, who is the victim here?' as Arjun would ask. I think of Mrs Arjun Bedi. Arjun hardly ever talks about her. Maybe, beyond an accommodating hate for each other's goodness that a long-shared life gifts, they have found something short of love, a talent good enough—and perhaps even equal to love?—to suffer each other's presence? Maybe. I am profound tonight. The closest I have ever been to life's secrets is today. I am a medium for Kali.

It's the pox.

'Neem leaves help, you are lucky, it's Kali Mata's love,' the kind hotel manager says—when did he come up? Now you understand what I mean when I say love is like hate? Or, did I say that? Elizabeth shimmers like the memory of things that have not happened; a radiance of impossibility. 'Soak neem leaves in hot water and pour it over your body,' the manager says, 'it helps the itching'. He exits, and then enters, unfathomable hours later, with a forest of neem leaves. The bathroom smells of neem. The bed, too. I think I may not recover. I feel old. My body is a mass of sores. 'The curses are coming out of the system,' the manager smiles. 'Kali Mata loves you.'

When the worst of the chicken-pox is over, Anand turns up, on behalf of himself and the school. 'You should have called earlier. Why didn't you call me earlier?' Anand says.

'I sent a couple of emails to the warden.'

'I know. You look charred.' His friendship wets my eyes. He is in good spirits. 'I called my friend, the manager. We discussed neem. Nothing like traditional medicine!'

'Thanks, Anand.'

'I won't ask you about Elizabeth Madam.'

I turn my face to the wall. Elikalimata. She turned me verminous, and small. My soul creeps into the black mole on my right toe. In my weakened state, Elizabeth could dispense with me an easy conscience. How I served her. Little empowers a despot like devotion and faith. From absolute loyalty and faith come absolute punishments. Has everything been said before? I am about to weep. The purity of my love is destroying me. I keep my face to the wall. 'Anand, you are my only friend.'

Ruth Reprieved

Elizabeth decided to shift to a nearby guest house. It was called The Ikon. It seemed discreet to move to another address, even if the place followed the universal trend and misspelled its name, than stay in her rented place. She packed her suitcase and dragged it down the steps. While negotiating the second flight of stairs she felt sick in the pit of her stomach and sat down on the steps. Before she could lay a preventive finger—and a single restraining finger was all that might have been required—the suitcase tumbled down the staircase. Elizabeth watched at first with academic eyes as the trolley-bag fell head over heels, skidded, skipped a step or two and then landed, its top open and her dear clothes spilled like secrets out into the open. The enormity of her loneliness struck her. 'Like Ruth among the alien corn,' Elizabeth thought, 'like Ruth among the alien corn with a spilling suitcase'. She went down slowly, picked up the stuff, and put it all back in, its order all messed up. Elizabeth had spent some time arranging the clothes. She was normally deliberate in her movements, a trait she developed, she would think in her less charitable moments, to cover up her impulsive nature. But now that time spent in arranging her clothes inside the bag seemed to make no difference to the utterly unpredictable reality that she found herself in. It might have been her, not the suitcase that tripped and fell. And she was pregnant. After a minute or so, Elizabeth went down the steps. When she lifted the suitcase, she found one of its wheels had broken. She would have to lug it then. 'Ruth among the alien corn dragging a suitcase after her: keep the camera rolling on Ruth to find more in the frame.' A little way off, her eyes caught a black lace bra, the wayward source of all her problems—she might well think—and felt a deep pity for it. 'Keep the camera rolling.' She shoved the bra into the suitcase and stepped out, just in time to see the cab she had called for drive up. 'The Ikon,' she said to the driver, and was sick for England. She missed the calmness of Kris.

'Yes, madam, I know where you want to go. It's all there on my map,' the driver said.

He was a huge man, and his head nearly touched the roof of the car. He wore a saffron shoulder band, perhaps in solidarity with the ruling right-wing party. Elizabeth wished she had not broken off with Kris, who believed human relationships are best avoided—and then proceeded to have one with Elizabeth—because they carried the unique germs of misery. Humans infected each other. 'Emotion,' he said, 'was a virus transmitted through words. Men, women, and children would have been happier before language was invented.' Kris was 45-odd years older than Elizabeth, a retired academic in physics. 'The fate of the individual was the result of a million chances brought into play by utter strangers,' he would say with a look of helplessness. 'That was why Man's destiny was collective. Their first meeting,' Kris said, 'happened probably because of the ISIS bombing Aleppo.' Elizabeth and Kris were both waiting for their turn at the Barclays ATM at Marble Arch when a big-built, bearded man jumped the queue. 'Indian, Pakistani, or Syrian,' Elizabeth had wondered. 'It was remarkable how they all looked the same.'

'Excuse me,' Elizabeth said, 'It's my turn.'

'I am sorry,' the stranger said, 'it's a bit of an emergency.' His face showed worry and tension.

'Well, you should have requested the lady,' said a calm voice from behind Elizabeth.

Elizabeth turned. A tall elderly man, with wrinkle-free skin and olive complexion, was staring steadily at the interloper. He had small, jet-black eyes. His silver hair was parted low on one side.

'You can't just jump the line,' she turned back to the interloper.

'You are making a big thing of it,' the bearded man said. He looked frantically around, as if for an interpreter, a translator not so much for the language as another country, culture. Someone to interpret his alien manners and anxieties.

'There's a way of going about this,' Elizabeth's new-found friend said.

'This won't take a minute.'

'This is England,' Elizabeth said.

'Yes, England,' the man threw up his hands. 'With all this glass and steel and manners, you have shut us out.'

'I'm going to shout for help.' The greatest threat to the West from East was chaos.

'No,' the man said, 'there is no kindness here in this country. Only order.'

'Then you shouldn't be here.'

'You have everything,' the man said, his voice loud and bitter. 'Everything. You took it all from us. For hundreds of years. We have a right to be here.' He turned and walked hurriedly away, pulling his cap tight over his head.

Elizabeth took out the money from the machine. Her fingers fumbled. To be insulted despite being British and a woman. He could have hit her. Killed her even. These things happened just like that. She shook her head.

'Kris,' the man behind her said.

'Elizabeth. Thank you for your intervention. Wasn't that strange?'

'Yes, rather. Maybe not so strange in India or Africa. Makes you want to think about things like immigration policies, don't you think?' Kris looked around, spotted a joint. 'I feel like coffee. Would you…?'

'Yes, yes.'

They walked into a cafe with black chairs and green tables.

Elizabeth noticed how still Kris was in everything he did. She watched him sit down with minimal movements. No *chi* possibly blocked in there.

'Are you always like this? So calm?'

'At my age, there is no need to hurry, is there?' He spread his napkin with great care.

'That man was in a mess, wasn't he? Like he was trying to claw his way in. Which country do you think he was from? Syria? Turkey?'

'Can't tell. But every time the West plans a war, now they know it's more than about dropping bombs. Little Aylan Kurdis by their hundreds might wash up on their shores face down.'

'That's cruel. Please don't think I am against immigrants.'

'I am one myself. From India. Decades now.'

'You are more native than me then. But he really was rude.'

'Did he push you?'

'Did he push me? No, no. He just shoved himself between me and the machine. Me and my money, after a manner of speaking.'

'See? Exactly the issue with refugees: the hordes are positioned between you and your resources.'

'No, that's not fair.'

'I guess not. Well, pushing you would be assault, I guess?'

'Yes, but if he had pushed me, I would have remembered the weight of his body. I would have remembered where he touched me.' Your body carried the burden or its memory long after the weight was lifted, didn't it?

'Maybe he had an emergency.'

'Still...'

The waiter came. 'What will you have?' Kris asked.

'What about you?'

'Banana chocolate cake and black coffee. I'm vegetarian.'

'Same for me.'

After that, Kris didn't say anything for a long time.

Elizabeth stirred.

'You don't have to say anything,' Kris said. 'I'm good with silence. I am not working your mind.'

'No, I was wondering, suppose that man was a terrorist? Or a refugee *and* a terrorist?'

They watched the people passing by on the pavement. Terrorists and victims moving in a flock.

'Suppose he was? A terrorist may still be in an emergency in relation to the ATM.'

They both thought about the man walking fast.

'Yes. To pay for a bomb? Where do you live?' Elizabeth asked.

'Oxford. Or maybe his daughter was in the hospital. Or his lender was harassing him.'

'Oh, yes.' Elizabeth sipped the coffee. 'Oxford! I live in Oxford myself.'

'We are neighbours, then.'

'Are you on your way there?'

'Just now? Yes. Would you like a ride back?'

'That would be kind of you.'

Kris finished his coffee and placed the cup carefully on the table. 'Would you like to go to Paris?'

'What?' Elizabeth laughed.

'Just kidding.'

They fell silent again.

'Paris. Really?'

'Yes.'

'How?'

'I have my car parked here somewhere.'

'By car? By car!'

'My passport is in the car.'

'Ah. For the moment, Oxford would do just fine.'

They laughed at the mischief of it.

Kris folded the spotless napkin in a rather meditative process and kept it back on the table.

'It's a good thing we met,' Elizabeth said.

'To know what it means to have met, we have to take it ahead, I guess. It was long in the making, like Aleppo.'

As they made their way out, Elizabeth noticed Kris walked with slow but firm steps. Kris eased the car into the traffic.

'If you want the sun, I can pull down the top,' Kris said when they were out of the city. It seemed to them they were already in Paris. They were there and here at the same time. The Thames flowed over the Seine.

'That'd be nice.'

'The sun and the trees travelled with them. The car was full of sky.

'Elizabeth was glad she was not a refugee. Glad she was British. There was power in country, race, gender. That was the truth.

'What do you do in Oxford, Kris?'

'Nothing. I stopped teaching physics years ago. You?'

'I taught literature in a school for a while. But I am interested in cultural studies, stuff like that. I often wonder if terrorism is more a cultural issue than religion.'

'Not much point in having an opinion on the issue, is there? There are so many, as it is.'

The road wound through fields. Elizabeth wondered if he was too cynical and distant for her taste. She didn't think age was a problem. Sex might be. But she was not hung on sex, was she?

'Where in Oxford are you?' Kris asked.

'Burlington.'

They exchanged numbers.

'Things begin with numbers,' Elizabeth said.

A little later, Kris agreed. 'They often end in numbers, too.'

'How do you remain so still and silent?'

'The good silence is when you don't talk to yourself,' Kris paused. 'Mine is an act. Don't be taken in by it.' Kris looked at the cows grazing on the fields on either side. 'Animals are very good at it. You get to learn a lot just by watching them.'

'Do you keep pets?'

'No. I am afraid of getting attached to them.'

***

'Ikon, Madam. Your destination,' the cab driver said.

'I need to go to another place after this. Could you wait?' Elizabeth asked.

'A pleasure, Madam,' the driver said. 'Just change the final destination in your Uber booking.'

Elizabeth went in to keep her luggage in her room. She eyed the broken suitcase warily, as if it would betray her again. She could buy another. But she was fond of this one as it had travelled with her a lot. When she got back into the cab—the driver making a bit of a show opening and closing the door for her—she asked the cabbie if he knew of a place for fixing suitcases. 'I could fix it for you,' he said, Elizabeth was not sure what to make of the offer. She nodded at him, and thought she would buy a new suitcase after all.

'Do you know the way to Kabuki?' Elizabeth asked.

'The clinic? Everyone knows the way to Kabuki. Not to worry,' the driver smiled at her in the mirror.

'You don't know a thing about me,' Elizabeth thought. She felt superior in her distance and unknowability. She wondered what kind of life the driver led. The framed identity card on the dashboard said he was Ram Yadav. She eyed the saffron band again. She had no great interest in Indian politics. Or any politics. Elizabeth worried about the pregnancy test. She no longer thought of Ruth. There was only a mounting anxiety that crowded everything else out of Elizabeth's mind as she neared the clinic. There was a slight stink of sweat in the cab (the driver, not the passengers, surely, was the source?), which moved in spurts and starts. The traffic was not just heavy, it was bad. Yet, once upon a time, in the 1970s, Osip had said, there was a bus from Connaught Place to Moscow. How long would that take?

Forever, if it were in service today: cars, buses, motorbikes, auto-rickshaws, cycles, tractors got in the way of each other, and yet, they moved ahead in mysterious ways, one wheel at a time. Pedestrians ran across the road, some carrying banners and the Indian flag. Bikes came in from nowhere, crossed them, and triumphantly climbed on to the footpath.

'So much traffic,' Elizabeth said nervously.

'There is a protest rally today at India Gate.' Ram Yadav said.

'That's why? Protest against what?'

'Some political measure. To protect Hindus in their own country.' The driver did not seem to approve of the protest.

'Why not Muslims?'

'Muslims can go to Islamic countries. Where will Hindus go? Are you Christian?'

'Yes.'

'American?'

'British.'

'Same thing. Why are you going to Kabuki?' The driver grinned as if he knew a secret.

'Just take me there.'

They had hardly got past one jam, when they got stuck again. This time it was a small tight procession. Inside the procession though there seemed a ring of bare-bodied men, whipping themselves. They lifted their right leg first, brought it back, raised the left, brought it back, and whipped their bleeding backs. Their hair and foreheads were wrapped in white cloth. Was it Muharram? But this was not the

Muharram month, she thought. She could not watch the violence for more than a moment.

'Shias,' Ram Yadav said. 'Very few in number, very large headache.'

'It must hurt them, no?'

'Madam, ordinary folks are capable of great violence, giving and taking. They could kill.' Ram Yadav honked.

'How much they use the horn,' Elizabeth thought.

'But the Hindus too have public processions.'

'Not like this.'

Elizabeth didn't argue. She had seen in Bombay people walking with a deity on their heads, their mouth pierced through either cheek with a thick, iron needle. A whip-wielding, horn-honking, god-rattling people. Who would want to bring a baby into a world like this? 'I am getting late.'

'I am trying, as you can see.' Ram Yadav honked even more fiercely at a nearly immobile tempo packed with gas cylinders. 'There would be less traffic, too—if we got rid of the riffraff.'

By the time they reached the clinic, Elizabeth was nearly collapsing with anxiety. She had expressly asked Sangita not to get in touch on the phone with her about the results. She wouldn't be able to take it if the news turned out to be true.

Indeed if she was pregnant, she would ask for an immediate abortion. As soon as she paid, Ram Yadav jumped out and opened the door for her. He towered over the car. Elizabeth was not sure what to make of the exaggerated gesture of courtesy. Everything he did seemed to be hinting at something else. She came out from the other door.

'Should I wait?'

'No, thank you.'

'I could wait.'

'No, I am fine.'

'Please give me a good rating. At least four stars.'

Elizabeth ran inside Kabuki. Waiting for Sangita at the reception, Elizabeth checked Ram Yadav's Uber profile. 'Ram Yadav knows Delhi inside out and is great at conversations,' it said. Elizabeth gave him one star. Not satisfied, she reported him menacing. Then slowly regretted it. A moment later she tried to undo the comment in vain. She put her vacillation down to anxiety.

Elizabeth needn't have hurried. She was told Sangita would be late. She was coming in from Noida and had to make her way over a bridge on the Yamuna, a scene of yet another protest—or was it related to the one Ram Yadav was talking about? Would Elizabeth be interested in acquainting herself with the Astro-Club meanwhile? The Astro-Club was on the first floor. It was very popular. It helped to figure out an auspicious time for conception and birth, aligning planetary arrangement with human destiny, making new lives less fraught. Elizabeth hesitated, then walked up the stairs and into the Astro-Club, where a young man was lecturing, presumably, a group of parents, a kind of introduction to the course. He checked his phone and punched a number—date, month, year—that flashed on a large screen on which were drawn the planets. Wasn't that her date of birth? Yes, it was. Elizabeth held her breath. The young man scribbled: 7.30 am.

Elizabeth was born in the second half of the day. A narrow escape, then. 'I hope none here present shares this date of birth and time,' the young man smiled. 'Now, this lady or man is in a little trouble. They have their sun in Aquarius and the moon in Aries. That means they usually have their way. Their Mercury-Uranus-Venus-Mars conjunction is likely to mean an active sex life...'

Elizabeth walked out. She sweated despite the air-conditioning. Someone asked her to sit in Sangita's cubicle. She sat there, thinking how quickly she could catch a flight out of India. She had wanted to go and visit an old friend, an artist, in Bombay before she left, but she didn't think she would do that now.

'Sorry, I'm late,' Sangita said. 'It vas very bad, the traffic.'

'No, it's fine.'

Sangita took out an envelope from a drawer, pressed it close to her chest, and holding it in both hands offered it to Elizabeth like a gift.

Elizabeth read the report. It was negative.

Elizabeth wanted to weep, but converted the urge into a warm handshake with Sangita.

'You are happy?' Sangita asked.

'Yes, we make mistakes. It would be terrible if we couldn't correct them ever.'

'Yes, ve make mistakes.'

'What's yours?' Elizabeth wanted to ask Sangita. But she only thanked Sangita again. They shook hands once more.

The Darwinists

Because Anand and I had left early, we had escaped Delhi city limits before the traffic picked up. But the effort of travelling exhausted me. Without Anand, I might still be at the hotel.

'Thanks, chief, for everything,' I said.

'My pleasure and duty, comrade. How are you feeling?'

'Irritable. Uncertain. Angry.'

'That's normal these days. You need to attune your energies with the Universe. You understand entropy?'

'That things if not helped tend to slip into chaos?'

'Sort of. You could minimize the rate of entropy. Do you want to? '

'No. But how?'

'I am on the job. How to harness the energy from the cosmic rays and replenish your resources on a steady basis and fight entropy. In short, how to save the world.'

'The world can't be saved.'

'You need a life coach. I will be one soon.'

'I am heartbroken.'

'You should have called me when Kali Mata started blessing you.'

'The manager was very kind.'

Anand cleared his throat. 'We haven't settled the bill.'

'Ah, yes.' I had thought Anand would have settled it.

'That's fine. He is a friend.'

'I will settle it. This month I am running short.'

'Every month, kiddo,' Anand said. 'We run short every month.' He shook his head cheerfully.

The taxi slowed down. We had gone past Bijnor, and a by-pass led us into the highway. A minute later, we saw a white Mercedes lying on its back in the field, its wheels up in the air.

'They race along these roads at night. Look at that. No one would have got away. Anything over sixty on the highway and you are asking for trouble,' the driver said. 'There is a drinking joint every five minutes of the road. And the sisterfucking potholes! Real craters.'

A fleet of thunder approached. A bunch of women bikers roared past. The driver looked at them in amazement.

'I need to buy a Bullet,' Anand said, when the dust that the bikers raised had settled. 'Bullet's a good bike. Heavy, but good. Ever ride one?'

'No.'

'Solid. Like you know you are going somewhere and you will reach there.'

'Expensive, I guess.'

'I want a red one. Cherry red.'

'Do you have someone in the army?' the driver said.

'No. Why?'

'Army guys get it cheap. Special quota. Or talk to a politician. The politician always knows someone in the army.' He took his hands off the wheel and clasped them together to show how thick the politicians and the army were.

'My father was a politician.' Anand winks, as if to say his father was a trick.

Anand's father was the late Mr Andrew Andrade, a member of parliament who went for an election campaign in a rather remote part of India and had an affair with Anand's mother. A few weeks later, Mr Andrade had turned inaccessible to the pregnant woman. His thugs told her since he was Catholic, he didn't want the pregnancy terminated. He would take care of the child if the mother made no claims and disappeared, and he was doing her a favour because his wife Yolanda naturally did not approve either of her husband's indiscretion or the arrangement. Anand never met his mother or father. Before Anand reached school-going age, Mr Andrade had died of a heart attack on a plane.

'Even better. The sisterfucking politicians control the army,' the driver said.

'Did you get to meet Elizabeth Madam?' Anand asked, looking out at the flat countryside.

'No. The guard said she was not there. Maybe she left for England?'

'Don't be too sure. It's cheaper to live here. It would be easier for her to get a job too. Indians love to flash a bit of white skin in their schools. Everywhere. The Arabs do the same thing.'

'How do I locate her? Not that I really want to.'

'Talk to your friend, Arjun Bedi? He must know a lot of people.'

'I threw up on his carpet. I haven't met him after that.'

'You can't let a carpet come between you and your love.'

We fell quiet.

'I think I will take a gap year. Maybe go to England.'

'A gap year? Like a break between years? In search of…?'

'Did I say that?' Would Elizabeth have left for England? I lowered the window glass. The deodars and pines had begun to show up, like the tail of an army. Fresh, fragrant air filled the car. 'Not a soul about. Good to ride along.'

'Yeah. A Bullet,' Anand nodded at the smooth road in approval. 'Phut-phut all the way up to Dharamshala.'

'That's pretty high up.'

'Political, OB. Every Tibetan there is plotting at the humiliation of China. Free Tibet, remember? We are reluctant to grant autonomy to Kashmir. But they don't mind Tibet taking birth as a nation against China's wishes.'

'Is the Dalai Lama a spiritualist or a nationalist?'

'Both? You know what sells in this godforsaken country? Salvation. Moksha is an experience. Value for money. It's the pineal gland, I keep telling you.'

Anand's interest in the third eye—the pineal gland, as he called it—began when the biology teacher had mentioned the dormant gland in passing. It inspired him to do some research of his own. He found out that Descartes believed that the pineal gland was the 'seat of the soul'. Anand stuck what Descartes said on the back of our room's door:

> My view is that this gland is the principal seat of the soul. The reason I believe this is that I cannot find any part of the brain, except this, which is not double. Since we see only one thing with two eyes, and hear only one voice with two ears, and in short have never more than one thought at a time, it must necessarily be the case that the impressions which enter by the two eyes, or by the two ears, and so on, unite with each other in some part of the body before being considered by the soul. Now it is impossible to find any such place in the head except this gland....

'Not love?'

'Love?' Anand laughed. 'All body and possession, OB. My long years on this planet have taught me what humans are after. It's either money or salvation. Are you planning to go over to Oxford?'

'No.'

'Never mistake passion...' Anand paused to think it out, '...for a purpose.'

'Why not? The French president Macron went after a woman like that. She was much older to him.'

'Macron, huh?'

'Emmanuel Macron. Fell in love with his teacher when he was 15. She was 39.'

'He is the French president, OB.'

'Not when he was 15. You know why this country will never catch up with France?'

'Because they won't let you shack up with your teacher?'

'They will label him a pervert here. But because he is in France, they are all so full of fucking admiration.' Ha, I knew my countrymen. '"Ye, churls and chuts," as Arjun would say. It's not Macron and his love life. It's an idea... Remember that Korean movie we watched on YouTube? Kim Ki-duk's *Moebius*?'

'That one! Wife attempts to castrate faithless husband, fails, and then castrates teenage son, on whom father transplants his penis? Bizarre.'

'Dark corners of the human mind, Anand. There would never be a Kim here. We are just too decent, I guess.'

'It had no subtitles!'

'That's because it had no dialogue. I don't think you got the movie, Anand.'

'Easy, OB. I am your friend. The only one, as you said. You mustn't antagonize me.'

'Anand, you are a good friend, but you are not very bright.'

'Well, you are irritable after your blessings. Oxford is posh. Macron and Kim will not get you there and get you a meal.'

'True.' I rolled my head on the back of the seat and closed my eyes. Gloria was not likely to give me that kind of money. She was tight on funds, and she had always been mystified, she said, about her husband's perennial penury. 'Your grandfather never made enough. Nothing in the bank,' Gloria would exclaim, enraged at the unreasonable financial situation. 'That's what. His mysterious and long-missing brother sent some money occasionally from Britain for your education. He was regular in the beginning. Then erratic. But he did help, and I am grateful. He was the one I should have got married to, except it was clear he didn't like me the one occasion I met him. We were more or less the same age, I believe. There are communists other than your grandfather in this country. They all seem to be living well. No one ever asked me how I manage to run this house. Have you any idea what it takes?'

Gloria did eventually discover that her husband had hidden away the little he made in the pages of the books in his library. One day, Gloria had stumbled on the treasure while dusting. Between pages 141 and 142 of volume one, *Das Kapital* had a hundred-rupee note. Another big note on page 254 of *Anna Karenina*, with whom Gloria vaguely identified. Late in the evening of the same stupendous day, between pages 126 and 127 two notes of Rs 10 in Stalin's *Economic Problems of Socialism in the USSR*. It was then a matter of time, she would say in her lighter moments, before she figured out that there was a small bank right there in Mr Menon's library. Gloria later said she considered the serendipitous event a just reward for her many lifelong disappointments with her husband. And she introduced Tolstoy and Marx, among others, more as personal bankers than writers to Makkam, who knew no one more powerful than my grandmother. The library had over 10,000 books. There would be more up in the attic, she would say, money, and valuables, and perhaps—she would pause before she said the next word—weapons, but it would be a search, with all those old trunks, cobwebs, and dust. After *that* day, Gloria and Makkam, who was literacy-challenged, would spend a lot of time in the company of books.

'My grandmother is against ideas like a gap year, anyway,' I said to Anand.

'Ah, yes, the gap year. So from where…?'

'Steal?' Murder? I smiled. It hurt. I had boils on the inside of my lips too.

Anand was lost in thought for a moment. 'I can't depend on that bitch to give me any of my father's money either. You know what? I have a fight ahead of me.'

'You shouldn't call your mother a bitch,' I said.

Anand grunted in annoyance. 'Not my mother.'

'Unless Ms Andrade pops it. Then you are rich.'

Earlier in the year, Anand had squeezed in an advertisement declaring Ms Andrade was dead, and the principal had come across her obit on the fifth page of *The Tribune*, while she was travelling. It had merely informed her she had died of a 'massive heart attack', and that she was survived by her son, Anand Andrade.

'She is just not the dying type. I tried suggesting the option to her in the obit that I put in, remember?'

'Yes, rich people die last.'

'Oh, accidents can occur. And the good thing about accidents is that they can be made to happen.'

I thought about the Mercedes on its back.

'Please stop the car...' Anand tapped the driver's shoulder, who had his headphones on. Anand held up his little finger.

The driver parked the car to the side of the road.

'Let's take a piss, OB. Let's irrigate the earth. In Israel, they encourage men and women to piss on fields. They are a tough race.'

We watered a tree, taking turns.

'Have you any idea, Anand, why you lift the little finger when you want to piss?'

'Why do you raise your forefinger in warning?'

'Well, at least we know when someone raises the middle finger, we are fucked. Or about to be.' I zipped up. 'I have a boil on my dick. I have boils everywhere.'

'Hurts?'

'Not so bad now.'

'Dick reminds me. You know Father Roderick is dead?'

'The school priest? Really?'

'Yes. Things have happened in your absence.'

'How?'

'Heart attack. Dropped dead while he was giving a sermon. Curled up down on the floor like a comma of his interminable sentence. It was quite incredible.'

'See? That's all there's to it. So unreal.' Ten steps you are with me, the next, gone, as M. said. 'Can't eat like that. Shouldn't.'

'Mr Roderick? Yes. He was sort of breaking bread all the time.'

'Have you seen the violence with which he breaks a scone? Or bread? He tears it apart.'

'You are a great observer of humanity. Possibly the greatest. Mrs Roderick, the stammering curser, came to school in a wheel-chair. They were waiting for their son David to arrive from the US for the burial. He would have got in early this morning, I think.'

'She has Parkinson's.'

'She shakes out curses from her heart now. People are best dead before they are sixty. The old should give way to the new, but quickly.'

'You sound like Arjun. That's Nazism.'

'Darwinism. All your modern management theories are based on the survival of the fittest.'

'Who calls the top CEOs Nazis, though?'

'Because it's about money. Profiteering makes modern Nazis look like businessmen. You have no idea.'

We walked back to the car. Overhead, the sky darkened. The weather had changed without warning. A wet wind blew. When we got into the car, heavy raindrops flowered on the windshield. I thought of Father Roderick underground. 'Listen, Anand.'

'You have an idea for my Bullet?'

'Yes. And for my Oxford trip.' I glanced at the driver. He was all right; he was listening to music, outsize headphones on. 'How about…' I reached for my hip flask. I was going to be a Darwinist. 'Why not dig up Father Roderick and hold him to ransom?'

'Eh? Is that a plan? Anand shook his head. 'And how do you dig up a coffin? They bury them deep, you know. It's hard work.'

Was this the way young men thought? How did they talk? Like me. Like Anand. Without the leisure and luxury of the actual allotted years that justified theft, murder, and love. We learned to talk ahead of our time exactly as Macron at 15 must have; if only because an adult-sized problem had presented itself before *its* time.

'No, it won't work. You are too weak. I can't do it alone,' Anand said.

The rain started in earnest, and Anand's eyes took on a new alert. 'And because they are great believers, the family would want the body back in the grave and at rest with Jesus? The whole operation, including collection, should be over in 12 hours—6 PM to 6 AM.'

'How much do you think they will pay us for returning the body intact?'

'Is this for real?'

'I need the money.'

'Oh, well. The Rodericks are rich. Five lakh? Not even $10,000. It's nothing for his son making money in dollars in Chicago. On the lower side, in fact.'

'That's right. Good Christians can't let the body rot.'

'True. But if they call the police?'

'Mrs Roderick is very ill.'

'But that's no guarantee.'

'I doubt if the Rodericks will involve the police. The police never figure in the afterlife of the faithful.'

'We should talk only to the son.'

'It's your idea.'

'I am floating it. Can't I think aloud? I can't execute it.'

'Well, I will be the executioner. And this is for a cause, isn't it? There's a guy who can help us dig.'

Anand had bought into the idea just as I was extricating myself from it.

'Who?'

'Idris Abbottabad. He's a part-time thief. Used to pass off as a train attendant. On the run from the police now. Part-time motorcycle mechanic, too. He is part-time everything.'

'A name like that.'

'As if yours is any less weird. His forefathers come from Pakistan. It's not his fault, you know.'

'In Kerala, people are routinely christened Lenin and Stalin. In Goa, Kennedy is a popular name. So is Churchill.'

'But no one anywhere in their right mind calls a kid Osip.'

'You know about M., only because I told you.'

'Roderick is a good idea. Think about it.'

'Well, I don't know.' No matter how acute our financial need, the exhumation of Father Roderick is a fantasy; it seems like a TV serial: *Stranger Things*. Kids doing adult things.

We listen to the rain as the taxi winds its way up the hills.

Yes, it's a good idea.

No, it's a bad idea.

Yes, it's a very good idea.

Connections

On a Saturday, Elizabeth and I slip out of school early in the morning, take a ride in her car to Delhi. A second-hand Maruti Swift, green body with blacktop. Green leather with black trimmings. A green weekend with black clouds hanging low, and rolling over the landscape. Elizabeth is wearing the green cotton sari in which she made her first appearance in school. Elizabeth drives, one hand on the wheel, the other on the gear. She hums. When the humming becomes truly repetitive, I tell her so. Elizabeth glances at me, amused.

'All right, let's listen to something good.' She fumbles with the radio. A bar of music fills the car.

'Shostakovich, 1937,' I sit up. 'Stalin said his music was so awful no one could even whistle it. Shostakovich wrote the 5th in response and the Party applauded: A Soviet Artist's Reply to Just Criticism.' I laugh uncontrollably, as if the music we heard over the radio was a vindication of my shortcomings.

'I don't know a thing about western classical music.'

'This one begins unmistakably. Like an alarm going off in a factory.'

'I listen to music only when I dance. *That* kind of music.'

'My grandfather said the best of everything beautiful died with the twentieth century. Everything then was more than itself, he said, everything was symbolic.'

***

'Every object is laden with meaning, little Osip,' my grandfather would say, and he would take my hand and go for a walk over the dykes squaring off the paddy fields. The frogs croaked. A tiny spider fell from nowhere and caused ripples in the shadowed pools of water in a clearing. A slimy, algae-like plant trailed its hands below the water. All around us the paddy was lit and waving against the rain clouds billowing over the blue hills of Thrissur. I stared at the spider. There were more ripples. Death struggles. 'So much is going on here, grandfather.'

'And each thing is something else. Let's go back. It will rain anytime. And my umbrella is full of holes.'

He stood still, looking at the funerary horizon. From the distance, a small group of people made way toward us over the ridges. We waited under the low, overcast sky. The paddy looked almost black in its greenness. They reached us at last. Three rugged-looking people with bloodshot eyes. One of them carried an axe on his shoulder. They bowed to my grandfather.

'Is it done?'

'Yes, Comrade,' the one with the axe said. He was short and stocky.

'Disappear for a few weeks,' my grandfather said. 'The Party will take care of everything. Lose your axe.'

'Yes, Comrade.'

We watched them turn back the way they came. A few steps down, the short man flung his axe into the distance. I saw it describing an arc in the air, but could not see its landing.

***

'Think of the Beatles and it just could be true.'

'My grandfather used to listen to him when the mood was upon him. Usually in the rains. Shostakovich and, for some reason, K. L.Saigal.'

'K. L. who?'

'Saigal, the first of the great Bollywood playback singers.'

'My friend in Oxford is a great fan of Shostakovich—"both haunting and cautionary at the same time," Kris said.'

'Are you still in touch with him? With Kris?'

A car overtakes us recklessly from the left. Elizabeth sticks a middle finger at the driver. 'Male drivers are the worst,' she says. 'Do you mind turning off the music? I can't concentrate on the driving.'

I try the knob. But the volume only goes up. This is a problem, I know. I can't carry out simple things without botching up. I get confused, my coordination skills are not the best. 'Oh,' I say.

Elizabeth reaches out and turns off the music.

'My grandfather had a long trip to Moscow long back. Came back with a great number of classical records. You know those big black LPs?'

'They are back in fashion. The ones your grandfather brought must have been heavy.'

'The Customs gave him a choice between the records and some rubles.'

'And he chose the records.'

'Yes.' And Gloria would say, 'He should have brought the rubles.'

***

It was 'the trip that spun Mr Menon around and caused his brain to slip and slide,' Gloria would think aloud for the hundredth time, crossing her legs and swinging one over the other, back and fro, 'because it was a mystery that grew with time. And to date, I am not sure what exactly happened to him. Except, of course, now I know he was in love with a woman. I knew he was ready to give up everything for her, including the Revolution. And I had to live with that, too; that there was someone else far more valued than me for him, though I was slaving for him.'

My grandfather had disappeared into the white vastness of Russia. Gloria had made several calls to the party office which had sent him there. 'There's no news of Mr Menon. It's been a month since he's gone,' Gloria said to the Party secretary.

And the party secretary would joke, 'Mrs Menon, our comrade is having a ball. Vodka, caviar, great women.'

'Women?' He was not just a moral coward, he just didn't have it in him to love, or even the fibre to lust after,' Gloria would think.'But he should be in touch with me, surely?'

'Maybe he got married to one Comrade Tamara Maximova? Or, maybe he is training to be a cosmonaut? Ha ha. Don't worry, Mrs Menon, he will be back.'

When months, years, later, Mr Menon returned—as he alighted from the plane, he had briefly held up his fingers in a V sign—he looked relieved but drawn, and he had lost weight.

'What did the V mean,' Gloria had asked herself. 'That he had returned safely home at last?' And, Gloria said, her husband's first sentence in the car was what sounded like a dissident's quote, because she had later come across the same words somewhere: 'They are knee-deep in the blood, the black Marias, the mysterious phone calls, the back-to-back funerals. The State. The Party. The Mob. It's all true. Thank God he's gone, and Khrushchev is in.' And Gloria would think Mr Menon was still naive, despite all that happened to him. That he still had hope. 'He was a joke,' she would think, 'a poor, red joke.'

***

The Maruti bumps over an unmarked speed breaker.

'Why don't they paint the speed breakers yellow?' Elizabeth asks. 'And they are so sharp. You could break your spine going over them. You know the problem with India?'

'No.'

'Never mind. It will sound racist.'

The trees speed past us.

Elizabeth steps on the pedal. We pass by a drive-in-restaurant. We reverse, pull in.

Elizabeth asks for coffee at the counter. She gives her name as Katrina Kaif, a Bollywood film star. When the coffee is ready, the girl at the counter calls out, 'Katrina Kaif', and everybody looks up. Elizabeth smiles at me. She is completely charming. 'Where are we going?' I ask her finally when we get back into the car.

'The National Gallery of Modern Art. There's a show you might be interested in.'

'Whose show?'

'Brijesh Kapoor. He is a great Indian artist. Divides his time between London and Mumbai. I know him. A lover of the sea.'

'Will he be there at the show tomorrow?'

'I don't know. It has been on for a while now.'

'Why did you change your name back there?'

'It's nice to be a star at least for the space of a coffee, don't you think?'

'Where do we stay tonight?'

'In separate rooms. The same hotel.'

***

The exhibition at Delhi's National Gallery of Modern Art is C-O-N-N-E-C-T-I-O-N-S. The middle of the letters is cut by razor wire. Against a backdrop of stacked logs, a series of giant black-and-white portraits of young girls and boys. Half the face of each portrait is that of those from war and pogrom survivors. The catastrophes range through the World Wars, Partition of India, Kashmir, Korean War, Vietnam, Serbia, Rwanda, and Syria. The other half of the faces are that of youngsters from Indian slums. The faces look on at the world with hope and despair with their dichromatic eyes. They unsettle you. The names of the models are given beneath each portrait. Faint strains of *Mama Son Tanto Felice*, 'Mother, I am so Happy', the music that the Einsatzgruppen played as the concentration camp prisoners buried their comrades, haunts the air. There are 12 portraits. I spend a little more time on the 11th. One half belongs to a girl. A girl with a small mole at the left corner of her mouth. I look for her name. And look again. Ava Lenk. The other half is Abdul Aziz from Dharavi. I run a finger over the girl's name.

'Please don't touch the artwork,' says the bearded man curating the show.

'Who is Ava Lenk?'

'Who Ava Lenk?'

I point to the portrait.

'The idea of the show is that but for the aspect of mass shootings, the deprivation of millions of Indian children is on par with warlike experiences. No food, no water, no future.' He continues to read out from the brochure: 'Time is still. It's the events that toll through it. The same events with slight variations.' The curator looks up. He seems satisfied. 'Is that what you wanted to know?'

'No. I wanted to know who Ava Lenk is.'

The curator sighs. He takes out a diary from his pocket and consults it. 'Ava Lenk was in the Lodz Ghetto in the early 1940s. Poland.' The curator looks at both of us carefully. 'Anything wrong?'

'No. I thought I had seen her somewhere.'

'You are too young for that.' The curator focuses on Elizabeth. 'Isn't he?'

'I don't know. An old man far in his teens. A bit odd, too.'

'Funny,' the curator puts the Diary back in his pocket.

'Is Brijesh around?' Elizabeth asks.

'He is in Bombay.'

'Oh, I was going to surprise him.'

We drive back in the evening. A full moon chases us through the trees. There's little traffic on the road winding uphill.

***

Mr Menon met Ava on his trip to the Soviet Union. She was his guide before both of them disappeared for a while. From what he said later and over many years, Ava's father, a peasant originally from Ukraine, had been an official with the Bund, a Jewish socialist organization. They had fled the collectivization drive of Stalin. In 1940, she and her family were rounded up with others of Jewish origin and moved to the Lodz ghetto. Her mother starved to death. A year later, Ava's father, advised to flee Lodz because he was on the hit list, tried to escape to the Russian-occupied area of Poland; he was caught and killed. Ava continued somehow to stay alive in the ghetto until the early months of 1944. Ava had an affair with an officer from the Einsatzgruppen. Ava survived, possibly because of him. In mid-1944, she was transported to Auschwitz, where she decided there was no God. The Germans selected Ava for a labour camp near Hanover. In January 1945, the labour camp was dispersed. Ava and her fellow prisoners were marched to Bergen-Belsen. 'Here there was not only no God, but also an absence of man,' she told my grandfather. The barely living and the decomposing dead were put up in the same huts. Ava contracted a burning fever. She thought her end was at hand. When she regained consciousness, she discovered the camp had been liberated. She was taken to Switzerland. She waited there for over two years before she could get the papers processed for her immigration to Russia. Ava worked as a janitor in a training teachers' college. Here she was caught for sleeping with a student and was denounced by the college authorities, as—at that point in time—sex was an event that could transpire only after signing up at the Registrar's Office. Further proceedings in punishment stopped in early 1953 as Stalin died. Later, she quit, when the man in charge of de-kulakizing her extended family in Ukraine became the head of the department, and she made a living conducting trans-European tours for war-horror visitors. In St. Petersburg, on a trip, my grandfather ran into her; and returned in that mysterious daze, as if he had fought a secret war all by himself.

***

Elizabeth turns the car up a steep, narrow, dirt road and cuts the engine at the lip of a cliff. The sky is clear, the air cool. She gets out, stretches her limbs. I shiver. After a while, I too step out of the car. The moon is reddish gold, and big. The leaves glint and gleam as if they are dipped in oil. Elizabeth and I lean our backs on the car and gaze at the deep midnight blue of the sky. The stars spread deep and wide, perfectly spaced and beyond reason. Elizabeth puts her hand around my shoulder. A vague sense of sharing an understanding thrills my blood. Elizabeth draws me closer to her. We can hear our hearts beat. No. We can't. We kiss.

'Not so hard,' Elizabeth says. Her breath is fragrant.

'It's not easy,' Elizabeth loosens my belt with one hand.

'The belt?' My voice is thick.

'The belt, too.'

Her hands curl around my stiff penis. She pulls it out. I sigh.

'It's just that...' Elizabeth leans against the side of the car, pulling me into her.

She is lonely. That's what she is trying to say. I know.

She runs her reckless thumb over the tip of my penis. I shiver.

'You are circumcised. Not Hindu?'

'I don't know. Does it matter?' I say to Elizabeth, who is not listening.

'The sari,' Elizabeth whispers.

'Yes?'

'Don't dirty the sari.'

'This is my first time. Second.'

'What was the first like?'

'A handjob in a spa in Bombay.'

'Doesn't count. Let's take off the clothes.'

I step out of my trousers. I am good and hard. Above us, the sky is deep. Wisps of clouds fray between the stars.

Elizabeth guides me into her. 'You don't love me. But you may after this. And it would be bad for you.'

She is soft, warm, moist. Like the earth in spring.

'A little lower, yes,' she gasps.

I am being taken hold of, and navigated into another gravitational space.

'We've blown it.' Elizabeth grips my butt.

'Yes.'

We move to and fro, desperate to break the body borders between us.

'You have no idea what can come off Shostakovich, do you?' Elizabeth says.

'No. Yes.'

My mind stops.

The moon screams.

A Colonial Invasion

Weeks after Kali Mata's blessings, I check into Singh's Palace, following a call from Arjun. The manager is on leave. His assistants are warm and hospitable. They give me one of their best rooms which is not saying much, except that it has an extra window that is boarded up. I lie in bed and open M.'s *The Egyptian Stamp*, and begin reading. 'Parnok ran…more than anything in the world, he feared to attract upon himself the displeasure of the mob…' and, a moment later, find myself snoring profoundly. My phone rings. It is Arjun. He is waiting below in a cab. We drive to the Foreign Correspondent's Club. The campaign against him has resulted in the cancellation of his columns and directorial posts. 'How am I supposed to find work, earn a living?' he asks the ruins of Delhi as we ride.

M. said the same thing when he was freed from his four-year exile in Voronezh in 1937, before he would be arrested again and exiled socially and physically in 1938, for the second and last time.

'M. never stood trial,' I say to Arjun. 'They just ostracized him.'

'Why do you now talk of dead people and of the distant past, distant lands,' Arjun asks, 'this is not the time, I am not in Russia; it is not snowing here, can't you see? This is not that white land wasted by famine and despots and revolutions and ice. I am here and now, I am no M.'

Wrong. Of course. It takes everyman's past to arrive at this moment. Somebody's future is our past. We are nomads wandering through time. And in our mind any event from any place can recur, and it becomes us. But all I say is: 'But if they think you are a bad man…a transgressor…'

'Who?' Arjun asks, 'who? I am not a good man, I admit, and my genius is to be hated, but all this ganging up and trying to muzzle me…it is not legal, it is not constitutional, and, who, who are *they*? Scented Saints? The French Guillotineers? The Commissars of the Peoples? A sentence I wrote, a joke I cracked—I know you won't believe me—is the most traumatic event in the life of some woman, or man, as the case maybe, waiting to be outraged? Nothing more painful has happened in their lives besides this…this breach of drawing room decorum?'

Would Arjun cry? The tinted glasses of the cab filter the day. Summer has begun. The days hazy, the air thick like muddy water, the pollution fantastic.

The FCC is a pretty, old-fashioned bungalow on a quiet lane off Mathura Road, just behind the massive Supreme Court in Central Delhi. Its main gate faces Pragati Maidan, Delhi's convention center, which has recently been demolished because the government wants a better building.

Bigger and better. Nationalist, too. Names of historic roads are changed overnight because they are called after Mughal rulers. Someone proved under laboratory conditions that the cow exhales oxygen, a news item which provoked Arjun to ask, 'From which end?'

At the FCC, we sit in one of those inner rooms, which must have been someone's bedroom a few decades ago, and wait for Mitali Jain. We order a drink. On the TV on the wall, above a well-populated fish tank, Avlok Dutta is obliterating the permanent representatives of anti-nationals on his panel. 'I will expose you today, Faizal Rashid,' he says. 'I have had enough of your pro-Pakistani sentiments. Tell me one reason why an Indian cannot buy land in Kashmir?' Faizal Rashid tries to say something in defence; something along the lines that Himachal Pradesh also does not sell land to outsiders; but he is drowned as Avlok Dutta unleashes his hounds on him, having already lowered Faizal Rashid's audio. Arjun shakes his head. 'Deep in the heart, just about every Indian is a fascist looking out for his Fuhrer.' He mutes the TV.

Before we finish our drink, Mitali makes an entry. Mitali is in her 30s; she is slim, and her dark brown skin radiant. Her large eyes are luminous with understanding. She wears a grey sari with a golden border, and carries herself with great dignity.

Mitali Jain looks at the TV and says, 'Papa is an admirer of Avlok Dutta. A great admirer.'

'OB, Mitali is the de facto editor of *India Post*. You want a job as a journalist, she is the person. That is, if and when you become a graduate, which I doubt.'

'Are you the one I should talk to for a job?' I ask Mitali.

'No longer. My father has finally hired a CEO who doubles up as the Editor.'

'That way he does away with one post and saves money,' Arjun nods. 'And who may this be?'

'Arun Dudani. He sits in Bombay mostly.'

'Never heard of him.'

'He is from the corporate sector. Fast-moving goods.'

'Soap. Shampoo. News. The time-tested transition.' Arjun nods to himself.

'My father believes anybody can do anything if he has common sense.'

'True citizen journalism.' Arjun takes a sip of his whisky. 'I need a column, Mitali.'

'I have been reading about you. You have so many enemies. Quite impressive.'

'He really did go far,' Arjun imitates the crowd he believes is baying for him. 'It was to be expected. He wasn't one of us, after all.'

'Let me see what I can do, Arjun. Papa may think a columnist like you might be the thing to prop up the paper. Papa believes everybody is guilty of something, and that one must play on that. But one thing: he is not afraid of anyone.'

'Mr Dudani has been in for how long now?'

'Just a few weeks. You haven't met Mr Dudani, of course. He is unintentionally funny. And wears a heavy perfume. I always look for a halo of flies around his head. And he likes tight green trousers and slim-fit high-collar shirts. Long teeth. Hollow cheeks. Says "At the intersection of ambition and scarcity is innovation." Things like that.'

'I am already in love with him.' Arjun orders a round for all.

Mitali's phone rings. 'Yes, Papa. Where are you? ... You called twice? ... No, I am sorry, it was on silent mode... Oh, please stop shouting, Papa ... Today is your white suit day. You can't shout ... Yes, yes, just give me a minute.' Mitali switches off her phone. 'He is waiting outside in the car to pick me up. Thanks for the drinks, Arjun.' She smiles at me. 'And Mr Osip Bala Krishnan has been silent.'

'He is a Russsian poet, but will not admit it under interrogation.'

Mitali smiles at me to say Arjun is being Arjun again.

'Next time we must meet without Arjun,' Mitali says.

'A young man wise beyond his age. Wise beyond the ages even. Speaks in tongues, if at all.' Arjun assumed a mock-serious expression, which for him was serious. 'Experience is the name people give to their mistakes, as the wise say. This man here today especially is much older than he was yesterday, having fought more wars with the world and himself in the interval.'

'Oh, I expect no one to be normal. My father's training.' Mitali laughs. 'Besides you haven't met my niece. She is 16 and talks like my aunt.'

'Run along before your father breaks in here.' Arjun gives Mitali a parting hug.

'See you soon, guys. Now, whom has he fired, I wonder?'

***

It was hot. Arjun and I stepped out of the FCC with a bottle of beer in hand. 'I am not insensitive to the irony of my position in approaching Mr Alok Jain,' Arjun said. We waited at the zebra line for the green man to come on, so we could walk across to the other side, towards Pragati Maidan Gate 7. 'Welcome to the Delhi International Book Fair,' a giant banner fluttered over the gate. Around us, cars and rickshaws honked without a break. It was past seven. I saw Elizabeth emerging from the gate. Was it Elizabeth? Not just a bright conjuration of my mind? Because there was a man in front of her. And her head would pop up and vanish behind his shoulder. Then the man abruptly turned to a side—yes, it was Elizabeth. She had a carry-bag out of which books burst.

I handed over my bottle of lemony Bira to Arjun and ran through the traffic to the other side.

'Hey,' Arjun said.

Elizabeth saw me. She seemed transfixed. 'Oh no,' she said when I reached by her side.

'I came to your place a few times.'

'OB! You begin with accusations. For God's sake!'

'I had to meet you. I had to.'

'To make it more painful for everyone?'

'The baby…?'

'So this is Elizabeth?' Arjun said. He had finally made it across the road. The beer bottles in his hands glinted as he raised them in greeting.

'Who's this?' Elizabeth asked.

'Arjun Bedi. He is a famous writer.'

'So famous he has to be introduced,' Arjun panted.

'Where are you staying, Elizabeth?'

'Use your Google Map.' Her face was red with anger and embarrassment.

'Elizabeth wants to be left alone, Osip.' Arjun said. 'The boy has been a bit desperate.'

'I don't know if it's a good idea for me to be talking to you, Mr Arjun Bedi.'

'Arjun is a great friend,' I said.

'You are right to plead the fifth,' Arjun said to Elizabeth.

'I suppose you confide everything to him?' Elizabeth shook her head at me accusingly.

'Well...'

'So long. I've ordered a cab,' Elizabeth said, looking around.

'Not fair,' I thought.

An Uber cab drew up at Gate 7.

'My cab,' Elizabeth said and half-ran towards it. Her hair streamed in the air. It had grown longer. She was that thing, a perfectly formed, perfectly cruel human, who knew exactly what effect she had on me. As Elizabeth pulled open the door of the cab, one book spilled over, face down, but she did not bother to pick it up. The driver eased the cab into the traffic.

I ran after it, wondering what might be the book she dropped to distract me, like a lizard's tail.

Pragati Maidan is on Mathura Road, and a few minutes later came the Purana Qila, a sixteenth-century fort. In Delhi, one millennium rubbed shoulders with another, and the simultaneous prolificacy of civilizations never ceased to bewilder you; events and histories, molecules of time, passed through each other inextricably like waters meeting and flowing. Far ahead, Elizabeth's cab was slowing down. She cared, then. I saw people flying past me; the great, summer dusk falling like a shutter over the Fort; trees turning deep as caves. Elizabeth's cab stopped. Horns blared. Elizabeth stepped out of the car. She calmly walked to the side of the road through the milling traffic and stepped up on to the footpath and turned in my direction.

'Sher Shah is watching, so behave.'

Purana Qila was built by the Afghan king, Sher Shah Suri, who ruled Delhi bloodily in the sixteenth century. Monuments. Ruins. Blood. The story of each great city. Right alongside the Fort was a lake. Once it was a moat. Little boats could be hired, and you could go up and down the lake till sunset. After that, the Fort closed and the revellers departed; the guards retired to their tin houses inside the Fort and continued watching news or porn, 'the two secret and interchangeable career aspirations of the hardworking Indian,' Arjun said. The small boats painted yellow, red and bright blue, and loosely tied to their moorings bobbed. Elizabeth took my hand. 'I thought you would understand and keep away.'

She seemed to have got older; sounded older too. 'Want to go on a boat ride?'

'They will catch us,' I said.

'The name is Blonde. James Blonde.'

We untied a boat from the stake and stepped on the pedals. I could see the last of the day's light rippling along the top edge of the fort in the water in a livid red line. When we rounded the corner of the fort into the farthest reaches of the lake and over the shadows, Elizabeth stopped pedalling. After a moment or two, I stopped, too. It seemed I had no will independent of Elizabeth's.

Elizabeth dipped her fingers in the water. 'The lake doesn't look dirty in the dark, does it?' She put her arm around me. 'Look, you are several old men when it comes to everything, except yourself.'

'I'm a little off, maybe.'

'A little?' She laughed.

'There's no baby?'

'What will I do with a baby, and a boy for its father?'

'I thought there was a baby and you had flown to England and…' If I knew she was in India, I might have not have had poor Father Roderick dug up.

'I bought eight books today. If I hadn't, you probably would not have run into me.'

'Yes. One you dropped on the way.'

'Did I? But I didn't know this was what I was going to do with them. Because the life I am leading seems to be more complicated than the one I read.'

I was curious for a fleeting moment to know what the titles were. But it seemed a detail without consequence in the larger scheme of things. Like a prisoner trying to remember the title of a movie just before he was hanged.

Elizabeth took out the books one by one from the bag and, covers down, stacked them by her side. 'Ready?' she asked. She nudged the top one into the lake. It fell into the water with a plop, and slowly sank. She did it seven times. The boat bobbed. 'I have drowned all the nameless babies. A kind of Medea act.'

A late crow flew over the wall of the fort. 'We have our own Medeas. Why should it be all Western archetypes?'

'Because we are the West. We are very powerful. And it is our duty to civilize the East.'

'The grandest period of colonial expansion was between 1876 and 1915.'

'I wish I was born then.' Elizabeth laughed.

'During those years the French empire grew 20 times the size of France. Belgium—80.' I had become a nationalist of sorts to get even with Elizabeth. 'But Britain was the most rapacious; it outgrew its size by 140 times. Look at what the Enlightenment gave you—slavery, Colonialism!' I felt momentarily good, having scored against the powers that be.'

'I suppose by Britain, you mean me,' Elizabeth said. 'And because of us, you now have electricity, cars, and the railways.'

'Well…'

'We can't help it, we just must improve the lesser peoples of the world.'

'What I am trying to say is we don't have to know about Medea.'

'What are you talking about?'

'Our myths.'

'What about them?'

'*Mahabharata*'s Shantanu is the great-grandfather of the Pandavas and Kauravas, the warring cousins. Shantanu falls in love with Ganga, the river goddess. And she tells him she will stay with him if he asks no questions about her conduct.'

'That's great. She is what it is all about.'

'The king agrees. They have seven babies. Ganga drowns them all. When the eighth is born, Shantanu says, "No!" Ganga leaves him. The saved baby grows up to be Bhishma, a great warrior, and a celibate, and without whom the great war may not have happened.'

'So?'

'It doesn't have to be always Medea and Oedipus and...'

'You are free to write what you want. A lot of people do, I believe. I don't know about your myths. I don't need to.'

'But we have to know yours, see? We have to know your cities and street names. We have to know your gods and writers. But you don't have to. Elizabeth, you are always deciding for me.'

'We are having a great anti-colonial evening.'

'I am sorry.'

'Your board exam will start soon.'

'I will probably be going home for the study holidays.'

'Good.'

'And the baby…'

'I aborted. I suffered so both of us are free.' Elizabeth stared at the massive fort. 'Is it only Muslims and Christians who have theological problems with the idea of abortion? I had asked you once, but you never answered, did you? Are you Hindu?'

I was adopted. My grandfather had gone to make a speech at the local orphanage, and he had found me staring at him as he passed through the dormitory. 'Not to worry, Osip,' he said. 'I will take you home with me.' At the end of that evening, when my grandfather asked the orphanage officials about taking me home, they waived the usual paperwork and entrusted me to him. He was Bolshevik Menon after all, the Revolutionary leader with a great past; there would be no Party without him. 'Everything went off fine,' my grandfather said, except when he reached home with me in his arms. Gloria had screamed, 'I don't know how to take care of babies, you know that. You should have asked me. This is a child, not a puppy. And where's the money? A baby is bloody expensive. And... and, we are so old.'

'Does it matter? What should we do?' I said to Elizabeth.

Wouldn't you like know the titles I drowned?'

'No.'

Elizabeth rubbed her cheek against mine. 'Your cheek is wet.'

'It's the lake.'

'Have you have been swimming while I was busy expanding my colonies? '

'We could be together.'

'I can't get involved. That's how I stay free. Have you sailed ever?'

'What? No.'

'You must sail. The other day I was in Mumbai and I went sailing on a private yacht. A short break to put it all behind me.'

'Whose yacht?'

'Brijesh Kapoor. Remember the artist?'

'C-O-N-N-E-C-T-IO-N-S.'

'He got in touch. He has been here for some time now, he said. He is quite a guy. He made some money from that show of his, and so he decided to buy a yacht. I was with him for a few days.'

'A yacht?'

'Yes. Someone told him you could get the shell of a twin-hull cheap in South Africa. Well, Brijesh being Brijesh, he flew to Joburg, got the shell for a song, fitted it out, hired two men, and sailed back to Mumbai. It took him two months, he said. He learned the ropes on the way.'

'Where did you go?' Why does jealousy feel like murder?

'Off Mumbai, we went far out.'

'Really? How long were you out sailing?'

'We spent a few nights at sea.'

'This is a yacht with bedrooms and all?'

'Two bedrooms below the cabin on either side. You've got to go down a few steps. The cabins are tiny though.'

Tiny and cozy.

'So when we got out to sea, Brijesh put up the sails. The main one and the other. It was cold and windy. I didn't think it was going to be that cold, off Mumbai. And then I remembered I had brought no jacket with me.'

'This is a good moment to push Elizabeth out,' I thought. 'Let her follow her books.'

'But Brijesh had an extra one, so that was fine then. The night on the sea is something else. All those stars. There are so many, and you hear nothing but the water and the wind.'

I trailed my hand in the lake.

'You must do all those things before you become a father.'

'Let's turn back.' Elizabeth started pedalling.

I sat still. Let her pedal all by herself. Let her steer the boat to the shore of my ruins.

'A good man helps his partner,' Elizabeth said.

We slipped the knot over the stake and got back on the ground. There was no one about. We waited in silence. When a rickshaw—its tail lights on—came by, Elizabeth hurried into its shiny, pink, laminated cabin.

The rickshaw moved ahead. Elizabeth waved. Just the hand. A moment later, Elizabeth put out her head and said something. I could not catch her words. The rickshaw receded, its red tail-lights blinking like the bloodshot eyes of the night.

A WANDERING CORPSE

The world tumbled about inside Ms Yolanda Andrade's head. David Roderick had called to say he had parted with Rs 5 lakh to a gang of corpse kidnappers, whom he suspected were her students. The corpse was that of his father, that fat paraph of a priest. All the actual transactions had taken place seemingly through a fumbling third party, whose face was covered, David said. He could give more details when they met. He chose not to inform the police because matters relating to the school and church were best handled discreetly. After all, he was a former student of the school.

'But…,' Yolanda had nearly fallen off the new red, overstuffed, Godrej executive throne with its custom-built back to ease her prolapsed disc condition. 'What are you saying, Mr Roderick?' She found it hard to address him in this honorific fashion. He had once been her student. 'They took out the body? And held it to ransom?' The reputation of the best school in the Kasauli hills was about to take a beating? 'But how do you know? And why did you pay before consulting me?'

Yolanda perspired at the prospect of *The Tribune* breaking the news—it had carried her obit and was unapologetic when Yolanda pointed out that she was alive—and the hostile Parents-Teacher Meeting as a consequence. A scandal of Himalayan proportions loomed before her. 'When did it all happen?' She looked in amazement all around her book- and trophy-lined office for hope, anchorage.

'Well, the last few days have been tough. You were travelling, I was told.'

Cowardly fate conspired against her, mostly in her absence.

'We are not reporting this to the police yet. Father Roderick had a lifelong relationship with your school.'

'Yes, they were nearly inseparable.' Yolanda recalled the dinners when the gravy train would invariably levitate to Father Roderick's side. 'But who? How did they…?'

'They must have had some professional help. The mortal remains…the body of Father Roderick had been taken out of the coffin, and whisked away and hidden. They then called in for the money.'

Whisked seemed too light a verb in this context, but English, Yolanda recalled, had never been David's forte. 'Horrible, horrible. But how do you know our boys did it?' Our boys. Our gangsters? She was aware of rage replacing the shock.

'Because of the way they spoke on the phone. You know the school sing-song intonation?'

'That...that's really guesswork, you can't take that to court.' But this man might. She recalled his face: a determined billygoat wearing thick glasses.

'And the tarp they packed the body in had the St George's seal. That faint green watermark.'

'Oh my God.' Yes, St George slaying the dragon. A battle which the saint seemed to be ever losing. 'Does Mrs Roderick know? It would be hard on her.'

'No, that's another reason why I paid up. Can't have this sort of thing up in the air, can we? The body has been restored to its rightful place.'

Or to the rightful owners, the worms. 'What would you like for us at the school to do, Sir?' From Mister to Sir. Yolanda's self-degradation seemed to her complete.

'I want the school to reimburse me.'

'But how can we be certain our boys did it?'

'If one of your students is suddenly conspicuous in his consumption, you've got your man,' David said, choosing his words carefully. He was a slow, deliberate man. 'Of course, your boys did it,' he thought, 'that tarp now!'

'These days a residential school is the hotbed of evil,' his father had told him last year. 'You have no idea, son, how things have changed since your graduation.'

'Indeed, as in the US, so here, by 13, the kids became adults,' David thought. 'Adult size, adult minds. Their shoe sizes!'

Anand? A bolt of lightning, hundreds of kilometres long, coursed through Yolanda's blood. Of course. Anand had been riding around on a gleaming red Bullet. She had thought it was probably borrowed. He had been wanting to buy one for long. Poorly worded and falsely humble appeals to her generosity had been made and ignored. Her shocking death on the train had been one of the consequences. But the less said about that, the better. 'I'll gouge his eyes out,' Yolanda muttered to herself.

'Did you say something?'

'No, I…I'll keep an eye out.'

'Ah, yes, of course. But I need to be reimbursed.'

'Please give me some time, Sir. Just a little time. We need to confirm your…your fears.'

'I have to return to the US next week.'

'Before that, I will get in touch with you, I promise, Sir.'

'How am I to go about this?' Yolanda thought. The school was her life's work. It had been hard to get the institution up and running in a man's world. True, Mr Andrade had helped with the licences and connections. But the actual work of making things happen was her lot. And she had done an excellent job of it, Mr Andrade would tell Yolanda, when he was pleasantly high, which happened nearly every night. They should be raising a statue to her in the hills in honour of the services she had rendered to society, Mr Andrade would say, looking deeply and without meaning into her eyes, the way he must have looked at every woman, and there had been many, Yolanda knew. But he was right. She deserved respect and recognition. Maybe even a statue. Why not? Instead, she was being dragged through the mud for no fault of hers, thanks to her late philandering husband. It all went back to him; every single one of her travails could be easily traced to him. Who seduced her when she was little more than a girl? Mr Andrade. How did she become so aggressive? Mr Andrade. How did she develop a distrust of the world? Mr Andrade. How did she…? Mr Andrade. Yolanda had no doubt about who was responsible for changing her fate and personality. What a free, lovely, curly-haired, wonder-eyed Goan girl she had been, and now…that girl had gone missing. How? Mr Andrade. And then that affair. The cherry as it were on the cake. Mr Andrade and *that* woman had fun. In the fullness of time, one died, and the other was asked to vanish, in reverse order. And she, Yolanda, who had nothing to do with the folly, had to suffer. Bad karma? Mr Andrade was the synonym.

Yolanda had been restrained even in the face of extreme provocation. When Anand published the obit on her, which she had accidentally read on the Bangalore-Delhi Rajdhani Express, she had wept in horror but precipitated no action. She had again put the interests of the school before everything. Imagine reading about one's death while travelling on business. If the train attendant, young Idris, had not brought a timely cup of tea and massaged her toes to prove she was not dead, she may not have survived the news of her death. Well, that day had turned out to be even more bizarre before it ended, what with poor Idris being arrested, a mistake no doubt, a mix-up to be sure, he was such a kind, helpful boy…but this exhumation and extortion were a great deal worse because the whole school was involved. She gasped at the enormity of the damage. Surely, the institution was more important than an individual? Any individual?

'Sorry, the signals are weak here, and your voice is breaking,' David said.

'No, Sir, I can hear. We will resolve this to your satisfaction, Sir.'

'How? I am sorry, but time is of the essence. If my mother gets to know of this, she could die of shock.'

'I understand, Mr Roderick, I am reeling from it myself.'

'Please take action on the boys, Madam,' David said.

'Yes, Sir.'

'The study holidays had started. Would Anand be on campus? Where else could he go?' she thought.

'This is a matter of great concern to us. And I will get to the truth of it. I'm so, so sorry, no son should be subjected to such an experience.'

'No father, too. We owe the dead a decent burial.'

'Yes, for that, we start with the living,' Yolanda simmered. She had to confront Anand. There seemed no other way. She began saying something—something weak, yet another apology—into the phone, and realized David had cut her off. She had been slighted again.

Voices

In the basement, I am watching a clip on Twitter where the curator of an aquarium in Seoul is describing how an eight-year-old female tiger shark has swallowed her five-year-old male companion. The curator, who sports a Kim Jong-un haircut, has shot the whole five-minute sequence on his cell-phone and put it out on social media. You can see the male disappearing into the mouth of the female slowly, as she swims around without too much fuss. There has been a territorial dispute between the sharks and the older one has had enough and begins swallowing the rival, who is also her mate, unfortunately. 'She will, most probably,' the curator says, 'regurgitate him in a week.' He stares at the camera doubtfully. 'Liebestraum is more powerful than sex. Or love. That's what the sharks are telling us.'

The phone in my hand comes to life. It is Anand. 'Hey, man,' I say.

'Home and dry?'

'Not dry.' When I landed in Kochi, the nearest airport to Thrissur, it was raining. It has been raining since. The airport looked like a lake. I had booked a pre-paid taxi at the airport. 'We take only cash,' the girl at the counter said, pointing to a sign, Tender Exact Change. Cash was no problem, thanks to Father Roderick, and Idris Abbottabad who had done everything from digging up the body to wrapping it up and stashing it away, and putting it back in. 'It's the rain,' the girl said. 'The network is erratic. It's water everywhere here.'

'I won't be back until another week, Anand. Where are you?'

'Shangri La. I don't have a home, remember?'

'You must come down here.'

'Too late now. Listen, can you do us a favour? Drop everything and come back?'

'I've been here just a few days. I am a long way off. This is another country almost.' From Delhi, you could reach Kabul faster than Kerala. Does that make Afghanistan part of India?

'It's about Elizabeth madam.'

'What about her?' Nothing to do with the corpse, then.

'That's what I am trying to say. Maybe you can't hear me because of the rain?'

'I can hear you very well.'

'Madam and the corpse. It's all about the same thing, you understand?'

'No.'

'Just come, will you?'

'There are no flights out of this place. Bad weather.'

'There are always flights. Catch one tomorrow. This is serious.'

'What?' The line goes dead. I try his number. It's busy. He must be trying mine. Or maybe it's the rain.

***

'Bala,' Gloria Innaley shouts from above, 'Baalaah!'

'Yes.'

'What are you up to down there? It's almost night. There are important matters to be discussed. Not that you are keen on taking responsibilities.'

'What's it?' I sense a plot to ambush me.

'Come on up.'

I go up. Up here, there's only a little more light, a kind of gloaming, coming in through the slatted window, into the high-roofed, cobweb-cornered hall. Gloria is sitting at her writing-table. 'No newspapers and no TV. Do we exist? The power has been off and on.'

'It's the rain.'

The power comes on. Gloria clears her throat. 'Bala, it's about your grandfather. Your grandfather is better off in a retirement home. It will make no difference to him— if he is not pretending.'

'Yes.' No. Surely, one must still be sick to pretend like this?

'Yes, what?'

'What would you like me to say?' I think I have a headache coming.

'There you go stonewalling. I want to start living, do you see? I'm losing it. Can I begin to live, please? Am I asking for too much? I am tired of my small town family sacrifices. That's all I have been doing. My life has passed me by.'

Yes, an ambush. 'Isn't it too late?'

'You haven't changed at all. As aloof. As insensitive. As helpful as ever.'

'You are a celebrity in these parts with *A Revolutionary, In Retrospect*.'

'Ah, you saw those three who came here yesterday to invite me for the Nirmala function.' Gloria nods in appreciation. 'They got their copies signed. But you saw it. You were behind the door.'

'Was I?'

'Yes, hiding, eavesdropping. You are so like your grandfather. Paranoid.'

'It was quite something, the story they narrated.'

'About Nirmala out in the fields being attacked by a leopard...They said L-E-O-P-A-R-D.'

'Yes, and Nirmala killing it with her sickle, the Marxist party symbol. They stressed on the sickle, did you notice? As if it was the Marxist party that killed the animal.'

'I liked the last part best. About Nirmala reaching home late, all wounded and bloody, and her husband saying, "You are late for cooking dinner; all of us are famished waiting for you?"'

'It was funny.' Droll. Very droll.

'But, you see they are very earnest people. One of them said the leopard was male, too, and I must connect that with patriarchy in my speech somehow, he said. And all the while he was looking in the direction of your grandfather's room, the leopard in residence.'

'You are going for the function, then? Very good.'

'Yes, of course. I need distractions. Only, I must expect someone from the crowd to ask me something about your grandfather, about *our* great political past. Mostly tales that the people would like to read about a hero of theirs. I have a tough time keeping up with all the grandiose half-truths that I wrote about him in the book.'

'Oh, but no one asked you to, grandmother. You were free to speak the truth. You still are.' The right side of my head feels squeezed as if in an iron clamp.

Makkam appears from the kitchen and gives Gloria a clean handkerchief. 'Thank you, Makkam.' Gloria blows her nose.

'Maybe you should have a drink, Madam Mother.'

'Isn't it too early?'

'It's raining. One stiff drink will help.'

'All right, if you insist.'

Makkam bares her long, narrow, yellow teeth in appreciation, and goes around the old dining table of teak and glass, towards a low cupboard where my grandfather's clothes are ironed and kept, preserved from the guerrilla war waged by insects, by means of camphor balls, and reaches into the recesses to draw out a bottle of Old Monk rum, also camphor flavoured. Makkam pours out a large drink with obvious relish, so her boss turns more tolerant of the world, whose many flaws could be blamed on Makkam.

'Please. No one can speak the truth. Because there is no such thing. Only approximations toward it, as I know only too well.' Gloria considers her toes for a distant moment.

'How memory metamorphoses the motive!' She reaches for the rum.

'You have no idea what it was to live and work in those days, do you, living with a legend? The Revolution was around the corner. Every day was momentous. A car backfired. It was the revolution. When the House of Soviet Culture crashed, right across our home and office in Trivandrum, you were not there, of course, you came much, much later, we were certain reactionary forces had bombed the building. It was the Revolution in reverse! Things kept happening down the decades, false alarms, of course. And then the Berlin wall. It crashed around his head, let me tell you. It all began with that Russian trip, as you know. Still, a hero to all, despite his murderous politics.' Gloria acts as if she is about to get up; she raises her hips a little from the chair, and then sits back. 'No, I don't think I can put him away in a home. I am stuck with him for life.'

I worry if she will expand the bit about murderous politics. But she is too distracted.

'None of that comes in your book.'

'No, I don't think you understand. If I set about correcting and criticizing him, I would have been lynched out of the nostalgia for what was not there. The Party here is the Mob. Not that the Communists or any of the others did anything for him once he lost it. It's like they know he was turning against them secretly, and he didn't know what to do with his rebellious thoughts. He thought the Party could read his mind. Of course, they could. We can all read each other's thoughts. Absolutely. He tried not to have thoughts. He *was* paranoid. Delusional. It's all in the head, isn't it?' She points a strong, square finger to her head.

'But you brought him back into reckoning.' Should I tell her I am not feeling well?

'Well, that can't be the purpose of *my* life. I cannot be rationalizing forever all that he did, or not did. I should be writing about my life. The life I lost. For him. Just consider my name, Innaley. Yesterday. Very symbolic, don't you think?'

'You should write about it,' I say without conviction.

'Oh, don't make this into a question of an easy choice. That Camus drivel about everyone having a choice and staking one's life on that choice, to live and fight. Half a billion Indians are working their backs off to earn a meal. Choice!'

'I didn't say anything about a choice.' I press a hand to my head.

'All my life I have suppressed my talent for this man. I could have been an All-India Radio staff singer. A star! I could have retired with a pension! They invited me. Sent around a car for an audition. But no, I had to take care of the guests, the house, dictations. It was carnage. Day after day, the same lamb was slaughtered. That's what it was. At the altar of the Party, they sacrificed me, a woman and an artiste. Can you tell slaughter from sacrifice? But is anyone interested? No. They want to hear me sing his praise in rosy rhymes. That golden period! Hell, I just might write that sequel denouncing the present work.'

'Maybe after his death?'

'It's a thought.'

'When is he back from the Majlis?' The Majlis Ayurveda Health Centre was on the outskirts of the town, on the way to the beach toward the temple town of Guruvayoor.

'Late tonight, I think.'

'Who's with him?'

'Treesa. The only good that's come out of his lifelong love for paupers and prostitutes is her. He is no longer active as the President of the Prostitutes, as you know. But, for Treesa, he is still the leader.'

Mr Menon's fight for the rights of the Sex Workers' Association (SWAX) came late in the day when his people had forgotten him, because, he said, the Party suffered from Alzheimer's. On an afternoon of brilliant clarity, it occurred to my grandfather that nobody was doing anything for sex workers. 'Not bleddy saxy,' he said, imitating someone only he knew. He began going to their meetings and protests. The sex workers loved him. On good days, he spoke of their rights in the town square and on public platforms. Not as he used to, but a little haltingly, with Treesa jogging his memory from the sidelines in alternately heartening and heartrending whispers. And one day, despite his increasing infirmities, they had elected him as their leader for life.

'Is that Ayurveda place doing any good to him?'

'Not really. He believes it's some sort of KGB arrangement and the masseurs are torturers. I think he is deteriorating.'

'Hmm.'

'Are you all right? Have you been regular with your medicines?'

'Yes.'

'Been seeing or hearing things?'

'No.'

'But, the constant hum in the head, waxing and waning?'

'Of course not. I think I will do some reading.' I turn to go back down to the basement.

'Stop running away. I won't be there for the next few days. I have joined the election team of the Party. "Please help us, Comrade Gloria Innaley," they said. And I did. I am just filling in for your grandfather. I may leave late this evening. I hope you realize, I have no alternative at this late stage but fight for a new life. I am tired of this vague longing for my missing self, sadness, and a constant alternation between excitement at possibilities and exhaustion from life-long disappointments.'

'I'll take care of him.'

'You needn't worry on that account. Treesa will be there, unless she has a client.'

The phone in my pocket vibrates. Anand. I ignore the call.

'Don't let Treesa take over the house. She is nice, but you know how it is. Nice has nothing to do with anything. I know she uses my toothbrush once in a while. And I have bought her at least two in the last three months.'

***

Late in the night, I faintly heard a car coming to a stop, and then dug deeper into my sleep. I waited, but sleep would not come; the ache had risen like cake inside my head. I went up to see if my grandfather had returned. There were subdued noises. Were they in my head? Dr Ratnamali Nair once told Gloria, 'Hallucinations, auditory or optical, at some level reflect one's inner reality.' The lights had gone out again. Mr Menon's study was lit by a lantern and deep with shadows. I found him sitting up in his bed. Where was Treesa? When he saw me, he placed a finger over his lips. I stood still at the door, the Troitsky Bridge—part of the room out of my line of vision, and a jumble of voices humming around me.

No, there is no real Worker's Way, no *Rabochi put*, he said. Because the worker eventually goes where the capital is. So there was no time. He had to shrink history, Comrade. He had to telescope time, had to compact the development of a hundred years into 10, 20, bending time to his will. There would be violence, blood, death. What did you think this was? There was no place for misfits. For Jews. For poets. For outsiders. No assembly line runs with a spanner stuck in its belts.

Another voice, thin and fraying, familiar as one's own—but issuing from a stranger's throat: '*картошка*. Kartoshka. Potato.'

What tuber is more epic? Mr Menon turns his head in my direction. '*Поэт голоден*. Poet *goloden*. The poet is famished. Do we have anything in the kitchen?'

Had it stopped raining? What day was it? What time? What's this buzz in my ears? I turned, went, past the hall, through the passage, into the kitchen. The steelware gleamed in the pale moon filtering through the skylight. I found two potatoes on the sideboard. I washed them and put them to boil. I watched the bubbles. I drew a knife from the rack and peeled the potatoes. I saw my fingers had grown and that I was far removed from them. It was as if I was wearing someone else's glasses. The potatoes were hot to the touch. I cut them neatly into pieces, first vertically and then horizontally. I shook salt and pepper over them. I picked up the heavy red porcelain plate, turned, and walked into something.

'Ahh!' I yelled, and dropped the dish. I struck out with my hand in anger and fear.

'Are you mad?' Gloria shrieked. My hand had already connected with her face.

'What's wrong with you?' Gloria said, her hand over her mouth. She was bleeding a little from her nose.

'I…I'm sorry. I thought…'

Gloria lit a candle.

I looked at the potato pieces strewn on the floor laced with red bits of china. 'I thought you had gone. That's what you said. I thought it was someone else.'

'Who? Are you crazy? Just like him. I hate all of you. Hate, do you understand? You people ruined my life.'

I bent over to collect the crumbs.

'I'll do that. You will make a mess of it,' Gloria nearly screamed.

I sat down on my haunches. I had a crying need to hide. But my migraine, or whatever it was, had gone.

Old Enemies

The impact of Father Roderick's abducted corpse, Yolanda thought, was comparable only to an earthquake. Like the one in Mumbai years ago, when she was there on a visit. Yolanda shuddered at the recollection of that seismic event. She was in a bra and skirt and plucking her eyebrows, when the mirror on the wall of her hotel room shook. She had hurried down the steps of six floors and run across the reception, her ears ringing with terrified screams. Outside, there was a ring of people by the garden looking up at the Sun & Sand hotel shaking. 'What are they waiting for?' Yolanda had wondered. 'For the building to fall on their heads?' And then she had joined the suicidal voyeurs. A window had come down, rather lazily floating in the air, and had decided to fall into the pool at the last minute. There was a crack on the perimeter wall. But no one had got hurt. As the clients and the staff stood staring at the building, waiting for it to crash, they had felt one more tremor under their feet. But that was it. And, with recouped life, returned the trite, attendant distractions. Yolanda had realized that she was not wearing much. Walking naked on the streets had been one of her recurring nightmares. And it had come true. She noted with alarm that all the frightened spectators around her were seemingly in their finery.

She had returned, crimson-faced, her hands crossed over her generous breasts, and taken the slowest elevator, walked down the longest corridor, toward the loneliest room in the hotel, her room. She had decided then she was never going to bed again without her best clothes on. This morning too she had not been sartorially wanting. But, as she listened to David's description of the misfortunes faced by his father's body—restored to its grave *and* decomposing even as they spoke—she had felt naked again and shaken. There was a killer of sorts about, a defiler of corpses, and he happened to be her stepson.

***

Anand waited in the reception of Yolanda Andrade's office. He sat down on one of the wooden chairs lined up against the wall, stood up, and sat down again. He tummy-breathed to calm himself down. The receptionist glanced at him once and went back to her work. She seemed to enjoy his discomfort. Anand switched to loud nasal exhalations. It was all about breathing; in-breath; out-breath. If you were one with the universe, and the universe breathed through you, things had to fall in place. *Ayam Atma Brahma*. 'This *Atman* is the *Brahman*,' as they said on the yoga channels. 'Don't resist, go with the flow'. If this *Atman* was the *Brahman*, why was he in this room? Anand popped a stick of chewing gum into his mouth. The receptionist watched him; he offered her one. She declined. A green light flashed over the door. When he had been issued the summons, he had guessed what it would be about and had called up Osip again. Would the rains delay him too much? Anand hoped not, for his friend's sake. And, of course, for his own sake. For humanity's sake, let's say.

'You can go in now,' the receptionist said.

It was a large room. Its size never failed to impress Anand. Trophies and medals that the school won in sports and contests glittered on a wall shelf. Books, mostly inspirational biographies, lined another. The morning sun poured in through the four large windows. In a corner of the room, a Feng Shui waterfall soothed the nerves, presumably, of both the chastiser and the chastised. A desk of polished teak, the size of a ping-pong table, took up the centre of the room, behind which his stepmother sat on her Godrej throne. She seemed preoccupied. Anand blew the mint into a bubble and burst it.

Yolanda looked up, removed her glasses. 'Sit,' she said pointing to a chair.

Anand sat. He felt momentarily like a dog. Silence, except for the waterfall. Was Feng Shui a real science?

'We have a problem,' Yolanda said in a small, careful voice.

They stared at each other like atavistic enemies. Between them lay the late Mr Andrade's enormous, if invisible, dick. 'My father the motherfucker,' Anand thought. He wondered what he would do if he ever met his mother. Cry? Laugh? He had never felt like making an effort to find her. He had been rejected at birth. Disqualified. It was not his fault. Most things, Anand had begun to realize, were not his fault. 'A problem, Madam?'

Yolanda smiled, then let it curl around her mouth until it died and was reborn as a bitter sneer. 'Unfortunately, yes.' The obit had passed through her mind again, silent as a funeral. Yolanda could not put it behind her. It had been hard to digest that she could be hated enough to be wished dead. Hate was endlessly draining. But the feeling of exhaustion was soon replaced by a seething fury. Look at him. How dare he? Who was he to hate her? What gave him the right? He was wanting in every respect. A liability to her, to the school, why, even to himself. Even an utter stranger would have known at first glance the grace and goodness that was at the core of her being. Idris! If only Anand had been Idris! Someone who allowed the goodness in others to come to the fore. Someone like Idris. They were pretty much the same age, give or take a couple of years. How gentle that boy was. Unlucky, too. That day— the obit day—on the train, Idris had sat by her, massaged her feet gently, and reassured her she was alive, despite *The Tribune* informing her otherwise. He had got her tea. It had been too sweet. But Yolanda hadn't complained. That night on the train, out of gratitude for Idris's warmth and care, Yolanda had offered him a small—perhaps too small?—monetary reward. He had refused. Everything could not be measured in money, he said. They had sat side by side in the otherwise empty coupe for long in consolatory, companionable silence, despite the stuffy smell of sweat wafting out of Idris's grey railway uniform with yellow lettering.

'You know, Idris,' she had said, 'I have been afraid of travelling by plane since my husband died of a heart attack on one.'

'They had no doctors on board, Madam?'

'No. I guess when your time is up, your time is up.'

'Inshallah.' (Idris's next question was, 'How many wheels did a plane have?' but he had not asked it. Idris also wanted to ask, 'What happened to human waste while in flight?' He did not think it likely that it all went down the hole on to the fields below.)

'The great thing about your community, Idris, is that you are all such great believers. Such faith. That must help.'

Idris only smiled.

Idris had beautiful red lips. Like a girl's.

'Yes, belief helps.'

'For the poor, what was the other way to be?' he asked. As Yolanda listened to his story, her heart went out to him. Idris's family—his mother, grandmother, two elder sisters, and a younger brother—was dependent on him since his father had been lynched, like so many others, by a mob a few years ago for dealing in the beef trade. While they had chased his father down a dead-end alley with sticks and stones in hand, Idris was watching a Salman Khan movie at the *Globe* in Daryaganj in Delhi. When he got out of the cinema hall, he had switched on his phone.

'There were 16 missed calls from his father, 16 stabs to the heart,' Idris said. Idris had never been to a cinema since. 'Everything is the will of Allah,' Idris said, but he wouldn't presume to understand His workings. 'We have to believe, Madam.' A world without God was impossible, even if it conspired to murder his father.

Shaken, Yolanda could only manage to say, 'Yes, of course.'

In the morning, when the train reached Delhi, Yolanda had looked out for Idris and was shocked to see him being escorted out of the platform by two policemen. He was wearing a skull cap. 'Wasn't he the train attendant?' Yolanda said aloud.

'No, a petty train thief,' someone said, 'masquerading in an attendant's uniform. These guys; can't trust anyone, especially a Muslim, their loyalty lies elsewhere, with Pakistan maybe.'

And Yolanda had thought, 'No, not Idris, he was an angel of a boy, must be some mistake.' She would pray for him. Later, Yolanda would blame herself for not intervening on his behalf with the police. But it was too much trouble, given how rude and suspicious the police were. She had a life to lead, despite Anand wishing her eternal rest, which was what the subtext of the obit was. 'Text, not subtext,' Yolanda corrected herself. 'And this,' Yolanda now sighed, looking at Anand across the table, 'was the life that the munificent God had gifted her'.

'Yes, a serious issue has come up. A very serious issue. And you are responsible,' Yolanda said.

'I, Madam? I am responsible?'

'Yes. Please explain yourself,' Yolanda said.

'Explain what?' The bubble gum was no longer sweet, Anand decided. Should he excuse himself and spit it out?

'I see you riding around a new Bullet.'

'My friend's. It's a nice bike.'

'The friend gave it to you for free? Very generous of him.'

'Just borrowed it, Madam. He is a good friend.'

'Who's this?'

'He runs a garage.'

'Can you bring him over?'

'But why?'

'Because I believe that bike is yours.'

'No, no. I don't have the money for luxuries. All I get is what you give.' All you give is what I get.

'I would like to see the papers for the bike.' She hoped she didn't sound like a traffic cop. One had to be careful with this boy.

'I don't have them on me. But I can ask my friend.'

'How long will this take?'

'He is in Delhi.'

'Father Roderick's body...'

'I saw him die. Just dropped down. Life!' Anand felt like blowing a bubble. A big, white one that encompassed the room and its owner.

'The father's body was dug up and held for ransom. It was returned in the school's polythene cover. Someone broke into the stores. Father Roderick's son, David, believes boys from this school did it. And you are riding a new bike.'

'The just are not rewarded,' Yolanda thought, 'look at me'. The cross she had to bear. The crosses: the night after David called, she had persuaded him to accompany her to the cemetery. 'Paying you back your money is not the problem, but we are in it together, Mr David, both of us are victims,' she said. 'I need to see the plastic, Sir.'

'Well, the body went back to rest in the plastic,' David said, after a longish pause. 'We didn't want to unduly disturb the corpse.'

'How awful. But I need to see it for myself…you are a science student, you will understand the importance of direct observation.' And confirmation, of course.

'All right, tonight, then,' David had said,' I will come with my men.'

'Oh,' Yolanda said, 'I don't know if I can stand the smell.'

Later that night, at the cemetery, her nose and mouth covered with a peach-scented scarf, Yolanda experienced a mounting sense of martyrdom. She would deserve that statue richly. She looked around. So many dead. Including her husband. But she was alive. A survivor. A perverse sense of pride and power swelled her heart. Those who lost the battle were down under. She was standing upright—on their shoulders; on their heads even.

David had been supportive—after a fashion, which she could classify only as curiously academic. He was always good in biology and physics; she recalled that David had once toyed with the idea of studying for medicine, before his father persuaded him to take up computer engineering. 'A much cleaner trade,' Father Roderick had explained later to Yolanda.

'The body would be discoloured, and the teeth will bulge out of the face because the skin would be all gone, you see,' David warned her.

'That's good to know.'

'The skull takes the hit first. Because of the sockets. The worms lay eggs in all those holes. They go nearly berserk over sockets.'

'Do the nails and hair grow?' Yolanda voiced an old fear. She hoped the scarf would muffle the question even as she uttered it.

'No, no, that's a myth, I think. The skin just gets pulled away. So the nail and hair look longer. I believe the intestines would have been eaten away by Clostridia and Coliform bacteria. The smell is because they break it all down into hydrogen sulfide and methane gases.'

'Clostridia and Coliform sounded like two evil sisters from a Greek tragedy,' Yolanda thought. It seemed to her she had become David's student, a rather reluctant one. Yet another cross. Pile it on, God in Heaven. 'But we don't have to open the polythene cover, do we? We just have to see if it has the St. George's seal. Unless the seal has gone in somewhere under the body or inside the folds.' Yolanda prayed for small mercies. She had heard of corpses moving about within the confines of the coffin, shuffling off the mortal coils like a suit. 'If there was no seal, I'd be so happy,' she thought. Then everything would be back to normal, the earth a safer place. If only she hadn't insisted on the seal on all school inventories. She was a control freak, that was what, and now she was paying for it. She should start trusting people more. It all came down to that.

In the event, the St. George seal was right there on the priest's face, a nightmare wrapped in opaque plastic. The light from David's torch rippled slimily over what was once Father Roderick.

'All right, I have had enough,' Yolanda said. She had seen it all by now. She watched the coffin with its sad burden slowly disappear back into the earth.

'Well, now you know,' David said.

How insufferable another's triumph is. It occurred to Yolanda that David might be enjoying the outing.

'Show me the papers of your bike in a day or two.' Yolanda said to Anand. 'No more than that, do you get it?' Was that cutting enough? 'The matter will brook no delay.'

'Of course, Madam. But where do I come in?'

'That's what we are trying to find. Alternatively, you can explain it to the police.'

'No, not the police, please,' Yolanda thought.

Anand shook his head at the unfairness of it all, but said nothing. The Feng Shui water fell on their rocky silence.

'You may go.'

Anand got up.

'Tall boy,' Yolanda thought. 'Looks like his father, too.'

When Anand reached the door, Yolanda called out his name, like a warning.

'Yes, Madam?'

'What you get when you pass out is my discretion. Just remember that.'

Anand manoeuvred the gum to the tip of his tongue so he could blow it out into a big bubble...no, not a good idea. He turned and walked out of the door. He stuck the chewing gum on the door handle. He had decided on a course of action.

Shark Waters

It was night and raining when I reached Kasauli. The road up the hill was slow, slushy. The state transport bus took its time, honking, grunting, stopping. Climbing again. The rain reached in and ran in small currents up and down on the dirty steel floor of the bus. As we took the main turn at Dharmapuri, toward Kasauli, the back of the bus erupted into an abusive quarrel for a few moments when a passenger opened his umbrella under the leaking roof, and another protested because it was in his face. The conductor had the bus stopped at Sri Prem Kishan Tea Stall, persuaded them to go out with him in the rain—the three of them huddled under the contentious umbrella—bought the two men cigarettes and tea, and made peace. They smoked under the awning of the shop, lit with two candles, looking at the bus in the rain. When they got back in, both passengers shared the umbrella.

Anand made me a cup of tea. 'It's cold here, huh? How was home, warm and good?' he winked. He closed the windows. Then he said, 'Brrr,' and ran to the door and closed that, too.

'The tea all right? How was home?'

'All right.'

'Is a bad home better than no home? We will never know, will we?'

'What about Elizabeth?' I asked.

'I am going to make you rich,' Anand said. 'Very rich.'

'Anand!'

'Elizabeth madam is fine. Just fine. Should we first discuss the schemes that will make you rich so that you can live with her happily ever after? My friend, the future is bright.'

'Begin with Elizabeth.'

'No, I am serious. Listen to my plan, will you. This theory of mine, Holistic Metaphysics, is now fleshed out. I will be brief. It's called the 7 Routes to Happiness. Each colour has a distinct frequency or vibration due to its wavelength, or energy. Red, for instance, has a larger wavelength than blue. My idea is to tap the spectrum of colours for their energy and prop up the dying cells of the human organism, and thus reduce entropy. How, you are wondering?' Anand smiled. 'You have heard of Georges Lakhovsky, of course? A genius scientist who was wasted on us humans? He says a living cell is an electromagnetic entity, which is activated by cosmic light rays…You see where I am getting at? No, I don't want to burden you with the details. It's all quite connected…But you get me?'

'No.'

'You've come back quite crabby.'

'Say it, Anand.'

'This is a desperate country, OB. My Holistic Metaphysics, call it HM, will do very well, I feel.'

'What happened to the corpse?'

'Listen. This is money. We set up an HM institute.'

I sipped the tea. The room depressed me. 'Anand, what the fuck, man?'

Anand grimaced, and came and sat beside me on the bed. 'I had a meeting with Yolanda madam.'

'Why?'

'We have been exposed.'

'The corpse?'

Anand got up and walked to the door as if to prevent me from fleeing. 'Yeah, that fucking corpse. And the Bullet.'

'I knew that Bullet was a bad idea. I told you. So soon after...'

'You didn't tell me.'

'I did.'

'No, you didn't. In any case, the corpse was worse than the Bullet. The Bullet was the effect, the corpse was the gun.' Anand laughed in admiration at his own word play.

'I told you it was a bad idea.'

'No. you said it was a good idea. At least, you thought so.'

'I said I couldn't do it. I said drop the idea.'

'Then how did we get around to doing it?'

We were silent. The silence of two desperate men.

'What are you going to do?' I asked Anand.

'The question is what are we going to do? Because you had no problem taking your share of your money.'

'But I am not the one who is riding around on a fat bike and showing off. '

'There you go. I can explain the bike away. But we shared the money.'

'You went and got the money.'

'Idris. Idris collected the money.'

'Fuck Idris.' No, that wasn't fair. Idris had worked very hard. And he had seemed reliable. 'Is Idris trustworthy?' I had asked Anand. 'He is running from the law, who could be more trustworthy than a petty thief on the run?' Anand had said.

'What I meant was, you masterminded all that, remember? I was recovering. You did everything. The kerchief over the mouthpiece scene in a telephone booth? You translated how much Rs 5 lakh was in dollars to David, remember?'

'I was doing you a favour, OB. A bloody favour.'

I took a deep breath. 'What's the way out?'

'Madam believes I did the mischief.'

'How did she come to know?'

'Son David had a revelation. He identified the plastic sheet that we used had the St. George's watermark at the time of the hand-over of the corpse. We needn't have wrapped up the body in anything at all. See what comes out of a little concern for a fellow corpse? The thing is Yolanda madam will cut me out of any money coming my way, besides dismissing me from school.'

'So? What are you asking me to do?'

'Listen, OB. You have to weigh in for me here...hmm... tell me, what's your star?'

'What? Aquarius.'

'I see.' Anand checked his phone. 'Just as I thought. Only good things to happen to Aquarians this week, it says here. You are protected, OB. Your colour for the week is orange. Wear it and your electromagnetic activities would shoot up.'

'Anand, this is serious trouble. I can't handle it. This is jail.' I started sweating. The enormity of the crime hit me only then. Nothing justified it. Why did I go in for this? Why? Of course, I knew why.

'Calm down. They won't go anywhere near the police. It's a matter of reputation, don't you see? This woman is all society. She will not let the secret out. This is just a personal thing between her and me.'

'What action do you think she will take on me?' If Gloria got to know?

'I guess they will suspend you. Something light.'

'They won't let me take the boards.'

'I guarantee you. They won't do that because it will be a scandal again.'

'You are in it equally, Anand. And you have been showing off that bike of yours like a…' I got up and opened the window next to the bed. A sheet of rain came in, hung in the air like a curtain.

'It will all come out well. Just you go and talk to Madam.' Anand opened the door, put his head out to see if anyone was eavesdropping. He closed the door and leaned on it. 'Please close the window. The rain is coming in.'

'Let's meet her together.'

'Look, I don't want to do this to you. You are the only friend I have got. I swear you will get off lightly.'

'I am not taking the rap all on my own.' I sat down on the bed heavily.

'Well, I am not the one who slept with my English teacher, OB.'

'What?'

'If you don't step up, I will have to talk to Yolanda madam about you and Elizabeth madam.'

I hurled the cup at him. He ducked. I watched the cup shatter against the door, exactly at the spot where Anand had stuck his Descartes quote on the pineal gland. Anand stood there, his mouth open, and I saw myself disappearing slowly, inexorably into it, just as one shark was consumed by another in the aquarium show.

The Mass Destruction of One Life

When I arrived at Whispering Woods, there were already people in Arjun's living room. The smell of alcohol and tobacco mixed with perfumes licensed the air. The hall was packed. It was late, though guests still trickled in.

'But you had a birthday party earlier in the year!' I said.

'This is the roaring '20s. We hurtle from one drunken party to another.' Arjun put an arm around me. 'That was for Maina. This one is for me, but it is quite political in its purpose. I must fight by all means the daily and mass destruction of my one life. With silence, cunning, and parties, pagans and vegans all welcome!'

'URF?'

'They want to see blood. The crowd needs to see fresh blood. It has a way of turning everything into a sport.'

It seemed unfair to ask him for help.

'Everything all right?' Arjun asked.

'Well...'

'What's it?'

'The thing is...Can you come to my school?'

'What for?'

I told him in an urgent whisper, every word I uttered more absurd than the one preceding it.

'This is serious business, OB. How did you get into this mess? You are worse than me. But I am afraid I can't get into this, not now.'

'You are a famous man. A great writer.'

'Fame is what they can use against you. Remember what I told you some time back? You wouldn't believe it, it is organized frenzy.' Arjun looked around. 'These little parties I throw are my way of holding on to what little I have. It's a dangerous world now, anyone can work out their revenge from rest rooms, you understand? These are toilet revolutionaries,' Arjun grimaced. 'But, what the hell are you up to? An affair with your teacher followed by murder?'

'No, not murder. Exhumation.'

'It's as good as murder. Hell, it is worse!'

Three retired men of the military came up to Arjun and wished him happy returns loudly. Their chests were covered in stars and medals. The shorter, thickset one, with a luxuriant, twirled mustache, seemed always one step ahead of the other two.

'You must formally join our political party, Arjun Saab,' the short general said, staring hard at Arjun. But his eyes twinkled. 'You promised.' They had, it turned out, recently started a political outfit at the behest of Arjun.

'Ah, my generals,' Arjun said. 'India's best.'

'We registered the party. You can't back out now,' the second man said.

'The New India Political Party, NIP,' the third said.

'RIP?'Arjun said.

The generals laughed helplessly, holding on to each other's shoulders.

'Arjun Saab, Arjun Saab,' the leader shook his head as if Arjun was too much. 'Really, you are our star. Our torch. Our…' He looked around at his friends for help, but they only smiled in encouragement.

'Of course I will join NIP. On one condition, but.'

'What's that?'

'I'll be the treasurer. For life.'

They all threw their heads back and laughed again. They were an uproarious bunch.

'Jokes aside, Arjun Saab, the retired soldiers of this country can no longer bear to see the nation going down the drain. It's as you might say, RIP India or NIP India.' The short general said. 'We are looking for a writer with the rank of a general.'

'All right then, I will be your Maxim Gorky.'

The generals raised their eyebrows.

'He was the head of Union of Writers under Stalin,' Arjun said.

'M. applied to him for two sweaters and a pair of trousers. He didn't get the trousers, I think,' I said.

'This is Osip Bala Krishnan. He is Russian,' Arjun repeated his old joke.

They ignored me.

'Let's talk about NIP.'

'Aren't we all a bit too old to start a change-India party? Mind you, I am not talking about me,' Arjun said.

'You will bring the average age down, Arjun Saab,' the second general said. Everybody laughed again. One of the generals shook his head as if to say this is just too much. He had tears in his eyes.

'Really, we are as good as the young,' the short general said. 'I challenge anyone here to hand-wrestle me.' He looked around the room, but mostly in the direction of a woman in blue jeans and kurta. There was a bespectacled young man with her, holding her wine glass as she was answering a call; her other hand was in a sling. 'What corruption! Moral, financial, physical. Is this what our founding fathers sacrificed their lives for?'

'Are you addressing me, or my neighbour, general?' Arjun said. 'Careful. That's Dev and Diya. They represent the rights of the underprivileged and head a social media campaign against me. I have some trouble on the patriarchal front as you might know.'

'Love thy neighbour as thyself.' The general with tears of joy in his eyes said.

'Love thine own neighbour, not mine,' Arjun said.

This time the three generals nearly doubled up with laughter. The short general put out a hand in the direction of Arjun, pleading with him not to be so funny. 'I may be gazing elsewhere, but I look up to you.' The short general said, straightening up. 'As for the campaign against you, it is chaff in the wind, Arjun Saab. Nothing will shake our faith in you.'

The short general hugged Arjun briefly, and turned their attention to someone seemingly important entering, a politician, from the white *khadi* he was wearing, and marched toward him.

Arjun swallowed a drink neat and gravitated to Dev and Diya, who had moved out into the balcony. I straggled along by Arjun's side in grim fascination. 'I have had to work on through someone to make them come here,' Arjun whispered. I later learned that the 'someone' was the old man with the German shepherd. He was Diya's uncle—and Arjun's friend—and the couple were living in a flat of his in the building, a rent-free arrangement, Arjun said.

Dev and Diya were stiff, and it was clear they wanted to stay by themselves. They had done Arjun a favour dropping by.

'Dev and Diya, Thank you for coming.'

'We will be only a minute here.' They seemed assured and self-sufficient in the strength of their good intentions.

'Of course. I know you are fighting a good cause. And this is perhaps not the time to ask…'

'No,' they said in unison.

'I am not a tactful person…'

'We know that, don't we, Dev?'

'I knew this was why he insisted we come. Don't tell me I did not warn you.' Dev said to Diya.

'I can't help it, and I didn't think I would say it, but all these daily mass mails to publishers, festivals, editors…,' Arjun said.

'Well?' Diya said.

'It seems so much work.'

'Mr Bedi, please don't worry about our workload. We will stop when you apologize,' Diya said.

'Apologize for what?

'For your nude dancing and provocative comments and sexist columns. There were many good people in that party. They are deeply offended.'

'It was a rave party…so many years ago.'

'But only you were nude. And you put your arm around a victim's waist.'

'I was wearing something, not much, I admit, but something.'

'But you were the only one nude,' Dev said.

'There were others in other rooms.'

'Mr Bedi, a writer must represent the spirit of his age, and overcome it. You have failed,' Dev looked away in resignation.

'At a seminar, you said, "What's everybody's problem with the dick!"' Diya said.

'It was both a joke and a question,' Arjun said.

'Your whole discourse is wrong,' Diya shook her head.

'And your columns! We can't allow that kind of writing. You may think it is daring and intellectually provocative. That is your vanity. It is just bad form and poor taste.' Dev shook his head of long curls. 'And one poem that turned up on my computer last night, something about the Dark Spider.'

'"*Dolomedes Tenebrosus*: Spontaneous Male Death" was the title. The dark spider eats the male partner after sex.'

'You called the female spider a "b…h". Language is a social tool, Mr Bedi,' Dev said. 'There are norms to be observed. These are sensitive times. There is a historical correction to be made in favour of the female gender…'

'In favour of Dalits and children, too.' Diya's large, earnest eyes left no room for doubt about her commitment to her cause.

'In favour of the wronged people. What we stand for is a certain much-needed correction in patriarchal politics,' Dev said. 'We are conscientious citizens of this country, Mr Bedi, and we can't let a few things happen on our watch—even if the government is not of our choice, and we have no executive powers,' Dev's eyes bored into Arjun's. 'We have an obligation toward civilized society. But this is no place to talk about such matters, is it?'

'You are depriving me of my right to earn a living, in effect. That's not a constitutional or even a liberal thing to do. Any accused has the right to speech and work. In any case, you are not the court,' Arjun said.

It appeared to me that the intended reconciliatory meeting was not going the right way.

'If the State is regressive, and the institutions are failing us, the citizen must step forward as the culture dispenser. There's no space in *our* world for exploitation of any kind.' Dev said.

'You know you are guilty, don't you, Mr Bedi?' Diya said.

'I…'

'The fact is your kind of voice has had its day,' Dev said.

'Our speech is a composite quote of the history of the oppressed peoples.' Diya took a sip of her wine, and looked challengingly at Arjun. 'No more regression. Not even inside a man's skull.'

'This is nothing personal, Mr Bedi. We just can't legitimize men like you. We must take leave now. We thank you for your hospitality,' Dev said. 'We must be leaving now, Diya?'

'If you apologize, you will be setting an example. And there will be more to follow in your wake leading to a change in the patriarchal norms that are at the root of all the problems we are now facing,' Diya said.

'How will my recanting help me with my lost positions? I am damaged beyond repair.'

'Think of those whom you damaged. Confess before more accusations surface. Even as we speak, there are people working on your case,' Diya said.

'You are putting me out of my world. Are you a career revolutionary? Maybe you have a book coming up out of all this? Because, I refuse to believe that a verbal transgression on my part is the most traumatic incident...'

'...In your victim's life?' Diya said. 'We would rather believe your victim than you.'

'Maybe you are not fit for the world, which you may think in your vanity as yours, Mr Bedi. The new world does not want to read you. We will make sure of that,' Dev said.

'The new world you are building then is one step short of burning books.' Arjun's voice was thin, as if he was no longer interested in defending himself. He stood there, clutching his whisky tight: short, defiant, disintegrating, top to toe, invisibly.

'It's not the books we are burning so much as the awful world you built,' Diya said.

I coughed by way of distraction. 'That phrase "composite quote" is from Nadezhda Mandelstam. She uses it in her memoir.'

'And who is this young man whom you are corrupting?' Diya asked.

'Why don't you go out into the terrace, Osip?' Arjun said. 'Mitali is out there somewhere.'

I turned to go.

'Arjun Saab!' The generals were waving to Arjun to join them. They seemed to have surrounded the politician and cut off his mobility.

I walked out onto the terrace through the large sliding glass door. White and red bougainvillea grew wild over the trellis. The flowers looked painted, and brittle; almost as if they were made of paper and stuck to the air. High above, the stars shredded the sky.

'Hello, OB,' Mitali said, blowing smoke in my direction.

Mitali gleamed like a dark flame. The whites of her eyes flashed against her glowing skin. We hugged like old friends.

'You are out here alone,' I said.

'Smoking,' Mitali said.

'Nice party, you think?'

'Arjun keeps throwing them. In Delhi, no one misses out on a party. Not a good career move. How's school? Or is it college?'

'School.'

'Of course. Arjun has been seriously recommending you for an internship at the *Post*. Finish your boards.'

I didn't tell her about my possible suspension, pending inquiry. The boards seemed out of reach. 'Help me,' I wanted to say. It struck me I never said what I wanted to say the most. And why? 'I think I have a trust deficit problem.'

Mitali laughed. 'That will be handy for you in the *India Post*.'

'Thank you so much for the offer.'

'Too soon. Just send me a small sample of your writing whenever you are ready.'

'Is that how you choose your people?'

'I expect you are looking for a paid internship. If so, my father will eventually get to know about it, and he is sure to ask on what basis you were chosen? He is a micro-management freak when it comes to money.'

'Is Mr Dudani still there?'

'Mr Dudani's fortunes have dipped since we met last. My father switches his affections fast. That's how he keeps them all in their places. Anyway, I don't think Mr Dudani is the one to quit so easily. He is what they call a corporate survivor. The one thing they don't need is pride. But I think he is interesting because he is selfless.'

'Selfless?'

'Mr Dudani believes in the cause of his wife, Surimol, an art-house film director. He believes she is a genius. He funds her projects. That's his career objective.'

'Is Surimol a genius? I have never met one, you know?'

'Let Arjun not hear it.'

'Is she really?'

'I have no idea. It doesn't matter. It is what inspires Mr Dudani. He believes his wife's art is bigger than him.'

'I will be at your door as soon as I finish my exams.'

'Whenever you feel up to it. There is such a dearth of talent in the paper. No one much cares though. Yesterday, they carried "chief secretary shitted" instead of "shifted." Painful.'

There was a crash of glass in the hall.

'What's that?' Mitali ground her cigarette underfoot.

'The party has started in earnest, maybe.'

'That's not just one glass.'

We went back into the hall.

Mrs Bedi stood swaying in a loose, long black half-sleeved shirt that reached a little below her knees. Large red flowers bloomed on her shirt. Her thin, bare legs ended in a pair of black high heeled stilettos. She wore a brown butch wig, slightly pulled down to one side so her shaven head just above her ear could be seen, a bald criticism of the celebrations around her. Her lips were scarlet. She looked like a ruin lit up. Mrs Bedi had knocked down most of the glasses on the bar. The shards seemed so much a part of the silence in the hall. There was a short plastic tube hanging loose from her nose, and a blue patch on her left arm, where some sort of invasive procedure seemed to have happened recently. The guests spread out in a ring around her in caution.

'Stop the music,' Mrs Bedi rasped.

'There's no music, madam,' the nurse, the one with the big nose, said. She had followed her patient in alarm.

'A woman is dying in this house, and this man is partying,' Mrs Bedi said, shaking an angry, trembling finger at Arjun, who wore an expression of pale, perplexed concern.

'Mrs Bedi, you should not exert yourself,' the nurse said, 'they are just having a drink. Come to bed, Mrs Bedi.'

'Mrs Birdie do this, Mrs Birdie don't do that.' Mrs Bedi mimicked the nurse. 'Why can't I have a drink?'

'Oh no, Mrs Bedi.'

'No? If no one offers to pour me a drink, I can manage one on my own. Thank god, I am not a cripple yet, though that's what everyone would like me to be.' Mrs Bedi poured herself a drink. Her hands trembled. 'Sorry to disappoint all of you. Still, like air, I'll rise.'

Arjun took a step in the direction of his wife, and then stopped uncertainly, stealing a glance in the direction of Dev and Diya. Dev seemed busy with his phone.

The three generals were manoeuvring their way to safety, toward the exit, their backs to the door. The politician stood, contemplating, a fat, well-fed hand placed over his paunch.

Silence raged like cancer.

Mrs Bedi downed the whisky and dropped the glass on the floor. 'Ha,' she said, when it didn't break, its fall partially cushioned by the carpet. Mrs Bedi stared for a moment at the rolling glass. 'Can't even drop a glass properly.' She looked up at the room with its people racing away from her at the speed of light. 'When you live with a man for more than half a century, and you have nothing good to say of him…no, the only thing you can say of him is that he believes in nothing…' Mrs Bedi gazed at her husband with contempt. 'You charlatan.'

The nurse looked on, worry writ large on her face,

'Maina,' Arjun said.

Mrs Bedi turned to face him squarely. The tube from her nose fell to the floor. 'Do you believe in anything at all? Because belief is indispensable to integrity.'

'Yes,' Arjun said.

Mrs Bedi addressed the gathering. 'He believes! He has faith. Faith, hope, and charity. A true Christian soul. Ha!'

She tried to step on the glass, which rolled away at touch. Mrs Bedi smiled awfully at her defeat. She could not crush a glass underfoot. She looked up at the gathering. 'He doesn't believe in awards either. Why? Because he doesn't get any.' Mrs Bedi laughed mirthlessly. 'Ah, you know what he believes in? He believes maybe in electricity. That's the kind of eternal thing he believes in. Electricity. Water. Columns. Gross is what he is.' Mrs Bedi was lost in thought for a moment. 'When he first met me, barely out of college, how he looked at me! With such…such licentious...' Mrs. Bedi looked at her husband in appeal.

'Licentious familiarity,' Arjun said.

'Licentious familiarity. And I told him, a woman is always more naked than a man.'

'Mrs Bedi,' the nurse said.

Mrs Bedi shook her head in desperation at the cards that fate dealt her. 'And he is stingy. He fed his guests almonds fallen on the floor. That was three years ago, I remember. I told him not to. He just winked, and fed them those dirty almonds.'

'Maina, you are not well.'

'Oh, I am very well, very, very well.' Mrs Bedi fixed Arjun with a stare.

'Maina…' Arjun said.

'Let me show you what your great men are made of, your rebels, genius writers, intellectuals,' Mrs Bedi said, looking around the hall.

'Maina, let me take you back to your room,' Arjun said gently.

Mrs Bedi ignored Arjun. She panted with the effort of it all. She made her way to a chest of drawers to the far side of the room with fast, faltering, noisy steps; by the time she reached her destination, she seemed exhausted.

'Let's go,' Mitali said in my ear. But she did not move.

Mrs Bedi gathered her breath, and pulled out a drawer. Halfway, it stuck. 'Ha,' Mrs Bedi said. She tugged at it with all her strength. The chest shook. Mrs Bedi's breath was loud, ragged. We looked on as if hypnotized. It was like a movie. The drawer suddenly came unstuck in her hands. Mrs Bedi staggered back, steadied herself. She looked at us with a horrible smile, inviting us into her confidence, and at the same time holding us in judgment. Her wig had further slipped to one side. A cobweb of blue veins appeared on her forehead. She dipped both hands in the drawer, scooped, and threw out its colorful contents. She repeated her gesture. It took a moment before we realized that they were condoms.

Condoms of all colours and textures, and a few tablets. She scattered them in the air. 'Pearls to the swine,' she said, 'pearls to the swine.' I saw Dev was shooting the scene on his phone.

'Please, Mrs Bedi, come away, please,' the nurse said, full of remorse. Her big nose twitched.

Mrs Bedi tried to blow air into a condom, but could not succeed. 'Apple flavour.' She flung it weakly in the rough direction of her husband, who was chewing his lips. 'My medals for living a dutiful life. He fornicated while I lay dying, and I die now, almost a virgin.' Her voice no longer had the initial edge though.

Mrs Bedi leaned her weight on the chest of drawers and tried to take off her shirt, but could only manage to remove the first two large, glittering top buttons. We could see on her chest the keloids of a surgery. 'I can't even undo these buttons,' she said softly, her fight quite gone. She hung her head down, her hands to her side. Whatever keyed her up seemed to have wound itself down.

Arjun took another slow step towards Mrs Bedi.

'Please don't, Sir,' the nurse cautioned.

Arjun put up a restraining hand, continued to move towards the chest of drawers. 'Maina,' Arjun said.

'When he first met me, he quoted Neruda,' Mrs Bedi said to no one in particular. Neruda. What were the lines, Arjun? The blue stars. Have they faded?'

'Tonight I can write the saddest lines. Write, for example, "The night is shattered and the blue stars shiver in the distance." The lines are still there, Maina. But we are not.'

Mrs Bedi did not look up. 'They will never give you an award. They hate you.'

'My dearest Maina.'

'I am slipping through my fingers. I am flying away from all of you.' A sob cleaved Mrs Bedi's body.

Arjun hugged her.

Mrs Bedi leaned her head on her husband's shoulder. 'I don't want to die.'

'There,' Arjun said, 'there.'

'Keep me here.'

'There Maina, there. It's all right. '

Mitali and I went out on the terrace and had another drink. She had fixed Arjun a weekly column. There were mails and phone calls to Alok Jain, too, she said. He could not care less. But Mitali could not find a moment to break the news to him. 'These Delhi parties!' Mitali said. 'They can make you or break you.'

***

A few days later, as Arjun and I came down the broad wooden steps of the school's administrative block after our meeting with Yolanda Andrade, Arjun said, 'I am quite impressed by your school. It's very well run.'

Arjun had come to the school after all. I was overwhelmed, but felt challenged to express my gratitude.

'Except that every second student seems to be of a criminal bent of mind.'

'Just the two of us, Anand and me. I am sorry.'

'Well, we don't know what the others are up to, do we? You are, of course, as guilty as your friend except for the blackmail part about Elizabeth. What were you guys thinking of, really, exhuming that poor priest?'

'Father Roderick? It was...just a joke. It just kept growing big. We only thought of how to get it done.' The most bizarre idea turns out to be a game of how to get it done, once the premise is accepted. One doesn't ask why it should happen at all.

'Your principal doesn't think it's a collective effort. Just you. I had to blackmail her.'

At first, Ms Andrade had refused to meet Arjun. 'In that case, I might as well write about this incident in one of my columns. A lot of parents and rival institutions would be interested.'

'Well, you are no saint, Mr Bedi, I know about you.'

'Well, unlike you I have nothing to lose, Ms Andrade.'

'What do you mean?'

'Osip's roommate's connection to your late husband. Viral stuff, Ms Andrade, truly viral stuff. Social media is nothing if not a vast tabloid newsroom. The demand for instant outrage, to feel good at someone's expense, is insatiable. I should know.'

'It's just gossip.'

'I am sure. But what's gossip? The processing of probable information. Just the kind of thing social media does for a living. Except that each mouth and ear add and delete a little to it.'

Arjun had placed his *Post* column with his mugshot on the table. 'This is a nationalist paper, read by the government.

And I can write what I want in it so long as it is not against Ram. You are running a private school in the name of St. George.' He had paused. 'Has anyone done a public auditing of your school?'

'Anand has nothing to do with any of it.'

'That's a matter for investigation. He certainly will have to explain the sources of that bike.'

'He showed me the papers. The bike belongs to his friend,' Yolanda lied.

'I see. Can I meet him, the friend?'

'I'm afraid that's not a good idea.'

'The truth is, when it comes right down to it, all of this is just guesswork, isn't it? Someone saying someone else is guilty of something...? Are you suggesting Father Roderick's body dug itself out of the hold, went to the stores—and why wasn't the place properly locked and guarded, why? Another mystery resulting from an administrative lapse, no doubt—wrapped itself in a school tarp and hid in the bushes? We have no idea what happens after death, do we, madam? That is if, indeed, the father was dead before he was buried. He could have been murdered for all I know. I would like to see the death certificate.'

'What do you mean? Someone must have it. Father Roderick fell dead in the middle of a sermon. A lot of people saw him die.'

'Nevertheless, I can ask the police to reopen the case. He might have died of poisoning. Think of the headlines. Do you have a copy of his death certificate, coroner's report, anything? I should be asking the local police to reopen the grave, ask for a post-mortem report. This whole thing appears to be a mystery. And there's this Anand's connection with your late husband.'

'No, that's not advisable,' Yolanda said after a pause. Mrs Roderick will have the certificate, she was sure. But a moment later she wasn't.

'And you have just the word of the dead man's son that there was foul play with the body?' Arjun said.

'I examined the body and the sheet covering it.' Yolanda's voice broke. The very memory of the night made her cringe. Would any principal have gone through such an experience? And she was from such a good family. 'No, don't even go there,' Yolanda thought; she was out alone braving a ruthless male-dominated world. She cursed her husband again silently. The patriarchal penetralia of Mr Andrade was attached to every one of her sufferings. This bearded old man sitting before her was another manifestation of the same problem.

'Exhumation without court sanction and police presence is a punishable crime.'

'Oh, please...'

'All of it makes for great reading material. A perfect scandal. And, no doubt, a great reflection on the august institution of which you are the head.' Arjun had smiled kindly at Yolanda. 'And you have no real proof to pin down the boy waiting outside as the kidnapper of the body.'

'Anand said...'

'Well, if he is called in as a witness, a lot of personal stuff will come unstuck. That would be even worse for the school. And for you.'

'"Dirty old scoundrel," your principal must have thought,' Arjun said, as we stepped out of the building into the sun. The air was warm. I felt light with relief.

'What a lovely place,' Arjun said. He walked up the quadrangle to an Alder at its center and read out its name carefully: *Alnus Nepalensis*. Then he turned around and said, 'Anus Nepalensis. Hehe.'

I walked him to his Ambassador, which looked like a mausoleum on wheels. Its tires were new. 'How is your…situation?'

'Ah, that. There seems "certainty in degradation," as T. E. Lawrence said.'

Arjun took off his turban and threw it into the back seat. He scratched his head. 'They will revoke the suspension. You take the boards and get the hell out of this place. They won't touch Anand because the principal's reputation is at stake. Philandering politician husband, the image of the school, her social standing, etc. What she does with Anand is her problem. You keep away from him, though you must be as guilty as him.'

'I would very much like to buy you a gift.'

'Oh, well, get me a good walking stick. They make good ones here. A walking stick with a lion's head, and a good grip on the ground. My knees are killing me.' He got into the car.

'The corpse idea just happened. It's not me.'

'Nothing happens like that. Jesus.'

He started the car, began rolling up the windows. 'Consider how the real world works.'

'How?'

'On two things. What you can do for people and what you can do to people.'

'Yes.'

'Think about it. Think about how many blackmails are at work here so everyone is happy including you. And your friend.'

'I'm not happy. And Anand is no longer a friend.'

'That's because you can't tell happiness if it sits on your head and tickles your ears.'

'I'm getting out.'

'Yeah, but not to a crack house or a jail.'

'No, of course, not. Travel a little, maybe.'

'Europe? Elizabeth? Are you out of your head?'

'Just travel a little.'

'Newrope! Newrope! To hang yourself with! At least, finish the boards.' Arjun shook his head.

I waved as Arjun's car slowly moved forward, trawling the trees against the sky in the windshield. There was a lot of sky today, and a great number of trees. I wondered what happened to the driver, Kishan.

***

I met Anand during the boards. He had grown a beard. He smiled as if everything was all right between us. I nodded. Nothing broke so bad as the bond between two kindred souls. The secrets that brought us together drove us apart. How good a friendship it was, its value could be measured only by its absence. Was I responsible for it? I didn't think so. Yes, the corpse plan was mine, may be but not its execution, surely? I was not going to be burdened with that part. The injustice of it all! No, I was not unaware of my part in the plan. Still, I had warned Anand, had I not? Did I not tell him in the car it was dangerous; to forget it? No? I certainly felt as if I did. Surely, my tone would have implied it? It was not Father Roderick's corpse that gave no one rest—for sure that was an irritant; it was Anand's threat to expose Elizabeth that ruined it all. Well, at least now, I had the money to go to London, in pursuit of Elizabeth. Who knew what that would bring? Love, happiness, life. Get on with the boards, yes. One fucking thing at one fucking time. Don't worry about your secrets. For god's sake, everyone had secrets? Consider Yolanda madam. 'Yolanda Furioso,' Elizabeth used to call her, because she was so imperious. She was a repository of secrets. Elizabeth, too. Anand, certainly. Arjun, of course. Mr Menon. Gloria. One lived by one's secrets. One died of them even. Ah, that was the reason why I felt so betrayed when Anand threatened to squeal. I could have killed him then. I shivered that I had been, for a moment, so close to murder. It had taken only a moment to discover another man hiding in me. Each carried so many in him, perhaps.

On the day of the last examination, in an awkward coincidence, Anand and I handed in the answer papers at the same time and walked out of the hall.

'How are the exams treating you, OB?' Anand said.

'Scrape through.'

'Same here. No head for studies, you know me. I'm taking a gap year.' Anand said, 'as you suggested.'

'Good.' Our footfalls echoed in the corridor. I could not recall my suggesting Anand take a gap year.

'I am heading for Dharamshala. A life of spirituality awaits me.'

'Is that where you are going?'

'Riding my Bullet all the way up.'

'Your mother good with it?'

'Stepmother. I don't ask her permission to move around.'

'I am taking a gap year, too.'

'London? Not to see madam? Sorry, I didn't mean that.'

'At least, I don't make a habit of blackmailing my best friends.'

'One. One friend and you are losing him.'

'Some friend.' Nothing he said would placate me. It would be all motivated by his need to destroy my relationship with Elizabeth.

'OB, I had no alternative.'

'No, you are a Darwinist.'

'We can forget all this and continue as before.'

'We are done,' I said.

'You are your own worst enemy. You got a gun cocked and ready to shoot your own feet at all times. A great marksman. Oh, well. I can drop you wherever.' He pointed to his bike.

'No, I am fine.'

'We all make mistakes. We move on, you understand?'

'I could have been in jail.'

'Me, too. I am just like you. Just a wayward bastard.'

'Speak for yourself.'

'All right, you are just crazy, I understand. Loser.'

I hit him. Only, I missed. Anand sidestepped and gave me a push in the direction of my momentum. I fell hard. I grabbed his feet, and it struck me that from a distance it could be construed as one man prostrating before another. Anand shook me off. In the position I was in, I could only wait for his punch. He held it. 'You miserable, self-righteous, self-indulgent, self-deluded, self-pitying, pompous prick,' he said.

His eloquence surprised me. We looked at each other with the kind of misgiving only people who could help each other bring on themselves to suffer. From where I lay, I watched Anand take a low, flamboyant U-turn on his bike and ride past the parking lot, past the driveway, and out of the gate—into the world of lamas and prayers and maroon togas. And none of it would likely mean a thing to him. Despite the fact that he got the better of me, I knew I did the right thing. I had said no to his friendly overtures. My left elbow hurt. The skin had broken, and the flesh was scraped, too. A little bit of blood seeped out. I took a spot of it and placed it on my tongue. It was sweet and salty, and smelled of iron. I lay in the dust and thought of Elizabeth. And the earth went mouldering around the sun with me and the mountains and everything else as if not a heart was broken, not a speck of dust was out of place.

Epistles

'My dear Ms Hill,' I began yet another mail, which I may or may not send. It said, again, how lonely I was. How I loved everything about Elizabeth. Everything. Love makes us all sound uniformly inane, no? Its mode of survival is clichés. 'I remember every moment of every day of our togetherness.' Our togetherness! It failed to strike me then that the shared past was what Elizabeth was fleeing from. I sent the mail in a burst of impotent anger. The morning after, I regretted it. And found that, thankfully, the mail had bounced.

Days later, I sent another mail along the same lines. But not so pathetic, I believe. There was no response though. It might have gone into spam. From there to trash. From there to be deleted forever. 'Serves you right,' I thought. But in yet another mail, I changed tack. Instead of talking about me, I wrote about Arjun and Maina, the party scene. I was full of pity for Arjun in my letter. To show how understanding I was of the plight of others. The truth was that I did not feel anything for Maina. Her cancer had seemed a distant if excessive oddity, and I certainly did not approve of her exposing Arjun by pulling out the drawer and showering the room with condoms. Was Elizabeth reading my mails?

I followed up with yet another mail. It addressed Elizabeth formally, in a desperate attempt to wrest back from her a bit of self-respect. And I turned an academic in the process. I reminded her of the riveting Romeo and Juliet lectures she delivered in class. She had called the play the first full-fledged teenage rebellion in literature. Romeo and Juliet were the Permanent Generation Next. I had pointed out that at 14, no child asks what's in a name, no girl spouts great poetry, no Romeo speaks like, well, Romeo. Original? Very, if you read the words upside down.

'My dear Ms Hill,' I continued the rather formal mail, and not quite sure of the point I was trying to make, and then, a little disoriented, I sent the message, thinking, 'Oh, be damned.' I had adopted an accusatory tone all through and it registered with me only too late, after the 'undo' command had come and gone. This mail did not bounce. But there was no response either. I gave up. I was free of Elizabeth, the name of the mind-virus that had silently evolved and mutated since the Big Bang to lay me low; I could not believe passion came into existence from the dead first minerals. I was free at last of my overwhelming need to be with her—if only just for one forgetful minute. When those deceptive and fleeting moments of freedom expired, I was back at the computer, helpfully informing Elizabeth that I had turned 19, going on 20, a real man and now, a veteran almost in a world where children became soldiers and killers, before they were boys and girls; teenagers dropped out of school to become multimillionaires, and novels with 15-year-old psychotic killers became best sellers. I found out the next, sober morning this particular mail had not been sent. It was in the drafts. The next minute, I sent it. I could not resist another act of abject surrender to her. One could never worship Elizabeth enough.

***

My dear Kris,

I am back. As in, I am back. India did me good. Can't say if I did the same for India. I met a lot of interesting people, whom, of course, I may not want to set my eyes on again. I know you are doing well, and that my prolonged absence must have contributed to the centring of your being. But you know me. I can't let a good thing be. I am in London—for the moment, at my cousin's pad. I may make a trip to Edinburg to my estranged mother just to say hi. I am in two minds about that, of course, as she is in three minds about everything. It is such a joy to breathe the sweet, awful London weather and the vulva-smelling Thames air after India. It's only when you come back that you truly realize what you have been missing. I will understand if you are not too eager to see me. I am afraid I am attached to places, but not to people. Not much anyway.

Elizabeth.

Dear Elizabeth madam,
An editor has been shot in Srinagar. He is not the first, of course. This is the third journalist killed in Kashmir in the line of duty in as many weeks. There have been very many arrests all over. The personal liberty of the average Indian is in question. But what's more important, personal liberty or national security? What's the point of the second without the first? Have I said to you that Arjun is a free speech absolutist? 'What's a nation for if you can't speak freely against it,' he says. Across the border there has been shooting and bombing. War? The separatists are up in arms as well. Is this India's Spanish Republic moment regarding Kashmir? Arjun thinks so. I have no choice but to become a reporter now. That is the least I can do. But I am not sure if I would be published. 'To write is not to obey orders,' Arjun says. May I request you to pray for me? Be safe in Oxford, away from it all.

Last week, my grandfather insisted upon meeting a few of his friends. This was not possible as they were all dead. 'I have the addresses of all the dead voices,' he later said. In his head, it is some other time, and he is walking on some other street and knocking on some other door, which, after a fashion, no longer exists, my grandmother says. I am not wholly convinced, naturally, as I often experience time as a loop. Yesterday, my grandfather went for a walk along Petersburg's Kamennoostrovsky Prospekt (which M. once described as 'irresponsible', where even 'cocoa could be bought and the 'maniacal automobiles' of the

1917-Kerensky government crazied past the Georgian shops). My grandfather said he had arrived at the street too late and missed his appointments and was astonished, later still, watching people in cafes reading Chekov in the light of the deep blue summer night of Petersburg, and Gloria, my grandmother, had to break the news finally as he went on and on that that he had got it all mixed up, and he subsided to sleep.

OB.

P.S. I admit I get things fundamentally wrong. Until today, I thought it was Kinhaza. It is Kinshaza, of course.

Dear OB,

This is bad news. Both about your grandfather and Kashmir. He must be hallucinating. Or are you? You are not proposing to go to Kashmir right away, are you? You need to graduate before you become a full-fledged reporter, I think, no? Do they insure conflict zone correspondents? I am in London just now. Will be here for a few weeks before I go to Oxford. It's summer here, but pleasantly cool in the evenings. Take care. I will be out of reach for a while. A long while.

It is Kinshasa.

Elizabeth.

My dearest Elizabeth,

Welcome back. When do we meet?

Your old man,

Kris.

My dear Elizabeth madam,
'India is a shell democracy. All institutions are pulled inside out,' Arjun says. I have resolved to dedicate my life to set things right. We live on the edge as all the developing world does. Kashmir is still restive. 'Kashmir is a nationality,' Kashmiris say; India does not agree. Higher up in the Himalayas, Tibetans claim to be a nationality; China does not agree. I wonder what someone like Stalin would do in such circumstances. He was, as you might know, the People's Commissar of Nationalities. I am hoping to travel to London, soon. The choice is between Kashmir and London. It will be nice to meet you.
OB.

OB,
It's not a good idea for you to travel to London, I am afraid. Why London? I will not be able to meet you. Do not look me up. I am taking care to erase myself from all social media. Not that I was ever active. I just want to be left alone.
Elizabeth.

Dear Ms Hill,
I have no choice in the matter. You can't forbid me from coming to the UK. I have applied for a visa. I have my rights. The meaninglessness of my existence argues for its termination. Or travel.
OB.
P.S. Arjun says we are living in the age of reaction, not tradition.

The last mail bounced.

The Naked Shopper

Elizabeth, naked, pulled a chair close to the mirror in her room. She turned the chair around and sat straddling it. Elizabeth had often found her reflection more comforting than her real self because of its inaccessibility, which could be, at a pinch, seen as her freedom. Today's mood swing was triggered by Osip's mail, which took her back to India. Her need to be free sometimes hurt people around her. She didn't mean to. But she was not like, say, Sangita, withdrawn and melancholic, seemingly reluctant of self-assertion, afraid to let go. Elizabeth recalled her night out with Sangita in Delhi before she left for London. The night when both of them shared the sensation of flight, freedom. Freedom was flight, wings willed. Sangita was not yet perhaps 40? But Sangita had wavered in her flight when very young, and her wings had withered, and she had been grounded.

***

Elizabeth and Sangita had met at the Tamasha Bar, at Connaught Place, frequented mostly by young people, all seriously looking for a way to stop, Elizabeth thought, their flight midway; relationships ended up doing that. The music was loud, and so the only intimacies possible in the place seemed sexual or, so universal they were meaningless. Sangita and Elizabeth had found a table at a corner. 'You've grown your hair,' Elizabeth shouted, looking at the thick, long hair with some grey streaks in it, framing Sangita's face. 'Suits you.'

Sangita smiled. She carefully drew out a wig from her shoulder bag. 'I wear the doll's vig in the clinic. It's like a part of the uniform.'

'Like what, did you say?' Elizabeth asked.

'Uniform. Like a part of the uniform.'

The wig lay on the table like a furry, little dog.

'I wanted to have a drink with you before I flew out.'

'Out vhere?'

'What? What did you say? Speak a little louder, please.'

'Flying out vhere?

'London. I am at home there.' Elizabeth looked around the bar. 'What will you drink?'

'Beer's good.' Sangita restored the wig to the bag. 'You can't make a home of Delhi. It's a place for jobs. Not for living and growing old.'

'Where are you from?'

'Purvanchal Pradesh. Not at home there either.'

'Oh, yes, you told me that.'

The beer came. Kingfisher Ultra. Elizabeth found it sharp and good. 'Nice beer.'

'I am not a great beer person.' Sangita smiled.

'Whisky?'

'Bloody Mary. It's like a badly behaving tomato juice.'

Elizabeth laughed. 'I am a bad girl. So.'

'Vhy bad? Because you fell in love?'

'Not love. A mistake maybe. We make mistakes, right?'

'Yes. Sometimes just one. But enough to last a lifetime.'

'Sex complicates everything. Men are better at handling it than women.' No, not true, Elizabeth thought. Consider Osip. But Osip was not a man yet, was he? No. he was a very old man. Old men.

Someone at the next table turned around and looked at Elizabeth. She realized she was almost shouting. Sex was a naturally loud word. She pulled her chair closer to Sangita's.

'This beer is going to my head,' Sangita said.

'Bad-behaving hops.'

'Ve have a local variation in the hills. Ve call it fermented water.' Sangita sat back, stretched.

They smiled reassuringly at each other.

'I had an affair with a boy,' Elizabeth said.

'How young?'

'A student of mine. I was a school teacher.'

'An affair is an affair.'

'You don't judge. Thank you,' Elizabeth said.

'Who am I to judge?'

'You don't have male friends, if I may ask?'

'I don't want to. It is best this way.'

'You know, my theory is that soon men and women will form secret societies and circulate documents and studies on each other.'

'Vhy?' Sangita looked surprised.

'There's where it is all going. Estranged Gender Age.'

'I don't know about these things.'

'They are already doing it, I am sure. That day I was at a loss when you said you had a baby whom you seemed to have written off.'

'He must be grown up now.'

'You don't want to know about him?'

'No, not really.'

They fell silent. All around them noises had increased. They ordered another round.

'I think I'll have a Bloody Mary now,' Sangita said.

'Of course.'

'When are you leaving India?'

'Next week.'

'Some countries are good only for a vacation.'

'Well, I wasn't having a vacation,' Elizabeth thought. But Sangita was right. Elizabeth had a place to go back to. A more settled world against which her individual acts of anarchy could be waged.

'You are right.'

Sangita was silent.

Did she resent my freedom, Elizabeth wondered. She felt the initial warmth they shared was cooling off. They listened to the music. A Bollywood song with slow, strong beats.

'Let's dance, shall we?' There was a small square of dance floor at the far end of the hall.

Sangita surveyed the hall. 'No one is dancing in this bar.'

'Oh, they won't mind. Everybody is looking for a change in rules. We just have to break them nicely. Come on.'

'I am not very good on my feet.'

'This is not a reality show,' Elizabeth pushed back her chair and extended her hand.

'All right, give me a minute.' Sangita pulled out the wig and tucked her hair under it. 'Just in case someone shot a pic,' she said.

They moved out on to the dance floor and began swaying to the slow music, a riff of something at once familiar and strange that turned their movements dreamy. A spotlight came on. As they got into the rhythm of the night flowing through their veins, the music too changed: first into fast Latino, and then into frantic Punjabi. Their bodies pulsed, their hands reached for the spotlight of a moon, their legs took on a new life in their own right, and their hair whipped and sieved the air. Someone turned the strobe lights on. The lights cut them up into slices, and each part of their bodies was a fast altering print of skin, lit and textured; their limbs and features, independent of face and body, embossed the blue and violet air. Lines of lights swam around them. The drinkers had stopped talking office gossip and politics. They clapped their hands faster and faster.

'I have to stop,' Sangita panted.

'Don't, I will take you home. This is when you must go on. See, these guys and girls are joining us. Leave the world behind us. Let's fly.'

They saw that the chairs and tables were being pulled back to make space for more dancers.

'I am breathless,' Sangita said.

'You must dance more often.'

'Hold me if I fall,' Sangita laughed for the first time.

'You won't. Do you regret?'

The beats had become furious.

'Yes, everything,' Sangita's face was flushed. Sweat poured down her face.

'You can't regret this. You are not even here.'

'I can't go on.'

The music built up in an apocalyptic crescendo and then crashed.

Elizabeth and Sangita walked back to their table.

'Now ve rest,' Sangita said.

'Yes, now we rest.' Elizabeth nodded. 'But let's take a selfie. It didn't happen if it was not clicked.'

'I vill keep the vig on if you don't mind.'

***

Osip's mails, now. Elizabeth widened her eyes in the mirror. What's happening with him? The business with him was not over yet, was it? Yes, it was. That verse was chanted, the chapter closed. *Talaq*. *Talaq*. *Talaq*. Elizabeth didn't like it that she was brooding. It was best not to dive into the subsumed potentials of one's personality, thinking obsessively. Elizabeth decided to go out and buy a hat. Or a book. No, not a book. Or lipstick. Shopping was like taking a vacation from herself. 'Spare me most of all the pain of being loved; to be loved again and again, to kill it again and again,' Elizabeth thought, getting up from her chair and pulling on a sweater. Her nudity bored her, her thoughts even more.

Om Mani Padme Hum

Anand sat next to the window at Dharamshala's Freedom Cafe and listened to the short, wiry Wang Chok, a black bandana around his forehead, which he had sworn not to take off until Tibet won freedom, working his Free Tibet followers.

Free Tibet, Free Kashmir, Free Speech; Anand did not care.

Free Tibet assembled on Friday evenings at the cafe. The cafe was a squarish room, up a shoulder off the steep Khada Danda (Standing Stick) street. From the low wooden roof of the cafe hung lamps shaped like nests. The walls were painted in green. The cement floor was red, and cracked. At the far end of the hall, against the wall leaned a shelf with little dolls on it. There were more people than the usual today. 'Why would anyone fight for a nation of their own?' Anand thought. Why take the trouble? His nation was India, and where did that get him? They were killing those who fled their nations on the border in America and elsewhere, too. First, you fought for your nation, then you fled it. Surely, at least some of the refugees crossing into America from Mexico must be descendants of freedom fighters?

Outside, it was getting dark over the Dhauladhar mountains, and deep among them, here and there, lamps shone, the distant specks interspersed with those of the cafe's, superimposed on the glass wall. He was in two worlds at the same time. Anand shaded his vision with his hands: yes, he was the medium through which the real and the unreal and whatever in between floated. When his vision became clearer, he saw that the roadside-vendors had shut their shops, their wares all packed up in large, blue plastic bags, and set to be carted away on the back of their tricycles, most of which had large wooden carriers. Where was Sheetla Devi, the girl who preferred the quiet of mountains to her rich and quarrelsome parents' home in Delhi? Though he found it not advisable to admit, he missed her.

The Friday a fortnight before, Sheetla had come over to Anand's table soon after Anand had interrupted Wang's speech with one of his questions: 'What makes you think India will prefer Tibet to China? Why would India antagonize China?' Everybody had hushed him. Sheetla had hushed him the most, one slender hand on her chest, one finger on her thin lips, her long-lashed eyes wide with warning and worry.

'Freedom begins as a wish if you will.' Wang replied to Anand. He had taken the trouble to come over to Anand's table. 'To take the edge off the question,' Anand thought.

'Once India's freedom too was a wish. We don't expect a physical war between India and China for our freedom.

But India is our host, and we naturally expect India to talk on our behalf…' Wang smiled. 'This is only your second or third time here. Keep coming, my friend, and you will get to know us better.'

'Dialogue, yes, dialogue,' Sheetla said to Anand, as an aside, when Wang had turned and gone back to his friends. She seemed excited at the thought of a nation taking birth right in front of her. 'You should not be so rude to Wang. He is working for a great cause.'

'You don't need a nation. We are all bigger than our borders.' Nation. If India invaded Sri Lanka the next day, would Sri Lanka be eventually India? Or Bangladesh? But Anand was not interested in these large, political issues. He just wanted to survive, to succeed. He hoped he sounded reasonable to Sheetla, so something emerged from the accidental meetings in a strange place. He had been a little out of sorts with himself of late. The future appeared uncertain.

'Are you talking about cosmic citizenship? My family guru once said if we are all part of the absolute being, why should we have borders?' Sheetla spoke very quickly, in a distinctly American accent, having spent most of her formative years in New York. She had come across to Anand as open-minded and impressionable, just the right kind of person, he observed. 'But, again, how can you not have nations? It's like saying we don't need families. You don't have a choice, do you?'

'I'm just talking for myself.'

'Ah, yes, cosmic citizen,' Anand made a mental note. The cosmetics of citizenship were for the rich. For those in the exports and imports business, perhaps. The nation was good for invoicing purposes. What's it to a boy whose ration of milk was mixed with water and shaken in a bottle before him like some magic potion and tasted like defeat? What's it to a boy who lay on a thin mat on a floor cracked like a hundred lightnings slept beneath it, and woke up to strangers issuing orders, day after day? What country would that be? How about a nation of orphans? 'Tell me,' he thought, 'tell me where the borders passed in that country, where it began and ended? What would be that nation's name? India? Sudan? Tibet?'

'To move up, we must leave behind the things below,' Anand said.

'You truly sound like my guru.' Sheetla's eyes rested on him hopefully.

Anand and Sheetla met for coffee elsewhere, and at the Cafe on following Fridays. She always arrived well before the meeting began: 'When you enter late, everybody stares at you as if in punishment,' Sheetla said.

But tonight there was no sign of Sheetla. Anand did not wait for Wang to end his speech, which was certain to mention the Chinese occupation of Tibet since 1951, and the great trek of the Tibetans to India in 1959, and the eventual setting up of the Tibetan administration in exile in Dharamshala. He was now familiar with the plot. Wang repeated his introduction every week for the benefit of newcomers. Was there anyone Anand knew? He looked around for Tasha, the tall guy who played guitar and chain-smoked, whom he had met the other day. They had had a rough chat. Tasha had said his songs were full of anger and resentment for his land, though he was based in Edinburgh. So, if Tibet became a nation, would Tasha come back? No, not really, because he had a lung problem, and the air did not have enough oxygen for him, but in Edinburgh they appreciated his homelessness, Tasha said. 'Fraud,' Anand had thought with grudging admiration. Tasha had quickly excused himself and vanished.

Anand made his way out of the little cafe. Outside, the cold hit him like a wall. He went down the three steps leading from the shop down to the narrow Mall Road packed with its long, narrower shops and paced around, waiting for Sheetla's arrival. Across the road and over the deep chasm, the Himalayas rose in silhouette, the heads of the mountains poking up in the air from under the black blanket of the night. The vastness of the prospect made him shiver. It was as if those parts of the brain responsible for the ego were melting away, and he was in touch with the mechanics of the universe. Like a glimpse into the Design. Into the divine. Anand had been working on himself. One never knew when enlightenment happened. But one had to be ready for it. Could his pineal gland be getting activated even without his knowledge, even as he stood and stared at the Himalayas? He could not lock eyes with the vastness that was before him for long and not be changed. A few minutes later, he snapped himself out of the trance, turned up the collar of his jacket and trudged the narrow road toward his lodgings. He was disappointed that Sheetla hadn't turned up. As he turned the corner, past a Buddhist monastery, he heard a faint voice over a distant speaker waxing and waning in the wind, inviting all brothers and sisters to step in and be cured of their aches.

***

'Is there life after death?' Sheetla asked Anand, one evening. They were sitting on one of the benches at the rear of St. John in the Wilderness. The small 18th-century British-built church—granite walls softened by ivy; green, slatted windows that would not open—was located on the slope of a hill a couple of kilometres down from the town centre. The British dead, from another time, lay around them under marble slabs, each with inscriptions that tried to capture the posthumous perfection of what was once a fallible life. It was only in death that life made sense, that man became worthy of respect, if only because he could be considered as having tried his best, and be given the benefit of doubt, of forgiveness hidden in praise. Redemption was salvaged, Father Roderick would preach—in borrowed words, no doubt—from life's irreversibility with forgiveness; but forgiveness was hard, he said between noisy spells of mastication, because being mortal we could catch the essence of another only in his passing. 'Ah,' Anand thought, 'we caught your essence when you passed away'. From epitaph to epitaph the churchyard stretched its cold body before Anand. He briefly wondered about Father Roderick's corpse. 'Life after death?' Anand turned to Sheetla. 'Yes, we are living it.'

Sheetla laughed. 'No, seriously?' She reached out and touched him.

'Yes, seriously.'

They gazed at the mountain stretching in waves, up and down, like the hem of a gown. A little later, after they were conscious of the silence that the mountain was creating all around them, they went up the steps cut into the side of the hill and walked up the narrow dirt road.

'I live up there. Come and have a glass of wine anytime,' Sheetla pointed to a little cottage of slate stone and glass as they turned a corner down a distance.

'That'd be nice. Maybe next Friday?'

'Why Friday? There are seven days to my week,' she laughed. 'Oh, well, Friday it is.'

Anand watched Sheetla run up the steps to her cottage. How old would she be? In her mid-20s? At the top, she turned and waved. As Anand retraced his steps to his room behind the Tourism Development Centre, and as the night quietened, he could hear again that recorded voice in the air, which could be mistaken for poorly rendered azan, urging him to step in and be met with immediate relief. Anand hesitated, then followed the voice to its lair up a dirt track. Less than five minutes later he was at the mouth of a beat-up, wind-ruffled tent, pitched in a clearing in the grass on the steeper side of the track. An old-fashioned tape recorder attached to a small loudspeaker assured the world again and again that Dr Hiteshwar was in possession of wondrous, pain-relieving extracts from mysterious plants higher up in the Himalayas: 'Come, my dear brothers and sisters, come, step once into this tent and step out healthy and happy. You have pains, Dr Hiteshwar knows. You have aches, Dr Hiteshwar knows. In the bones, in your spine, at the back of your neck, inside your head, aches, aches, aches. Step in and be cured. You are unable to relieve yourself, which ought to be a most pleasurable task. A cure awaits you. Dr Hiteshwar invites you to visit his Himalayan Herbal Travelling Hospital. Enter with tears, exit with smiles.'

Anand went in.

In a corner, on a dirty mattress lay a semi-naked patient on his stomach. He seemed to be sleeping. Idris—for it was he, even in this dim light, under his turban and full beard, it was unmistakably Idris—had just given him a massage. A yellow, smoky lantern suspended from a hook overhead cast a melancholy pall over the procedures. The many potions in jars stood in rows on the ground. On the back wall of the tent was painted a Lord Shiva in meditation, his head encircled by a serpent. A crescent moon was balanced on his hair. The central stake of the tent was disfigured by several nails, and from each of them hung framed endorsements of famous people like the Dalai Lama and Narendra Modi, testifying to the efficacies of the Himalayan Herbal treatment.

'Come, come,' Idris said.

Anand looked around for a place to sit, but there was none.

'Where's the pain?'

'No, I don't have any pains, Idris.'

The recorded voice droned on, unaffected by the outed identity.

'Ah. I thought you won't recognize me.' Idris dropped his voice to a whisper.

'Because you wear a turban? You are on the run still?'

'They came to Kasauli, Anandji. The bloody cops. I had to vanish. It is Allah's will. I now take care of sick people here.' Idris switched off the tape recorder.

The world quietened like a pack of dogs had stopped howling.

Anand hesitated for a moment, looking at the patient. He whispered. 'Not because of the corpse?'

'No, no, the train robbery,' Idris threw up his hands in a silent plea to God.

Anand experienced relief. He looked around. 'These medicines work?'

'They all work. What kind of question is that?'

Anand walked to a corner of the tent where a large jar stood, inside of which was a dead cobra, tightly coiled, in some preserving brown chemical. 'What's this?'

'That's a cobra,' Idris lowered his voice even further.

The patient on the mattress stirred.

Idris turned to him. 'I see you are awake. You are all right now. Apply the oil I gave you on the abdomen, and your cramps will go.'

The patient sat up and looked around for his clothes.

Idris pointed to them, piled to a side of the tent. They appeared rich with shadows and creases like fibre-sculptures.

The patient got up to go. 'How much?'

'50,' Idris said, 'think of Lord Shiva when you hand the money over to me.'

The patient paused at the exit. 'They will go, won't they, the cramps are quite terrible.'

'Warm the oil a little before you apply. Have only good thoughts. Buy a gift for your wife. Anything at all will do. Keep her happy. Helps. You will be all right.'

'Make a lot of money?' Anand asked Idris when they were alone.

'Everybody has one pain that is unique to himself.'

'What's that Quran doing under the mattress?' Anand smiled.

Without taking eyes off Anand, Idris tucked the Quran deeper under the mattress, out of sight. 'It's Shiva country up here.'

'It is strange to run into you here.' Anand said.

'Got to make a living.' Idris looked around the tent, the ramshackle abode of his double life.

'What brings you here, Anandji? No trouble from that night, I hope?'

'This and that.' From miracle cures to miracle-man, Idris was only one step short of a real career. 'No, no trouble from that night. The Father is at rest, finally. You did a wonderful job.'

'God's will. You paid me. All's well.' Money, it had often occurred to Idris, was a false notion. Most people did not have it. Surely something was wrong with a world that thought up money, but could not have enough of it ever.

'Your trade has a lot of potential.' Anand took a tour of the therapeutic shelves.

'As long it lasts. I have a family to take care of.'

'Yes.'

'You will be discreet? About me? They will lynch me here if they get to know.'

'Not to worry on that score.' Anand turned to go.

'We will meet again. I stay close by.'

'Inshallah.'

Anand walked back to the main road, away from the tent of miracles, thinking his plight was not so different from that of Idris. Just that he was running away from another kind of life. A group of Buddhist priests in maroon gowns passed him by, chanting *Om Mani Padme Hum*. He stopped to watch them. What were the monks running away from? They were young, and resembled each other in the wisdom they had found. All around him mantras of salvation reverberated. One of the monks, not much older than a mere boy, smiled at Anand as if he wished to share the gift of his enchantment. Anand bowed to him. The street lamps threw a weak, yellow light on the road. Just enough to see the next step. Anand picked his way carefully, the chants rising and falling ahead of him, almost like a lamentation of faith, leading him on.

A Meeting of the Minds

It's another late summer's day in Oxford. The evenings are brilliant, and pointless. The trees pointillist. The four bottles of Indian rum that I brought with me, out of thrift, have been drunk long ago. The pound is expensive. This is an ill thought-out-expedition. I have run out of my medicines, not that I was at any point regular with them. This is The Dewdrop, on Woodstock Road, where I am sitting. I dislike England. The language, culture, jokes. The superiority at the bottom of everything like a layer of sediment. The racism and nationalism of the coach drivers. The social distancing at the heart of a colonizing, formalist culture. Here I have disliked and loved Elizabeth with such despair the last so many days—breathing in the petrol perfumery of the Oxford air, stepping over the rainbows on the diesel-stained road—that it is almost a self-sufficient act in itself. This evening I am thinking of just one thing: how to make it all look not stalky and scary if and when I run into Elizabeth again after my self-defeating confrontation with her at the Refugee Studies Centre, Oxford, earlier in the day.

***

Before I left for England, I called up Gloria. She was not at home. Treesa answered the phone.

'Hey, Treesa, where's my grandmother?'

'Small Sir? It's good to hear from you. Gloria Mother is away at the Party office. I hear you are going to England.'

'Yes, for a while. Happy birthday, Treesa.'

'How did you know, Small Sir?'

'The alert came on my phone.'

'Thank you for remembering little things like when I was born,' Treesa giggled.

'No, no, Mark Zuckerberg cares.'

'Mark, who?'

'A guy who makes a lot of money because he knows everybody's birthday.'

'Mark? Anyway, we girls are taking the President to lunch today in celebration.'

'Is he up to it?'

'Yes, very much, today he is good enough for the Revolution; in fact, this morning, he recommended setting fire to the collector's office.'

'It's not such a bad idea. Often, I too feel like it.'

'Sometimes, I think he knows what he is doing. Because the other day, I saw him coming down from the attic with a small packet in his hand.'

'But he can't climb the steps.'

'I don't know about that. There's a rope to hang on to. And he still has strong hands.'

'What was in the packet?'

'I don't know. You know how he is. The attic is full of his old things. All those boxes. And then yesterday, he expressed a wish to sit on the swing as well.'

'The one in the back?'

'Yes. So I thought he would probably enjoy his day out.'

'Where are you guys going, Treesa, which restaurant?'

'To Qutub, that's what we can afford, and they know us and the President. You remember Qutub, don't you?'

Yes, Qutub, the Mughlai restaurant that offered discounts to my grandfather for old time's sake, and whose menu once challenged Treesa's skills as a translator and established her as the leader of the gang. Years ago, on an afternoon of brilliant clarity, my grandfather had taken the executive council members of the Sex Workers Association to Qutub, located on one of the narrow quarrelsome lanes running down from the center of the town toward Thrissur railway station. Qutub was narrow and long like a corridor, ending in a hot and noisy kitchen. The waiters shouted out orders into the kitchen like execution commands. Mr Menon asked for the menu and when it came, after fumbling with it for a few moments, passed it on to Treesa, saying, 'Here's your wedding card in English.' Treesa was more equipped than others to choose the menu as she had studied up to high school. She read out: OUR CHINESE TREASURES, and then subsided into silence, because what followed was only partly the language she had struggled at in school, and partly it was not to be learned anywhere in the world, Qutubese. There was Chiangling, Chicken Hong Kong, Quba Mutton

Missile Peace, Miami Chinkey in Double Bed, Stalinthal Shammi Kebab, and Chicken in Green Lake, said the menu card that she brought home, like a memento. That noon, Treesa perplexed her curly hair, already like spring, further still with her pensive fingers. When she looked sideways at my grandfather for guidance, she found him malevolently eyeing the proceedings. Treesa had prayed to Our Lady of Dolores, she said, as she had to do right by other SWAX members and their hard-earned money and ordered, her heart in her mouth, Chicken in Green Lake and Steamed Rice. When the food finally came, Treesa was relieved to find soft chicken nuggets floating like islets in an edible but oily green sea.

'Yes,' I said to Treesa, 'I remember Qutub.'

'Well, there is where we are going.'

'Have a good time, Treesa, and please take care of the President. He likes you very much. But you know that.'

'Of course, Small Sir. Gloria Mother knows you are going?'

'Yes.'

'Gloria Mother is becoming very powerful these days. The Party wants her to lead the women's rights campaigns.'

'Oh.'

'I will pray to Our Lady of Dollars so you will have a good trip.'

'Dolores.'

'Yes, Dollars.'

***

Elizabeth, it turned out, had newly joined as a research associate at the Refugee Studies Centre, Elizabeth House, just a couple of kilometres from my hostel. I went. Elizabeth House was an ancient, two-storied mansion with large windows and a gabled roof. The events it hosted were on display on the notice board in the reception area, a copy of which I had already seen at my hostel lobby this serendipitous morning. The notice mentioned Elizabeth as the contact person.

Elizabeth saw me at the back midway through her act but did not falter for a moment at my accusatory stare, which I had carried intact in my heart all the way from Delhi, before she continued her introductions. The backdrop of the stage had a blown-up photograph of a three-year-old Aylan Kurdi lying face down on sand on the shores of Kos, the Greek island, to which he and his family had fled from the northern Syrian town of Kobani, where the Kurdish people and ISIS had fought. A caption over the photograph said: 'Remember Aylan? Has Britain Progressed?'

The seminar raised several issues, mostly humanitarian. 'Why are refugees fleeing their home countries?' Because of 'geo-politico religious' events. 'This was a tragedy,' the speakers said, 'created by man'. Who dropped the bombs in Aleppo? Man. 'Not woman,' one of the speakers pointed out, 'but man'. People always moved; that was the story of mankind. The problem now was there were too many borders. Growing British insularity was adding to the problem. A mother separated from her child could be traced to a signature in Washington or Moscow; to an isolationist administration in Westminster. Migration was a result of political policies. A migrant was not a refugee. A migrant was one who made a home of another country. A refugee was one who fled his country because of persecution or violence and was seeking asylum. The seminar focused on the forces that created refugees. Wars. Global warming. Politics. A world that created refugees also had the moral responsibility to take care of its consequences. We abhor Nazism and Stalinism because it separated man from man, killed millions on the basis of categories. Jews, Reactionaries, Slavs, Poles. Why are we not condemning some of the largest migrations and dislocations in human history just because we see its instigators are disguised as nice people like us? Canada had declared itself to be the first post-national state. What are the lessons to be learned from that country?

An impassioned seminar. Almost pious. And through it all, I could only think of me, not the boat people, not even little Aylan. I was a refugee of the heart. The Refugee. What did it matter if it was war or love? Isn't love a legitimate, if old-fashioned, reason for a borderless world? Yes, I was in agreement with the seminar. Down with walls. If all of humanity perished except you and another person (Elizabeth and I, say), would you still dot on your nation? It was not Ithaca, it was Penelope, surely? When it was question time for the audience, I raised my hand. Elizabeth ignored it until after the panel fielded two questions, and an elderly man in a hat in the back row said, 'The young man there has had his hand up for long, please allow him to ask his question.' Elizabeth had no option but to come near and hand the mic over to me.

'Thank you,' I said, feeling like a victor, my rights as a refugee, momentarily at least, vindicated. 'My question is to the whole panel. What's your opinion on Kashmir? Would you consider those fighting for its independence be given refugee status in Britain? Or would you think the idea of an independent Kashmir went against the territorial integrity of India?' Though I trembled with foreboding in articulating the point, it no longer held any personal significance for me. Indeed, I had no position on India. I did not care. Kashmir was just a coded message to Elizabeth. Hadn't I written to her about becoming a Kashmir correspondent? The three panelists looked at each other as if to say, would you like to have a go at this? One man, the least vestiges of the sub-continental accent in the way he spoke, got up and said the seminar was not about Kashmir and that spies from Pakistan had infiltrated Oxford academic circles. There was consternation. Elizabeth brought the house to order, and invited the panelists to respond. After a moment's pause, the first speaker said that my question was perhaps valid, but delicate. Anything they said in this regard would be misinterpreted by India. The issue was larger and did not allow itself to be limited to a specific region. It was an international humanitarian question. I nodded as if that made sense.

'Any other questions,' Elizabeth asked the audience. I raised my hand again, not quite sure what I was going to ask. I was ignored. I stood up, determined to make a point, terrified at the attention that my transgressive comment received—I would have naturally broken some convention—especially from my fellow-detractor, (a patriot, clearly), but then sat down, because I had forgotten what I was going to ask. The question that would bring the evening down with a crash, show them all up, and I had forgotten it. When the seminar wound up, I hung around, hoping with a heart that pumped hard enough for two that Elizabeth would come, dropping the mask she had assumed for the evening for, in her heart, surely, she appreciated the fact of my being there at Elizabeth Mansion as proof of a passion that crossed a continent without a second thought? It occurred to me that I might have invented love all over again that day. Not fully, but substantially. No one felt the heart's wound as deep as I. But there was no sign of Elizabeth. A few guests had been invited for drinks afterward—after having shared the trauma of the damned and the drowned, perhaps, they had earned the right to dunk their sorrow for humanity in dark wine—and it looked like Elizabeth had joined them in spirit and letter. I was not one of them. My solitary passion fermented in the bog of my bitterness. Wine in my mouth would turn into vinegar. I got out and walked to The Dewdrop. I sat outside on the bench in the lawn, had a few drinks. I watched the evening go down. My spirits sank with it. I was alone again to grapple with the permanent eclipse of my heart.

Monologue of the Eclipsed Heart

I get up from the bench in the lawn and go into The Dewdrop to ask for a glass of beer at the bar. Just to put the whisky down. It has grown cold as the night, dragging the stars after it, journeyed eastward. In the hall, it is warm and crowded. Who are these people? What do they know about…about what? Did you ask what, Dear Reader? Suffering, that is what. Suffering from what? Suffering myself, if you must know. No, you won't get it. Never mind. I owe no one anything. I came into the world alone. I shall go from it alone. I wished I had a sense of humour. I stumble. My shoelaces have come undone. It could happen only to me. That was the kind of luck I had. There are so many people around. But only my shoelaces have come unstuck. I bend down and tie them, aware my ass is jutting comically out into the air. Someone pokes it.

'Fuck you,' I say, straightening up turning around. But see no one. An accidental penetration, then. I finish with the laces, sit on a high stool, drumming on the bar, and ask for a whisky, having changed my mind. I down the whisky, ask for two more. I am equal to anything now. Bring it on. I listen to people talking. It is not just English, though English itself sounds foreign here. Indeed, there are times when even words from one's mother tongue sound strange as one utters them, like one is masticating nuts and bolts. What was it like before Man invented language? There are 6500 now. Imagine 6500 different ways of calling water, water. It must have been quieter for sure before speech began, haha. Listen to the babel in the bar. Rising inflections. Winged vowels. Stony consonants. Gibberish. A babel of babblers. A jubilant bunch of Chinese students dominates a corner. '*Hui jia*,' one of them keeps repeating. Another translates it to his English friend: 'Going Home'. Somebody is going home. A send-off party. From another table, someone says, '*El tiempo es malo Inglés*'. Yes, the English weather is bad.

'Can I have one more, please?' I hear myself asking. I am speaking English the way Indians speak it. Fast. All the syllables stressed evenly or equably ignored. My blood speaks the cadences of my birth. *Hui jia*. Home. I have half a mind to go back to India, to Thrissur. Or, end my life, right here. Take your pick. I see no meaning. No point. I close my eyes, imagine myself as not being there. The stool I sit on is vacant for a moment. But before you register it, someone else has occupied it. Life goes on, like water closing over the spot where a man has drowned. It makes no difference to the dead man either. Indeed, he didn't know the difference when he was alive. Why? Because we did not get in touch with universal consciousness, Anand would say, 'Your breath is the regulator of the consciousness. It is the socialized self that you are trying to live, not the real thing.' Forget Anand.

Let's talk about me, the drowning man. Comrades, I have lived too much with too little for too long. The world owes me more, I deserve more. But I see no prospect of a change in the turn of events. Might as well call it a day. Yes, suicide is an option. A matter of will. I look around. I relate to nothing. Could I be an alien? Suddenly, the urge to end it all assumes urgency. What might be a good way to snuff it? I gaze at the mirror on the wall at the back of the bar. *Qui est ce monstre*? I look tragic. Wasted. A flower nipped in the bud. In the bed, too. I am arrogant with the forebodings of my end. End it here. Tonight. My prescience of my end renders me superior to all. Here's my last day—in a sealed cover. A man in a hat nods at me in the mirror behind the bottles. Wasn't he at the seminar? An Indian, to be sure.

'You will never see anyone wearing a hat like that in India. Where's the rabbit?' I ask the man at my elbow.

'The rabbit is cooking,' he says.

'Strange we wear no hat in India, why is that?'

'It's a hot country, you should be wearing several,' he says, 'all kinds of hats, but don't take mine, please.' He nods. 'Do you resent the world today?

'I resent everything every day.'

'Ah, you are the last angry young man. And naturally, you have been discovered in an Oxford pub. Here's to you,' he raises the glass, 'to anger, exclusion, and revenge.'

I nod.

'Man has a moral obligation to be happy, they say. Are you?'

'No, but does that explain the wars?'

'I am fundamentally an unserious person. Especially today. You will excuse me?'

'It must cost you friends.' I think of Arjun. In a message, Arjun said, his literary agent had expressed his inability to represent him, even as he grew 'deaf of eyes and blind of ears.'

'It doesn't gain you any in the first place. Have I seen you around here before? I don't have a mind for faces.'

'I am new to these parts.'

'Like Arabs to Alaska? Which college?'

'No, no college.'

'That's good. India?'

'Yes.'

'Stay nearby? Sorry, I am extra curious today. Extra garrulous, too.'

'Yes, close by.' I could not recall my address. 'It's terrible not to know where you can return,' I tell him. I rest one side of my face on the bar, the cold of the counter sobering me, hoping my address will come back to me. So this is what my grandfather is going through every moment of his life. To think of a word with the meaning fled, to feel the meaning without a name, to experience an object as a shade of memory. What was in his hands when he came down from the attic?

'It will come back.'

He has even teeth, slightly discoloured. He removes his hat and places it on the bar. His silver hair is parted low on one side. His eyes are small and sharp. His face shows no wrinkles. It's like time is breathing very close to his skin, but won't touch it with its iron brush. And I have seen him before, in a familiar place perhaps. I am not sure where. At the seminar? At home in Thrissur, a younger version of my grandfather? But many people resemble each other at some angle. Ah, he was at the seminar, yes. He intervened for my right to speak. The great Kashmir question that I raised.

'That's what happens in war years. No one knows the way back home for sure. The odds are so heavy, the memory of home turns into a dream.' He smiles. His mouth assumes a recognizable shape.

'Are you by any chance Dr Krishna Menon?' But the man belonging to the hat is busy with his phone. I make my way down the aisle towards the far end where an electric fire splutters blue butterflies into the air. A spiralling metal staircase floats into view. It leads down instead of up. My eternal search for the solace and quiet of the men's room. The smell of sulfide in the urine gives me a high, serves to silence the mind. To pee, or not to be. An omelet for Hamlet, please. I go down the steps. If I had a gun, I might just do it, yes. But results can't be guaranteed, sorry. Consider the case of one of Stalin's sons, Yakov Dzhugashvili who tried his luck with his revolver and was only wounded, to the derision of his father. What would you do to get a father, what would you do to get him out of your life? The smell from the piss room is strong. But it seems I have narrowly bypassed the place, and entered a passageway leading into a small courtyard, up a short flight of stairs, to the backstreet. Ha. A man and a woman are kissing. How did we come to this, tell me? Some 250,000 years after walking out of Africa, here we are, kissing in the open. No shame? It's drizzling. The rain falls on the lovers, makes them shine, dim lights glint off them. The quality of kindness is never strained, it falls from heavens light as manna. I stare hard at the rain. What falls, goes up. Now water, now cloud. In the distance, I can hear, but faintly, what began as a soccer anthem fading into one of war. When exactly did the transition take place? Drunken songs of soldiers about to be slaughtered fade as they march on their creaking boots. A heavy sense of apocalypse renders me utterly dysfunctional. No, I won't make it. The unmitigating awareness that he was doomed, Seamus Heaney said of M. The knowledge is liberating, too. The rain abates for a moment. 'And Jimmy will go to sleep in his room again.' That line for sure I heard now with startling clarity. Must be the jukebox back in the hall coming alive. The song of those who died before their time in the Second World War. Wasn't that Jimmy-line from the 'White Cliffs of Dover'? Vera Lynn? She was alive the last I heard of her. Over a 100-years-old, she would be now. But in these days of the internet, death somehow seems not so final; the departed pop up at the click of a button; maybe the internet is the other kingdom? 'Music is the powerful overflow of vicarious feelings,' Elizabeth mocked once. She is a dread detractor of Wordsworth. He was a man who related to rocks more than humans; was he, maybe, a geologist at heart? The rain hardens. I find my way back, but it takes me time. The labyrinthine English pubs.

Next time I must bring with me a ball of thread. I observe with surprise that the jukebox is indeed there, but that no one is playing it.

'Sorry, I went looking for the washroom.' I tell the man in the hat.

'You couldn't find it, of course. They keep shifting its location, teaching drunks responsibility, I guess.'

'Churchill used to wear a hat like yours.'

'I see you know that currently fashionable war criminal intimately. That was my hat he wore,' he says. 'Not a hero, maybe. But was Winston a mass murderer as they would like to portray him now? How the norms of ethics change.'

'I have to think carefully through what you said,'

'The time is coming when all heroes will eventually be seen as villains. The cult of the great men is all but over.'

'"It's the hour of the crowd," as my friend would say.'

'Who's your friend so wise?'

'Arjun Bedi. He is in Delhi.'

'And what's your name? Utter at least half of it? Mine is Kris. Krishna Menon.'

Kris. My grandfather's brother, of course. I drain the glass. 'Osip Bala Krishnan.'

'Oh, well. He places his glass carefully down. 'My fears always come true. Our paths have curved around the earth and now crossed. And we never come alone, do we? We bring with us everyone we know. Everything, too.'

'That's so true.'

'A whisky for my nephew, grand-nephew, and me, Myriana,' Dr Krishna Menon tells the plump, smiling girl behind the bar.

'I can remember where I stay,' I emerge momentarily triumphant from my chaos. Room number 9. Ground floor. A square block of a hostel with high walls. The road running parallel to Woodstock Road. I can't remember the name of the street, still. But I know my way back. I know where I must return unerringly tonight with the retinue of my selves.

'Now you see the kind of things that come out of this,' Kris touches his hat.

'Happy union,' Myriana places the refilled glasses on the counter.

'This is Osip. His long journey has ended at my narrow gates, as the Germans said of the concentration camp prisoners,' Kris informs Myriana.

I am back in the basement, for a moment—the moment out of time. The isms march in mud-caked boots. Whole nations in search of continual tragedies, uniformed men who plod on through slush and snow over often imaginary borders—rubbish strips of land where the wind flees without stopping and silence reigns emptied of heart. The innocent rivers, where fish once congregated in prayer, carrying collapsed cathedrals downstream. Armoured vehicles. I could weep for the world. I place my head on the bar, weep.

'You had a drop more than you should, maybe. Let me take you to the taps. Wash your face, and let's get something for you to eat.'

Later, as we finish our dinner, Kris asks: 'Have you watched the night sky? It's very clear these days.'

'No, not really.'

'You should. It's then that you realize that not everything has to make sense.' He draw four stars on a paper napkin, scribbles something, and passes it to me. 'My address, written in the stars, for you.'

I look up at him in a daze.

'The wise say stars are the alphabet of god, each constellation a story. It's just that there are too many to make sense.'

Love, The Word Known to All

I sat down at Cheers, a cheap coffee place near the Oxford Railway Station, not bigger than a stall, where I had found myself in my aimless walks this mid-morning, and where you could stand around round plastic tables in red and white, and have a coffee and a croissant for one pound. One side of the place was red bricks, and the other a mirror. The man behind the counter was young and bald, and had a face that invited confidences. I bought the coffee without looking him in the eye, and placed it on a red table. I had a headache coming. Its source was precisely at the centre point behind my eyelids. Soon it would radiate around my head. I checked my phone, read again the message from Arjun. Dev had posted the party scene where Maina was having a meltdown on social media. Diya shared the post with a kind of dissenting note. She said that it was a personal moment at a private party, and, ideally, should not be put out; but Arjun was a public figure, and his wife's 'observations' about him were helpful to understand the domestic abuse of the 'benevolent patriarch'. She said she would have more to say on the issue in a forthcoming book. Dev had masked Maina's face in his video.

'The terror comes in waves,' Arjun said. They had come up with another case where he had asked an artist if she were her own nude model. Arjun said he did ask the artist the question, but it was out of genuine curiosity. 'Today,' Arjun said, 'I awoke to hear someone moaning, like a hurt animal, and found it was issuing from my throat, so I will go and apologize to them and see if this thing can be stopped, but what's there to stop now? You see, Osip, although one needs forgiveness or appreciation from no one more than one's detractors, and though their file on me says I am well versed in the English language and the uses of irony, I say it all quite plainly: I am tired, and I must learn to die with this, though Dev and Diya have offered a forum on their online portal for me to apologize. Hmm. This offer Osip, was preceded by an anonymous call on my landline. The caller, a male voice, merely said, "Hello rapist, good morning" and cut the call. And, so, I ebb and eddy toward my exilic status, which I console myself is an essential stage of a writer's evolution, but equally, I am aware now, that even this thought could be an assuagement of my vanity. In short, I am no longer sure of myself. Stay good, and let me know if you need anything, money, etc.'

I sipped the hot coffee. English coffee always smells better than it tastes. A heavy-set woman in a tall black hat, black leather jacket, and black high boots came in with two black poodles, talked to the man behind the counter in a whisper, laughed, and left, glancing at me. The cold air was heavy with perfume in her wake, and triggered the first stab of my blinding headache. I leaned my head against the mirror. 'Poor Arjun,' I thought. I could not think of a repentant, apologetic Arjun. I closed my eyes to contain my headache.

'Now I present to you my 1935 poem, Ode to Stalin, seeking his forgiveness.

"Though I am not yet worthy of having friends,/Though I am not sated with bile and tears, / I still seem to be seeing him in his greatcoat, in his cap, / On the wonderful square, with his happy eyes…//."'

'Gladen'kii stishok. Facile doggerel.'

'Yes, nothing in the great Russian language, with all its wide vowels and gushing sibilants, justifies or accommodates it. The language fails when the poet is false to his situation. And the situation here is stark, simple: there would be no reprieve. Only more Siberia from the big man, and there is enough Siberia for all to go around with, and mocking laughter of other doggerel writers.'

'Are you talking to yourself in a foreign language?' the man behind the counter had come around, and was now considering me with his kind, bulbous eyes.

'No. I was thinking of something.'

'I thought I could hear your thoughts, mate. I don't mind, except the customers might take fright.'

I picked up the coffee and left, my head on fire, carefully stepping over the little puddle of poodle piss on the floor, mystified which one of them did it and exactly when. It seemed the woman in black had come a long time ago.

***

How is Elizabeth? I don't know, though I am stalking her. I know what time she arrives at the office in the morning. She does not come out for lunch. By six, sometimes seven, in the evening, she will emerge, like light, and I can see the world suddenly brighten. Mostly Kris picks her up. She knows of my presence, I believe. It is just that she will not acknowledge it. I don't blame her. The other day I caught sight of a tramp in the shop window and, a moment later, saw he was myself. I warmly greeted him. My beard was a beehive. My hair had grown up to my shoulders. My clothes were rumpled. I looked like a refugee on his last legs. Last laceless shoes.

On the day I wore my military-green jacket—picked up from the flea market, in a tired gesture of affiliation to my personal jihad perhaps—despite herself, Elizabeth looked in my direction fleetingly, with professional pity, the kind of Red Cross disposition that she and her kind must reserve for, say, the Boat People, or the Rohingyas on yet another boat to yet another island, before I turned my face away, unable suddenly to meet her gaze, and affected a stoop uncharacteristic of an angel's descendant, as if I was someone else. I had fallen. I had risen. How tragic. How comic. It's a game both of us are playing, in which Elizabeth dictates the terms because I am at her mercy—and this is

England, after all. Perhaps she is testing how far I would go before she calls up the police. How we reduce infinite options of life into just the one we can't handle. I blame Kris for complicating my life beyond comprehension. Who knew when I set out from India, I would run into Kris? That he was the lover of my lover? Nevertheless, as I keep my watch on Elizabeth, my heart expands. I am aware of a new quality to my consciousness. This is what the Buddha must have experienced. I feel one with the underclass of the world; I am the martyred saint of the migrants and marginals. I know what a day without a meal is. I know despair by its smell; sadness by the sound of its footsteps. I know what it is to be the one sailor out on the ocean with one flickering star in the sky. I know hope. Yes, it's love, the word known to all. Yet how it is happening only to me. I am blossoming in my love for Elizabeth. I have lost everything, and in my loss, I no longer fear the world. I have surrendered, and I am, therefore, free. I would like to share the abundance of my freedom with the world. In my green jacket, as I walk back from my stalking post, past the Bodleian, I open my arms wide and warm—wider and warmer than the spirit of the 12 million books that the library houses, and every single book is about me (surely?)—to humanity, offering solace to the damned, ready to embrace the wretched, undo every harsh judgment ever passed. And, alas, humanity sidesteps me, a hand up in defence, alarm in its eyes.

***

The days in Oxford flow, one into the next. What explains my obsession? I have thought about it, but there is no one good answer. The more Ms Hill spurns me, the more I desire her. More a need to worship than even desire. And, what feeds me, strangely enough, is a kind of optimism. The hope that Elizabeth understands and appreciates the depth of my need for her, if not now, then soon. That she exists just for me. That much is obvious, is it not, Dear Reader? Surely, she can't pretend none of it happened?

***

No sign of Elizabeth for five days. I couldn't just go into her office and ask the receptionist. I worried. I hesitated. I ventured into my next chivalrous enterprise. I borrowed an old cycle no one seemed to be using from the hostel and pedalled down to 71 Norham Gardens, a small, two-storied house with a courtyard in front, and a little garden in the back. I pushed open the gate, hoping it would not yield. A sensor light came on and threw the shadows of my cycle and me on the gravel. I froze, and felt as if a guard from a watchtower would shoot me dead any moment. Barbed wires rose and bundled the air around me. I was filled with dread. What might I discover? 71 Norham Gardens was a museum of curios. After all, Kris had shared a bed—or so I imagined—here with a woman who just might have been my aunt, and with whom I had slept.

Kris opened the door.

'Yes? Looking for someone? Ha. Osip. You have changed. Come on in,' Kris said. His eyes were sharp as shards of glass; surely, they miss nothing? He wore a light blue V-neck sweater and a pair of black trousers. The clothes sat on him very well. I followed him. It was a rather spare room. A black sofa opposite a TV on the wall. A floor lamp. A long narrow rosewood table with curved legs. Two rosewood chairs on either side of it. A black reading lamp stood to a corner of the table. A telescope on a stand by the window. No books. No papers. Strains of classical music spilled from somewhere above. We sat on either side of the table.

'All well? Are you all right for money?'

'Yes. Why do you ask?'

'Basics. Your grandfather never was good with the gold.'

'Thank you for funding me.'

'Now and then. No consistency. I know a young lady who believes duty is passion prostituted,' Kris said. 'A fine, young lady.'

We were quiet for a minute.

'How's my brother? I haven't met him in, what, a lifetime?'

'He is not what he used to be, I guess.'

Kris reflected for a moment. 'It's strange how distant my brother and I are with each other. Would you like something to drink? Tea?'

'Could I have a drink?' I was assailed by a fear that Elizabeth might appear at any moment. I thought I could catch a whiff of her perfume in the air.

Kris went in and came back with a bottle and a glass. He carefully poured out a finger of the scotch. 'It's too early for me. You go ahead. Besides, I am expecting someone.'

Who?

I stirred to go. Anything could happen. That apocalyptic feeling. Why did I come? I wanted to see the space Elizabeth shared with Kris. If Elizabeth turned up, we would perhaps pretend not to know each other? But why should she?

'You don't mind my saying it, I hope. You seem sort of spaced out; are you?'Kris said.

'It's the place.'

'Or the whisky. You do drink a lot, I noticed. But a woman is not the reason, hopefully?'

'No.'

'Another drink?'

'Thank you. I'd better get along.'

'It might rain anytime.' Kris said, looking at the sky out of the window. 'Want to wait it out? Or stay here for the night?'

'No, I think I will make a run for it.'

'Drop by again. Now that you are here, I can't pretend you don't exist. Any weekday is good.'

But not weekends. 'Yes, thank you, you are very kind, Kris.'

Kris opened the door. 'I've changed a lot from the timid boy I was once. Your grandfather used to bully me around. He was older than me by 25 years. And my mother was a little ashamed, I think, of her mysteriously late product. It took me a while before I realized that my brother was not my father.' Kris was lost in thought. 'He was impossible with that naive energy and conviction for a great egalitarian tomorrow. How strange, nothing moves man so much as fiction, they say.'

I stepped outside. 'Have you changed?'

'For the worse, I guess. But change is a hard-to-measure thing, don't you think?'

I buttoned up my jacket. A few cold drops of rain fell on my face. They were heavy like a dog's paws. 'What was that about change, again?'

'Ah. Suppose, you stand before a mirror, say, for 30 years. You can't catch yourself changing, can you?' Kris smiled.

'Ah. That way.'

'One of the ways. See you soon.'

I wheeled the cycle out as it began to drizzle. At the gate, I turned to look. The door was half-open, and Kris stood straight, looking at me, one hand raised in farewell, changing without anyone noticing.

A Turn of Events

Summer is getting over. On a Friday, a little after 6 pm when it is already dark, the pubs beginning to come alive, and the long-bodied Burlington and Banbury buses plying the narrow roads, I wait in windy, inexplicable Oxford, with my mind half blown, behind a lamp-post, like an ill-trained spy, and see Elizabeth coming out, and I can see all of the smitten town turning to look at her. She presses the walk button as if the road belongs to her; the green man comes on. Elizabeth crosses the street. I count 20 and fall in step behind her. No Kris today.

Elizabeth and I make our way, separated only by our shared experiences. Doves break out from stones. The dark sky is low like a weighted-down canopy. Ancient college windows come to light as they have done for a thousand years. Elizabeth slows down.

'Have you been stalking me?' She says without looking back. We are going past St. Giles underground urinals, and we see a naked man being carried down the steps. 'They take Jesus out for a piss these days before he is crucified,' Elizabeth says glancing at the spectacle. 'Very kind of them.'

I hurry to catch up with her.

'Ms Hill, please, we need to talk.'

'No. You came looking for me at my office.'

'No.'

'The receptionist told me.'

'Only once.'

'You have been shadowing me. I should be complaining to the police.'

'I'm sorry.'

'It's awkward for everyone. Go back.'

Has she moved in with Kris or not? Has he told her or not? What is it with people? You loved me once, I want to say. But it sounds like a threat.

Elizabeth and I walk up the road leading toward a close and large moon.

'I am thinking of taking up a journalism internship.'

'You mentioned that in your mail. Someone helping you?'

'Arjun. You met him.'

'Ah yes. That's good of him. What about your education?'

'I can always do it later. Online, or open university.'

We fall silent.

'You don't want to go to college right away? Is that wise?'

'A lot of people are doing it now, I guess. Journalism is the closest I can come to writing.'

'What are you going to write about?'

'I don't know.'

'Well, journalism is a starting point, I suppose.'

A cyclist in helmet and riding gear goes past Elizabeth, fast and close.

I try to save Elizabeth, pull her to one side.

'Jesus. I could smell his sweat,' she says.

'Yes, a starting point.'

Elizabeth puts an arm around me. 'OB?'

'Yes, Madam.'

'You didn't save me just now. You may have thought so, but you didn't.'

'Yes.'

'Your yeses and nos often mean the opposite.'

'No.'

'From what I can remember, not all your class was like you. Or was there a subculture I was not aware of? And you its hero?'

'No. We drank and smoked. That's about it.' And put in false obits. And dug up corpses. And extorted. And were expelled. And fell in love with our English teachers.

'Where's your friend these days?'

'Anand? He is in Dharamshala.'

'Yes, yes, Anand. How he tried to kill me.'

'Anand wants to become a millionaire godman.'

'You two were close.'

'We have a few things in common.'

'Like what?'

I tell Elizabeth about Anand's antecedents, glad we are talking at all. 'His mother is from Purvanchal Pradesh. But he hasn't seen her since a baby.'

Elizabeth stops in her tracks. 'Listen, there's this woman I ran into in Delhi. Sangita from Purvanchal Pradesh. She had an affair with a politician and had to give up her child to save his career.'

'Oh.'

'You must tell your friend,' Elizabeth says.

'I will.' Anand wins again.

'You don't sound enthusiastic.'

'But are you certain?'

'How can I be certain? What's the harm in informing him?'

We walk on.

'When I was a kid, my teacher asked me what would I like to become, and I said I wanted to become a mother,' Elizabeth dilated her eyes. 'I wanted to have children and tie their shoelaces and sent them off to school.'

'We go past a pub.

'Would you like to have just one drink? To Anand and Sangita?'

'Yes, that'd be great, Ms Hill.'

Ms Hill and I walk to The Gardener's, near St Antony's College.

We find a table next to the window. In the light of the lamp overhead, Elizabeth glows. 'See, this is what I keep telling you. Everyone is in it together. We don't know who holds the key to whose life.'

'You never said that before.'

'Oh, shut up, OB.' Elizabeth laughs. 'Aren't you calling your friend, break the news? Maybe not yet, do you feel? I can try connecting with Sangita. That's what I will do.'

'Yes.'

Elizabeth sips her whisky. 'This is just guess-work. But I have a feeling about it, you know.'

'Yes.' Could we talk about us, please? Should I tell her about my meeting with Kris? Is the timing correct? But I can't hide it either. 'I want to tell you something.'

'Tell.'

'I met Kris.'

Elizabeth turns pale. 'Oh no. That lovely man. But why?'

I look away. Ah, just as we were doing good. 'He is my grandfather's brother. I first met him at The Dewdrop. No, at the seminar.'

'Jesus, I should have known.'

'I didn't mean to, but it just happened.'

'I guess Oxford is a small town. Everyone runs into each other.'

'I didn't say a thing about you.'

Elizabeth appears a little relieved. She shakes her head. 'OB, what are you even doing here? I fled your country. You. I can't handle this.'

'I shouldn't have gone to your house.'

'You went to Norham Gardens, too? What's wrong with you?'

'I didn't know it was your house.'

'It's not my house. And that's not what I am saying.'

'Yes, it's terrible. And he loves you. It keeps him going.'

'People get on with things. You are stuck. Go on, get a life.'

'That was an accident.'

'You are an interminable accident.'

'I am fighting a whole bloody war all the time,' I blurt out, 'you have no idea what it's to be me.'

'Bring your voice down. Your war, like your love, is a delusion.'

'No.'

'Take my word for it.'

'You are not a delusion.'

'All that you think about me is. It's all in your mind. I'm done with this. You are a kid. And I don't want to be lost in your self-obsessed drama.'

'I am not a kid. I am past 19.'

'Way past? A dirty old man? And not quite all there either.'

'The old man is the one with whom you are sleeping.'

Elizabeth carefully folds the napkin and places it on the table. 'I am leaving.' She pushes back her chair against the table and gets up.

'I have come a long way.'

'One more rude word and I'm gone, I promise you.' Elizabeth sits down.

'Sorry.'

Her expression softens. 'All right, I'll have a refill. I could do with one.'

The bar is crowded. I wait for my turn. A middle-aged man to my right is talking to a young woman. 'Let me tell you a story?' 'Yes, Bill,' the girl says. 'There was this guy one day who paid his kids' fee at school, helped his mother—with whom he had strained relationship—to pay back a loan, bought groceries, and in the evening went into his room, closed his door, and slashed his wrist. He was found in time and taken to the hospital. A month later, he is standing next to a terrific girl, the nurse who took care of him, and they are waiting at the counter for a drink.' 'Bill, thank you, but do we have a point here?''Yes, I had to nearly die to be here, with you, Tess.' 'Oh, Bill.' When I come back with the drink, Elizabeth is not at the table. No, she can't just go like that. Of course, she can. No, she can't. I sit down, wait. A long time. When I have given up on her, Elizabeth returns.

'OB, I went out for a smoke. This has to end. Now. I have decided.'

Around us, the pub hums. A hundred drinks. A hundred stories.

'We…we could be happy.'

'No. I don't want to be happy with you.'

I don't understand her. At all.

'It's for your good, OB.' Elizabeth places her hand on the table, palm down like a mouse. A slender beautiful mouse. In the children's home, we would sleep on long, narrow straw mats in rows after rows, and when the lights were turned off, white baby mice would start falling from the wooden beams supporting the tiles, on our stomach, chest, face. They would just lie there quiet, tiny, helpless things with pink feet and closed eyes, and I would wonder how they found their way back to their mothers. When the mice fell, we could not make any noise though we wanted to, because big women with sticks would be walking around ensuring we slept. We slept with the mice on top, and somehow some would have vanished in the morning; some still slept on your stomach, as if you had given birth them. You plucked them and kept them on the side. Some kids squeezed them dead. It must have been some kind of fun, innocent at some level.

'What you need is not me, but a doctor. Or better still, a nurse.

'What for?'

'You are...' Elizabeth stopped short.

'I have a condition. I share it with my grandfather.

'What do you mean?'

'A non-genetic mental disorder. *Folie a famille.*' I look at my glass. How to make it short, say it is just a sign of the times? That I am not the only patient. Social media, the new world, works on shared disorders, Arjun said. What was the hashtag but a sign of the secrets of a given group? Each in his lunacy hoped another would share what he transmitted, validated his view. So the world could be understood a little better, owned a little more, turned a little less threatening. The more people you got around you, the more normal you felt. 'It's like sharing an outlook. Everybody has it.'

'No, everybody does not have it. You are talking about a psychosis.'

I place my hand on top of hers. On the mouse. My hand trembles a little. It's the alcohol. Or the possibility, the prospect, of my future. 'Can't we stay together?'

Elizabeth pulls her hand from beneath mine as if she has been touched with a hot iron, and slaps me hard. My left cheek stings.

People turn in our direction.

A man comes up to our table and asks, 'Is this Paki giving you trouble?'

An old lover of Elizabeth?

'No,' Elizabeth widens her eyes. 'Thank you, Tom. He is Indian.'

'I mistook him at first for a Kenyan. He is dark enough.' Tom considers me gravely. 'Behave, this is not India, or Kenya,' he tells me at last and returns to his friends.

'Stop messing around with my life,' Elizabeth empties her drink. 'For god's sake.' She sits back.

We have another drink.

'Listen. I don't believe in love.'

I look at her. A dog trying to figure out his moody mistress. Does one have to believe in a thing to be it?

'It's an excess, do you see, but not real.'

'Why?'

'It makes you feel like eating ice creams and makes you miss your bus, but wars still happen. As do riots and arson. Love! Love is not peace, do you see. Everyone loves at least one other person. And still there is so much violence. They all have loved and would kill other loves.' There's a glitter in Elizabeth's eyes, a glitter cold and sharp as knives drawn out from a heap of snow. 'Do you understand? It is better to be young and not be loving.'

'No.'

'Let's take a walk, take stock of two lives slipping into debauchery and depredations. A walk will help.' It seemed she has turned a corner and seen a new terrain.

I rub my cheek, gratified. I believe we are turning the corner together.

An Awakening

One evening, when Anand thought Wang's righteous wrath had gone on for a bit too long, and not a little envious of the adoration he managed to generate at will, Anand raised his hand.

'Yes, Anand, please feel free to interrupt me,' Wang smiled.

Heads turned in Anand's direction.

'I don't believe in nationalism.' No, he believed in success, recognition, money.

'Who's asking you to believe in it? But this is not the forum for disbelievers, I am afraid. This is Free Tibet.' Wang raised his fist. Everybody in the room raised theirs in solidarity. Wang nodded in appreciation of his followers. 'We welcome you as an honorary Tibetan, Anand.'

The men applauded.

'Aren't you proud to be an Indian? Indian!' Wang expanded his hands to indicate the greatness of the concept.

'Oh, you don't know the half of it,' Anand thought. Why should he be proud of a nation that denied him a father and a mother? The awful, adrift sadness of his situation overwhelmed him. Free Tibet was the kind of mission Yolanda perhaps would send money to on a good day. To Tibet's freedom, but not, he reminded himself, to his. It was not clear to him how a notion could be preferred over a human being, over himself, in fact. 'No,' Anand said.

Wang looked at him with concern. 'Are you all right?'

Sheetla laid a restraining hand on Anand. 'You are running a temperature,' Sheetla said, 'your body is hot, and you are wearing just a light pullover, Anand.'

'Anand, my friend, we believe in the idea of an independent Tibet. What difference could you have with that?' Wang asked.

'You want a land to go back to. I want to flee the land I was born in.'

Anand heard people laugh. He thought of Osip. Where had Osip fled? To a country more alien than the one he was born in? It seemed to Anand now that Osip was not looking for Elizabeth so much as a cause to belong, to be part of a thing larger than himself, to lose his identity in it. But to reduce that cause to a geographic location? Surely, you did not belong to a place, did you? You belonged to a father, mother, lover. And in his case, there was no one. Like Osip. Like Idris. Would a man on the run, say, Idris, be proud of the country that lynched his father and denied him his god? A refugee in his own country? There seemed so many of them.

'Why on earth should I believe in your idea of a nation?'

'I am not sure one man's personal experience can be defined as the heritage of the collective. But let's take this conversation offline? When you are well, we shall have a cup of coffee and talk about it.' Wang glanced at the CCTV. 'But just to be on record, India is our brother. A generous big brother.'

'Not for me.' Anand got up from his chair. He did not care if he was being recorded. He swayed a little on his feet from a sudden spell of vertigo. For a moment there was no time, and it was not an entirely unpleasant sensation. There was only a deep, dark spinning void as he fell through it. He put out his hands to balance himself.

'You might be living off India. Not me.' Anand said.

There were groans in the room. A dog that had wandered in barked.

'Let's go,' Sheetla got up.

'No one sends me a free cheque in this country.'

Someone booed. A bunch of stocky men moved toward Anand.

'Easy there,' Wang said. 'Everybody take their seats.'

'What are you fighting for? A piece of barren mountain land without enough oxygen for...for a lizard?'

Someone threw something heavy at Anand. A shoe. It hit Anand's shoulder and lay at his feet, its mouth open. A shoe with a hole in its toe. The feel and shape of nationalism. Anand picked it up with an effort; it seemed way below his reach. He showed it to all. 'This is what you do to me for dissent. Why should China not use force on you for your opinions?'

There were more catcalls.

'Explain this shoe to me.' Anand trembled. Yes, it's the fever, he thought, Sheetla was right.

Chairs scraped back.

'Tibet is our birthright, and we shall die for it,' Wang said quietly.

The cafe broke into cheers. Anand and Sheetla heard the commotion behind them as they opened the door. Outside, it was snowing, out of season, and the cold took their breath away. 'My clothes are too exiguous for this weather,' Anand said to himself. Exiguous had been a joke since the day Sheetla showed Anand an essay, '*The Saint*' by Somerset Maugham—'Somerset who?' Anand had asked—on the great Ramana Maharishi, whom Maugham had met near Madras in 1938. Maugham had published his essay 20 years after meeting the Maharishi, and 8 years after the saint's death, in 1958, so naturally one didn't know how truthful the account was, Sheetla said. She read out the part about Maugham's description of the yogi: 'Though he wore nothing but an exiguous loincloth he looked neat, very clean and almost dapper...'

'Please wear an exiguous loincloth and look dapper, Anand,' Sheetla said.

'But,' Anand had asked, 'what's exiguous?'

'Meagre,' Sheetla said.

'That was not a Tibetan who threw the shoe, it was someone else.' Sheetla consoled Anand. She put an arm around him as they staggered up the road against the driving snow.

'It doesn't make any difference.'

They walked on for a while, away from the town lights. The mountains seemed so close, he could stretch out a hand and touch them. When they came to an open expanse of snow, Anand knelt, shivering. He could not go on. A snowflake had more weight than him, more mass, more mooring. It knew where it came from. He looked up at the low, dark, laden clouds. Most of the universe was made up of dark matter. What you see is what you can't see. But beyond everything there would be a source of blinding light. Because he could now see it. The wart at the centre of his brows seemed to open like a third eye. He sat down in the snow.

Sheetla sat down beside him and cradled Anand's head.

At her touch, big sobs broke out of him like vigorous birds from a broken cage.

'I am sorry, I can't remember crying ever.' Would Sheetla withdraw her gesture of intimacy at his self-exposure? One's weaknesses came back to haunt one in various disguises as another's strength. One could not share them with anyone. Indeed, often, these preceded your arrival on earth. Yolanda knew all his vulnerabilities. He had always felt naked in her presence. But Sheetla was not like Yolanda. There was nothing in her to fight against. There was no resistance, the hostile force that defined for him the rest of the world.

'You should cry more often, that's what tears are for. No one saves them for the future. It's not money, sweetheart.' Sheetla giggled, as if the snow and the words they exchanged were going to her head.

'Yes,' Anand said into the hollow of her fragrant shoulder, bending his head down into a chalice of exotic vapours.

'Someone at last,' he thought, 'and out of nowhere; someone who cared for him. A spirit of the mountain?'

'Yes,' he said into her hair, his mouth dry.

In the distance, from below, they heard Idris's voice promising medical miracles. 'Give me a cure for what I am,' Anand thought. The snow thickened. How silently it fell. Without complaints. Falling down and away from the sky, never to go back. He belonged to the snow, to the skies from where it fell. He felt Sheetla's hands going around him in a tight hug. This is what it was, then. To be human was to be hugged, maybe? A part of him surrendered to that part of Sheetla vanquishing him so effortlessly. But he could not give himself up wholly to it as another part of him awoke to the demands of survival. The great pretence that one played at just to be. The game that reduced the exceptional enterprise of life into the framework of moves and counter moves, of masks. 'Something is happening to me,' Anand said. 'I see it now.'

'Quiet, Anand. I am with you.'

Spasms shook his body.

'You really are running a temperature!' Sheetla hesitated a moment, and then lay beside him.

'My molecules are realigning.' His Kundalini was being awakened, its serpentine coils straightening to pierce through the seven energy centres to enter the Sahasra Chakra, the top centre point of his head, sublimating his self with the cosmos. Indeed, the cosmos was the lack of self. He would not be surprised at all if his pineal gland had begun to activate itself. They watched the sky: a vast black bird shaking down its white feathers. Around them, the elements gathered their whisper in the wind. *Aham Brahmasmi.* The Eternal is the Self.

A couple of weeks later, Anand would have a long, orange gown designed for himself with the black lettering on its back saying: *Aham Brahmasmi*, and explain to an anxious Sheetla his plan of taking India by bike and teaching people the power of now—how to arrive at now by means of the Agya Chakra, the pineal gland.

Beside him on the snow, Anand heard Sheetla catch her breath.

'I know now,' he said.

'Yes.'

He appreciated that she did not question what it was that he knew. We are together, he thought, and we are not. I am here, and I am not. He was just a medium in which the universal in him replaced his petty social self. He felt he was ageing instantaneously to a new wisdom.

Sheetla held him close. The crushed snow under them melted in their bodies' heat. Anand surrendered to the demands of the fever.

The Wandering Jew

I measure my time by Elizabeth's absence and presence. She is the hourglass through which the sands of my life pour. I pay a price for my utter dependence on her to be fully alive to the moment. Since that night at The Dewdrop, Elizabeth has slapped me once more. We have crossed a line, so necessary to form a bond. The second slap happens on a happy, drizzly, bewildering evening when, hand in hand under an old-fashioned—so old-fashioned, it is new—grey umbrella, we are waiting to cross the road, and Elizabeth is saying how her idea of the special seminars at her institute is taking off. 'I am looking forward to the next one, and you must come. You will like it…oh, my god, what are you doing?'

What am I doing? I am dashing across the road, pulling Elizabeth by her hand, a red Burlington coach missing us by a breath, and the driver shouting abuses at us. The umbrella, crushed against the bus, has been snatched away from my hand. In short, I'm trying to kill us. It might have been an accident. But Elizabeth has already accused me and, since I tend to believe the worst of me, I naturally think I must have engineered it. The truth also is that the bus was irresistibly close. I had been unhinged for a moment at the thought that I might lose Elizabeth again. You see how the joy of possession gives way to despair. The awful coexistence of contrary feelings, as we already said. Well, once across the road, I turn to look at the bus, as if it has a design on us, and I see disapproving English faces pressed against the window glass. Their expressions suggest that suicide and murder are a betrayal of English manners; a breach in decorum leads to tragedies. Wait, just a minute, isn't that Dr Krishna Menon? No? The bus stops for a moment ahead, revs as if working itself up to a greater rage, then moves forward.

'What's wrong with you?' Elizabeth slaps me. 'This is England,' Elizabeth says. 'There are rules.'

'Yes. I am sorry.'

'What are you trying to do, OB, just what the fuck are you trying to do? Get us both killed?'

I am in the wrong, but does a suicide attempt—if it is that; it may have been murder, seen in another light—warrant slapping me? When does violence qualify to be a solution? It seemed important to know.

'I am sorry,' I repeat. 'Why do you slap me for the slightest offense?' I want to ask Elizabeth, but desist for fear of offending her. You can try killing people, but may not offend them verbally? Odd, but that is what I am doing. 'Ethics is relative,' my grandfather said: 'What would you choose, little Osip, a few dead now to keep many alive tomorrow? A little ugliness now for an eternity of beauty?' No, this is an extreme parallel. I can't seem to relate to anything but extremes these days; my analogies are far-fetched. Perhaps I am not well, after all. I am not surprised Elizabeth can't understand me. We may move in the same society, but even in the same stratum we live in different times, don't we?

'Was that Kris?' I ask.

'Who? What?'

'One of the guys looking out at us?' I say, pointing at the fuming bus vanishing in the distance.

'Kris doesn't travel by bus normally.'

I see Elizabeth, yet to recover from the narrow escape, is reflecting on the possibility, nevertheless.

'I thought that was Kris.'

'I can't get over what you just did.' Elizabeth shakes her head. 'Kris on that bus would be the icing on the cake.'

'Should we not be talking to him about us?'

'What about us?'

'Aren't you living with him?'

'No.'

'He should know that we know each other from before?'

'Whatever for? He is not my local guardian. OB?'

'Yes?'

'I don't owe anything to anybody. So try not to guilt me. Or make me stop a moving coach. I am not the usual type, all right?'

'I didn't see the bus. It was the umbrella.'

'Christ. Of course, you saw it. It was a big bus. And red! Well, I shouldn't have hit you.'

'Happens.' It doesn't escape me that I am able to provoke her to extremes. I am not entirely powerless, then, over her, though it is the twisted power of the victim.

'No, it's inexcusable, please forgive me,' Elizabeth says, kissing me.

I am not there in the kiss. I am abstracted. Still, I am grateful that an act of abuse has brought Elizabeth and me closer still. There is intimacy in violence, distance in decency.

'I am losing my self-control. I source my violence to you. Sometimes your actions make no sense at all.'

Ha. Is she the victim? Or is it me? We walk in silence.

'Well, we were talking about the seminar,' Elizabeth says finally as we draw abreast of the Jewish Studies Centre.

'Oh, yes.'

'The one coming up is special.'

'Why?' Shouldn't I have picked up the broken umbrella from the road? Questions, questions. It had lain there in the rain like a vulture with a broken neck.

'Ava Lenk.'

'Ava Lenk!'

'She is on the panel of speakers. I got her through Brijesh. You remember Brijesh, don't you?'

'Yes.' How can one forget one's lover's lover?

'Well, we are trying to get some funding done, and we are building bridges with the Jewish community.'

'What's the seminar about?'

'"God on Trial." Has God broken his covenant with the tribe? First, they will screen an old BBC production by that name, a movie about a bunch of Jewish concentration camp prisoners debating the existence of God in the context of the extreme privations of their race, and then there will be a discussion.'

'Would you please introduce me to her?'

'If you haven't succeeded in pushing me under a bus before that.'

***

By the time I reach Elizabeth House on the 'God on Trial' day, the screening has almost got over. The night before though, I watched the movie on the Net, and I found it too theatrical. Two of the listed speakers for the evening are professors. They are of the view that since the Promised Land of Israel has been delivered, the covenant is not broken. The brutal experiences of the race are just a test of faith. I ignore the professors. How they talk. And talk. I have eyes and ears only for Ava. With the same calm, wide-set eyes that she trains on us, she once searched the frozen ground, under the low, bleak skies scarred by barbed wires, for breadcrumbs in the Lodz ghetto; eyes that scoured the farthest reaches of hell. Ava barely in her teens, then, cast already in the mold of a woman ancient enough to have lived through all of history. Ava appears quiet, graceful. She carries a walking stick, but her frail body hardly rests its weight on it as she walks up to the stage. She has many deep channels on her face. A wedding cake left out in the rain. She doesn't volunteer to speak much. Just before the end of the session, dominated by the garrulous professors, someone from the audience asks her opinion and, Ava says, in a low, gruff voice: 'There is no God, and that it is often doubtful if there is even Man'. The denial draws sibilants from the 30-odd people in the hall. She quotes Paul Celan, the Jewish, war poet, reversing the Judgment day: 'Pray Lord, pray to us, we are near.' Ava chooses not to elaborate.

When the event is over, Elizabeth introduces me to Ava. 'Osip Bala from India.'

'A poet?'

'Not even Jewish.'

'Wasn't it Marina Tsvetaeva who said every poet is a Jew?'

'I think you two will have a lot to talk about. I will see you before you leave, Ms Lenk,' Elizabeth withdraws to circulate.

'What are you doing here?'

'To meet you.'

'I am flattered.'

We fall silent—to the shared great years between us.

'Ms Lenk?'

'Yes?'

'There's something I wanted to ask of you.'

'Yes?'

'Not here, if you don't mind. Would you mind if I called on you?'

'Why? You should be meeting women much younger?' She gazes at the professors who are talking to a group of animated students. 'How old are you? 20? Older?'

'Yes.'

'Old enough. But, by all means, drop by. Next Saturday. I stay alone. 119, Summer Town.'

***

Ava's is a typical Summer Town residence. A narrow row house, with four wide steps from the lane that leads up to a red door, and a shining brass knob. Ava answers my knock and looks at me, shading her hand over her eyes, against the sun setting behind my head.

'Osip,' I say.

'A password for our times. Come on in.'

I sit in an old divan placed against the wall. The room is clean and bare like a rabbi's prison cell, except that an old cycle with a wicker basket attached to the handlebar stands in a corner, its chain hanging loose. I notice a lift-chair fixed to the railing of the stairs, awaiting its only passenger.

'Some tea?' Ava asks. 'Or, you prefer a drink?'

'I am fine.'

'All right, I'm going to have a cup.'

She goes in and, a few minutes later, returns with a tray. 'Anything specific I can do for you? Please be direct.'

'Do you recall one Menon from India? In the 1960's. You were probably living in Moscow.'

Ava's eyes narrow. 'I was a guide to the ruins and monuments of war. 1961, I think, when Narayan came. A brown, handsome man full of revolutionary fervour. What has he to do with you?'

'He is my grandfather.'

'Oh.' Ava stares at the cycle.

'He was missing for a year.'

'Three. I think.'

I see. Three. 'What happened?'

'Well, if I tell you about it you will not think well of me afterward. Not that it is important.'

'Was he with you those years?'

'The first 6 months, in St. Petersburg. I had run into him at a Kremlin function, where I was briefly a translator. We got to know each other well. As well as possible, let's say. I found him naive and his zeal sickening. Later, I took him to people who suffered from the famine and the wars and the purges. It took a lot to make him take a second look. You had to literally turn his head. He was soon disoriented. What he read or knew was not what he saw. One night in Moscow, he got drunk, went and spat on Stalin's bust. They arrested him, put him in the Lubyanka.'

'But they had got over Stalin by then. Khrushchev had exposed him, dismantled the system.'

'You would be surprised. Stalin is forever. There is a bit of him in every leader. Think of your country, maybe. Essentially a despot anywhere is the State.' Ava took a sip of her tea. 'You can't get Stalin out of Russia. That's how the thing works. '

'And you did not help him?'

'No, I denounced him as a spy. I was already in their

bad books. My family were kulaks, rich farmers. You are, of course, aware of the great purge, 1937, the collectivization drive in Ukraine, which killed millions? They shot you if you held back grain from the State or you sowed seeds too late. Or did not clap enough when the commissar said something. Or clapped too much. I took Narayan to Ukraine and made him meet the survivors.'

I imagined my grandfather, uncertain, at a mass grave of the de-mobbed dead, the snow falling on him from a dark, circling sky.

'My kulak connections keep coming up whenever needed. It is not just here, don't get me wrong. In your country, too, if you are picked up for random check all you ever did would be interpreted in a different light. It's so easy to read a pattern in any man. Besides, I was also a decadent. I had an affair with a student at a Teachers' Training College. I had suffered enough. Best to denounce this stranger and get on with life, I thought.'

'But his party? They did nothing?'

'I believe between his party and the one here, they arrived at some understanding, and it was agreed they won't talk about him. He had complicated it further by confessing to the violence, arson, and murder that he supervised or carried out on behalf of his party in Kerala. Besides, Moscow would be funding his party in Kerala. They used to do that a lot in those years. There would have been strings'

'And he went insane inside the prison?'

'He gradually fell silent. But not before he spent a few months in an asylum.'

'All that for just spitting at a statue?'

'You could be in life-long exile or in the prison forever for little or nothing. How many must be in your jails for shouting a slogan or reading the wrong literature? That's the whole thing, you understand? Because we are all guilty of something. There would be a taint. They found he was spending a lot of time with me investigating the Soviet excesses. He had to be a spy. Or, he could be read as a spy, or a reactionary. It doesn't matter. He denounced himself, of course, before they let him go. And I denounced him in my turn. And I was denounced by others. Denunciations go always in a circle.'

'But the party back home accepted him.'

'Better that way, don't you think? No fuss. Everybody continues as if nothing has happened. People disappear into the fog and step out of it.' Ava gathered her breath.

'Were you lovers?'

'Were we?' Ava pours out more tea. 'Are you sure you don't want any?'

'I am good.'

'Well, love, hate, I don't know. A bit intimate for sure. A kind of mutual understanding of the body and mind that only strangers thrown together by chance have, maybe.' Ava places her cup back on the tray. 'I derived a sadistic pleasure in disabusing him of his notions. That made him more dependent on me. I read out to him his forbidden poet, Mandelstam, in Russian. We all have a forbidden writer, you know. And then took him one day, just to see him squirm, to Nadezhda, the poet's wife, at her little flat, 14 Bolshaya Cheremushkinskaya Street, Moscow.' Ava paused, scratched her forehead in sudden confusion. 'Or maybe it was another flat, I can't remember, she was moving about a lot then. This was about a decade before she published her memoirs, where she mentions a foreign visitor without naming him. Narayan was in two minds after that about the Party. "As a man is, so he sees," as Blake said. I took him by train to Vtoraya Rechka, on the way to Vladivostok, where M. died in exile, back in December 1938. "How does one survive at all if you are an artist?" Narayan said. His desecration of the Stalin statue came after that trip. "But you don't need art," I told him. We all know that, don't we? You just need bread, milk, and quiet. In any big crisis, the artist would be the first to be dispensed with. He is a burden morally and financially. That trip seemed not to impact him much at the time. It was all just an icy vastness, you see. It was like...like some great music silenced out there in that endless, white cold. Does that make sense? I was subjecting him to the humiliation of truth. Narayan grew dependent on me to figure out things that he thought he already knew, and realized he had got most of it wrong. The peeling away of the tissues leaves you finally with just the one thing you can't handle: the naked heart. You would think it all unreal, perhaps. But these things happen all the time. I bet in your country there are hundreds, thousands, languishing in jail for sedition or some other equally indefensible charge; indefensible because the crime was not committed. Or it was committed thinking it was not a crime, but as the exercising of a right. I don't know.' She placed her hands in her lap, palms up, and stared at them, short of breath. 'Everywhere, a myth is always at work. There is no power without a mythology of it.'

It's dark. Ava hasn't bothered to put the lights on.

'Give me a minute,' Ava gets up on her feet with an effort.

She goes upstairs in her lift-chair. Ava clicks on the lights on the landing. The stairs collect shadows.

When she comes back, she places something soft in my hands. 'What's this?'

Her stripes. I run my fingers over the cloth. 'Shadows in the fur,' M. said.

'What I wore in the camp. My mother used to think heaven and hell were out of proportion. That the actions of humans did not deserve such extremes, she said.'

'I'll tell him about running into you.'

'Narayan? He is not likely to register, is he? In any case, all of it seems to have happened to other people.' Ava glances at her watch.

'It's late. I had better go, Ms Lenk.'

'How are you going back? Uber?'

'I have my cycle.'

'Yes, cycles are useful.' Ava opens the door for me.

'So long Ms Lenk.'

I pedal slowly. When I reach the beginning of Woodstock Road, the back tire bursts, and I leap to the ground. There is a rumble in the northern sky. I lift my head from the road and watch out for the next sortie of Stukas. They come low and screaming, and I bury my head in my hands. The centuries surround me with fire, fed by pride in race, nation, and faith. I lie on the road, head cradled in my hands. The road is cold. I inhale deeply the smell of gasoline and wait for the tanks. It is my war, but the others started it before my time. The earth ruptures all around me. The map of the earth is a network of human fault lines. Minutes pass. The tanks don't come. When my head is clear, I pick myself up and roll the cycle back to the hostel. I am the Jew wandering through the ages.

Look Mother, How They Keep Us Waiting

After much deliberation, Aanand had altered his name by an additional 'a', indicative of his bliss, post-enlightenment. But one old grief still clung to him. The one that stopped his journey and brought him back to Delhi from his one-man roadshow.

He sat by the large window of a Cafe Coffee Day outlet and watched from under his cap, the guard opening Kabuki for business at 10 am sharp. The guard wore a fake military uniform, and carried a long, country-made gun over his shoulder. Aanand placed a hand on his fluttering chest. 'Calm down,' he said to his heart, which had been not in control since he read the short mail from Osip informing him about Sangita; the message cautioned him not to hold Elizabeth or Osip responsible if the information proved to be incorrect. Elizabeth madam suggested that he, Osip, get in touch with Aanand. 'So Osip is with Elizabeth,' Aanand had vaguely thought before the implications of the mail fully hit him. 'Sangita who? Where?' He felt sick, as if a deep pit had opened in his stomach; there was a rush of bile into his mouth. He spat it out, shut his eyes;

he ignored the sudden ache behind his eyes, just beneath the brow.

The mail had arrived right in the middle of his successful All-India Deep Life Tour, when he was about to reach Belgaum on the border between Maharashtra and Karnataka. There were people gathered on either side of the town's main road to welcome him. Aanand wondered if it was his designer robes that invoked the flattering public attention, or the assuredness with which he held out the prospect of self-actualization in a poor country, so corrupt and confused morally and materially that it did not know what corruption and confusion were, clamouring for mutually exclusive dividends like success and salvation. An escape, in short, from the petty and vicious business of living. The kind of people that mostly came to his sessions wanted to believe in God, whom they probably experienced more like a rumour that might turn out to be true if they didn't pay sufficient attention; heaven could turn out to be true. Although most of the people who flocked to his meetings seemed to belong to the middle-income group, of late the wealthier set had begun trickling in.

On the road, as Aanand rode, he saw the poor of the villages living hand to mouth; still they did not grudge the man who owned the land they tilled for more years than they could remember. In another country, there would be murder. Here they committed suicide. Indebted farmers ending lives in their thousands was news only when their numbers surged in the fallow season. The poor explained to themselves the terrible lives they led as karma. Aanand could not fully comprehend their stubborn faith in Lord Krishna or Ram, given the great deprivations the gods seemed to visit on them if only by an absence of their active intervention. Why make so many millions pay for the sins in their previous births, especially since they could not remember their other lives?

Almost every second week, there was news about Aanand's events in the local media in Bikaner, Surat, Nagpur. When there was nothing new to say, they still carried his photograph with a caption that aspired to be clever but fell perhaps a little short. The pictures often showed Anand riding his bike in orange robes flowing in the wind, under headlines like 'Bliss on Bike' or, 'Monk Bites Bullet'. Anand would travel through the day, stop in the evening by whichever town he was transiting through to explain how yoga began as a science founded by Shiva—Aadi Yogi—himself, and how it liberated the practitioners. Yoga initiated them into the awareness of vertical consciousness—Universal Being—as opposed to horizontal consciousness—social being. All you needed to do was to activate the chakras, culminating in the opening of the pineal gland, and access the cosmic energies.

'Guruji, what to think of while breathing in and out?' someone would ask.

'Why must you think about anything while breathing? In fact, when you become aware of your breathing, you stop thinking.'

'We have so many thoughts, Guruji.'

'Not thoughts, worries maybe. Feel the sensations of your abdomen, or nose, hands, feet. Feel the act of breathing. The rest will take care of itself. Thoughts might still come, but they will lose their power over you.'

The seeker's eyes shone with hope.

'Keep the spine upright, breathe in using the navel muscles, give them time to fill your chest and let it go into your head, to the third eye, and as slowly breathe out. In-breath, out-breath. Feel your breath. You will find your rhythm.'

'It's very difficult, Swami.'

'To breathe? Try stopping it.'

The crowd tittered.

'In breath, out-breath,' Aanand repeated. He took in the crowd. A flash of genuine sympathy went out from him to them. Such despair to be happy. What has the world done to them? What have they done to the world?

They closed their eyes.

'The present is full of possibilities,' Aanand said, almost talking to himself. 'To realize it, you must stop thinking. Camping in the past and worrying about the future are caused by ignorance. We will help you to get rid of ignorance. *Tat Twam Asi*. You are That.'

'Do all of us have to be physically present in your sessions?'

'Well, teleportation will do equally well.'

The crowd laughs.

'I meant my mother, who is too unwell to come for the satsangs, Guruji.'

'Ah. Well, soon we will have a department which works and prays for those who are unable to do it themselves. Depending on your mother's karmic destiny, we will devise a mantra, which will be written and chanted on her behalf 10,000 times a day by a team of professionals, and she can watch it on video.'

Aanand hoped no one will ask him who's the 'we' yet? Right now, he was all by himself. But people had been approaching to join his team. Some highly qualified. Some just looking for a job. Among the second group was Idris. He had made several calls of appeal. He was on the run, he reminded Aanand. And he could not go back home; his father's killers were waiting for him; his mother and sisters had moved to his uncle's home in Faisalabad, far from his village. Aanand had said, as gently as possible, that one's God often limited one's prospects. Idris was a Muslim. That cut short a lot of avenues even before he was born. This was Hindu country. Just about every religion, as they said, had an official home country. Why not India for Hindus?

Aanand looked out. The trees outside glinted and glowed like chandeliers in the last light. He had come far in a short time. This morning, one Mr Arun Dudani, representing the media baron Alok Jain, had called him up and offered him a verbal contract. 'This is just a chat, a causerie,' Mr Dudani said, after introducing himself as the Chairman's Chief Executive Servant.

'The Chairman,' Aanand made a mental note.

'Yes,' Anand said. Say yes to everything and take the risk? He must refer 'causerie' to Sheetla.

'If you allow me, we could do FaceTime. We cut the costs of travel and time, and in the Chairman's world, time is money.'

'Sure.'

A minute later, Mr Dudani appeared on the screen, standing behind an executive chair and looking down at Aanand, his neck stretched tight as if by an invisible rope over the buttoned-up high collar.

'There you are. You look younger and more handsome than I remember from media photographs.'

'Thank you.' Aanand placed his hand on his heart in false modesty.

'And you are all over the place.'

'Just carrying out a mission.'

'The Chairman thinks you will go far. He believes in the idea of spiritual India. It's a huge market, and as yet under-tapped, he says.'

'Mr Alok Jain is a visionary businessman.'

'Yes, a great visionary. And if the Chairman believes a man will go far, he will.' Mr Dudani wet his lips. 'The man has no choice. The Chairman's vision is ineluctable.'

'Yes.' Ineluctable.

'Now, here's the deal. Considering your potential as a brand, the long years ahead of you, and the crowd you are pulling across the country, the Chairman has an offer for you.'

'Yes?'

'We buy from you the rights to broadcast your yoga and meditation sessions.'

'Yes.' As man separated himself from God in all that he did, so money needed to be separated from man. The first was tragedy. The second was art.

'Now, if that takes off…*if*,' Mr Dudani raised a finger in warning, 'if that takes off, the sky is the limit. The sky. Together then we launch herbal products branded Aanandam.'

'Herbal products?'

'Shampoo, toothpaste, soap. But cheap. We sell cheap. It's an economy of scale, you understand? We will be at a loss in the beginning. But the Chairman is ready to take that hit. Desi is the market of the future. Buy Indian, be Indian.'

'And what do I get in return?'

'Good question. Free publicity, a flat cover-fee.'

Is that enough? What did he need most? 'Why don't you help me build an ashram in Delhi or Gurgaon?'

'Ashram?'

'Aanandashram. Yes. I am sure you have land in these places.'

'That's an idea for sure.' Mr Dudani clasped his hands together, at an arm's distance, in front of him, as if they did not belong to him. 'I am not in a position to say yes or no to that. An ashram is a real estate decision, not media and content, not my department.'

'We can have an arrangement for you to recover the real estate expenses as part of my fee. In instalments, of course.'

'Hmm.' Mr Dudani hawked his throat.

'You could shoot the sessions there live. Good for you, good for me.'

'As I said, it's an idea. But I have to refer to the Chairman on this.'

'You contacted me,' Aanand reminded Mr Dudani. 'I am in no hurry.'

'Give me a little time. The Chairman is acquiring land in New York for a spiritual park. A spiritual park! And then he flies to London for an honorary doctorate in London. Well-deserved, of course. He is a pioneering businessman, after all. Once he is back, we start the paperwork. Meanwhile, I hope to visit you in person soon.'

'You are most welcome, Sir.'

'I will be in touch. The Chairman's word is the law for me. The law.' Mr Dudani clasped his hands above his head and stretched. 'Where have I caught you now in your whirlwind tour? When are you planning to pass through Delhi?'

'Just now? In Belgaum. Another month, and I should be back.'

'Yes, all right then. We can't let the Chairman down. All of us depend on him.'

But just a day later, here Aanand was, at Delhi's South Extension, watching out for a woman who might be his mother, based on a photograph that Osip sent, a night selfie that Elizabeth Madam had taken with Ms Sangita Ering in a bar. He had cut short his trip at Belgaum and taken a flight to Delhi. Aanand took deep breaths looking unblinkingly in the direction of Kabuki. How was he supposed to cross-check the information—short of asking Ms Ering if, indeed, she was his mother: 'Greetings, Madam, are you my mother?' And why should she affirm or deny these deep and almost mocking questions from a stranger?

Aanand had changed his robes for a pair of blue jeans and a white shirt. He had been living in those theatrical costumes long enough to feel stripped of his powers on their removal. He trimmed his hair and shaved his beard. 'My hair grows fast,' he thought. In an emergency, he could always use a wig. Or a fancy turban. 'What was more important, your mother or your career? Career, of course.' He looked around. No, there was no one watching him. It didn't make sense to draw the attention of the people to an up and arriving swami spying on a woman who might be his mother. All it took to portray him as a pervert was a tweet. When Aanand had recovered from Osip's cryptic mail, his first instinct was to call up Yolanda. He might not like it, but Yolanda was the bridge to his past. Aanand carefully worked out a conversation in his head:

'*Suprabhatam*, Yolanda madam. Aanand speaking.'

'Aanand!'

'All well, madam?'

'Christ. Yes. Where are you? I have been seeing your pictures all over the newspapers. You have become a star just in a few months.'

'How have you been, madam? The school doing well?'

'I am all right. Yes, the school is doing fine. It doesn't need me. No one does, I am finding out.'

'Now you must live to realize yourself, madam.'

'Teach me, Aanand. You have earned an extra 'a' in your name now, I see.'

'I am just an instrument, madam. God has been generous.'

'Yes! Who would have thought? Anything I can do?'

'Actually, yes. It's about my mother. I suppose I do have a mother?'

'Of course, Aanand, what a thing to say.'

'Would you have any idea where she is, Yolanda Madam?'

'Yes. I was waiting for you to ask.'

Yolanda would proceed to give Aanand the details, and confess her willingness to share with them some of his father's wealth. But that was not the conversation Aanand had.

When Yolanda had picked up after the fourth ring, all he could ask after the preliminaries was a visceral, 'Do you know where my mother is? Any idea at all?' Aanand heard Yolanda's sharp intake of breath.

'What? Your mother? No, no. Aanand, you never showed any interest before.'

'Is she in Delhi?'

'I have no idea. I am sorry. And you should not be searching for her.'

'What does she look like?'

'I am sorry, I haven't met her ever.'

'You have absolutely no clue? She never got in touch with you?'

'No. That was part of the understanding, remember?'

Yes, an understanding. An understanding of this sort always benefited the stronger party. 'Just how could you do that to a helpless woman,' he thought, as he hung up.

Aanand glanced at the Cafe's wall clock. Five past ten. The minutes dragged. The weight of his personal history was slowing time down. At 10.10, he saw a woman in a short shirt and jeans walk with unhurried steps into the clinic. Ms Sangita Ering? Though he was only across a narrow street, he could not be sure. He waited for a few more minutes, then hurried down the loosely carpeted stairs, and stepped out. 'Would Ms Ering have left when he was negotiating the steps? No,' he thought. 'Banish all anxieties. Be grateful. To who?' He glanced at the tiny florist's shop wedged in an orphaned doorframe, next to Kabuki. Gullu's Flowers. The young shop owner was sprinkling water on the roses. Gullu smiled at him with one part of his mouth like a line that had gone wayward. Aanand pushed open the glass door of Kabuki and was immediately conscious of a calming flute in the air. 'He must have music like this,' he thought, 'in his ashram. If and when.'

'Yes, can I help you?' The receptionist, a middle-aged lady with a bluish bucktooth and painted lips, asked him.

'I would like to see Ms Sangita Ering.'

'Ms Sangita Ering is busy. Is it professional?'

'Yes.' So she is here. Whoever she was.

'This is regarding?'

'My sister wanted to thank Ms Ering for a favour.'

'She is expected?'

'No. She is abroad.'

'I will see if Ms Ering is free. We don't encourage personal visits.'

The receptionist attended a call in a voice that came the closest to an answering machine.

'No, the doctor is not in yet,' she said into the phone. She pointed Aanand to a sofa.

'Take a seat. Who should I say has come?'

'Osip Bala Krishnan,' Anand said.

He walked toward the sofa, sat under the sign: NO CASH. NO NARCOTICS. Anand saw that there was a photograph on the sidewall of Ms Sangita Ering under the label, 'Employee of the Week.' Sangita appeared grim in it. 'That's a wig she is wearing,' he thought. He studied the features. 'Besides the high cheeks they both shared, there seemed little in common. And why wear a wig? Absurd.' Aanand felt breathless. He looked up at the receptionist. She was preoccupied with her computer. 'Had she spoken to Sangita about him? Had she any idea, what was going on around her; the people whom she greeted every day? The secrets that they carried about them, making them live double and triple lives? Perhaps, it was the secrets that made us all too human? The little and big lies that turned us new from moment to moment, inventing purposes to go on. Aanand looked at the Employee of the Week again. 'Look, mother, how they make me wait for you.' There was just a door between the two of them.

And a wall.

And a man. Mr Andrade.

And the world.

Aanand got up and left.

Out on the road, all of it seemed unreal. 'Mother.' He said the word aloud as if it were a thing. An object. A woman. One who let go of her baby, like a balloon over the sea. Bye, bye, baby, go away, it's for your good, the wind will take care of you. And Aanand had turned out like this, a young man, who could bring himself to believe in no one. Who neither laughed nor cried. Who was afraid to love. Who only wanted to be rich. Whose fault was it? Who made the wrong decision to sleep with a man out of her league? What was she thinking? And what if Ms Sangita Ering was his mother? What will come of it? First tears of remorse, no doubt. Later, perhaps the sharing of experiences, and consolations of a common pain. Then, a lifetime of recriminations that hard fought for unions brought. But…there would be love. With all its defects. The thing that made people depend on each other, tamed them, made them stand in line for each other's ration. Aanand could not conceive of love and its softening effect on him. He was nothing without anger and vengeance, he knew. He looked around. The traffic had picked up. People moved about with purpose. Normal people. Just like him. Plotting at career moves. Hoping to buy a shirt. Wanting to kill their spouse. Throw a mug at their boss. People hallucinating normal life. Looking for love and life, fucking these up when they got them. Ordinary people. Each one insane in his own way, and at large. Just containing it drove them crazy. Aanand wanted to be back where he belonged, back with the anonymous B-grade town crowd looking up to him as he doled out the eternal. Back where no one asked him about his origins; or held out love like a red flag. Back where there was a future, but no past. 'Make a run for it, Guruji,' he told himself. 'Run fast and far.' Instead, he bought flowers at Gullu's. A bunch of yellow and crimson rosebuds.

'Have I seen you somewhere?' Gullu asked.

'Yes, I am very famous,' Aanand smiled.

He went back into Kabuki, aware this was the first time he had bought flowers in his life.

'Oh, there you are. I was looking for you,' the receptionist said. 'You just disappeared.'

'I went and bought these flowers.'

'They are beautiful. Let me talk to Ms Ering again. Please don't vanish.'

Aanand sat on the same spot on the sofa. A health magazine on a side table told him the best coital position to conceive a boy was missionary.

A minute later, he was aware someone was standing next to him in a kimono.

'You vere asking for me? I am Sangita.'

Aanand got to his feet. 'Osip Bala Krishnan.'

'Vat can I do for you? Please sit,' Sangita said.

They sat down, the rosebuds blooming between them.

'My mother is a good looking woman,' Anand thought, 'and mild-spoken, her English broken and lilting.'

'I dropped by to express thanks on behalf of my sister.'

'I am sorry, I can't seem to recall who your sister vas.'

'It was a little over a year ago. It's the baby's birthday today. She had come for some tests and consultation and you were very kind and reassuring.'

'That's so nice of her. So many patients come and go. Very few have the time to keep in touch. Vat's her name?'

'Sheetla. Sheetla Balakrishnan.'

'Sheetla? No, I am afraid I can't recall anyone by that name. All vell with her?'

'Yes, she is a single mother. The girl is fine too. They are in the US.'

'Single mothers have it tough.'

'Yes.'

'What do you do? Still in college?'

'I am a salesman. Ayurvedic products.'

'Isn't that a racket?' Sangita smiled.

'It is one of those things. Are you from here, Ms Ering?'

'Purvanchal Pradesh.'

Aanand felt nauseous.

'But I left the place years ago. Decades. Never returned.' Sangita lowered her voice a notch further. 'We are not allowed to talk about personal things during office hours.'

'Of course. I am sorry. Here, my sister sends flowers to you.'

Aanand lifted the foil-wrapped bouquet, and handed it over to Sangita.

'They are so beautiful. Thank you. Vhat a gift to begin the day!' Sangita shook her head in disbelief. 'But I have vork to do.'

They got up.

'I will be off then.' He realized he was a little disappointed that she did not look like Mr Andrade.

'Are you from Delhi?'

'No. I am from the hills. I rarely come down.'

'Oh, vell. Thank you again. And give my regards to your sister and nephew.'

'Niece.'

'Yes, niece.'

They shook hands.

At the door, Aanand turned. Sangita stood looking at him, the roses held close to her heart.

'My sister will be happy to know I met you.' Aanand opened the door.

The world enveloped him with its fierce and focused purposelessness. People. Cars. Auto-rickshaws. Dust. He was safe at large, away from the one person who might tell him who he was. And whom, he knew, he would never see again.

Scherzo. Lullaby. Serenade

For a fortnight or so Elizabeth Hill disappeared. She must have had enough of me. I didn't blame her, though I thought her conduct erratic even by her own standards. I waited in street corners from where wafted perfumes mixed with the welding odour of the crowd: unwashed human bodies, beer, petrol, and English sewage; women wearing black walked past me with hair streaming in the wind; men with backpacks looked at me with suspicion. When the cold got too much or when my feet were exhausted, I wandered into unwelcoming coffee places.

A few days later, Arjun would wire me some money with a note saying Maina was on the ventilator. His novel, four years in the making, and the only one he had written, had been rejected by publishers. 'Maina was right Osip, I am no genius, just a mediocre, if wayward, writer. Began with a bang, perhaps, but must end, muttering into my pillow, how none of it matters.' Dev, Diya, and others of the Union had summoned him for a meeting. Diya asked him if he had read Michel Foucault on the problem of subjectivity and the State. He hadn't, he told them. 'Well, never mind,' Diya said, 'it was up to the progressive rights groups, like the Union, to resist, and forge a people's state, virtual though it may be, but no less real, through social media and related technologies; group identity—people agreeing on norms of acceptable politics and social conduct—was crucial; and in this sadly Arjun was a misfit; actually a threat, sorry.'

'I do feel like a sinner, Osip, and every time I see a woman now, I try to think of God, altogether a new state of mind for me, because lust, which was once an aspiration, is now almost a punishable thought. No doubt my head has been tampered with, and the fact that it was indeed lust persuades me to believe the worst of me, though I know there is a trap there, too, because it is easier to mistake a hard opinion of oneself for the truth—for surely truth would always be unpleasant?—rather than be justly charitable to one self. I can't be *that* bad. But myth or malaise, we all have one, and whose unravelling is inseparable from the process of becoming ourselves,' Arjun said, 'and so I shall not apologize, for they are sure to equate an apology with admission, best to take comfort for the remaining years of my contrarian life as a much wronged man; there is no redemption without self-deception, perhaps.'

Arjun continued to remain cancelled then, but I had not paused to think about him. Elizabeth had consumed me like fire, even though I knew that Elizabeth was a project fuelled by my ingratitude, and fed by others' charity. Charity, and found meals. Like this morning, at a coffee place, when I ordered a coffee and while waiting for it, I saw a plate of half-eaten vegetable sandwich, which I gobbled, hoping no one would notice. I had had nothing since morning. I skipped lunch, drank, made friends with a street dog whose eyes seemed to laugh at the humans around him, and was full of antics. I bought him a bun and, in return, he loved me for a whole minute, like only a dog could, and disappeared. Late in the evening, I went for a walk. The sky had begun to shake out the first stars. I stepped around a clutch of Arab-looking refugees with their blankets pulled tight down over their heads and their shabby bags pitched around them. The homeless smelled like snot mixed with coal. When it was night, I made my way to Kris's place. I wasn't looking for him. I was looking for Elizabeth, though she had told me she did not live with him, before she went missing.

I crossed the path of light on the gravel, pressed the buzzer. 'Would I be bothering Kris?' How pious of me. And the truth was, my concern for him was genuine. Like that of a professional killer who did not want to unnecessarily hurt his victim. So, would I be bothering him, turning up at his door without notice? Yes, this was not India. You did not just drop by and pleasantly surprise your uncles and aunts—angles and ants, Anand would mime—in their various states of chaos. This was England, hag-ridden by formalities to exercise rigour over impulses. Manners were a means not to shock people, hold society in place. I pressed the switch twice. Listened for sound of movement. Nothing. The air condensed on my forehead. I shifted my weight from foot to foot, leaned on the wall, turned to go. The door opened. It was Elizabeth. Did she lie about not staying at Kris's then? Of course. Or has she moved in recently?

She stared at me for a moment. 'Oh, OB.'

'Hello. Long time.' I felt weak with desire.

'What are you doing here?'

'I....' Looking for you. Always looking for you.

'You can't be here.'

'I didn't think you would be here.'

'Where did you think I was?'

'Not here.'

'I had to move house on short notice.'

'I came to say bye to Kris. I am going back, Ms Hill.'

'To India? Come on in. It's cold.'

Elizabeth wore a white sweater and nothing else. Her legs gleamed. I followed her in dread and awe of what she might offer or withhold. She could do anything with me, and I would feel it was just. She led me past the dim-lit hall with its solitary table and the shuttered telescope. Through a short passage, up the stairs, into her bedroom.

'Are you feeling cold?'

'No.' Yes.

'You look pale.'

'I feel pale.'

She took my face in her hands and kissed me, as if she was throwing it all away.

'I missed you,' she said.

'I haven't thought of anything else.' I said.

'What else is there for you to think?'

'War,' I thought. It was love and war. Variations of a theme.

'That's true.'

'I know this is wrong. But this makes me feel alive.'

'Why is it wrong? I really can't tell.'

'Because it has no future. And you are my student.'

'I am no longer your student.'

'Anyway, here we are.'

And precisely at my grand-uncle's house.

'Are you wondering about Kris?'

'Yes.'

'He is a good man. But how fast one outgrows one's mentors.'

'Because he is old?'

'He is a beautiful being.' She said it in a way that implied: and this is what we do to beautiful beings.

Elizabeth kissed me. I returned the kiss. At first softly. Then hard and clinging. Demanding more. A moment later, our bodies took over. There was only an overwhelming need to give and take. Elizabeth removed her sweater. She worked her way down, bit my nipples, counted my ribs with her tongue.

'I like that,' I said as she unzipped my jeans and took me in her mouth.

'I like it, too. This is a good way to speak. And the mic is in my control.'

'Check, check. One two cha cha cha.'

We made love. Fucked the universe to a stop.

'Just in case you are wondering, OB. That was the great

spiritual fuck people try to live for and write about. You get to see it mostly in movies.'

'Really?'

'Trust me. Of course, then you sort of forget it. And look around for the next great spiritual fuck. What are you thinking?'

'Will you come with me to India?'

Elizabeth turned away from me.

'Ms Hill?'

'Will I come with you to India? No. Do you like India?'

'No.'

'Do you like England?'

'No.'

'Why don't you like the country in which you are born?'

'Why doesn't the Bogong stick to New South Wales instead of traveling 1000 kilometres to the caves in Victoria and then flit back?'

'Bogong what?'

'A moth.'

'You are not the Bogong. Besides, it always goes back, you said.'

'Only to start again.'

Have you been reading up on butterflies?'

'Just a bit that I remembered. If everyone liked the place they were born, the first man would not have walked out of Africa.'

'The first woman.'

'The first woman.'

'Do you belong here, Ms Hill?'

'More than any other place. The sun here is mild and many-hued, you know. The reassuring smell of bad machine coffee and McDonald's burgers in town centres, and the way everybody smiles at you without looking you in the eye when you are in their way. And the Islamic pious reading out Quran in market squares. And every third person has a running nose. It's all very comforting. This is the people I like to return to after adventures.'

'Consider me an adventure. Please come with me.' I traced her back with my finger. Her spine was so straight.

Elizabeth turned to face me. 'And how will we live?'

'I will look for a job.'

'Man of the house. But, no. It won't work out.'

'Arjun said the chairman of the *India Post*, Alok Jain, will be in London for an honorary doctorate. I know his daughter.'

'I see you are in touch with him.'

'He has been a great friend. His wife is on a ventilator.'

'Oh. I am sorry to hear that.'

'He wants her gone, he said. Exit from pain, you know?'

'This is good post-coital talk.'

'Sorry.'

'Go on.'

'Cancer is awful, isn't it?'

'Can we stop talking about death, please?'

'Yes.'

'You are too young for a full-time job.'

'When 15-year-olds fight wars, they are not too young.

When a 19-year-old takes up a job, it is not done. I can vote and fuck, but I can't be going to an office? I am going on 20 now.'

'Have you ever voted?'

'No.'

'There. And who said you can fuck? You shouldn't be fucking, too. Why don't you stay back?'

'It's too expensive. The college, too, if I get around to that. And no one will give me a job here.'

'Oh, well, let's have a drink.'

'To what?'

'To your job? When is the doctorate function of your friend?'

'Not my friend. Friday.'

'I'll come with you.'

Elizabeth shifted her weight and lay by my side. When she came a moment ago, her lips parted and eyes closed, she had seemed like someone else, a beautiful stranger in touch with her primal being, beyond reach. At that moment, I could have committed murder for her. Or theft. In a way, I was doing both. But I felt no remorse. No guilt. It was just dare. And truth. We lay in bed, naked, willing Kris to come; waited for him to make that terrible entry through the trick door of time into this room, into doom. But Kris refused to make an appearance.

We looked for our clothes in the dark. Elizabeth wore my briefs over her head, before throwing it in my direction. I wore her bra, and it didn't look good on me. We got dressed. 'Is this the right time to end our lives?' I asked her. It felt like the perfect moment. I had an image of us both, holding hand in hand, stepping over a skyscraper's ledge, deep in conversation.

'Why, no, not for me.' Elizabeth took my hand in hers. We made our way down the steps. Elizabeth flicked on the kitchen lights. Kris stood leaning on the counter, drinking wine.

'There you two are,' Kris said.

'Oh my god.' Elizabeth said, but she did not let go of my hand.

'Go for the Merlot,' Kris pointed his glass at the bottle beside him. 'Napa Valley. I just opened it. Nice and dry. Some whiskies and wines do not travel well. This one does. '

'I think I had better go,' I said.

'You've been to Napa Valley, Osip?'

'No, Kris.'

'California. Heaven on earth. Where are the places you have been to?'

'Kerala, Bombay, Kasauli, Delhi.'

'Oxford,' Elizabeth said.

'Oxford.'

'You have been to Bombay? Did you tell me about it before?' Elizabeth said.

'Spent a couple of weeks there on a summer vacation. I didn't like the place. Too crowded. Too noisy.'

'Yeah, too everything. You must like Oxford the most, young man,' Kris said.

'How long have you been here, Kris?' Elizabeth asked.

'Long enough, I think. It's my home, remember?' Kris said. 'Let me fix you guys a drink.' Kris handed a glass to us each, poured wine. 'To the teacher and to her disciple,' he raised his glass and downed it. 'Come, sit. The kitchen table is meant for three.'

'Let him go,' Elizabeth said.

'Why?'

'I am responsible for this.'

'You are not responsible for anything, Elizabeth. You can't be responsible. Not in your nature.'

'Kris, I am sorry.'

'You are?'

'The fact is you have become the crabby old man you never wanted to be. It is terrible what people end up as.'

'So you are not sorry. You are just repelled by old age, that's all it is. I understand, ' Kris looked at me helplessly. His impotent rage seemed to have given way to resignation. 'She is the world I am fading from,' he said.

I thought of Maina.

'That's not the way to look at this.' Elizabeth said.

'But why does this still feel like betrayal?' Kris asked.

'Because for all your wisdom you are seeing me as yours.'

'You chose to come and stay here.'

'How does that translate into a right of proprietorship? Or a curtailment of my personal preferences?'

'Proprietorship? Me?'

'This space is your world. This is the space in your head. In there you have granted me a few liberties.'

'You are the victim, I see. So, what are you doing here under my roof making love to my grand-nephew? You realize that soon enough his raptures will bore you?'

'Relationships don't work to prescriptions, Kris.' Elizabeth caressed my head. 'You are embarrassing the boy.'

'A small price for him to pay for being your man, I am sure...Hardly a boy.'

Kris poured himself another drink. 'How long has it been going on? Since your Kasauli days?'

We waited as the wine filled the room with its sound.

'I thought you were spiritual, Kris. It turns out you are an impostor. All this silence and meditation and order is a sham.'

'Everything is spiritual, don't you get it?'

'No.'

'Fucking the daylights out of each other. Which you two just did. I could hear it all down here. I bet at some point it turned spiritual, whatever trash you mean by that word.'

'I must be going,' I said.

'You came to my house without my permission. The least you can do is to ask my leave before you run out.'

'OB, stay. I'll come with you.' Elizabeth said.

'Will you come with me to India?'

Elizabeth looked at Kris for a moment. Then keeping her eyes on him, said, 'Yes, of course.'

Kris suddenly smiled and his face relaxed. It was as if a decision of life had been reached for him and he had no responsibility in the process. 'Have you been in touch with Thrissur?'

I wondered if he was about to insult me in some intimate, familial way. 'No.'

'Well, I got in touch with your grandmother.'

Alarm bells rang in my head.

'I said you were fine. That we met. She was worried. "He needs care," she said.'

'Thank you, Kris.'

'Shall we go, OB?' Elizabeth asked.

'How's my brother?' I asked Gloria. "He is in 1956," she said. "Moscow, February 25, to be precise."'

'Oh. Khrushchev's secret speech at the 20th Party Congress where he denounced Stalin as a mass killer and a cult leader.'

'Ah, yes.'

'He has got a copy of that speech in the back of his bottom drawer.' I felt instantly closer to Kris than Elizabeth.

'Well, he now believes that the copy in there has been replaced with a tampered one. He says it is a part of a plot to undermine Stalin's legacy.'

'I wish I was with him. He talks to me.'

'Maybe it is time you returned, helped him locate the original document.'

'OB, finish your drink and let's go,' Elizabeth said.

'There is nothing as representative of these times as a young, beautiful woman who knows her mind, out to live her life.'

'You are just jealous, Kris.'

'Yes. Add to it the fact that as you grow old you lose your right to demand anything. Old age should be banned.'

'Are you done with your insults?' Elizabeth asked.

'No.'

'Tough. Let's go, OB,' Elizabeth said.

'Elizabeth,' Kris began, and then stopped.

I saw an old man in the throes of love, an affliction that could strike you at any age. I had thought that one's immunity rose with the years, that the heart resisted as it greyed the visions of vistas of happiness that passion and beauty conjured up. But I was wrong. One's innocence never ended. Nor hope.

All through the exchange, Kris never raised his voice. His words were clear and strong. But I had never seen such sadness stare out of a face. It was like the last, slow farewell of a man to his fondest dream. I worried if he would end his life. I would have found it correct, too, if he stabbed us with the kitchen knife in the rack by his side. I had seen Kris glancing at the rack. The thought might have crossed his mind. Murder was no longer an incomprehensible act. It could even be just. Instead, Kris smiled at us. He took his phone out. He pressed a button. A moment later, the room lilted with the tenderest of sounds longing for the woman who danced in your hands and, even as you held her and moved with her, she slipped away elusive as a shadow into the receding horizons of one's life, where began another's world, taking her promise of eternity to *him*, to continue the endless waltz of hope and loss, beauty and love. The phone seemed connected to invisible speakers.

'Shostakovich. Waltz No 2. Original score, 1938. Made popular as the soundtrack of the movie, *Anna Karenina*,' Kris announced with a bow. 'Everything a man can feel for a woman, Elizabeth, no matter what his age or race, is here. Scherzo. Lullaby. Serenade.'

We listened, entranced. For a short while we ceased to be ourselves; we were in the presence of a thing greater than us.

'Dance, Elizabeth?' Kris asked gently.

Elizabeth seemed to think hard, her face flushed from wine and embarrassment. She looked at me.

'Please dance,' I said. I saw that Kris's love was indistinguishable from a great loss, a death almost.

'Let's go into the hall,' Elizabeth said.

The music followed us.

Kris was a graceful dancer. But soon he was slowing down.

'Come on, OB, join the gang,' Elizabeth said.

'Nope. I am short of breath. You two go ahead,' Kris said. 'Three can't waltz anyway.'

'We weren't waltzing. Kris, another minute won't kill you. Quick, OB,' Elizabeth held out her hand, without letting Kris go.

I took it. 'I don't know how to dance.'

'It's letting go,' Kris said.

I joined them. We held hands, but did not move well together. So we stopped.

Kris walked toward the telescope. 'It's a clear night. Osip, let me show you a few stars.'

'He doesn't want to be alone,' I thought. 'How did we come to this?'

'I have never seen the sky through a telescope,' I said.

'We see more,' Kris said, 'much more than the naked eye is meant to see.'

The Contract

Kris insisted that he drive us to India House, Aldwych. 'I have to be going to meet someone in London anyway to plan for a trip. And the three of us will get time to talk,' he said.

Elizabeth and I had decided that we would skip the honorary doctorate ceremony of Alok Jain, and go for drinks and dinner later in the evening. We avoided the subject of Kris in our conversation. 'One betrayed in love; one's happiness was often at the expense of someone else's,' Elizabeth said; there was only a limited supply of the stuff.

In the car, on the way to London, Elizabeth and I were tense, like children apprehensive of quarrelsome parents in a captive space. Kris whistled. But his one eye twitched. I could see Elizabeth did not like the whistling, though he was doing a good job of it.

'Please stop whistling, Kris.'

'From the Ryan Gosling movie, *Drive*,' Kris said. 'There's something inside you, it's hard to explain; they're talking about you, boy, but you're still the same.'

Kris stopped whistling.

Elizabeth turned her face to the window. No one could be as bored as Elizabeth when the mood was upon her.

We hit the Expressway. Farmlands opened up on either side.

Kris asked, 'When are you guys off to India?'

'Soon,' Elizabeth said. 'We have yet to buy the tickets.'

'I am looking for a job,' I said. 'I need a job.'

'You get a job without a degree these days?' Kris asked. 'Looks tough to me. Especially in India. They believe in degrees.'

'As an editorial trainee to begin with. In a newspaper,' I said. 'OB knows the daughter of a news baron, Alok Jain.'

'The same guy whose event you are going to? I read somewhere the doctorate is conferred on him by a group of non-resident Indian shopkeepers.'

'Is it?' Elizabeth said. 'Well, it's an honorary doctorate, isn't it? And we, the British, are a nation of shopkeepers, too. Why can't they get together and confer a doctorate? How racist!'

'And you are going to work for him, Osip?' Kris ignored Elizabeth, who was saying 'No' to him in so many ways. 'For this fake baron?'

'He doesn't have a choice, does he? It's all based on Osip's merit.' Elizabeth said.

'Isn't he too young, even if it is an honorary job?'

'He is going on 20. They are watching porn at 12, Kris, and waging war for a greener planet before they are 13.'

'Ah, yes, there are only babies and adults these days. No children.'

'I have written a sample piece for them. For Mitali,' I said in vague self-defence.

'Mitali is Alok Jain's daughter,' Elizabeth explained to Kris. 'What's the piece on, OB?'

'On Bombay.'

'Bombay! You should have written on Kashmir,' Kris replied.

'Why should he do that?'

'I know nothing about Kashmir.'

'Who knows what their stance on Kashmir is!' Elizabeth said.

'Only because you raised the question of Kashmir at that seminar, remember?' Kris explained.

'That seminar!' Elizabeth said.

'I have been to Bombay! I keep saying that.'

'Bombay,' Kris nodded. 'That city is long gone, too, isn't it? The garbage. The crowds. Those trains! The last time I visited Bombay was 20 years ago. I have not been to India since,' Kris said.

'Hundreds die every year in Bombay trying to get into a train. For just wanting to reach their workplaces. It's a tough city. I am not sure what I wrote is any good.'

'So long as your piece has no mistakes,' Elizabeth said.

'Would you like to take a look at it, Elizabeth? Before I send it?'

'Is it too long?'

'No. It's on my phone.'

'Why don't you read it out to us?' Kris said.

'He wants me to check it for mistakes, Kris. I was his teacher after all.'

'The things you taught.'

'Kris!'

'Sorry. Read it aloud, if you don't mind. We have time.' Kris said.

'Will you read it out, Elizabeth?'

'All right.'

I handed over the phone to her. 'It's just an impressionistic piece.'

'Never be on the defensive. They are all waiting to tell you how sorry a thing you are, don't lend them a hand,' Kris said.

Elizabeth cleared her throat. 'Bombay: shit and sea, the elemental exhalations of the city,' Elizabeth began reading, 'the hot air wrapped itself around you like a foil. You passed a lane lined with buildings that leaned this way and that, draped in washing, and fluttering like flags of a whole Republic on the move, back and forth, the unceasing passage assuring you of anonymity. You could live and die here every day doing the same thing, going to work, coming back to your room, a speck of dust in the shadow of a stone. There are 20 million people in Bombay. But no one has a face, except the film stars. They are everywhere. Then you turned a corner, and walked into the sea, deep, blue as ink. Narrow lanes opened out into sudden eternity. The view from the plane landing in the city tells you what it is. Bombay is mostly slums, and tall buildings that rise like a middle finger from a fist of huts. Bombay has only one direction. Down. To distract themselves from the relentless fall, the distraught men and women switched on the brightest lights at night and, during the day, turned on the loudest speakers for Bollywood music and songs in praise of Lord Ganesh. Through everything, dirt and grime hung in layers after layers like unwashed curtains of time. Tiny temples of powerful but unknown deities blessed bent bodies, the houses of gods built of spotless pink or blue bathroom tiles on the encroached road, the extortionist's paradise…'

'Elizabeth reads so well,' Kris said. 'She makes everything sound like confidential information.'

'Yes,' I was disappointed that Kris commented on the reading but not the matter.

'It's not bad, Osip. Just a little over the top.' Kris said.

'It's an "impressionistic piece", he said. I like it OB, though it is a bit choppy. You need to call it something,' Elizabeth advised.

'I will give it a title,' I said.

'So long as Mitali or whoever likes it,' Kris said. 'Why didn't you write about Delhi?'

'Well, if he did, then you might ask him, why he did not write about Kasauli?'

'Kashmir. Why didn't he write about Kashmir, I asked.'

'That's what I meant,' Elizabeth said.

'Yes, but Kasauli, I'd understand. No, I did not mean that, Elizabeth.'

'We will let that pass.' Elizabeth put a hand behind and around the seat.

I gratefully took it, though I knew Kris would be hurt if he saw the gesture.

'OB, just call it Bombay and send it off. Before you get to meet Mitali. Best not to wait for afterward.'

'Right now?'

'Yes.'

'Anyone interesting coming to your party? Literary types?' Kris asked.

'I don't know,' I said, looking at the beautiful double-deckers and cars. How well they managed traffic on these narrow roads. We had reached the city.

'This is not that kind of gathering, is it?' Elizabeth said.

Kris slowed down the car. 'Well, here we are. That is Bush House. That's where I have to go.'

'Drop us here then,' Elizabeth said. 'India House is just down the road.'

'Are you sure?'

'Yes. Good to walk.'

'All right.' Kris manoeuvred the car to the side of the road and cut the engine.

All of us sat in the car silently, waiting for something.

'Kris,' Elizabeth took her seat belt off. 'I know what you are thinking of me. You've got it so wrong. It's about freedom. Sometimes when I think of freedom, I can't even begin to see its limits. Every moment of life is yours. Imagine. And yet one must do one's all to own a few of them. Elizabeth opened the door. 'I am sure you two have things to say to each other.' She got out of the car. 'Being myself has been a wonderful performance with men like you around.' She looked cold and sad like a statue raised amidst a people who had failed to recognize its merits.

Kris turned around to look at me, 'Quickly, now that we are alone, there's something I would like to give you, Osip.' He drew out a yellow envelope from the pocket of his jacket. 'I want you to keep this.' His right eye, now grown smaller than the left, continued to twitch.

'Thank you. What's it?'

'A letter that your grandfather wrote. It reached me years after he sent it. A scrap of paper without a beginning or end. Open it whenever. It's yours for keeps.'

'I'm sorry, Kris.'

'For what?'

'For everything.'

'Ah. Me too. I feel foolish and even older than my years. Elizabeth is so grand. I vaguely realize what she says about freedom could be true.'

'Maybe she is sorry, too. She doesn't open up easily.'

'I didn't know I could ache like this at this age. But long after the grape is gone, the wine still seasons in the vat,' Kris smiled. 'I might grow a beard. Calm, bearded, and wounded.'

'What...' I hesitated, 'what had you expected from her?'

Kris considered his hands on the steering wheel. 'It sounds strange now that I am saying it. I wanted her to help me live.' He paused. 'And, maybe, die, too.'

On the footpath, I saw Elizabeth pulling her jacket tight around her against the cold. The city lights seemed to swirl around her.

'Is love just a need to share the same secrets with a different person?' Kris said, looking at a tourist couple kissing across the road on the other side. They had materialized from a roofless, red-and-cream Big Bus.

'I have been meaning to say, I would rather if she did not return to my place, though.'

'Oh. I will tell her. But her stuff…'

'She has a key. She could take her things out in the next few days. I won't be home for a week from tonight. I am going up to Scotland with my friend here,' Kris pointed at Bush House.

I got out of the car.

Kris lowered the passenger window. 'Say hi to your people from me. One day I will drop by at Thrissur if I don't pop it.'

'You really should. Bye, Kris. Thank you for everything.'

'And please don't let Elizabeth make you think I am an asshole.'

'No, I will not.'

Kris put his thumb up, rolled back the window. But he didn't start the car.

'Let's go, kid.' Elizabeth put her arm around me.

We walked down the footpath in the direction of India House.

Kris would be watching us. We didn't turn back to look.

***

The guest of honour, Alok Jain, was gracious, and high. He smiled a lot. He was stocky, of middle height, and swept his shock of silver-grey hair straight back. He had a charming smile. His left hand was slightly bent at the elbow, and was a little shorter than the right. He wore a silk, lilac tunic. Mitali said in my ears, 'When Papa wears lilac it means it's party time for all. So enjoy.'

'Mitali?'

'Yes, OB?'

'I sent you a sample of my writing.' Did it come out as a major accusation?

'I got it just a while ago. Arjun has been talking about you. You know his wife passed away? She was in pain. Someone called up and told me. '

'Oh my god. When?'

'This morning.'

I wondered about the empty carton of Mysore sandalwood soap.

'But the nice bit is that in a moment of clarity she had her nurse put out a post declaring her love and appreciation for Arjun. For all his faults, one of the kindest men she knew, she said.'

'Oh, good.'

'Gracious of her.'

'So this job...'

'Arjun believes you are talented. But, OB, journalism is not literature, it's proofreading. I glanced through your piece. How old are you now?'

'Twenty, soon. You wouldn't want a permanent London Correspondent for your newspaper?'

'Get real, Osip Bala Krishnan. No Indian paper believes news good enough to consume happens abroad. It's dollars and pounds, besides. But a dowdy desk job in Delhi or Bombay should not be a problem. The salary we pay you is for not being yourself through the day, when you are in your senses, you understand? Media is a dirty business, OB, it is not what you think it is. It works on orders from the top. It's tied in with a lot of things that have little to do with news.'

'I don't care.'

'I will introduce you to Papa and Arun Dudani, the CEO.'

'I remember Mr Dudani. Is he here?'

Mitali pointed her chin at a tall, wiry man in a purple coat who seemed to both appear and disappear all at the same time around Alok Jain. 'Watch out for him,' Mitali said, 'that is a man who will do anything to keep his job.'

Elizabeth, stepping back into the hall from the washroom, caught Mitali's eye. 'And that beautiful creature lighting up the far corner must be Elizabeth. I saw you two entering.'

The ambassador, a tall man with arms that reached just below his waist, announced that Alok Jain would be soon instituting a Chair in Indian Business Studies in University College, London. Alok Jain was a great man, the ambassador said. Alok Jain thanked the Ambassador and made a short speech.

A Chair in business studies was the least he could do, Alok Jain said. 'India always was a spiritual superpower. Now it is going to be an economic superpower. Thanks to tradition.

The liberals blamed the caste system for everything. They had no idea. The caste system helped social order and generated wealth. I am a banya, a Marwari Jain, we don't hurt a fly, but we make money, which involves a kind of metaphysical violence, I admit. Business is in my blood. I respect Brahmins. But the Brahmins respect my caste, too, because I know how to make money. Without trade, there are no Brahmins. Caste is just another name for trade specialization. The Indian Business Studies Centre will focus on our traditional strengths. Our glorious future is in our golden past.'

'India looks forward to its past,' Arjun had once said.

Later, Mitali introduced Elizabeth and me to Alok Jain. 'Papa, I mentioned our young friend here to you.'

'Yes, I remember. We do need people who know English.'

'It's murder and misery reading the *India Post* every morning,' Mitali said. 'The Chennai Cement Company, not Semen Company.'

'We are working on it,' Mr Dudani materialised, seeing his boss in conversation.

'You have been working on it for long, Arun. Take the young man on the desk in Delhi,' Alok Jain said.

Mr Dudani clapped his hands without making noise, like a movie clip with its audio cut.

'And, Arun, get me a good newsman. I know now you can't edit, though you have been pretending to be an editor for some time now.'

It seemed for a moment that Alok Jain would slip into monster-mode.

Mr Dudani smiled disarmingly and tried to vanish, but failed. He dug up his phone from his pocket and said he would meet the caller the next morning.

'Who are you conspiring with?' Alok Jain asked.

'No one. I never conspire, Sir,' Mr Dudani said, sounding pained.

'I bet that was a code, a secret,' Alok Jain smiled his charming smile.

Mr Dudani bowed. He had survived another critical moment in his career, perhaps.

The ambassador sneezed and said he had a cold coming; the only thing he was afraid of was the common cold, he said to laughter, and retired.

Mr Dudani touched Alok Jain's feet, as if seeking his permission and blessing, then took over the mic, and broke into an old Kishore Kumar song:

Mere mehboob qayamat hogi,

Aaj rusva teri galiyon mein mohabbat hogi.

'What do the words mean?' Elizabeth asked.

'My love, today is doomsday; in your lane, my heart goes unclaimed, astray…' I said.

'He sings well,' Elizabeth said.

'I am proud of you, Arun,' Alok Jain said, taking the mic roughly from Mr Dudani, and pouring some whisky into his wine glass.

Alok Jain's face was flushed. 'I'm proud of Kishore Kumar, too. Those who are here and not Indians will not have an idea who Kishore Kumar is. He was the greatest playback singer of the century. The greatest. We ate from the same plate, Kishore Da and I. When he died, not one foreign newspaper mentioned it. Not one. That's why I started my newspaper. To see the world from India's perspective. Mark my words: the set of conventions of our nation is changing, and changing for the better. We are in the process of reinventing the age of the *Gita*: karma, faith, and detachment.' He looked around at the solemn faces, a little confused at the course of the evening, and shouted into the mic, 'So let's celebrate the rebirth of our nation.'

As if on cue, the DJ played a couple of fast Kishore Kumar numbers. Everyone danced. Mitali stood in a corner, watching the proceedings. I saw Alok Jain going up to her and saying something. She shook her head. I saw his face change. A moment later, he almost dragged Mitali by her hand and danced with her, his hands open, looking at his daughter with benevolence, his hair comically dishevelled. Mitali appeared upset and angry, but she kept up.

The party wound down. Where was Elizabeth? There, at the far corner, talking to two men and a woman; they were drinking in her beauty—the men hungrily, the woman resentfully, no doubt. I made my way to the men's room, and washed my face. When I straightened, a man in a worn, black, broad-lapelled coat, a size too big for him, appeared in the mirror and handed me a towel. He wore spotless white gloves. He was of medium height, thin, bald, and had the face of a puppy with sad eyes. I buried my face in the neutral smell of the towel for a long safe minute, and dropped the towel into the basket. 'Thank you, sir,' the man said, looking like he had stepped out of a book, a story of great and unrecognized and dutiful suffering. 'Thank you,' I said uneasily, and got back into the near-empty hall.

Mitali arranged for a car to take Elizabeth and me back to Oxford. She came down to see us off. 'Arun knows Papa is so fond of Kishore Kumar and that song. I am sure that his performance was a part of his plan. That man...' She shook her head in admiration. 'Thank you two for coming.'

'Did they eat from the same plate?' I asked.

'Yes, yes, of course. Papa never lies.'

'I had a good time. And I learned about Kishore Kumar,' Elizabeth said.

'See you soon,' Mitali waved as the car moved toward the moon which was filling up the space between the tall office blocks with silver gelatin.

Lines From The Last Millennium

We got back to Kris's place just before daybreak. Elizabeth was very tired, and went upstairs. I would tell her about Kris's instructions tomorrow.

I remembered the envelope Kris gave me. I drew it out from my pocket and checked the contents. An Air India open ticket to Delhi. A cheque for 3000 pounds. I turned my attention to the other gift. An envelope with an old, black Lubyanka postal seal; the date on it had faded. Time and space eddied around me. I thought I could catch a whiff of tobacco in the room. I extracted a yellowing note from the envelope, folded four times over. It was written on both sides. My grandfather's hand: round letters, leaning to the left, marching backward in straight lines even as they stepped forward. It was in red ink, now turned pink with the years. As I read it, I saw in the rotting ink the rubric of a mind coming apart.

...Koba twirls his mustache, and then grabs his daughter Svetlana off her feet and lifts her; he kisses his daughter under the leaves glinting in the summer sun. A white swing

hangs from a tree in the distance, expectant, like a crib and its baby. His people are there to record his moment in the sun with Svetlana, when no one is conspiring to steal his power, which will happen any moment after he puts his daughter down; yes, the world is safe so long as Svetlana is in his arms. 'Papa, do you kill,' Svetlana asks. 'Only for a beautiful world,' Koba says, kissing her again, for a happy future. And once Koba sets the child on the ground, he will sign the death warrant of one million, two, three, four, or five; let's stop at five million, then, that's a good number, signing night after night with a blue and red pencil 'the names that he rolls in his mouth like berries', as the poet said, working long into the night, while the dead with their eyes open in the dark wait for the jackboots to ring on the dim-lit corridor to their cells: 'Tell me what have I done, Dear Koba, tell me comrade, I who fought the enemy at the gates with my bare hands, beat him back all the way from a blasted doorstep in Moscow to a bunker in Berlin where your blood brother the Fuhrer sat with a gun in one hand and a blonde in the other. I who sang the Internationale at the top of my voice with tears in my eyes; who carried your bust and planted it on the head of every peak in the Caucasus. I who took each word of yours, Koba, like a gift to the kolkhozes and courtyards of comrades waiting to be shot, turned in my deviant wife, sister, and child to the NKVD. Tell me, what's it that I have done to offend you, my dear Zozo; what crops have I infested in Ukraine with ticks; what spring I held down still-born in the seeds; tell me why you are doing this, your pencil hovering over my name in the list. What must I confess, what will set your mind at rest, so you can stop finally yourself, so the revolution can halt? Koba, why is my death necessary for you?

The note ended abruptly. It was unsigned.

I folded the note carefully back along the ruts of time and put it back in the envelope. 'Why is my death necessary for you?' That line was from Nikolai Bukharin, Stalin's loyal follower, and M.'s friend, just before he was executed. The smell of tobacco in the room had become stronger. Maybe it came from outside, a late pipe in the back-lane? I washed my face under the tap, hoping the tobacco smell would vanish from my nostrils. It didn't. I went up the stairs and crept under the blanket, inhaling Elizabeth's body like oxygen, until she stirred and said, 'I can't sleep if you do that.'

Call Me Idris

Idris looked well—even plump—and assured now, far from the haunted expression he wore when he had turned up at Aanand's sprawling ashram in the Aravalli hills in Gurgaon weeks ago.

Idris's appeals on the phone gradually had drawn little and then no response from Aanand. Best to sell up his business and land at Aanandji's ashram, Idris thought one evening—the third in a row that showed no sign of a patient at his dispensary of miracles. He found a buyer, Hemendra Singh, his only other competitor in the area to whom he was losing his business, if only because he could lie with better cheer. Hemendra Singh was a cut-throat quack, famous for his long dreadlocks gathered into a shoulder bag like a nest of wipers. Idris sold the tent, the oils, and the colorful ointments for Rs 6000. He had thrown in the fermenting cobra for free. It was contemptuously received by the new owner.

All his life Idris, like most of humanity, was motivated by the fear of not being able to eat. 'Show me a way, Allah, show me a way,' he had prayed. And Allah had nudged him in the direction of Aanand. 'So be it,' Idris thought. Gods were cruel only because they were helpless. A man had to lend a hand to his Maker at times.

Idris had fallen at Aanand's feet on his first appearance at the ashram. Aanand took Idris into an inner hall, and gently broke to Idris that his was essentially a Hindu ashram, and that a devout Muslim doing his prayers five times a day would not be well received, he was sorry.

'I'll keep a Hindu name, Hindol.' The Quran in Idris's bag thumped against his side at the constant betrayal of his god.

'There are a lot of Bangladeshi immigrants in Gurgaon and Delhi who change their names,' Aanand said. 'Mumtaz becomes Malati. Ajaz becomes Ajit. But the police eventually catch them.'

'I am not a Bangladeshi immigrant, Aanandji. I am Indian.' Idris paused. It struck him for a moment what might work here was blackmail. The corpse was a secret he could resuscitate to good effect. But his heart was not in it. There was no end to evil. A threat of disclosure might get a job out of Aanand, but sooner or later, it would get him in trouble. Nobody trusted a blackmailer.

For his part, Aanand considered the spectacle before him: a man reduced to barter his faith for a meal. How little he knew of Idris with whom he and Osip had shared a life-endangering secret? Did Idris have a girlfriend? Someone whom he wanted to marry? What was his future like? What was he beyond just being a survivalist? Did his massive uncertainties make him cry once in a while? And yet, he had been noble: Anand was grateful that Idris did not think of bringing up the night of the exhumation as a bargaining chip. 'No prayers in public, Hindol,' Aanand had warned. After all, in his room, with the doors and the windows closed, and with only the Prophet looking on, Idris could still be a Muslim, if he so wished. 'You could join as my personal assistant.'

Idris had nearly collapsed in relief. There would be water to bathe, food to eat, a room to stay. Inshallah. To his embarrassment, Idris found he was putting on weight within no time. 'Don't eat so much,' he told himself, 'don't eat so much.' It was not even great food, Rice, vegetables, curd. But somehow he could not resist the temptation. It was as if he was eating for the lean days that the future might yet bring. He watched his growing paunch with fascination.

***

One evening, Aanand, stationed in Delhi for the week, gets a call to reach Alok Jain's residence—a square white, unpretentious bungalow behind a high wrought-iron gate—in Chankyapuri. 'It's about the signing of a memorandum of understanding,' Mr Dudani's voice informs him.

'On my way,' Anand says. When he reaches the spot, there are already three cars parked in the portico. 'No trouble, we will park the car outside,' he tells the guard. 'You wait here,' Anand instructs Idris. 'Keep the air-conditioner running. Be comfortable.'

The business begins right away. Mr Dudani and Alok Jain's daughter, Mitali, are part of the meeting. 'We just have to put our initials on the pages for now,' Mr Dudani explains to Aanand.

Halfway through the meeting, reference papers related to the ashram are found missing.

'Not important,' Alok Jain says expansively. He is in a good mood. 'Let's have dinner. We can do those later. What's important is trust.'

'No, I will ask my assistant to bring them. He is in the car. The papers are in a folder in the back seat.'

When Idris comes in with the documents, Aanand introduces him to Alok Jain as his personal assistant.

'Hindol.' Alok Jain nods, 'Nice name. Musical.'

Idris bows and turns to go. Alok Jain, jovial for having concluded the contract, insists that Aanand and Idris stay on for dinner. Aanand says he is obliged, but it is getting late and maybe they can break bread another time? Alok Jain is firm.

'Let's harmonize our thoughts, Aanandji. It is not as if a special culinary effort has to be made for this. We signed a deal, now we have a little meal. My kitchen is frugal, but always open. Indeed, we don't believe in class or caste in this house, do we Mitali?' Alok Jain says, his eyes following a fly. 'Well, Hindol seems to have brought in a fly,' Alok Jain smiles.

Mr Dudani tries to shoo the fly away.

'The flies always remind Papa of his young street and market days,' Mitali tells Aanand.

'You know, Aanandji, I started with nothing,' Alok Jain says with a far-away look. 'I come from a family of traders. We were well-to-do once, and then overnight we were broke. The grain business just blew out of our hands. My father was heartbroken. And the burden of the whole extended family was on my shoulders. Some 40 people. Imagine. I was just 16! Think of it. Only the flies were my company. Hundreds of them flitting around the sacks of rice. All the way from Hissar in Haryana to Delhi and back. Everyday. A market of sharks! And I was 16!'

'Papa had an accident in one of those journeys.'

Alok Jain holds up his left hand. 'The truck crashed. The sacks fell on my hand. Had to have an operation.'

'You've built an empire, Sir,' Aanand says, 'A whole empire in one lifetime!'

'Single-handedly!' Mr Dudani says without irony.

'I create value. Money chases it. The only thing I have failed at,' Alok Jain looks in the direction of Mr Dudani, 'is the *India Post*. But we are not done with it yet, are we, Arun? We have big plans for our Delhi edition.'

'We are hiring new talents, revamping the edition,' Mr Dudani says. 'A young genius from Oxford is joining us soon.'

'Osip Bala Krishnan is not from Oxford. He is from some school in Kasauli,' Mitali says.

Aanand smiles.

'What I mean is, he is just now from Oxford,' Mr Dudani says. 'But we must hire as many Oxford graduates as possible.'

Mitali makes a face.

'Yes, we must get a lot of young talents around us. The paper should be a hub of ideas. I'll pay what they want. Arun, please go strong on talent recruitment.'

Mr Dudani makes a note on his iPad.

I never asked you, Aanandji, where are you from?' Alok Jain pours himself a stiff drink. 'Not that it is important.'

'I am originally from nowhere.'

'The provenance of India's godmen has always been something of a mystery,' Mitali smiles.

'Well, now he is our man. How's the ashram shaping up?'

'It's a great location and it's a very spacious farmhouse. We are doing very well, thank you.'

'I told you,' Alok Jain nods at Mr Dudani.

'We renovated it in double-quick time, Chairman. On a war-footing. I was on the site.'

'"Commanders must exercise restraints unnatural to war, and judgment often not required of young men." General William Westmoreland, Vietnam. It's war all the time, Arun. Ask me.'

'I am just a foot-soldier, Sir,' Mr Dudani smiles his humility.

'We must start televising Aanandji's sessions live soon.'

'Yes, Chairman.'

'The *India Post*, too, must give him space.'

'Yes, Chairman.'

'Dinner is ready,' Mitali says.

Aanand and Idris follow Alok Jain into the dining room, past a hall in white, bare and empty except for a naked

Mahaveera statue in white marble, at least 12 feet in height. Aanand could see only a profile of the statue from where he stood, for a moment, before he followed the others.

It's a vegetarian dinner. Sweetcorn soup, paneer tikka, dum-aloo curry, methi, buttered naan, saffron rice flavoured with ghee, and dessert: kaala jamun, and the Bengali sweet, sandesh. The room buzzes. The fly has found its way into the room. Idris swipes the air before his face. The fly seems to have focused its attention on the lone false Hindu in the room, Aanand notes.

Mr Dudani sits to the left of Alok Jain, one hand over his mouth, which is filled with food, the other wielding a violent fork half-buried in paneer. 'It's great food,' Mr Dudani says, 'But Aanandji, I see you are not having any?'

'The soup is just the thing for me,' Aanand says. 'And I think I will wait for all of you to start on the kaala jamuns. I can't resist sweets.'

Idris is enjoying his meal, perhaps too loudly. The second helping of the saffron rice is quite large. Around that high castle of rice, he distributes all the dishes, like a moat. With the free hand, he swats the elusive fly.

'You don't eat much, generally?' Mitali asks Aanand.

'He is a sannyasi, he has renounced the pleasures,' the Chairman winks. He has been drinking through dinner. In fact, he has hardly eaten anything. 'He is going to be a hugely successful sannyasi.'

'I thought in sannyas, the idea of success has no relevance,' Aanand says.

'Anything you do, you must do well,' the Chairman says. He takes a swallow from his glass, emptying half of its contents. 'You couldn't beat Mahaveera or the Buddha in renunciation, could you? The market for miracles is competitive. The basis of any success is sales, I keep telling Arun here. And the crux of sales is not the quality of the product. It is convincing people they have found a hope in the product. The great saints could do that. They persuaded whole peoples to do away with their mattresses and take to mats. You think that is easy? Selling is nothing compared to sacrificing what you bought. They sold penance and silence! The great saints would have succeeded in anything they set their heart on.'

Idris places his knife and fork down. A sort of surrender of his weapons to age-old customs: he begins to eat with his right hand, the hand that feeds the mouth. Mr Dudani's expression says he is critical of the forfeiture of the implements by Idris, who is now actively threatened by the fly buzzing around his face.

Idris follows the whirring fly with his eyes. He waves it away. But it keeps coming back, mocking him, kissing him, flying away. A cloud of wariness, of a good meal interrupted, steals over Idris's face. He watches the fly slyly, from a corner of his eyes. The fly hovers near his forehead. Suddenly, Idris claps his hands. He's very fast. He's killed the fly. Its soul fled, the mortal form of the fly lies in in state on Idris's rice. Idris picks the fly with his left hand and drops it on the table. He resumes eating.

'You killed! You killed in my house?' Alok Jain snarls. His face is flushed red. A childhood friend has been murdered.

Idris looks around frightened. What has he done? 'It was only a fly,' his face says. He masticates uncertainly.

'What's there is not what's there,' Anand thinks.

Alok Jain gets up, sways a little. 'I want that man out. And what's that mark on his forehead? Is he a bloody Muslim?' He pushes back his chair. 'No blood will be shed in my house. Not a drop. This is not an abattoir.' Alok Jain turns and walks out of the hall.

The room is heavy with silence.

Mitali recovers first. 'Sweets, anyone?'

'Kaala jamun for me,' Aanand says.

'For me, too,' says Mr Dudani.

'Me too,' Idris says.

***

Aanand decided to wait for a few days before asking Idris to go. He didn't think Alok Jain would rescind the contract with him for an incident like this. Aanand could always plead innocence; that he took the impostor in good faith. But, surely, it was appropriate for him to ask Idris to go—for his own good. As it turned out, a couple of days after the incident, Idris came into Aanand's office with his old, battered trunk with broken handles on the side. He had not come out of his room since the murder of the fly.

'Come, sit, Hindol,' Aanand said.

Idris put his trunk down on the floor. 'Call me Idris,' he smiled. 'I'm leaving, Aanandji.'

'But why? You mustn't take small issues to heart…'

'I had a dream.'

'What kind of dream?'

'The fly was no ordinary one.'

'Well…'

'It was sent by the Prophet.'

'The dream was about the Prophet?'

'Maybe it was not even a dream. It was a vision, Aanandji. A great person swaddled in white robes came into the room and said in a deep, but kind voice to me: "Allah detests it when two people relieve themselves uncovered and have a conversation. Have you been doing that my child?"'

'Yes, my Prophet,' I said. 'I am with the Kafirs, Prophet, the urinals here are built like that.'

'"If they peek, which they will, they can see your private parts?" the Prophet asked.'

'Yes, my Prophet,' I said.

'"Ask Al-Mughīrah ibn Shu'bah, my companion in travels. He will tell you I went far away from him to relieve myself. These are private things and, man or woman, modesty is recommended," the Prophet said.'

'Yes, my Prophet.'

'"Are you in the habit of cleaning your private parts after urinating, my child?" asked the Prophet.'

'No, my merciful Prophet,' I said. 'There are no wudu facilities in this ashram.'

'"Idris, you must know three stones are recommended," the Prophet said. "I take it you don't carry stones in your pocket into the urinals so you can clean yourself up with the stones?"'

'No, my peerless Prophet.'

'"It is as expected," the Prophet sighed. "Why are you with the kafirs, Idris?" the Prophet asked me.'

'You know why, my only Prophet, I am a poor man, and I have a family to take care of.'

'"Fool, if every poor Muslim took to becoming a Hindu for this reason, there would be no Islam," the Prophet explained.'

'I am clearing out, my Prophet.'

'"After the fly incident, then, you have had second thoughts, Idris?" the Prophet asked me.'

'Yes, my Prophet.'

'"I sent that fly, child. I have done my duty. Now, Idris, you must do yours," the Prophet said.'

'And then, Aanandji, the Prophet walked out.'

'A good dream. You have taken a decision, then?'

'Yes. I am a Muslim. Nothing will change that.'

'Go to the accounts, get three months' salary, and may God be with you.'

'Keep the money, Aanandji, Allah will take care of me.'

'Take the money and go, Idris. You will need it.'

Idris took a deep breath. 'Thank you, Aanandji,' he said and directed himself to the accounts room.

Aanand watched Idris shuffle away, one hand gripping the trunk, the other wading through the air, as if he was negotiating a knee-deep river.

'Idris!' he called out.

'Yes, Aanandji,' Idris turned.

'Where would you be going now?'

'I think I will make my way to Karim's. I will eat a mutton biriyani. I haven't had one in years.'

The Flip

I look in the mirror, fumble, and pull the one knotted tie that I have down my head. How do people tie a knot looking at the mirror? What could be more misleading? Elizabeth lies in bed and watches me, eyes wide in fake horror. Her nose is red. She is recovering from a cold. It's the air. Delhi's pollution changes the colour and shape of your organs.

Last night, she had a sneezing fit. 'I am sorry,' I wanted to tell her. What if she develops a fatal condition due to geographic dislocation? A place, besides being history, could be a disease.

We have been here more than two months now, and it has not been easy to adjust to my new role as man of the house and journalist. My anxiety levels have shot up. Anything can happen any time. The world caroms around me. A nearly perpetual sense of inadequacy in facing up to the quotidian world has reached a peak, and persuaded me this morning to wear a striped tie. I am hoping I will disappear behind it. Last night we watched Joaquin Phoenix's *Joker*, between two power cuts, about a dysfunctional man in a deranged Gotham city. Elizabeth did not like the movie: 'So unreal, so violent.'

'That's what it is,' I had said.

'Why are you slipping that silken noose around your neck?'

'Some function at the *Post*.'

'Who wears a tie to a newspaper office?'

'No one? Mr Dudani?' I take the tie off and hold it in my hand.

'Mr Dudani is an apparition. Come here, let me kiss you. No, but I will give you my cold.'

I go up to her. 'You are so beautiful. But you have a cold.'

'The combination is a trick I learned just for you.' Elizabeth looks out of the window at the trees filtering the morning light. 'I don't think I can make it to office today.' Elizabeth has joined Oxfam as a research associate. She gets jobs with impressive ease.

'I will go and get some medicines?'

'No, I will take a steam. It is just a cold. You know what?'

'What?'

'Delhi looks different from last I visited.'

'I can't tell. Have you come back to it with new eyes?'

'Ears and noses too.' Elizabeth's left eye weeps. She sits up to will into the air an elusive sneeze. 'Maybe because I have not been to this part of the city.'

'I have never seen a naked woman with a running nose.'

Elizabeth bursts into what might have been a laugh had not a bubble materialized out of her right nostril. It hangs there uncertain, like a tiny greenish balloon.

'It's rather sweet,' Elizabeth touches the bubble with the tip of her tongue. 'You know, in a kind of septic way.'

We have moved into a corner building in the well-leaved Nizamuddin East, behind the huge Humayun's tomb. Nizamuddin is littered with the ruins and relics of the Mughal empire. Mausoleums mushroom by the wayside. Monuments rise out of the ground. Ancient walls spring up and break off, suddenly not sure of what they are meant to guard. Our flat is a terraced two-room set—a hall, a passageway, a bedroom, and kitchen—accessed, from the street that circles a park, by means of a narrow, deep, unpainted staircase. Cracks run along the length of the staircase wall. Arjun fixed the place for us. 'The hall looking out on to the tomb has an air-cooler, but the bedroom has no AC. The furniture, chipped, heavy, apologetic, came along with it. 'You are set for now. Summer will be tough,' Arjun called in to warn before we checked out the place. 'But all day long you could have conversation with kings and ruins.' He said landlords in Delhi preferred married couples. Live-ins and Muslims went against their idea of law and order. 'Best to get married,' Arjun said, 'it would be easier to get a gas connection, too.' He hoped, he said, that I knew families stayed together because of gas, water, and electricity. Dogs, too. 'Get gentrified as couples do,' Arjun said.

'We need the gas Arjun, but Elizabeth and I are not a family,' I said, 'not yet.'

'Do you have an Aadhar card, or a domicile certificate, or a ration card, or a voter's ID, or at least a driver's licence?' Arjun asked, though he added that one must furnish any one card for the others and all the others for any one of the documents: 'One for all, all for one,' he said.

'I have a passport,' I said, 'and a PAN card.'

'Hmm,' Arjun said, 'your Indian-ness can't be proven by just one document or two, an endless paper trail is required, but let me see what I can do, I am not as powerful as I used to be, as you know.'

His status as an iconoclast has been further downgraded, he said, as an acquaintance had tweeted that her dear friend, Maina, told her that Arjun thought if married men had affairs, it was just sex, but if women had them, it was infidelity. Arjun didn't deny it, as he could not remember.

Didn't Maina's last words have any effect? 'No, not really, they seem to think I manipulated Maina. There are two ways to fall,' Arjun said, 'one was to fall from a height, the other was to fall through where one stood'; his fall was the latter. Arjun said he was now thinking of a novel, and he was glad to say he was writing at his best now. The idea of the novel was not really original, he said, it would all depend upon how well he wrote it; it was set in the near future and it was about how the Mob criminalizes non-conformity even at thought level.

'You can,' Arjun said, 'read a man's face and make out what he is thinking; in fact, the novel was about a man who has only bad thoughts—because he tries *not* to think them—and how he is on the run, even from himself.' The novel would be privately printed, Arjun said, as publishers, naturally, preferred writers with certifiable conduct, good people, in fact, with no police records or social media slurs; ah, he had begun to address himself as an asshole, so everything they said about him must be true. And if they searched on Google all they would find was what a one-thought monster he was, so he didn't blame them either. Let his last work be available, with luck, to only those few who look at writing and not writers, but at the end of it all, even more than the novel, Arjun said, he was looking forward to his death, preferably assassinated by an accuser who turned out to be false; he had thought he would be a footnote to history, but he was not even going to be an asterisk, oh well, maybe an asterisk after all—if his murder worked out the way he imagined it.

'I like it here, OB. It's quiet, and we have an emperor for a neighbour, it's more than one can ask for,' Elizabeth said through her cold. 'And I am planning to grow a little garden on the terrace.'

Because of her cold, her 'we' came out as b.

'But summer…? We are right on top, you know. It could get really hot.'

'Summer is still far. We will meet it with guns blazing. More immediately, OB, we need a cooking range.'

'We can't. The voltage is not stable. I asked the landlord.'

'Then you must get a gas connection,' Elizabeth sits up in bed.

Ah, gas again. 'Yes. This weekend. Now, I have to run along. They cut your salary if the machine records your entry is late by more than five minutes. See you in the evening.'

'Be careful. It's a wicked world.'

***

I go down the deep steps, past the first floor whose one window is boarded with old newspapers. No one stays there, I guess. Yes, gas, A/C, cooking ware. Soap. Toothpaste. Toilet brush. The list of accessories for loving and living together, I am finding, is endless and exhausting. It takes an adult. A team of adults. Since Elizabeth is a foreigner and a woman, I have to do it all on my own.

'That sounds racist and sexist,' Arjun said, when I explained my situation to him. 'Still, it is,' he said, 'true, too.'

'They look at her with different eyes,' I said, 'it is dangerous.'

'Yes, I know what you mean, the Punjabis, Keralites, and Bengalis all look at foreigners with different eyes, the same-different eyes, if I may say so,' Arjun said, 'the Biharis, too, not to mention Goans, Goa is the worst, Goa and Kerala.'

'But Arjun,' I said, 'I resent that I do all the running around just because I want to be with Elizabeth…'

…Which is proving to be difficult. I come back late in the night when Elizabeth is already asleep. I set out the next mid-morning again to the office in far-flung Noida, when she has left for work. We meet in transit. It is work at home, and double-shift at the *Post*.

***

At the *Post*, it was another world and it birthed chaos every minute. I found a confidante and a mentor in my immediate boss, Gautam Ta, short, pudgy, and wearing a golf cap over his bald head. He wore striped shirts and striped trousers to appear taller. He suspected the newsroom was bugged and that secret cameras spied on us. I didn't doubt him. He knew everything about The *Post*. Three years ago, Ta said, the *Post* had been launched with great fanfare, with the blessings of the government in power. It gave the feel and appearance of a great paper, too. The circulation went up to 600,000 in two years and was rising. The Chairman was happy. He had sunk in millions, but it didn't matter; the paper was visible everywhere. When the Chairman went for a meeting with the politicians, or to a government office to get a licence, or graced a social occasion, they said great things about the paper, and the Chairman was pleased with the thought that the *Post* had announced him before he entered the room. He had huge and diversified corporate interests: shipping, construction, packaging, garbage recycling, gunny sacks, entertainment. In all these sectors his newspaper came in handy. But it told on the Chairman that year on year, there was no revenue coming in from the paper; he was a businessman after all. The Chairman knew all the advertisers. Recently, on his return from a trip abroad, he asked them why the revenue was dry because the ads were there for all to see. They said the ads were being sold at fractional charges compared to the other big paper in the city, *The Times of India*.

'Why a fraction?' the Chairman asked.

'Because, sir, there was no response to the products advertised.'

'We sell more than *The Times*,' the Chairman said.

'Yes, Chairman,' they said, 'but no traction.'

'What do you mean no traction?'

'No conversion, Mr Chairman.'

'Why? '

'We don't know, Chairman, we just don't know.'

'I am telling you all this,' Ta said over a cup of tea late one night, when we had put the city edition to bed, 'so you know the lie of the land.' He grinned at the phrase. I noticed that Ta lifted the saucer along with the cup. He was happy that the front page had no mistakes. I had done the proofs. 'No one here knows English,' Ta said, 'though they speak in that language. They even write in it,' he said, 'but it is still not English.' Ta always carried an edition of Webster's dictionary in his pocket.

***

One day, when Mr Dudani was out on a tour, the Chairman walked into the newsroom. It was about 11 in the morning. Someone had sent him a photo on his cellphone of hundreds of copies of the *Post* dumped in a drain in the suburb of the city. The Chairman had a method of gathering evidence against his own employees from total strangers. He seemed to survive by surveillance.

'Where are the editors?' the Chairman asked. The nearly empty newsroom turned emptier. The Chairman was the kind of man who left a hush in his wake.

'They will come in the afternoon, Mr Chairman,' his secretary said.

'Whose cabins are these?' The Chairman pointed a finger at the row of nice, well-lit cabins.

'The editors' cabins, Mr Chairman,' the secretary said.

'How many senior editors?'

'Thirteen,' someone said from behind a pillar.

'Thirteen editors? And not one of them at work?'

'They come in the afternoon, Mr Chairman.'

'Bloody Brahmins and their cabins. I bet they are right now conspiring to bring me down.'

'We will cut off their ACs, Mr Chairman,' the secretary offered, making the air conditioners sound like balls, a muted sentence instead of the firing squad.

'Demolish the cabins. Now!'

'Yes, Mr Chairman,' the secretary said.

'Where's the Managing Editor who drives around a BMW at my expense, where's he?'

'He is out on a call, Mr Chairman.'

'Get him on the phone.'

The secretary got the Managing Editor on the phone.

'Put him on the speaker,' the Chairman said.

'Where are you?'

'Good morning Chairman, anything wrong? I am out on a business brunch,' the Managing Editor sounded surprised. Wasn't he supposed to do his work? The newsroom could hear the surprise quite clearly, like the tick of a clock.

'Why is this sisterfucking paper in the red?'

'You are asking the wrong man, Mr Chairman. The market is down, Mr Chairman, maybe?'

'The market is not down for the other papers? Their profits are up 20 per cent from last year.'

'Mr Chairman, when the market is down, most of the share moves to the first paper.'

'So who made this the last paper?'

'I manage the content, Mr Chairman. But I have been here just three weeks.'

'Who cleared the story on the garbage heaps in the Gazipur dump yard?'

'The one endangering the air-traffic because of the birds? I did, Chairman. The garbage pile was five floors-high. The birds were flying around it, posing problems for air traffic.'

'Yeah? And who owns the garbage dumps?'

'Well…'

'I own them. And I own this paper. And I pay your salary. And you carry a story against me. Should I laugh, or cry? Your activism comes out of my bank account.'

'I didn't know, Chairman.'

'You are fired, you get that? Fired. Don't come back to this office. You hear?'

There was a pause from the other side.

'Who wants to come back to your dump, Chairman?' the Managing Editor said.

The secretary cut him off. You couldn't have people talk back at the Chairman.

'Where's the circulation man?'

'He is here, Mr Chairman, in his cabin.'

'Where?'

'At the far end of the back corridor, Sir.'

The Chairman walked fast in the direction of the back corridor.

Someone asked the secretary, 'What's wrong? And the Chairman is wearing a white suit today. He should not be doing all this.'

'Shut up,' the secretary gesticulated, running after the Chairman.

By now, some journalists had started coming in. And online people as well.

No one talked.

The cabins had begun to be dismantled by workmen who had materialized from out of nowhere.

The Chairman came back into the newsroom dragging the circulation manager by the scruff of his shirt. They seemed to have already had a one-sided conversation. The circulation man's eyes were popping out like a doll that has been whacked hard in the back of the head.

'Motherfucker, have you been giving me inflated circulation figures?'

It transpires that hundreds of thousands of copies were indeed transported from the press every morning. But half of them were dumped in the drains of the suburbs; at an appropriate time they were removed by mysterious people and sold as scrap.

'Yes.'

'So you know. Which drain?'

'In Okhla, behind the railway station.'

'And you are getting a cut from the sale of the dumped copies?'

The Chairman turned to his secretary. 'Show him the clip on my cell.'

The Chairman's hair was all over his face. His pupils had reduced in size to a point.

'Yes, Chairman,' the secretary said.

The circulation guy stood, hands at his sides, face down, his shirttail out.

The secretary showed him the clip.

'That's proof for you.' The Chairman told the circulation manager.

'Yes, Sir.'

'You are fired.' Sweat ran down the Chairman's face. He pulled his tie loose.

The circulation chief turned to go back to his cabin.

'Out,' The Chairman said, 'Go home.' He turned to his secretary. 'Send his stuff home.'

The circulation manager changed his direction midway and headed for the door.

The Chairman focused his attention on the newsroom again.

'Where's that crocodile, Dudani?'

'He is abroad, Sir.'

He looked around the room and saw me. 'Osip Bala Krishnan?'

'Yes.'

'Take over the paper until further instructions.'

'I am an intern, sir.'

'So? Listen. Leadership is the readiness to commit violence first, and then stick to it. You just proved you will never make it. Go home to your mother. Who's the senior man here?'

Ta stepped out in his hat from behind one of the pillars. 'I am.'

'You take charge until further instructions. No news of the Opposition. No Rahul Gandhi ever on the front page, all right? No Arvind Kejriwal, either. What's your name?'

'Gautam Ta.'

But the Chairman didn't wait for an answer. He strode to a chair in the center of the newsroom. He sat heavily in it. He asked for a beedi. The secretary checked his pocket and produced one, and a light. The Chairman inhaled the beedi sharply. He held it for a long moment and let out the thick blue smoke in rings, watching his paper go up in smoke. An acrid smell filled the air. The sensor alarm went off. All the alarms sounded simultaneously. The showers started. The Chairman sat under his wrath-induced rain, smoking. The secretary produced an umbrella. He stood behind the Chairman holding the umbrella over him. The Chairman finished the beedi, looked at the dead butt, and flicked it into a corner. 'So much for the fucking journalists,' he seemed to say.

'It was mass extermination,' Ta said later, 'genocide; a pogrom, let's say a pogrom. And you know why he embargoed news about the Opposition? Because he is angling for an

Upper House nomination.' He shook his head at me. 'And you missed your big chance.'

***

Mr Dudani is back on top, following another uncertain spell in the office. 'It must help Mr Dudani that the Managing Editor has been sacked,' Ta said. Back on top at the *Post* means Mr Dudani has found a way to hang on in his job. When I mentioned this to Arjun, he only nodded. Then, the same weekend, when we met, he said he knew the inside story of the latest of Mr Dudani's countless comebacks. Arjun's source, he said, was a gossip journalist who paid servants of the rich and the famous on a monthly basis for private information, which he might then use to get favours in cash or kind. 'Have you been to Alok Jain's residence in Malabar Hill, Bombay?' Arjun asks, one glass holding a whisky, his chin resting on the walking stick I brought him from England. One of the two. The other is meant for Gloria.

'No.'

'Well, it's a majestic movie set, British-colonial period. You can't mistake it. Over the pillars of the gate are statues raised in memory of two late great greyhounds that your boss would feed himself. In the neighbourhood, the house is known as Dog House. Huge trees grow around the bungalow. Well-cared-for creepers hang over walls. A short driveway leads to the porch housing a silver Phantom, the size,' Arjun expanded his hands dramatically, 'the size of a yacht. Well, on the night of the incident, an attendant—the source of my source, if you must know—in a white shirt and white trousers, receives Mr Dudani at the door. Now the attendant is disconcertingly cheerful, and is overflowing with false humility, the kind of humility that servants of great masters flaunt, you understand, Osip. "Come, come, Dudani Sir, would you care for a drink before you meet the Boss, or…"'

'"Thank you, nothing, I'm good," Mr Dudani says.'

'Mr Dudani follows the attendant past a great hall with a well-stocked bar to one side, into another high, splendidly appointed room. The attendant points to a short flight of steps in the corner and asks him to go on in. Mr Dudani walks up the steps of polished wood, and after a moment's hesitation pushes open a tall door. It is one of the biggest and the most beautiful bathrooms he has ever seen in his life. All of it is Italian marble. Grey with green tesserae. It is hot. Through the swirling steam, Mr Dudani can see a giant marble tub at the far corner. And in it, covered in foam and bubbles, lies the Chairman, Alok Jain. The Buddha of the Bath. There is a glass of whisky in his hand.'

'"I am sorry, Mr Chairman, I didn't know…," Mr Dudani says.'

'"No, I wanted to meet you here," the Chairman says.'

'The tub helps Alok Jain's blood pressure, which spikes when he listens to Mr Dudani Besides, Osip, acts of cruelty are best carried out with kindness. From hidden speakers, the sound of Om reverberates in a beguiling whisper. Mr Dudani continues to stand, hands shoved into his trousers' pockets, staring at the long snout of his shoes. Should he have removed them outside, as was expected of a guest in a normal Indian household? Now it is too late.'

'"Arun," Alok Jain says simply, "you must leave. You have not delivered on your promises. The paper is bleeding me millions. I have never failed in anything I set out to do."'

'"Yes, the worst is happening," Mr Dudani thinks. By an effort of will, he tries to run in from the flank. "The content is Ms Mitali Jain's department," he says. As soon as Mr Dudani says it, his face shows regret.'

'"I am not talking about content," Alok Jain says. "It's product sales and revenues. The quality of the product is secondary for a first-rate salesman. I live by that truth. You know that."'

'"I have a few plans to improve that part of the business," Mr Dudani says, hopeful as ever.'

'"You have no plans, Arun. Or you have only plans. It is a shame how negative you were this morning to my suggestions about more editions to garner government tenders," Alok Jain says. "How can you forego the projected Rs 200 crore from tenders annually?"'

'"Mr Chairman," Arjun says, "nine more editions in just two months is not possible."'

'"Neither do you have plans, nor are you able to execute my ideas."'

'Osip,' Arjun says, 'the Chairman feels rage beginning to build in his blood through the fragrant bubbles of the bath. He settles deeper into the water. Under the foam, he caresses his penis pensively. It was a source of joy when he was young, with so many starlets ready to please him for roles in his tacky family serials. Mr Dudani, meanwhile, is fingering the contract in his hip pocket, his final weapon.'

'"Are you firing me, Mr Chairman?" Mr Dudani asks. He has a cunning expression on his face.'

'"What do you think I am doing?"'

'"Then you must send me an official mail," Mr Dudani says.'

'"Why? My word is good enough."'

'"Please refer Page 3, clause 15 of my contract," Mr Dudani takes the contract out from his hip pocket and shakes it as if he is airing a blanket.'

'"What? An exit fee, motherfucker? No, I am not firing you. You quit on your own."'

'"I am not quitting, Mr Chairman. You have to sack me."'

'"All right then, I won't fire you. No work will come to you. And no one will report to you."'

'"That's up to you, Mr Chairman," Mr Dudani says, "I am only your servant."'

'Well, Osip,' Arjun says, 'Mr Dudani folds the contract and puts it back in his pocket. He turns to go. When he is at the door, the Chairman shouts from behind. "If you have any pride, you will leave."'

Arjun puts his glass down. 'There is nothing as fit for survival as a man without pride. And Mr Dudani's lack of it comes from his love for his wife. And her art. Isn't patriarchy beautiful?'

***

I returned home from the office, past midnight. I took care not to put on the lights.

I sat on the bed.

'The gas has come,' Elizabeth said in her sleep.

Ah, gas. I went into the kitchen.

The red gas cylinder stood in a corner, sullen, shoulders rounded and sloping, but at the same time ominous; waiting. I poured myself a drink. Who was going to break its seal? I had never done it before. I approached the cylinder with caution. Its silence gathered around me like a red cloud. I waved my hand through it. My hand felt heavy and alien, as if it was parting water when it made the passage through the air. I sat down on the floor. It seemed the thing to do was to pull the nylon thread attached to the white plastic cap and then screw on the tubing from the stove to the cylinder's valve. It seemed simple enough. But I have always had problems with sequential processes, I reminded myself. Watch it. Something somewhere could go wrong. What if it exploded? Inanimate matter was not innocuous. Atoms exploded after all. I gathered the white nylon thread in my hand. It felt mean and merciless. In the right pair of hands it could be a lethal noose. I set my glass down. I pulled the thread at first tentatively, and to no effect. Then I remembered what the Chairman said about leadership and violence. I pulled the thread with all my strength. It only cut into my palm deeper than before. It shouldn't be so difficult.

I wrapped a kitchen towel around my hand and got back to the exercise that would assert my dominance in the as yet silent but deathly struggle over the cylinder.

'What are you doing, OB?' Elizabeth asked from behind.

'I don't know how to do this.'

'Pull it out in the reverse direction and up.'

The thread came away in my hand.

'Only in India.' I blamed the country. I looked around for a knife. 'Have you noticed how they pack food?'

'No.'

'You have to use real violence to open a packet of peanuts. Or anything. You could starve yourself to death surrounded by packaged food here.'

'That hard to open them?'

'Virtually impossible. Hand me that knife, teacher.' I pointed to the black-handled knife gleaming in the rack.

'No, not that. That's my Kamikoto. That's not for things like this.'

Ah, yes. The Kamikoto was an old gift from Kris to Elizabeth, 'to severe all ties with the world.'

Elizabeth handed me another knife. 'They issue only one Kamikoto per family, did you know that?'

'Really?' Wasn't one enough?

'Careful. Don't cut your hand.'

I inserted the knife's point into the bracket and leveraged it out.

The cap broke. I stepped back. I had done it.

'Bravo,' Elizabeth said.

We smiled at each other.

'How was your day?'

'Long. Many wounded. Some dead.' I said.

'Oh, dear.'

'Now place the regulator on the cylinder and connect the tube to the regulator valve.'

But the main valve of the cylinder did not yield.

Elizabeth went in to get her phone. She googled and read out the instructions sleepily. Why can't she do this herself?

'Open the catch, and press the spring.'

It took a sticky three minutes before I got the hang of it.

'Don't keep staring at my hands,' I said. Because as she stared at them, I was aware they were growing heavy inch by inch.

'Now screw the tubing into the regulator valve.'

'Easy,' I said, as the tubing fit in.

'Mr Clumsy,' Elizabeth smiled.

'I need a shower,' I said, my bleeding hands clasped behind me.

I waited till she stepped out of the kitchen. I took the gas-lighter and pressed the trigger. The stove did not light. I had been defeated. I will try again later then. Maybe after Elizabeth slept. I went into the bathroom. Stood under the shower. I watched the water run down into the drain in bubbles. They moved in fast trains. I watched them for a longish time. I bent down and touched one. It broke and was no more. I wondered where the bubbles went. Into the air, of course. What purpose did they serve? I squatted on the floor. There was only the sound of the shower now. The water had banished the world to a distant rumour. I turned off the shower, soaped myself carefully, and recalled that I had forgotten to bolt the door. Never mind. I turned on the tap, and found that the shower was dry. I wept tears of rage with my eyes shut against the lather, and hoped Elizabeth won't come in. She did, a moment later, laughed, and said there was a water cut. She handed me a towel, and I hid my face in it.

Inner Workings

I am waiting with the *Post* photographer at Aanand's spacious office in his Gurgaon ashram, south of Delhi, where I have never been to before. Gurgaon is a corporate city. Most of the Fortune 500 firms have an office here. And its demography is double-income, upwardly mobile. Metro. Rapid Metro. Flyovers. Underpasses. Malls. High rises. Food courts. 'Surrounded by the low hills of Aravalli, Aanandashram though is relatively better protected,' Ta said, 'from the air-conditioned invasion of the city.' A long private drive-way takes you deep into the valley, and to the ashram. I look around. Where I am waiting for Aanand is a large hall with deep windows. The walls are bare, but for a framed picture of Ramana Maharshi in a white loincloth, lying on his side, composed like a sculpture, looking into the camera and finding, as great men do, reassuring signs of the imperishable everywhere he looks. There are white cotton mattresses on the floor, with small round but thick meditation-cushions on them. Outside, the lawn is lush. At its center, a yellow ficus, pruned like a lampshade, radiates a golden light. The perimeter walls are guarded by the stately, sentinel kanju trees. The evening is clear and still like a lake.

I have tried my best to wriggle out of the assignment. But Mr Dudani will not hear of it. 'Two young people in a conversation!' he says, 'one who has made it so early in his life, and the other a relative failure. It's a dramatic contrast.' He says it jocularly, but I know what he is getting at. The young man who was offered an editor's post and did not grab it, that's me. Mr Dudani does not like me, I think. Which is as it should be. I am not the type people fall in love with. I don't like myself. I believe Mr Dudani is putting me to test with this interview. If I fail, he could report to Mitali that her candidate is not up to the mark, and score a point. I suspect he knows I have a secret life. Lives. 'Mr Dudani believes you are leaking information against him to Mitali,' Ta said. Indeed, if I fail, Mr Dudani could use it as Mitali's poor judgment of talent and play us both down against the Chairman, who always appreciates peer-betrayal. 'The *Post* is run like a spy network,' Ta said, 'just like any other newspaper; everybody tries to win his superior's confidence by sharing information about someone else, though it may not be a guarantee to his/her survival.' It is denunciation round the clock. At the *Post*, the Chairman's powers of discretion equalled life and death. Ta mentioned the incident, before I joined, of Robert Perriera, a political editor, who, after a heart stroke, did not produce much; the news eventually reached the Chairman who, in what was going to be an exit interview, stared so hard at Perriera that he slumped, a minute into the session, in his chair, dead. Before he eyed the man to death, the Chairman had asked if Perriera was having a paid vacation at the *Post* (he reportedly played the audio of a conversation that Perriera seems to have had with the editor of another paper in which he referred to the Chairman as the 'devil'). Later, when the Chairman was informed that Perriera was survived by his wife and a spastic son, the Chairman said that the heart, indeed, was an unpredictable thing, one must never trust it. When I mentioned this incident to Arjun, he said, '*Arbeit Macht Frei*.' The Auschwitz gate slogan. 'Work sets you free. That is what the Capitalist really believes in,' Arjun said. Mr Dudani, it was widely suspected, was the one who passed the information to the Chairman regarding Perriera's secret links with the anti-Nationals. A Dudani-engineered investigation 'found' that Perriera had been plugging for the Opposition. 'The accused walked about in a daze, unable to give any sensible explanation for their most simple actions,' Arjun had quoted Arthur Koestler, when I told him about Dudani's findings on Perriera.

'But Mr Dudani did this,' Ta said, 'only to show that he was a hard taskmaster. Mr Dudani was apolitical. The Chairman appreciated hard taskmasters.'

'Would this be after the battle of the tub happened,' I wondered.

'Aanandji is a corporate investment for the Chairman, so create a good impression with your story,' Mr Dudani says, as I leave his cabin. 'Your interview will be amplified across all media channels of the group. All. The new media functions like an echo chamber, you understand. We must make things happen, right?'

'Yes…'

'Things happen when we scream things have happened. Amplification. "Indeed, reality," the Chairman says, "is not what happens, but what we show to happen."'

As I wait for Aanand, I see out on the lawn, people come first in a trickle and then in droves for his famous Sunday Satsang, the meeting of good spirits. Aanand's satsangs are much talked about. Hundreds of people, either good or wanting to be good, flock to them. They cry, laugh, sway in ecstasy. Deep down, Mr Dudani had said as part of my briefing, 'We were all saints once, it is just that the world we built did not encourage that aspect of us. And we are the agents of that change.'

'Where's Guruji?' The photographer asks. Alka works for free at the paper. The *Post* is full of interns who work for free. Mr Dudani says it helps him to cut costs. (Ta says he suggested to Mr Dudani that the strategy just adds to the workload of the regulars because of the supervision involved. Mr Dudani waved him away, Ta said. I doubt if Ta would have really said it though.) But Alka is talented and quite a professional. She wants her CV to look good before she applies for a fellowship abroad: a photo essay on the power of the single woman in India.

'He will be along, I guess.'

'I have a date with my boyfriend. He is coming around to pick me up. He always knows where exactly I am.' Alka chews her thin red lip with her long canine tooth. She is very pretty.

'How?'

'Some spyware,' Alka holds up her phone to me.

'Isn't that scary?'

'Have you been in love?'

'No. Why?'

'It makes a lot of drastic things seem reasonable.'

'You could take a few snaps and leave, maybe.'

'I don't mind really. Guruji is a great celebrity. And he is so young and handsome.'

'Namaste,' Aanand says softly from behind.

I turn. Aanand looks splendid. Beard, hair, orange robes with black lettering. What does it take to fool a whole country? Hope.

'You look great,' I say.

'God's grace. All well?'

'Yes.' I feel stupid, small, inadequate.

'Fire your questions, please.' He smiles his detachment at Alka. 'I have a satsang to attend in 30 minutes.'

I ask the usual ones. I have lost all interest—if ever, truly speaking—in journalism since the Aanand assignment. Once, we dug up a corpse together, and now I am interviewing my partner in the crime. 'We will finish this in no time, Guruji,' I say. Both of us know what not to ask. Most interviews in media are like that, Ta would remark later. Alka moves around Aanand, clicking and frequently checking the snaps she shoots.

'What got him here?' I ask Aanand. 'What set him off? Isn't he too young to be wise? What's the future? For him. For the world. For the universe?'

Well, an inner calling got him here, Aanand begins. He had a vision in Dharamshala; it was elemental, like the snow. It released things in him. But he was always spiritual, even as a child. No, Aanand was not too young to be wise, Bhagavan Ramana Maharshi's 'death-experience' and self-realization occurred when he was 16. Indeed, a child was the most spiritual thing in the world. Because, you see, a child acts out instinctively from the innate knowledge: *Aham Brahmasmi*. As you grow old, you lose the child in you. Activating the pineal gland is a way of rediscovering that child, her first look at the world. After that, it's all memory of the first impressions. Aanand's pineal gland is now fully awakened. He is a cosmic citizen; the stuff of air, water, and fire. We are all spirit as matter. Aanand breaks off, as Alka takes leave.

'I hope you got some good pics,' Aanand says.

'Yes, would you like to see them?'

'No, I trust you.'

Alka nods at me. Her boyfriend has arrived.

Yes, Aanand resumes, he was aware that he was different even when he was young, did he tell me that already? His first awakening came when he was 12. No, borders do not contain him, us; we are free, we just don't know it. We are rare. We are air. In the future, countries will not have names. When everybody is rich and free, the idea of the nation will not count. Indeed, if you ran into an alien on Mars, you are not likely to say that you are from, say, India or America, but from Earth. Aanand smiles. But it is not a smile that admits of our school friendship. I had not wanted it to be acknowledged when I began the interview. Now I do. If he apologizes, I am ready to forgive him. But I am not quite sure what he should be apologizing for. All of it seems a grey area. Memory is a fog filling up a room, no object in it begins or ends but merely extends its presence and flows into each other, an amoebic entity. Someone comes and tells Aanand everybody is waiting for him out on the lawn.

'I must go now. Let's meet for a glass of water soon,' Aanand says. 'Would you like to attend the satsang? I can show you the way.'

'I don't care.'

'Ah, but you do. Your neuroses and depression are proportionate to your incompetency in facing up to the challenges that the world offers. People commit suicide mostly because they are unable to live the life they want. They want more, not less.'

'You and the Chairman have much in common.'

'Successful people are all the same. I'll give you a call and set up a meeting when we are not so rushed. A personal audience.' Aanand glances at the wall-clock.

'It had better be an early morning call.'

'Why is that?'

'Cellphones have been banned in the office. All incoming and outgoing calls are routed through a central server.'

'Actually, that makes sense. A lot of time is spent faffing. So, now the management can listen in on all conversations?'

'Yes, if they want to.'

'Well, I will find a way,' Aanand gets up, indicating the interview is over. 'OB, guess, who has been coming of late for the satsangs?' His voice is suddenly more familiar, friendly almost.

'Who?'

'Yolanda Andrade.'

'Really?'

'Things change, don't they? And how's your life with Ms Hill?'

'Did you meet your mother?'

Aanand's face darkens. 'No. It's stupid to go around asking a stranger if she is my mother,' he says.

'Are you sure?'

'OB?'

'Yes?'

'You are an asshole. You need help.'

'The way you helped me.'

'I tried. You are messed up. You are frightened. You don't...you don't have the tenacity of curiosity of life...'

'Tenacity of curiosity? Fuck you.'

'Fuck you, too. The alien in the room. Despite your misery, you think you are superior. You think no one understands you. It's the other way around. You understand no one. You must be aware of yourself and of the others. You are not aware,' his eyes shone with ardour and conviction.

Perplexed, I weakly say, 'Your people are waiting for you. For salvation.'

'Not just them. Potentially the whole world. Are you jealous?'

'No.' Yes.

'When you type the copy, don't forget the extra 'a' in Aanand.'

Aanand gathers his robes and walks out of the room in measured steps. At the door, he turns. 'Learn to listen to the wise. "Attention is the purest form of generosity," as Ramana Maharshi said.'

'Simone Weil, the French philosopher said it, not Ramana Maharshi. She also said group-structures, or organizations, are resistant to truth.'

'Ramana Maharshi also said it.' Aanand paused. 'Could have. Great people think alike.'

'Fraud.'

'Loser,' he turns his back, and walks away, his back erect, towards people waiting to listen to him, his old-fashioned wooden clogs clear and loud on the floor.

***

The green-shaded garden light on the terrace is on. The plants, bamboos mainly and creepers, have grown tall. Often at night, a luminous Elizabeth nurses them, purposeful and lost in the mini-forest lit by the moon. Why are things transparent and yet mysterious? I go into the house. Elizabeth is not at home. I switch on the lights, and see on my side of the bed a copy of *Time* magazine. I flip through it. On page 34, I stop. I see Ava Lenk, frail and wispy like a wind-torn cloud, staring out of a black and white photograph. The headline reads: 'The Last Nazi Trial'.

The report is on the legal proceedings against a wheelchair-bound Fritz Hanning, who was a security guard charged with being an accessory to murdering 170,000 people in the death camps. Ava is quoted as saying she cannot recall seeing Hanning, but she testifies to what she witnessed.

I put the magazine away. I sit on the bed thinking how fluid humans are. Like rivers reaching for strange and far shores; the same river, but the water all changed by the end of the journey. Hanning looks like just another old man. His face wears an expression of puzzlement: 'Was that I who did all that; how did I arrive here, stepping on so many dead bodies?' How do you hold a man responsible for a crime committed when he was someone else? I have seen that baffled expression at home in Thrissur. My grandfather and Hanning are of the same age. They resemble each other. Old men, like babies, look the same, perhaps. How is Mr Menon faring? I have been caught up. For a startling moment, my head clears, the buzzing sound in my ears subsides. I call up Thrissur. I listen to the ring, staring at Ava. Should I tell Gloria about her?

'Hello,' Gloria says.

'It's me, grandmother,' I lower my voice.

‘Why are you whispering, Bala? Where have you been? You don’t care for us, do you? I tried calling you a couple of times. Are you back?’

‘I am in Delhi. How’s he?’

‘How’s he? You don’t ask, how am I?’

‘How are you, grandmother? You sound good.’

Her words slur. She must be drinking. ‘You men have ruined my life.’

‘You’ve said this before, grandmother.’

‘It’s worth repeating, let me tell you because I will never know what I was meant to be.’

‘But you are doing good. You are famous.’ We have had the conversation before, surely? I am living in overlapping dreams.

‘Because of the book?’

‘That too. Isn’t your book doing well?’

‘Someone wants to buy the movie rights. After your grandfather’s death, I said. It won’t be for long now. How he started out. A rebel! A dreamer! And how he ended up a murderer and a mad apologist!’

‘No, he is not a murderer.’ Not just a murderer.

‘He had a hand in at least 23 murders. It’s all so long ago, and all for the party, of course. When it’s for the party, it is not considered murder, you see? It’s just an order to be carried out.’

‘There is no proof…’

‘Listen, I have washed his blood-soaked shirts. 23 times.’

I listened to the hum coming back in my ears, filling up my head like an echo-chamber.

'Makkam and I have decided to clean up his room. All those old copies of the *Pravda* and *Moscow News* in his room gathering dust. Lies and dust.'

'But I need them!' The pages of *Pravda* seemed endless, and every line of the paper, even every word, a lie, Ava said at the seminar, and all of it was god's truth to millions, and out of it came real things like blood and agony, and broken homes and new gods.

'Oh, well, we didn't make much progress, Makkam and I. You know why?'

'Why?'

'We found a gun. A sidearm as they call it. An old Russian revolver. That's when I remembered about the washing of the shirts.'

A revolver. 'Where?'

'Under the mattress on the far side, below the pillow.

It's marked 1938, and has a star carved in the matt-yellow handle.'

'But from where? Where did he get the gun from?'

'I don't know. There is no telling with him.'

'Is it loaded?'

'I can't tell. Maybe that was the gun he used to finish off his enemies. Well, in all that excitement we didn't get around to clearing the junk.'

'Wait until I come back.'

'We tried to remove the gun. He refused. So we let him be. But Treesa will do it eventually. She is quite tactful. When are you back? I don't have the first idea what you are up to.'

Gloria blows her nose. 'I am getting old. Every moment I am leaving everything behind.'

'You will live long, grandmother. Everyone in your family died old, you said.'

Gloria blows her nose again. It's the rum.

'Don't cry, grandmother.'

'I am not crying. Why should I cry? Bala, what will I do when he is gone?'

'You will be free to do what you want.'

'I no longer want to be free. You want to be free when you can do something with it.' She stopped crying. 'The good news is that I can read very well now.'

'You could always read well.'

'No, I had a cataract in my left eye.'

'You had an operation?'

'That's the thing. A couple of weeks ago, the rum glass fell from my hand. And a shard flew up right into the eye and removed the cataract. It was painful for a few of days, of course.'

'Imagine!'

'Hmm. I could have lost an eye. Now I can re-read the *Mahabharata*, after all. Tell me about you.'

'I have taken up a job in a newspaper.'

Shouldn't you be graduating?'

'I will.'

'You must know what's good for you.'

'Yes.'

'Bala, my drink smells of camphor.'

'Change the glass?'

'It's Makkam hoarding the rum where she keeps the clothes. She uses up too many mothballs. Why can't she keep the rum somewhere else?'

'You must tell her.'

'She doesn't listen. The other day I had such a fight with her. Then both of us cried and made up.'

I recall my grandfather telling me: 'Gloria and her servants have a very intimate relationship, Osip. I can't fathom it. They fight violently and then cry. In her younger days, both she and the servant of the day would square off against each other and beat their chests to show how much each was hurting the other. It's very cathartic for them, I guess. It's much better now. So don't worry if you hear them scream, OK?'

'It's good Makkam is with you.'

'She just doesn't like Treesa. She is threatened, and Treesa is better looking and more intelligent. Visit us before he dies, Bala. Hello?'

'Can you hear me?'

I disconnected the phone. The buzz in my head had grown more insistent. Where was he hiding that gun all these days?

***

It's Friday. My off. I sit up at my desk and try writing the Aanand interview. It's tough going. Halfway through, Elizabeth comes in from outside. She is in high spirits. 'How's my star student today?'

'All good, Teacher.' I get up and lie on my side of the bed.

'OB, you know what happened today? Sangita and I met after office.'

'Really?'

'Hold on. Someone by the name Osip Bala Krishnan came along a few months ago, and gave her flowers.'

'Aanand.'

'I didn't tell her that. The point is your friend met his mother and vanished without a trace.' Elizabeth removes her shirt and flings it into a corner. It's a bedtime ritual of abandon. The discarded clothes would be all over the place. I gather them in the morning and put them to wash. Resenting, of course. Naturally.

'Did you tell her about Aanand?'

'No. I thought I would only be complicating everything.'

'But why my name?'

'Because he doesn't want his identity blown? He is quite a guy, isn't he?'

Elizabeth dangles the bra in the air and flings it. It slides over the *Time* magazine on the table and falls to the floor.

'But he could have used so many other names.'

'It doesn't matter, does it?'

'I guess. Thank you for the Ava issue.'

'You read it?' Elizabeth stretches out on the bed.

'Do you think Aanand and Sangita are playing a game?'

'Whatever for?' Elizabeth ruffles my hair. Her breath is faintly laced with alcohol. She turns to her side and goes to sleep almost immediately.

I clasp my hands under my head and continue to lie in the bed. I turn and toss. I get up and switch on the computer. I resume typing out the Aanand copy. How anodyne it is. It explains nothing. Not one thing I know about Aanand figures in it. None of the *Post*'s corporate interests in Aanand shows up. By omission and commission, I help manufacture silence. Is this how it works? Ever a Kashmir-version of truth? A reality so suppressed and self-censored—by rent, Uber, gas, love. I go out into the terrace, walk among the mini-forest that Elizabeth birthed and nursed. I uproot the plants, one by one, and in silence. I cover myself in sweat and dirt. 'Beg,' I tell the plants, 'beg!'

I sit on my haunches amidst the wrecked vegetation. I apologize to the corpse of Father Roderick risen again from the grave.

Eye of the Storm

The ceiling fan is on. The water cooler is on. The exhaust fan in the kitchen is on. And it's no good. Early in the morning, I throw a few buckets of water on the terrace. The next time I look, there is just one tiny pool as if someone has wept. The tiles of the terrace spew out vapours, and the air over it shimmers, like silk. It's 10 o'clock on a May morning in Delhi. The concrete roof radiates heat. The bathroom, which one keeps always closed, is a furnace. Out of the taps run hot water. The clothes have to be peeled off the body. The landlord has been finally pinned down and prevailed upon to replace the straw-stuffed water cooler with an AC. 'It will come soon,' he says, but he is afraid the system may not be able to take the load; he may have to rewire the entire place. 'Nothing is easy,' he says.

'I don't feel like getting up,' Elizabeth says. Sweat streaks down her face. Their source, I think in a stupor, is the roots of her golden hair. Today would record 46.1 degrees C. Both Elizabeth and I have taken to wearing dark glasses indoors. In the hallway, we pass each other like tourists on vacation.

'Good morning, Ms Katrina Kaif.'

'Good morning, Mr Balakristoff.'

'How are you liking Tunisia, Ms Kaif?'

'Wrong time for a vacation here, Mr Balakristoff.'

'The camels are ready for your inspection.'

'Can you get me some ice and water, please, OB?'

I resent this demand immediately. I pour water out into a glass, drop into it three fuming cubes of ice.

'I can't take it,' Elizabeth sips the water. 'It's like living inside a pressure cooker.'

It's a madman's summer, breeding hostility. The white, breathless light of the day is broken by the burning yellow of the amaltas, the violet of the jacaranda, the white, red, and orange of the papery bougainvillea, the insane plants drawing blood from Delhi's summer, shaking their brilliant sap in the face of the sun, trees that betray the killing season, flowering Judases, swaying like torches in the loo from the Rajasthan desert. Each gust is a hornet's nest. The dust and sand sting your eyes, cake your throat, shred your skin. The sun is a delirium.

'Those are the flowers I can remember Delhi by. Those fearless flowers,' Elizabeth says.

I lie by her side, not touching her. Elizabeth is in her glasses and nothing else. 'I am doing my best to ignore the grating of this fan at one point in its oscillation,' Elizabeth says carefully. 'Just as I do India, whose grating points are legion.'

'It's the heat.'

'Even if I want to touch you, I can't, you understand, OB?'

Yes. Touch adds to the heat, to the grating. The weather makes us mourn. Moan. And I can see through my shades that it is not borders or skin, but the sun that separates us; a whole massive star. Elizabeth and I come from its opposite sides. 'Yes, it's hot. No one is in control.'

The furniture in the room, a cot, a table, a small sofa, and two chairs, Elizabeth has been shifting around so often, twice I have run into them at night. 'Why do you move things around so much,' I asked her, and she had said, throwing her hands up in the air, and eyes wide, 'I have control only over the furniture here.'

'In summer, the poor ought to have shelters. All those children begging out there, and the road melting under their feet,' Elizabeth says.

'It's like you need a shower all the time.'

'Listen, there would be a water-cut today. The landlord said the colony has made arrangements with private suppliers. You have to go down and get it up in buckets.'

Elizabeth should have told me this before? These are important things. She just gives me no notice at all. It has not been easy for me. I have to be constantly psyching myself up for the war of the chores. 'When is the truck coming?'

'Three, I think. I am not sure.'

I will be late for the office, then.

I am not having an easy time there either. The workload has gone up. And Ta says he will resign soon. I am lost without him. Ta says he can't understand news anymore. Too much violence. Too many groups. Too many patriots. Too much of the Chairman. And the government. The last two are the same, Ta says. How do you take a call on news? Recently

Ta graduated to a smartphone and discovered social media. And though he has only 20 Facebook friends, he is blasted, he says by a million simultaneous but contradictory realities. It is tyranny of the masses, Ta says. Ta believes social media has enabled modes of conduct that would have been considered mental disorders at an earlier time. Who knew madness was a mobile phone?

'What do you mean, tyranny of the masses?' I ask.

But he evades a direct answer. The day he quits, Ta says, he will throw his phone away. The day he quits. It hangs like a sword over my head.

When the trucks come, I bring up the water, sloshing it a little all over the steps. The landlord watches the proceedings approvingly and says he will fix water tanks on the roof for future emergencies. Those large, black cylindrical containers, you know, he burps, lifting his shirt over his hairy paunch to air it. He is genuinely sorry for the inconvenience; water is not usually a problem in this area. But he doesn't lend a helping hand as I go up and down with the buckets. He has no real reason to after what seems like a late, satisfactory lunch.

'How did Delhi deal with summers before air conditioning?' Elizabeth asks midway through my labours.

'Well, the rich would flee the place to the hills, or go underground,' I pant, pouring the water into a big, red plastic bucket, 'to the basement.'

The *Post* has just carried a feature. In earlier times, the article said, the wealthy would build *thekhaanas*—deep basements—and the whole family would move down in summer. The windows and doors would be curtained with roots of the cool, fragrant *khus* grass, frequently wetted by the servants. The man who magically supplied the water was called *abdaar*. The *abdaar* was in charge of khus, wine, sherbet, and water. I feel like an *abdaar*. The *abdaar* of A/61. *Abdaar* of anything.

'OB,' Elizabeth says, 'the connectivity here is so bad, do you think we should change the service?'

'I will call them up,' I say.

'OB,' Elizabeth shouts from the shower, 'there is no soap.' And I run to the corner shop.

'OB, the grocery bill is on the table. OB, there are no vegetables, please order from Smart'N Fresh. OB...'

'Arjun wants to know if we would like to go over to his place...' I pour the last load of water into the bucket and straighten up.

'In this heat?'

'Sunday. Brunch. I will take a day off.'

'You decide for us. I can't think.'

***

The AC doesn't come; and the landlord is missing. Elizabeth and I go to Whispering Woods. 'What's more liberating than prolonged social isolation?' Arjun asks lightly, as Elizabeth browses through his library.

'But, really, how do you feel, Arjun?'

'Oh, it's a bit like taking a man out to shoot every morning, you get used to it, I guess.' Arjun looks haggard. There are bags under his eyes. He is wearing shorts and a kind of sleeveless vest broad at the shoulder. We exchange pleasantries, drink beer.

On the TV, Avlok Dutta, looking fitter and better than ever, is in replay from the night before, continuing his eternal interrogation of one man. Arjun taps on the audio. 'Faizal Rashid, tonight I shall shred you, and since you know you are in the wrong, you might as well enjoy it: Are you a Pakistani agent or not? And what role would spies like you have in the new, strong India?'

Faizal Rashid shakes his head: 'Mr Avlok Dutta, you are doing violence to the idea of India. For the last time, I will tell you, I hold an Indian passport.' The other panelists begin speaking together, mostly against Faizal Rashid. But it is a babel, only a little different from the noises in my head.

'And how are you holding up, Elizabeth?' Arjun shakes his head and switches off the TV.

'Ah. I don't know. I don't know what I am supposed to feel. The heat makes everything look like a mirage. I feel sluggish. And the other night, they vandalized my terrace garden.'

'Who? Why?' Arjun asks.

'We don't know who,' I say. 'It's the heat. It does things to people.'

'Truly sorry to hear that. I could have someone call up the Nizamuddin police station and get them to scope the place if you would like me to do that,' Arjun says.

'No, it's too late now, I am done with gardening in this city. Plants are such helpless things,' Elizabeth says.

'Delhi is insane. There's no telling what happens next. Just a few days ago a boy and his father were lynched for taking cattle to the market. Right next to a police station, too. ' Arjun throws up his hands. 'Can't get it. These orgies of violence on the one hand and, on the other, the same bunch, more or less, dreaming of the great smart Magintogorsks.'

Elizabeth raises her eyebrows at Arjun.

'The Magnetic City. Stalin had this massive barrack socialist city of steel built in the Urals next to the iron ore mountains in the 1930s,' I explain to Elizabeth. 'Many died working at that dream.'

'I see.'

'But who could have destroyed your plants? That takes another kind of damaged mind.'

'We are shifting soon. I have asked some people in the office to help find a place,' I say.

'Don't say I did not warn you about the summer in a terrace-flat,' Arjun says.

'We had a good time in the winter, didn't we OB?'

'Yes.'

'How's the *Post* treating you?' Arjun asks. "It's my favourite paper now because they are the only people who allow me a platform.'

'Too much work. It's chaotic.'

'OB is stretched thin with the office bullshit, though he doesn't say much about it,' Elizabeth wipes the rim of the beer bottle with her hand. 'But his real problem is that he doesn't belong anywhere. He is unable to be a member of a group and further its interests.'

'A shame, a shame. The world gets along in groups. Be part of the herd or not be heard, OB,' Arjun nods.'

'I am fine.'

'I hear cost-cutting is the operative word these days at the *Post*,' Arjun says.

'Yes, the toilet rolls were missing for a day or two.'

'Ah, those white ribbons of honour. But isn't that a bit extreme?' Arjun says.

Elizabeth laughs.

'The women protested and now the rolls are back,' I say.

'But not men? The male species has no future, has it? At least, are you enjoying your work?'

'OB can't enjoy anything, can he, OB? It won't be cool.' Elizabeth says.

'Everyone in the office lives in fear of being sacked. The guy who is arranging the farewell-cake today is the one getting fired tomorrow.'

'Another beer?' Arjun gets up to fetch the beer. 'I hear poor Mitali is increasingly taking to spiritual retreats?'

'Yes, she goes for these long vipassanas. Can we stop talking about the *Post*?'

'I am a gossip, you know that,' Arjun grinned. 'How about some music?'

'Kishore Kumar, please,' Elizabeth said.

***

It is a little after 4 pm. Elizabeth and I step out into the evening, each of us holding a cold can of beer. We find it is already dark. The evening is not quite orange; but a bronzed saffron. A high wind chases leaves down from trees, rolls them off the ground in a ball and hurls them hard against the metallic sheet of the air. Leaves, twigs appear black like charcoal lines against the bronze of the day; the air buzzes like TV static. A dry leaf draws its rough edge across my face, floats away. It's a perfect summer storm. The air has cooled a little. But we can barely see each other through the dust. We walk a little, hoping it would blow over. But the storm only gathers strength. Elizabeth is excited, almost jubilant.

'Listen, OB, I like Arjun.'

'What? You like Arjun? I thought you found him overbearing and sarcastic?' I cover my mouth with my hand.

'Did I? But I saw him wiping his armpit with the corner of a cushion,' Elizabeth laughs, a little high.

'When did he do that?'

'When you mentioned the toilet rolls.'

The wind picks up.

'I have never seen a summer storm like this,' Elizabeth grabs my arm. 'Where did it come from? What a monster!'

'Rajasthan. A western disturbance in the desert.'

Hands clapped to our mouths, we laugh over the western disturbance.

'If you repeat any phrase three times, it turns funny,' Elizabeth says.

'But I said "western disturbance" only once.' We laugh again.

The wind tugs at our beer cans. We drink. We walk on. It dawns on me that we may have by now got our directions all mixed up. I remember having taken a turn toward Max Muller Road. If so, we should have reached Lodi Road by now.

'How are we going to get home at this rate?'

'Call Uber,' Elizabeth says.

The road is deserted. I take out my phone. A few drops of rain fall on it. I call Uber. I look around. Where's the landmark Habitat Centre? The wind nearly lifts us off our feet.

We hold hands.

'This will get over in a moment.'

'Let's take shelter somewhere,' Elizabeth says.

'Home is not far.'

'Check Google maps,' Elizabeth says.

I check the phone. 'The network is down.'

We stop in our tracks. Elizabeth has her eyes shut because of the dust.

We have stepped out of Arjun's onto Mars. We blind-walk for a while. It feels as though we are on an edge, pushed back from falling over by the force of the wind. I open my eyes, look back, take stock. His headlight on, a biker approaches us from out of the storm.

I show my thumb.

He goes ahead, looks back. Stops.

We run up to him. The biker is a big, burly man with his head wrapped in an orange scarf.

'Could you drop us somewhere near Nizamuddin East, if you are going that side?' I ask in Hindi.

He sizes us up, points his thumb in the back.

'Thank you,' I say, climbing behind him. Elizabeth squeezes herself between the backrest and me.

We ride along. The trees we speed past shake like they are having a seizure. The place looks empty, unfamiliar. My head is bowed, almost touching his back. He smells of sweat, alcohol, and cattle.

'Are we past the Habitat Centre?' I ask after a few minutes.

He does not answer. A moment later, he shouts, 'What are you and Madam doing on the road in this storm?'

'We went to a friend's place and found the world changed when we stepped out.'

'Not the right time for women to loiter on the streets.'

'No, no, we are not loitering. We just got lost.'

'Drank too much?'

'Just a beer.'

'Mind, giving me a sip?'

'What?'

'Beer. The one in your hand.'

'Beer?'

'Give me a sip of your beer? You don't understand Hindi?'

'It's not right to ask for a stranger's beer.'

'You are riding on a stranger's bike. If you don't part with that beer, we would be riding forever.'

'This is my beer. I don't know you enough to share it.' Elizabeth taps on my shoulder.

'But you two know me enough to bump a ride?

I hand over my beer. 'Have a sip. What's your name?'

He takes a sip. 'Ram…Ram Yadav.' Ram Yadav kisses the green and silver Heineken can. 'Ha,' he says.

Elizabeth taps on my shoulder again.

'Can I have my beer back, please?'

'It's my beer now.'

Ram Yadav races the bike through the thick of the storm. We are in the vortex of a death-well. Ram Yadav drinks up the beer to its last drop, tosses the can. It whips past us.

'Please stop the bike,' I say.

We have just hurtled past a red traffic light.

'This is fun,' Ram Yadav roars.

'Please stop. We are getting off here.'

'I forget how to stop,' Ram Yadav laughs dramatically.

'We want to get off,' I say.

'Give me another beer.'

'You just had mine.'

'Your girlfriend has one.'

'That's hers, Ramji.'

'All right, *behnchut*, I will show you whose beer it is.'

The bike is no longer on the main road. That much is clear. We are on a dirt path leading to a vast construction site rising spectre-like in the distance.

'Please stop,' I say. I consider choking him, but worry if the bike would crash.

'Give me that beer, you little fuck,' Ram Yadav shouts, and raises the front wheel for a long moment. Elizabeth clings to me. I hold on to Ram Yadav. Faced with mortal danger, you still hug your enemy. Ram Yadav brings the wheel down.

The bike goes up and down, trampoline-like, on the cratered ground. From acres of deep-dug pits, from the foundation of the earth itself, iron bars rise, impaling the whirling air. A mall? A Magnitogorsk of the future? Half-built and abandoned? 'The chronic and indeterminate condition of our country,' Arjun once said.

Ram Yadav rides the bike toward the very edge of the pit, past a bunch of frightened cows that appear in the swirling dust as their ghosts.

Elizabeth screams as the bike judders to a stop, its back-end rising before it nearly crash-lands.

'Give me that fucking beer,' Ram Yadav says.

'What do you think you are doing?'

'What did you think when you asked me for a lift? That it would be free? This is my territory, my place.' Ram Yadav arcs a hand over the site.' He suddenly turns to me. 'Your girlfriend is foreign, but you are Indian, right? Not a Paki? Do you love your country?'

'I…?'

'Yes, you.'

'I…'

Ram Yadav hits me in my face. I go down.

'Can't even say you love your country?'

I am terrified for Elizabeth. Can I hold him down until she makes good her escape? I size him up. He is a huge man in a long kurta and blue jeans, his face hidden from view; a form nearly wavering in and out of the storm, a demon spirit shaken out of the dust. No, he is too big for me.

'I am a British citizen. You will get into serious trouble,' Elizabeth says.

'I lost my job because of you. I took you to Kabuki, remember? And you turned me into a buffalo-milk seller. I had to sell my car. I used to drop my kids to school in it. My family was proud of me. And all of it disappeared because of one negative comment by you. Black-magic witch.' Ram Yadav makes a grab for Elizabeth.

Elizabeth fends him off.

I hold Ram Yadav from behind, around his waist.

'Motherfucker.' Ram Yadav shakes himself free, crooks his elbow around my neck. He drives a fist into my ribs.

Elizabeth picks up a stone and screams: 'Let him go.'

The pain makes me sit down. Elizabeth drops the stone and runs toward me.

'Are you all right, baby?

'Romeo and Juliet.' Ram Yadav walks up to Elizabeth, twists her hand behind her back. As she bends down to ease the pressure, he snatches the beer from the other hand. He shoves Elizabeth away from him. 'You smell good, bitch.'

Elizabeth stumbles and falls with a sob. The wind balloons her skirt. Ram Yadav empties the can into his mouth, squeezes it mercilessly, drops it on the ground.

'I can do anything I want, you get it?' Ram Yadav turns to me. 'Kill you, fuck your bitch. I am the king here. This is my kingdom. I do what I want.'

'I am a journalist.' The storm drives dust into my mouth. All around us the ruins roar with the wind.

'So?' He turns to Elizabeth. 'Where are you from?

I get up on my feet, find breathing painful. I help Elizabeth up. Do we get out of this alive? Rape and murder seem all too real possibilities.

'You want to punch me?' Ram Yadav offers his chin. 'Go on. You must be angry. Impress your lady.'

Elizabeth comes in between us. 'He is just a boy.'

'Not a man? Let's see. Boy, huh? That's a thought.' Ram Yadav takes a green-handled switch knife out of his pocket, and pulling me aside from behind Elizabeth, makes a show of tracing the outline of my groin with the point of the knife, 'I might check your toolkit to know if you are boy or man.' He brings his eyes to my level. 'But I am running out of time.' He lets go of me.

'Let's get out of here,' Elizabeth grabs my elbow and starts walking.

'Not until I give permission,' Ram Yadav plants himself in front of Elizabeth.

'I'm calling the police,' I take out my phone.

Ram Yadav snatches my phone, hurls it into the depths of the foundation. He is free to do whatever he wants here. His freedom comes from his readiness to commit the world to violence, to kill. He is the leader. And the mob. He is the citizen. And the State. The victim. And the victor.

'Go, get it,' Ram Yadav says.

'OB, don't go.'

'You had our beer. Now, allow us to go,' I say.

'This is not about beer, asshole. This is about my life, which this British bitch ruined.'

'Let us go, please,' Elizabeth says.

A phone rings. It is Ram Yadav's phone. He takes it from his hip pocket, looks at it. 'Hello, hello,' he says into the phone, '*behnchut, aa rahaan hun, yaar.*' He shoves the phone back into his pocket. 'On your knees, chut. You got lucky.'

I kneel.

'Say, please don't rape my sister.'

'Please don't rape my sister.'

'Say, please don't kill me.'

'Please don't kill me.'

Ram Yadav laughs. A corner of his face-wrap comes undone. He tucks it back. 'Give me your wallets.'

Elizabeth and I give him our wallets. He takes the money and hands the wallets back. 'See how just I am? All right, get going before I change my mind.'

The beer can comes back rolling on the ground, close to his feet.

He kicks it, misses it. He kicks it again. It hits my forehead.

Elizabeth turns in fury. 'Bastard,' she says.

Ram Yadav takes a threatening step in our direction.

'Let's get out from here,' Elizabeth says.

'I am letting you go,' Ram Yadav folds his knife, and restores it to his pocket.

He starts the bike, circles us once very low, and moves forward, the bike's tail-light in the shape of a lion coming alive in the gathering dark.

We look around the site. There is no one in sight. We can't see a way out of the place. We walk in the direction the bike exited. Heavy drops of rain, dragging down the dirt on their way down, fall on us. Elizabeth walks ahead of me with fast steps.

The storm subsides. Dusk has fallen. We have had two nights in one day. It begins to rain in earnest. This stormy evening does not begin with Elizabeth's abortion ride and her low rating of Ram Yadav as a driver. It is more than the personal history of Ram Yadav, too. It's a whole country turning. I would like to tell Elizabeth that, but it's so hard to explain, so hard to remember how it began, or where, the back and forth of the narrative, and its sideways slip, complicating the telling. Because we are part of the story we tell. I watch the distance between Elizabeth and me widen. I can't, don't, love her anymore. Where are we now? I can't tell. But I know the name of the road we walk is Shame.

A Moment in the Lives of: Russian Roulette

The morning after Elizabeth left for England, a month or so after the evening of the storm, Ta called to say Arjun had died of a heart attack, a little past midnight. The news reverberated inside my head like the drum beats of a world ending. The immensity of his departure struck me as disproportionate to the scope of my understanding. No, I thought, no. Delhi did not make sense without him. They had found him slumped at his writing desk, a half-empty glass of whisky at his elbow. Arjun could not write that last novel after all. But he had begun something on paper before he was interrupted by the white-gloved man (M., surely?) with puppy's eyes. A note that began: 'Dear D,' and ended there—as if he could not find the words for what he wanted to say. After that there was only a downstroke of his black-and-gold Mont Blanc pen, which they found under the desk, its nib broken.

***

All of next day, I lay in bed for as long as I could, traced Elizabeth's body on the bed with a finger and, on her part of the bed, under the pillow, discovered a strand of hair, a question mark in blue. That day, I did not go to the office. Or the day after. I thought of the series of accidents that brought us together, then parted our ways. But the Magnitogorsk stood out in that train of incidents, as if it was the terminus to which everything led, a meaning that had come about almost by its own agency, as a whole nation turned. Elizabeth had never mentioned that evening afterward, except the night before she left, when she came in from outside with blue hair and matching nails.

'What have you done with your hair, Ms Hill!'

'The same thing I did with my nails.' Elizabeth kept her shopping on the floor and held her fingers up. 'Do you like it?'

'It's blue! Blue!'

'The shade of my vengeance,' she smiled brightly.

'Ms Hill, you turned your hair blue because…?'

'Just a point of departure. Did I tell you I am leaving for England? Via Tokyo? I might as well see if I can meet Murakami in a kimono,' Elizabeth said.

'I feel terrible about that evening.'

'It is not your fault. It is not easy to know how to deal with a thug. We got away lightly.'

No, we did not get away lightly. We had not shared the same bed since that evening. It was like I had been castrated. It was like Elizabeth had been violated. I could have been braver. Courage was how little you cared to live in the world of another's making. 'I thumbed that ride.'

'I could just as easily say it all happened because I gave him a low rating.'

'But you went to Kabuki because of me.'

'Oh, never mind, that's all in the past. What are you going to do now?'

'I don't know. Go home, maybe. Take a break.'

'Get it all back.' Elizabeth said. 'And go on forward.'

I could not reach her anymore.

I watched her packing, her mystery somewhat lost. Then helped her, handing out things, folding her clothes. As ever, the moment seemed pre-decided, and presented to me as something that could not be improved upon.

Mr Dudani called up on the third day of my absence from office on my new, grey and black plastic cell phone, a tiny, cheap, nearly extinct Nokia model. 'You could drill a hole through it, and nothing would happen,' the shopkeeper said. The *Post* was bringing out a special supplement on petroleum products, Mr Dudani said. 'The Egyptian petroleum ministry is holding an exhibition and will be the main sponsor. They want a market in India. And we will be their media partner,' Mr Dudani made it sound like a wedding in his family. 'I am hoping to sign a three-year contract.'

'I am quitting, Mr Dudani,' I stopped biting my nails.

'But why? You are doing well.'

Egyptian petroleum products. The hot afternoon closed in around me like a box.

'Come and talk to me. This supplement could be a regular model for us if it does well. We could put you in charge.'

'No, thank you, Mr Dudani.'

'I am thinking of a new post for you. Supplements Editor.'

'That's kind of you.'

'The youngest Supplements Editor in the world. Why do you want to quit? The Chairman is happy with you.'

'My grandfather is ill. I am going home to Thrissur.'

'Town of temples and elephants, I know. I see a supplement there too, provided the temples sponsor it.'

'Would temples do that?'

'Well, the elephants won't.' He laughed. 'Kerala is famous for temples, don't you know? I would have to sell the idea to the temple administration, of course. They do have a lot of money. And we are a nationalist paper.'

'Yes.'

'Thrissur is home, eh? It is raining heavily there.'

'Floods. It is pretty bad.'

'Global warming.'

'Yes, global warming.'

'Take leave of absence. Resigning is way too drastic. And when you get back, good things await you.'

Mr Dudani had persuaded Ta, too, to go on long leave instead of quitting. When he came back, he would be getting a raise and a promotion, Ta said. Mr Dudani had finally understood that no one wanted to join the *Post*, Ta explained. Ta had come around to see journalism as just another job, like waiting on a table. Censored by the groups, the State, and the management itself, there was no real news or views worth carrying, he whispered under his hat.

'I am done, Mr Dudani.'

'Just like that? You just began.'

'I'm sorry.'

'I wish I were you,' Mr Dudani sighed. 'You have such freedom. You are the master of your own destiny.'

There was a pause. Would he talk about his wife, her art now? About his little-known sacrifice? I wished he did, and imagined us leaning on each other for support.

'What do I tell the Egyptians? They would have made out a pass in your name. And they offer free five-star lunch on all the days of the exhibition.'

'That's nice!'

'Call me if you change your mind. Eventually, there would be a Cairo trip. The pyramids! You would like the pyramids in the moonlight.'

***

When I reached home, the floodwaters had already receded, leaving a mark on the wall, a straight brown line, nature's watermark. It had been raining without a break for weeks, Gloria said, the roads and lanes had become waterways. I could still catch traces of an overpowering smell, the kind that the earth released when it is reclaimed from the sea for the first time; the detritus smell of salt, fish, discharge, elemental deposits of the deep. While it rained, Gloria had called up the press and allowed herself to be interviewed on a small canoe (which she had arranged) about a similar flood when her husband went underground as a revolutionary, in another millennium. A nostalgic story; the press liked it very much. 'But the TV cameras made the President angry,' Tressa said out of Gloria's earshot. The President stared hard at everybody whenever he was awake, especially the reporters. Then he caught a virus, Treesa said, that perhaps the waters had brought in or a dying fish coughed out, and overnight he had begun deteriorating.

A couple of days after my arrival, Treesa announced: 'The President no longer recognizes us, I know.'

I was not so sure, because in the afternoon he had called out my name and said in a clear voice, 'Where's that speech?'

Of course, he was referring to the 1956 Khrushchev speech. I took out from the bottom drawer of his table a broad, brown, envelope with several stamps on it; one, triangular-shaped and outsized, featuring the Kremlin, stood out. It was then that I saw the gun at the back of the drawer. A pretty little thing. I weighed it in my hands. It felt heavier than its size. I kept it back. Before I could hand over the envelope, my grandfather made a feeble noise deep in this throat, like a clock winding down to its last. Then he fell back against the cushions. I placed the envelope back in the drawer. I bent down and peered under the cot. No, Gloria has not thrown anything out. It was all there: records of great outbreaks of lunacy and genius, of mass delusions in Cyrillic. I saw an issue of *Moscow News* sticking out of the pile. I pulled it out. April 1986. I turned the pages, came across an article, crossed out in red. The headline read: 'A

Poisoned Cloud of Anti-Sovietism'. The report denounced the news about Chernobyl: 'A Premeditated and Well-Orchestrated Campaign', aiming to 'Cover up Criminal Acts of Militarism by the USA and NATO'. That had been crossed out, too. What conclusion did my grandfather draw? Chernobyl happened? The news was false? What was the truth he was taking to his grave, what world??

I spread Treesa's mat on the floor next to my grandfather's cot. Her pillow smelled faintly of soap, of carbolic acid mixed with rose. I fell asleep, and Columbus of constellations, I was cut adrift through the stars, the ones Kris explained so patiently as his heart lay in ruins inside him that night when we danced. The air rushed up inside my clothes, and I was floating and free. And the sky was vast, even, deep in all directions. I swung up past the conspiring planets, scaled the high peaks of the Plough, shimmied down the spine of Ursa Minor, elated. On the spikes of Cassiopeia, I hung up my military jacket. I was home. I was instructed by Kris to protect his daughter from fear and hatred, so Elizabeth could wear a yellow frock and run free all her years on the beach, her small feet picking their way through the little black crabs running around on the sands; the sands were white, white like sugar. There she was, grinning, real as a pinprick in the heart, running on the brilliant beach, the big bright blue sea breaking on her ankles and going back to the depths with a little bit of the earth, a little bit of her, too, and a little bit of all of us, and she was running fast now, the wind in her hair, the sand shining on her wet skin, her body tilting this way and that, her small hands extended like the wings of a plane, toward my grandfather.

'I think the President is gone,' Treesa awoke me.

I rested an ear on his chest, listened to the heart's feeble code of departure.

'Give him a drink of water,' Treesa said.

I poured a little water from his bronze glass, very carefully.

It trickled out of either side of his mouth.

'Farewell, my friend.'

Gloria called up the party secretary and insisted her husband be given a state burial. They did. When we returned from the funeral, Gloria said she wouldn't be surprised if they made her a minister in charge of the welfare of women and children. He had to go, she said, before something good could happen to her. In the car, on the way back, Gloria said she was not interested in a sequel to the biography of her husband—the longest personal disintegration in history, she said—but she just might reinterpret the *Mahabharata* from the perspective of Ganga who, in her opinion, should have killed the eighth child, Bhishma, as well, asserted her independence just one more time when it was most required, and thus avoided the great war.

'Do you have a pen,' I asked.

'You are not listening to me,' Gloria said.

'Yes, I am, you are going to be a minister, and you would like to rewrite the *Mahabharata* in Ganga's voice.'

'Yes, a minister, for sure, that's more than he ever was,' Gloria said, handing me her dark blue Parker fountain pen.

'Keep it,' she said, 'it is a gift, but you must shake it once before you start writing so the ink flows freely.'

I wrote out two cheques for whatever little money (Rs 26,312) I had in the bank. I divided it evenly between Gloria and Treesa. And wasted four leaves to get two correct. I kept the cheques on my grandfather's table and placed the Parker diagonally over them for a paperweight, conscious of the theatricality of the gesture.

***

I walked past the hall, through the passageway, into the kitchen, and out the back door into the veranda. Things took on an oiled glow as light flickered like candles between the leaves. The Elizabeth episode no longer weighed me down as it had only a few days back; it was more like a ring that had cut into the finger once, had now turned into a circle paling on the flesh. Other, more final departures seemed to have put in perspective Elizabeth's exit.

The swing was tied to a long sturdy branch of the mango tree. I tugged at the ropes. Gunny bags buffered the spot where the ropes went around the branch. They appeared sodden. A sprinkle of water drops hit my face like shards of cold glass. I settled on the seat. The way I was, I did not, in any measure of confidence, seem to represent to myself a choice. My years had lapped at my mind like an eddy of dreams. Did all that happen to me? I must swim ashore, or continue to be borne away by the currents. True, none of it appeared a justification for what I had now resolved to do. But, few things explained one's action as action itself. I went back a few steps on the swing and let go. When I came back to the midpoint, I pushed back against the moist earth and went farther up, rebounded. Back and forth. Rise and fall. I shook off my sandals. They lay at different spots, as if they had never gone on a journey together. Dusk fell. The hills departed. They would come back in the morning for those who survived the night. Arjun was not among them. 'The only way to go,' he said, 'was to go as if we had never been there, as if it was a nothing, like waves returning, sure-footed even as they ran backward, on the home-stretch, to the sea.'

Below, I heard Gloria call out to me, 'Balaa…' Her voice, kind, assured, and demanding trust, seemed to come from another world, the one I had just left with the house, the trees, and the hills in it, maybe because I was high up in the free, limitless air, before descending and moving past the lamp-lit windows to the other end, where all of it fell away from me again. When the swing stopped, I would go in and check if that gun fired through all those years at me. If it did, I would be the sea. If it didn't, I would be a wave rising, lit, in the brief sun. Either way, I would have decided the worth of my breath, answered the challenge of a word, my name.

Acknowledgements

This novel took me more than six years to write. It began as one thing, and ended up as another. In these years, enough for a million stars to burn out or be born, I have changed, too, facing many crises, and a little of which material, disguised, has found its way into the book.

Through these uncertain times, the one person, my intimate enemy and friend, who supported me has been my wife, Manjula Narayan. I have found this book not easy to write. One reason is that writing a novel, like any living organism, is an elusive process of metamorphosis. I owe my thanks to many friends who were patient with its endless evolution. Priya Bala, Achuthan T.K., Ankita Tandon, Dibyajyoti Sarma (who explained to me with a diagram over a cup of tea, at a wayside stall in Delhi, how to write a novel), Saaz Aggarwal who lent her intellectual resources and generosity of spirit unstintingly, Ravindran C.P, Dr Deepthi Murali, Joseph Antony, Shanu Athiparambath, Dr Padmaja Chellakere and the late P.V. Padmanabhan. I must thank, too, with pleasure, Nirmal Kanti Bhattacharjee, Trisha

Niyogi, and my editor, K.E. Priyamvada, at Niyogi Books, for the trust they have shown in *One Love*.

I have consulted many books for this project. A few need to be specifically acknowledged. Nadezhda Mandelstam's *Hope Against Hope* and *Hope Abandoned.* Osip Mandelstam's *Fourth Prose,* Stephen Kotkin's *Stalin* and *Magnetic City,* Arthur Koestler's *Darkness at Noon* and *The Invisible Writing* and R.K. Narayan's 'Elephant in the Pit'.

And I still remain, indebted, in varying degrees, to everything.

–C.P. Surendran